THE BALTIMORE BOYS

Also by Joël Dicker in English translation

The Truth About the Harry Quebert Affair (2014)

Joël Dicker

THE BALTIMORE BOYS

Translated from the French by
Alison Anderson

MACLEHOSE PRESS
QUERCUS · LONDON

First published in the French language as *Le Livre des Baltimore*
by Editions de Fallois in Paris, 2015
First published in Great Britain in 2017 by MacLehose Press
This paperback edition published in 2018 by

MacLehose Press
An imprint of Quercus Publishing Ltd
Carmelite House
50 Victoria Embankment
London EC4Y 0DZ

An Hachette UK company

A CIP catalogue record for this book is available
from the British Library.

ISBN (MMP) 978 0 85705 850 8
ISBN (MMP Export) 978 0 85705 688 7
ISBN (Ebook) 978 0 85705 689 4

10 9 8 7 6 5 4 3 2 1

Designed and typeset in Minion by Libanus Press Ltd
Printed and bound in Great Britain by Clays Ltd, Elcograf S.p.A.

In memory of . . .

Prologue

Sunday, October 24, 2004
One month before the tragedy

My cousin Woody is going to prison tomorrow. He'll be there for the next five years.

As I drive from Baltimore airport to Oak Park, the neighborhood where he grew up and where I'm about to join him for his last day of freedom, I can already imagine him standing outside the gate of the imposing penitentiary in Cheshire, Connecticut.

We spend the day together, at my uncle Saul's house, where once we were so happy. Hillel and Alexandra are there too, and for the space of a few hours we are again the wonderful foursome we once were. I have no idea how significant that day will turn out to be for all of our lives.

Two days later, I get a call from my uncle Saul.

"Marcus? Uncle Saul here."

"Uncle Saul, hello! How are—"

"Marcus, listen carefully: I need you to come to Baltimore right away. Don't ask any questions. Something bad has happened."

At first I think we were cut off and I call him right back: he doesn't answer. Since I keep trying, he does eventually pick up and says only, "Come to Baltimore."

He hangs up again.

If you find this book, please read it.

I want someone to know the history of the Baltimore Goldmans.

Part One

THE BOOK OF LOST YOUTH
1989–1997

1

I'm the writer.

That's what everyone calls me. My friends, my parents, my family, even people I don't know who recognize me in a public place and say, "Hey, aren't you that writer . . . ?" So I'm the writer, that's my identity.

People think that if you're a writer you lead a pleasant life. Only recently one of my friends was complaining about the long commute from his house to his office and he said, "Basically you get up in the morning, sit down at your desk and write. That's it." I said nothing, I must have felt too despondent at the realization that in the collective imagination my work consisted in not doing anything at all. People think you don't lift a finger, but it's precisely when you're not doing anything that you're working the hardest.

Writing a book is like starting a summer camp. Your life is ordinarily solitary and quiet, and suddenly you're being shoved around by a multitude of characters who show up out of the blue to come and turn everything upside down. They arrive one morning on a big bus then off they get, making a huge racket, all excited about the roles they've been given. And you have to deal with it, you have to look after them, feed them, house them. You're in charge of everything. Because your job is to be the writer.

This story began in February 2012, when I left New York to go and start my new novel in the house I'd bought three months earlier in Boca Raton, Florida, with the money from the film rights to my most recent book. I had made a few quick round trips in December and January to buy furniture, but this would be my first extended stay. It was a house with picture windows, overlooking a lake where people came on walks. It was located in a quiet, leafy neighborhood, mostly inhabited by affluent retirees; I felt out of place. I was half their age, but the reason I chose the place was precisely for its absolute tranquility. It was just what I needed, to be able to write.

My previous stays had been very short, but now that I had a lot of time ahead of me I went to Florida by car. The fact that there were twelve hundred miles of driving didn't put me off at all: over previous years I had made the trip from New York any number of times to visit my uncle Saul Goldman, who had moved to the greater Miami area after the tragedy that had struck his family. I could drive it with my eyes closed.

When I left New York there was a thin layer of snow on the ground and the thermometer said minus ten, and I reached Boca Raton two days later, in the balmy air of a tropical winter. On seeing that familiar décor of sunshine and palm trees, I couldn't help but think of Uncle Saul. I missed him terribly. I only realized how much when I left the freeway to head to Boca Raton, and I instinctively wanted to keep on going to Miami to go and see him. So much so, I even wondered whether my previous trips really were about furnishing the house, or whether deep down they were a way of reconnecting with Florida. It wasn't going to be the same without him.

My nearest neighbor in Boca Raton was a congenial man in his seventies, Leonard Horowitz, formerly a leading expert at Harvard on constitutional law, who spent his winters in Florida and had been passing the time since his wife's death writing a book he had not yet actually managed to start. The first time I met him was the day I bought the house. He came and rang at the door with a six-pack of beer to welcome me, and we instantly hit it off. He made a habit of coming by to say hello whenever I was in town.

I think he was happy to see me settle in for a while. Since I explained I was there to write my next novel, he immediately started talking about his book. His heart was in it, but he wasn't making any progress.

He went everywhere with a big spiral notebook; on it he had written in black felt tip, *Notebook No. 1*, implying there would be others. Whenever I saw him he was bent over it: first thing in the morning, out on the patio, then later at a café table in the center of town, always intent on his notebook. He, on the other hand, saw me going for walks, jogging, swimming in the lake, or heading for the beach. In the evening he came to ring at my door with cold beer. We sat out on the patio drinking while we played chess and listened to music. Behind us was the sublime landscape of the lake, the palm trees dusted pink by the setting sun. Between two moves he always asked, never taking his eyes from the chessboard, "Well, Marcus, how's the book going?"

"It's going, Leo. It's going."

I had been there for two weeks when one evening, just as he was about to take my rook, he broke off and said, suddenly sounding annoyed:

"Didn't you come here to write your next novel?"

"I did, why are you asking?"

"Because you aren't doing anything, and it bugs me."

"What makes you think I'm not doing anything?"

"Because I see you! All day long you sit around daydreaming, or doing sports, or watching the clouds go by. I'm seventy-eight years old, I'm the one who should be vegetating the way you are, but you're hardly a day over thirty, you ought to be working like mad!"

"What really bugs you, Leo? My book or yours?"

Bull's-eye. More calmly he said:

"I just want to know how you do it. My novel's not getting anywhere. I'm curious to know how you work."

"I sit out here on the patio and I think. And believe me, it's a lot of work. But you, Leo, you write to keep your mind occupied. That's different."

He moved his knight, threatening my king.

"Can't you just give me a good idea for a plot?"

"No way."

"Why not?"

"Because it has to come from you."

"Whatever you do, please don't mention Boca Raton in your book. I don't need to see all your readers coming around here cooling their heels to see where you live."

I smiled and added: "You don't have to go looking for an idea, Leo. The idea will come to you. The idea is an event that can happen at any time."

How could I have known that that was just what would happen, the moment I said those words?

I noticed a dog sniffing around down by the water's edge. He had a muscular, yet slender body, pointed ears, nose in the grass. There was no-one walking nearby.

"Looks like that dog's on his own," I said.

Horowitz looked up and observed the wandering animal.

"There are no stray dogs around here," he decreed.

"I didn't say he was a stray. I said he was on his own."

I love dogs. I got up from my chair, cupped my hands around my lips and whistled to call the dog. He pricked up his ears. I whistled again and he bounded up to us.

"Are you crazy?" Leo grumbled. "How do you know that dog doesn't have rabies? It's your move."

"I don't," I said, moving my rook distractedly.

Horowitz took my queen to punish me for my insolence.

The dog had reached the patio. I squatted down next to him. He was a biggish male, with a dark coat, a black mask across his eyes and long seal's whiskers. He pressed his head against me and I stroked him. He seemed very gentle. I felt an instant connection between him and me, just like that, and people who are familiar with dogs will know what I mean. He didn't have a collar or anything to identify him with.

"Have you ever seen this dog?" I asked Leo.

"Never."

The dog inspected the patio, then left again before I could hold him back, disappearing between the palm trees and the bushes.

"He seems to know where he's going," Horowitz said. "He must belong to one of the neighbors."

It was very muggy that evening. By the time Leo left, you could already tell, despite the darkness, that the sky was menacing. Shortly afterwards a violent storm burst, with impressive bolts of lightning on the far side of the lake, then the clouds opened in a torrential downpour. At around midnight, as I was reading in the living room, I heard barking on the patio. I went to see what was going on, and through the French doors I saw the dog, looking miserable and soaked. I opened the door and he bounded inside. He gave me an imploring look.

"It's fine, you can stay," I said.

He spent the night. When I got up the next morning I found him sleeping peacefully on the tiled floor in the kitchen. I made a leash with a length of cord, which was only a precaution, because he followed me obediently, and we set out to look for his master.

Leo was drinking coffee on his porch. *Notebook No. 1* was open in front of him on a blank white page.

"What are you doing with that dog, Marcus?" he said when he saw me putting the dog in the back of the car.

"I found him on the patio last night. I brought him in because of the storm. I think he's lost."

"Where are you going?"

"To put a sign up at the supermarket."

"So you really do never work."

"I'm working right now."

"Well, don't wear yourself out, buddy."

"Promise."

Once I'd put signs up in the two nearest supermarkets, I ambled down the main street in Boca Raton with the dog, hoping someone would recognize him. In vain. Eventually I went to the police station, and they gave me the name of a vet. Sometimes dogs had chips that could help find their owners. It wasn't the case with this dog, and the vet couldn't help me. He offered to send the dog to the pound for me, but I said no, and went home with my new companion, who was, I have to admit, particularly docile, in spite of his size.

Leo was on his porch, waiting for my return. When he saw me coming, he hurried over, waving the pages he had just printed. He had just discovered the magic of the Google search engine, and he keyed in every question that crossed his mind. For an academic like him, who had spent most of his life in libraries looking things up in reference books, the magic of algorithms had a special impact.

"I conducted my own little investigation," he said as if he had just solved the unsolved mysteries of the J.F.K. assassination, handing me the dozens of pages which would soon earn me the privilege of helping him change the toner cartridge on his printer.

"And what did you find out, Professor Horowitz?"

"Dogs always find their way home. Some will go thousands of miles to get there."

"So what do you suggest?"

Leo's expression was that of a wise old man.

"Follow the dog instead of making him follow you. He knows where he's going, you don't."

My neighbor had a point. I decided to take off the leash and let the dog wander. He set off at a trot, initially by the lake, then along a footpath. We crossed the golf course and came to another residential neighborhood I did not know that was situated on an inlet of ocean. The dog followed the road, turned to the right twice and finally stopped outside a gate through which I could see a magnificent house. He sat down and barked. I rang the interphone. A woman's voice answered and I told her I had found her dog. The gate opened and the dog dashed up to the house, obviously pleased to be home.

I followed. A woman stepped out the front door and the dog jumped up on her in a rush of joy. I heard her call him by name, "Duke". There was a flurry of affectionate greeting. Then the woman looked up and I was thunderstruck.

"Alexandra?" I eventually stammered.

"Marcus?"

She was as astonished as I was.

Seven years or so after the tragedy that had separated us, there she was. She opened her eyes wide and said again, with a sudden cry, "Marcus, is it you?"

I stood there without moving, stunned.

She ran over to me.

"Marcus!"

With a surge of tenderness that came perfectly naturally, she took my face in her hands. As if she couldn't believe it either, and wanted to make sure this was really happening. I could not say a word.

"Marcus," she said, "I can't believe it's you."

Unless you live in a cave, you're bound to have heard of Alexandra Neville, the most celebrated female vocalist and musician in recent years. She was the idol everyone had been waiting for, for so long, the woman who had revitalized the music industry. Her three albums had sold twenty million copies; for the second year in a row she had been named one of *Time* magazine's most influential people, and she was said to be worth $150 million. The public adored her, critics were tireless in their admiration. She was loved by young and old alike; in fact everyone loved her, and at times it seemed like the entire country was chanting their love and fervor, in four syllables: *A-lex-and-ra!*

Her partner was a Canadian hockey player by the name of Kevin Legendre, and now he came out the door behind her.

"You found Duke! We've been looking for him since yesterday! Alex was so upset. Thank you very much."

He held out his hand to greet me. I saw his biceps contract as he crushed my knuckles. I had only ever seen Kevin in the tabloids, which were full of his relationship with Alexandra. He was insolently handsome. Even more so than in the photographs. He gave me a curious look for a second then said, "You look familiar."

"Marcus. Marcus Goldman," I said.

"You're a writer, isn't that it?"

"Exactly."

"I read your last book. Alexandra recommended it, she really likes your work."

I could not believe this situation. I had just found Alexandra, at her fiancé's house. Kevin, who didn't really understand what was going on, suggested I stay for supper, and I accepted with pleasure.

We grilled some enormous steaks on a huge barbecue out on their patio. I hadn't kept up with the latest developments in Kevin's career: I thought he was still a defender for the Nashville Predators, but during the summer transfers he'd been recruited by the Florida Panthers. This was his house. He now lived in Boca Raton, and Alexandra was making the most of a pause in recording her next album to come and visit.

Only at the end of dinner did Kevin realize that Alexandra and I knew each other well.

"You're from New York?" he said.

"Yes, I live there."

"What brings you to Florida?"

"I got into the habit of coming here over the last few years. My uncle used to live in Coconut Grove, and I often went to see him. I just bought a house in Boca Raton. I wanted somewhere quiet to write."

"How is your uncle?" Alexandra said. "I didn't know he'd left Baltimore."

I avoided her question and merely replied, "He left Baltimore after the tragedy."

Kevin pointed at us with his fork, not realizing.

"Am I imagining things or do you guys already know each other?"

"I lived in Baltimore for a few years," Alexandra explained.

"And part of my family lived in Baltimore," I said. "My uncle, for a start, with his wife and my cousins. They lived in the same neighborhood as Alexandra and her family."

Alexandra refrained from going into details and we changed the subject. After the meal, she offered to drive me home.

Alone in the car with her, I could tell she felt awkward. I said, "That's wild, the way your dog showed up at my place."

"He runs away a lot."

It was tasteless on my part, but I tried to joke about it.

"Maybe he doesn't like Kevin."

"Don't start, Marcus."

Her tone was curt.

"Don't be like that, Alex . . . "

"Like what?"

"You know exactly."

She suddenly stopped right there in the street and looked me straight in the eye.

"Why did you do it, Marcus?"

I was having trouble meeting her gaze. She shouted, "You abandoned me!"

"I'm sorry. I had my reasons."

"Your reasons? You had no reason to ruin everything!"

"Alexandra, they . . . they're dead."

"And so what, is it my fault?"

"No," I said. "I'm sorry. I'm sorry about everything."

There was a heavy silence. The only words I spoke were to give her directions. Once we were outside the house, she said, "Thanks for Duke."

"I'd be really glad if I could see you again."

"I think it's better if we leave things like this. Don't come back, Marcus."

"To Kevin's place?"

"Into my life. Don't come back into my life, please."

She drove away.

I didn't have the heart to go home. My car keys were in my pocket so I decided to go for a drive. I went to Miami and, without thinking, drove through town to the quiet neighborhood of Coconut Grove, where I parked outside my uncle's house. It was warm outside. I got out of the car and I leaned against it, and stood for a long time gazing at the house. It was as if he were there, I could feel his presence. I wanted to see my Uncle Saul again, and there was only one way to do that. Write it.

* * *

Saul Goldman was my father's brother. Before the tragedy, before the events I am about to relate, he was, to use my grandparents' term, *a very important man.* He was head of one of the most renowned law firms in Baltimore, and his experience had involved him in cases that were famous all through Maryland. The Dominic Pernell affair, that was Saul. The City of Baltimore v. Morris, that was Saul. The case of the illegal Sunridge sales, Saul again. Everyone in Baltimore knew him. He was in the papers and on television, and I remember how in the old days it all really impressed me. He had married his college sweetheart, the woman who became my Aunt Anita. In my child's eyes she was the most beautiful woman, the sweetest mother. She was a doctor, a leading physician in the oncology department at Johns Hopkins Hospital, one of the most famous in the country. Together they had a wonderful son, Hillel, a kind boy with a superior intelligence; we were born only a few months apart and we were like brothers.

The best moments of my youth were spent with them, and for a long time just hearing their name made me swell with pride and happiness. Of all the families I had met until then, of all the people I had known, they seemed second to none: happier, more accomplished, more ambitious, more respected. For a long time life would prove me right. They belonged to another dimension. I was fascinated by the way they seemed to breeze through life, I was dazzled by their radiance, subjugated by their affluence. I admired their allure, their possesions, their social standing. Their huge house, luxury cars, summer place in the Hamptons, apartment in Miami, and skiing vacations in Whistler, British Columbia. Their simplicity and happiness. Their kindness toward me. Their magnificent superiority, which meant you couldn't help but admire them. They didn't inspire jealousy: they were too incomparable to be envied. They'd been blessed by the gods. For a long time I thought they were immortal.

2

I spent the day after my chance encounter with Alexandra shut in my study. I went out only in the coolness of twilight, to jog along the lake.

Not yet sure of what I would do with them, I decided to start compiling research and taking notes on the salient features of the Baltimore Goldmans' story. I began by drawing our family tree, until I realized I had to add a few explanations, in particular regarding Woody's origins. The tree quickly began to resemble a forest of comments in the margin, so out of a concern for clarity I decided that it would be better to transcribe everything onto file cards. In front of me I put the photograph Uncle Saul had found two years earlier. It was a picture of me taken seventeen years prior, surrounded by the three people I loved most: my adored cousins Hillel and Woody, and Alexandra. She had sent a copy of the print to each of us and on the back she had written: *I LOVE YOU GOLDMAN BOYS*

Back then she was seventeen, and my cousins and I had just turned fifteen. She already had all those human qualities that would make millions of people worship her, but we didn't have to share her yet. The photograph plunged me back into the labyrinth of our lost youth, long before I lost my cousins, before I became the rising star of American literature, and above all before Alexandra Neville became the celebrity she is today. Long before the entire country fell in love with her, with her songs; before, album after album, she enraptured millions of fans. Before she started going on tour, or became the long-awaited national icon.

Early that evening, true to form, Leo came and rang at the door.

"Is everything O.K., Marcus? I haven't heard from you since yesterday.

Did you find the dog's owner?"

"Yes. It's the new boyfriend of a girl I was in love with for years."

"Talk about a small world," he said. "What's her name?"

"You'll never believe it. Alexandra Neville."

"The singer?"

"That's the one."

"You know her?"

I went to get the photograph and handed it to him.

"That's Alexandra?" Leo said, pointing at her.

"Yes. In the days when we were happy teenagers."

"And who are the other boys?"

"My cousins from Baltimore."

"What became of them?"

"It's a long story."

Leo and I played chess until late that evening. I was glad he'd come to distract me: it helped me put my mind on something besides Alexandra for a few hours. Seeing her again had upset me. All these years I had never been able to forget her.

The next day I could not help going back to the streets around Kevin Legendre's house. I don't know what I was hoping. Probably to run into her. To talk to her again. But she would be furious at me for coming back. I was parked on the road parallel to their property when I saw something moving in the hedge. I watched attentively, intrigued, and suddenly good old Duke came out of the bushes. I got out of the car and called to him softly. He remembered me and ran up for a caress. An absurd idea sprang to my mind and I couldn't stop it. What if Duke could be a way to reconnect with Alexandra? I opened the back of the car and he jumped in. He trusted me. I drove off quickly and went home. He knew the house. I made him a spot in my study, he lay down and kept me company while I plunged back into the story of the Baltimore Goldmans.

*

The designation "Baltimore Goldmans" was the counterpart of what my parents and I were with regard to our address: the Montclair Goldmans, from Montclair, New Jersey. Over time, with the shortcuts that language takes, they became the Baltimores and we were the Montclairs. It was the Goldman grandparents who came up with these names in order to simplify conversation, so naturally they split our family into two geographical entities. That way they could say, for example, when we all went for the holiday season to Florida where they lived: "The Baltimores arrive on Saturday and the Montclairs on Sunday." But what in the beginning was just a tender way to distinguish us came in due course to express the superiority of the Baltimore Goldmans at the very heart of the clan. The facts spoke for themselves: the Baltimores meant a lawyer married to a doctor, with a son who attended the best private school in town. As for the Montclairs, my father was an engineer, my mother was a saleswoman in the New Jersey branch of an upmarket New York women's wear store, and I was a good little pupil at public school.

Even when it came to family pronunciation, my grandparents had ended up emphasizing their privileged feelings for the Baltimores with their very intonation: the word "Baltimore" seemed to have been coated in gold, whereas "Montclair" was smeared with slug drool. The Baltimores got compliments, the Montclairs criticism. If their T.V. wasn't working, it was because I'd messed it up, and if the bread wasn't fresh it was because my father had bought it. But the loaves that Uncle Saul brought home were exceptional, and if the T.V. was working again it was certainly because Hillel had repaired it. Even when the situation was identical, the treatment was not: if one of our families was late for dinner, my grandparents would decree – if it was the Baltimores – that the poor dears were stuck in traffic. But if it was the Montclairs, off they went complaining that we were systematically late. In every circumstance, Baltimore was the capital of beauty, Montclair that of can-do-better. The finest caviar from Montclair would never equal a mouthful of putrid Baltimore cabbage. And whenever we were out all together at a restaurant or a shopping mall, if we ran into some acquaintance of my grandparents', Grandmother would make the introductions: "This is my son Saul, he's a high-flying lawyer. His wife Anita is a top-ranking physician at Johns Hopkins, and this is their son Hillel, who is a little genius." Each of the Baltimores would then receive a handshake and a sort of bow. Then Grandmother would continue her recital, indicating my parents and me with a vague wave: "And this is my youngest son and his family." We would get a nod not unlike that with which you might acknowledge a doorman or domestic staff.

The single perfect equality between the Baltimore Goldmans and the Montclair Goldmans was to be found, during the early years of my youth, in our number: there were three of us in each family. But while the Bureau of Vital Statistics may have officially registered the Baltimore Goldmans as consisting of three individuals, those who knew them well will tell you there were actually four of them. Because before long my cousin Hillel, with whom I had always shared the burden of being an only child, was granted the privilege of having life lend him a brother. Following the events I will describe shortly, he would start going everywhere, no matter the circumstances, in the company of a friend you might have thought was imaginary if you didn't know him: Woodrow Finn – Woody, we called him – handsome, strong, tall, good at everything, attentive, and always there for you when you needed him.

In no time Woody earned a status all to himself among the Baltimore Goldmans, and he became both one of them and one of us – nephew, cousin, son, and brother. It instantly became so natural to find him with the Baltimores that – ultimate symbol of his integration – if someone failed to see him at a family reunion, they immediately asked where he was. His absence was troubling, thereby making his presence not only legitimate but also downright necessary, if the family unity was to be whole. Ask anyone who remembers those days to name the Baltimore Goldmans, and they will put Woody on the list without even pausing to wonder. So they beat us once again: in the match Montclair versus

Baltimore, where we had been tied at three all, the score was now four to three.

Woody, Hillel, and I were the most faithful friends you could find. My best years with the Baltimores were when Woody was there, from 1990 to 1998, a period that was blessed, but that also set the stage for everything prefiguring the tragedy. From the time we were ten until we turned eighteen, the three of us were inseparable. Together we formed a brotherly entity that was three-faced, triad or trinity, which we proudly referred to as "the Goldman Gang". We loved each other as few brothers have loved each other; we pledged solemn oaths, mixed our blood, swore loyalty, and promised undying mutual love. Despite everything that happened later, I will always remember those years as an exceptional time: the saga of three happy adolescents in an America that was blessed by the gods.

Going to Baltimore to be with them was all that mattered to me. I only really felt complete in their presence. Praise be to my parents who, in an era when not many children traveled alone, gave me permission to go to Baltimore on long weekends, by myself, to be with these people I was so fond of. This was the beginning of a new life for me, revolving around the perpetual calendar of school holidays, professional development days, or celebrations of American heroes. The mere prospect of an upcoming Veterans Day, Martin Luther King Day, or Presidents' Day triggered feelings of boundless joy. I was so excited at seeing the Baltimores that I could not sit still. Glory to the soldiers who died for our country; glory to Dr Martin Luther King, Jr for having been such a good man; glory to our honest, valiant Presidents for giving us a day off every third Monday in February!

To gain a day I got permission from my parents to leave straight after school. When classes were finally over, I'd go home quick as a flash to pack my things. When my bag was ready I waited for my mother to come home from work to take me to the station in Newark. I sat fidgeting on the armchair by the front door with my shoes and my jacket already on. I was early, she was late. To pass the time, I looked at the photographs of our two families on the table next to me. It seemed to me that we were as drab as they were brilliant. And yet the life I led in Montclair, a pretty New Jersey suburb, was a privileged one, full of tranquillity and happiness, sheltered from want. But our cars didn't seem as shiny, our conversations weren't as sparkling, our sun wasn't as bright, our air was nowhere near as pure.

Then I heard my mother blowing the horn. I rushed outside and climbed into the old Honda Civic. She was touching up her nail polish, drinking coffee from a paper cup, eating a sandwich or filling out an advertising order form. Sometimes all at the same time. She was elegant and always very well groomed. Pretty, nicely made up. When she came home from work, on her jacket she still wore the badge with her name and the caption beneath it, *Here to serve you*, which I thought was humiliating. The Baltimores were served; we were servants.

I scolded my mother for being late, she asked me to forgive her. I did not, and she ruffled my hair with tenderness. She gave me a kiss, leaving lipstick on my cheek, which she immediately wiped off, in a gesture full of love. Then she drove me to the station, where I took a train for Baltimore in the early evening. Along the way she told me she loved me and missed me already. Before letting me board the railroad car she handed me a paper bag with sandwiches she had bought where she got her coffee, and she made me promise to be "polite and on my best behavior". She gave me a hug and at the same time tucked a $20 bill in my pocket, and said, "I love you, kitten". Then it was two kisses on my cheek, or sometimes three, or four. She said one wasn't enough, whereas for me it was already too much. Now that I think back on it today, I'm sorry I didn't let her kiss me ten times whenever I was about to go away. I'm even sorry I went away so often; too often. I'm sorry I didn't remind myself how ephemeral our mothers are, and that I didn't tell myself often enough: love your mother.

Barely two hours by train and I was at the main station in Baltimore.

At last the family transfer could begin. I would take off my tight Montclair suit and cloak myself in Baltimore cloth. On the platform in the falling dusk she was waiting for me. As lovely as a queen, radiant and elegant as a goddess, the woman whose memory often, and sometimes shamefully, inhabited my young nights: my Aunt Anita. I ran up to her and put my arms around her. I can still feel her hand in my hair, her body against mine. I hear her voice saying, "Markie darling, I'm so happy to see you". I don't know why, but usually she was the one who came to get me, on her own. The reason was certainly that Uncle Saul generally finished late at the office, and no doubt she did not want to drag Hillel and Woody along. I enjoyed the moment as if I were being reunited with my fiancée: a few minutes before the train got in, I would adjust my clothes, comb my hair in the reflection of the window, and when the train stopped at last, I would disembark with a pounding heart. I was cheating on my mother with another woman.

Aunt Anita drove a black B.M.W. which was probably worth both my parents' annual salaries combined. Getting into the B.M.W. was the first stage of my transformation. I rejected the messy Civic and surrendered to the veneration of this enormous car, flashily modern and luxurious, and in it we left the center of town and headed for the fancy neighborhood of Oak Park where they lived. Oak Park was a world unto itself: the sidewalks were wider, the streets were lined with massive trees. Every house was bigger than the next one, every gate tried to outdo the next one with its arabesques, and the fences were excessively high. The people out walking seemed better looking, their dogs were more elegant, the Sunday joggers were more athletic. While our neighborhood in Montclair was full of welcoming houses, with no fences around the gardens, in Oak Park, the vast majority were protected by hedges and walls. A private security service drove through the quiet streets in patrol cars with flashing orange lights, sporting the badge of *Oak Park Security*, to ensure the residents' peace of mind.

Driving through Oak Park with Aunt Anita set off the second phase of my transformation: it made me feel superior. It all seemed obvious: the car, the neighborhood, my presence. The agents patrolling Oak Park were in the habit of greeting the inhabitants with a quick wave when they passed them, and the inhabitants returned the greeting. A wave to confirm that everything was fine and the tribe of rich folk could walk around in safety. The first car we met, the agent waved, Anita responded, and I hurried to do the same. Now I was one of them. When we got to the house, Aunt Anita beeped the horn twice to announce our presence before pressing the remote to open the two steel jaws of the gate. We went up the drive and into the four-car garage. No sooner was I out of the car than the door to the house opened with a joyful commotion, and there they were, rushing out to greet me with cries of excitement, Woody and Hillel, the brothers that life had never wanted to grant me. Every time I went into the house I would gaze around me in wonder: it was all beautiful, luxurious, colossal. Their garage was as big as our living room. Their kitchen as big as our house. Their bathrooms as big as our bedrooms, and there were enough bedrooms to lodge several generations.

Every new stay surpassed the previous one and only increased my admiration for my aunt and uncle and above all the matchless chemistry in the gang consisting of Hillel, Woody and me. They were like my flesh and blood. We liked the same sports, the same actors, the same films, the same girls, and it wasn't because we'd discussed it or come to some agreement, but because each of us was an extension of the other two. We defied nature and science: the trees of our ancestors did not share the same trunk, but our genetic sequences had the same spirals. Sometimes we went to visit Aunt Anita's father, who lived in an old people's home – "the death house", we called it – and I remember that his friends, who were a bit senile, their memories fraying, would constantly ask about Woody, and confuse us with each other. They would point at him with a twisted finger and unabashedly ask the same old question: "And this one here, is he a Baltimore Goldman or a Montclair Goldman?" If it was Aunt Anita who replied, she would explain, her voice overflowing with tenderness, "This is Woodrow, Hill's friend. He's the kid we took in. Such a good boy." Before saying that, she always made sure Woody wasn't in the room, not to offend him, even if you could tell at once from her tone of voice she was ready to love him like her own son. Woody, Hillel and I had our own answer to the same question, and to us it seemed closer to reality. Whenever, during those winters, in those corridors wafting with the smells of old age, those wrinkled hands clutched at our clothes and enjoined us to say our names, to make up for the inevitable erosion of their ailing brains, we'd reply, "I'm one of the three Goldman cousins."

My neighbor Leo Horowitz interrupted me in the middle of the afternoon. He was worried, he hadn't seen me all day and wanted to make sure everything was alright.

"Everything's fine, Leo," I reassured him, from the doorway.

He must have thought it was strange I didn't invite him in, and he suspected I was hiding something. So he persisted:

"Are you sure?" he said again, his voice full of curiosity.

"Absolutely. Nothing special. I'm working."

Then he saw Duke appear behind me; he'd woken from his nap and was eager to see what was going on. Leo opened his eyes wide.

"Marcus, what's that dog doing here?"

I looked down, abashed.

"I borrowed him."

"You did what?"

I motioned to him to come in quickly and I closed the door behind him. The dog must not be seen at my place.

"I wanted to go and see Alexandra," I said. "And then I spotted the dog leaving the property. I figured I could bring him here, keep him for the day, and take him home in the evening, and say that he had come to my place all by himself."

"You've got rocks in your head, bud. That's nothing short of theft."

"I borrowed him, I don't intend to keep him. I just need him for a few hours."

While he listened to me, Leo headed into the kitchen, helped himself to a bottle of water from the fridge and sat down at the counter. He was enchanted by the unusually entertaining turn his day had taken. With a radiant air he suggested, "Why don't we have a little game of chess? It will relax you."

"No, Leo, I really don't have time right now."

He frowned and looked again at the dog who was noisily slurping water from a pan on the floor.

"So tell me one thing, Marcus: why do you need this dog?"

"To have a good excuse to go back and see Alexandra."

"That I understood. But why do you need an excuse to go and see her? Can't you just stop in and say hello the way a civilized person would, instead of kidnapping her dog?"

"She asked me not to get back in touch with her."

"Why did she do that?"

"Because I left her. Eight years ago."

"Damn. No, that wasn't very nice of you. You didn't love her anymore?"

"On the contrary."

"But you left her."

"Yes."

"Why?"

"Because of the tragedy."

"What tragedy?"

"It's a long story."

* * *

The moments of happiness with the Baltimore Goldmans were counterbalanced twice a year when our two families got together: at Thanksgiving at the Baltimores', and over Christmas vacation with our grandparents in Miami. In my opinion these family get-togethers were more like football games than reunions. At one end of the field, the Montclairs; at the other, the Baltimores, and in the middle, the Goldman grandparents, acting as referees, counting the goals.

Thanksgiving was the annual consecration of the Baltimores. The family met in their huge, luxurious house in Oak Park and everything was perfect from beginning to end. To my great delight, I slept in Hillel's bedroom, and Woody, who was next door, would drag his mattress into our room so we could all be together, even in our sleep. My parents had one of the guest rooms, with a private bathroom, and my grandparents had the other one.

It was Uncle Saul who went to pick up my grandparents at the airport, and for the first half hour after their arrival at the Baltimores', the conversation revolved around the comfort of his car. "You should take a look . . . it's marvelous!" Grandmother said. "The leg room, I've never seen anything like it! I remember getting in your car, Nathan," (she was referring to my father), "and I said, 'Never again!' And so dirty, dear Lord! Is it so expensive to run the vacuum cleaner? Saul's car is like new. Those leather seats are in perfect condition, you can tell he really takes good care of it." Then when she had nothing left to say about the car, she went into raptures about the house. She explored every corridor as if it were her first visit, marveling at the superb taste in decoration, the quality of the furniture, the floor heating, the cleanliness, the flowers, the perfumed candles scenting every room.

During Thanksgiving dinner she could not stop gushing over the superlative dishes. Every mouthful was accompanied by enthusiastic noises. It's true, the meal was sumptuous: squash soup, tender turkey roasted in maple syrup and pepper sauce, macaroni and cheese, pumpkin pie, creamy mashed potatoes, succulent Swiss chard, delicate green beans. The desserts were not to be outdone, either: chocolate mousse, cheesecake, pecan pie, and apple pie with a thin, crusty pastry. After the meal and coffee, Uncle Saul brought bottles of strong alcohol to the table; at the time, their names meant nothing to me, but I remember that Grandfather would pick up the bottles as if they were magic potions and marvel at their name, their age, or their color, while Grandmother would pile it on about how wonderful the meal was and, by extension, their house and their lifestyle, leading to the Grand Finale, always the same: "Saul, Anita, Hillel, and Woody, my darlings: thank you, it was sublime."

I wished she would come with Grandfather to stay in Montclair, so that we could show her what we were capable of. One time I did ask her, for all that I was only ten years old, "Grandmother, will you and Grandfather come and sleep at our house in Montclair some day?" But she replied, "You know we can't come there anymore, sweetie. It's not big enough and not comfortable enough."

The second major annual Goldman reunion was held in Miami over Christmas vacation. Until we turned thirteen, our Goldman grandparents lived in an apartment that was big enough to accommodate both families, and we spent a week all together, never out of each other's sight. Our stays in Florida were an opportunity for me to observe how much my grandparents admired the Baltimores, those formidable Martians who, basically, had nothing in common with the rest of the family. I could see the obvious family similarities between my grandfather and my father. They looked alike physically, had the same odd habits, and they both suffered from irritable bowel syndrome, about which they had endless discussions. Irritable bowel was one of Grandfather's favorite topics of conversation. I remember him as gentle, tender, absent-minded and above all constipated. He went off to do his business the way others leave for the station. With his newspaper under his arm he would announce, "I'm off to the bathroom." He gave Grandmother a little parting kiss on the lips and she would say, "See you later, dear."

Grandfather worried that I too might be stricken one day with the non-Baltimore-Goldman affliction, the famous irritable bowel. He made me promise to eat plenty of vegetables with fiber and never to hold back my stools if I needed to do a "number two". In the morning, while Woody and Hillel stuffed themselves with sugar-coated cereal, Grandfather forced to me to stuff myself with All-Bran. I was the only one who was obliged to eat it, proof that the Baltimores must have had additional enzymes that we were lacking. Grandfather told me: "My poor Marcus, your father has a colon just like mine. You'll see, you won't get out of it. Eat a lot of fiber, son, that's the main thing." He stood behind me while I shoveled down my spoonfuls of All-Bran, and placed a hand heavy with empathy on my shoulder. This colon business made a big impression on me. I searched through medical dictionaries at the local library, watching apprehensively for the first symptoms of the disease.

This mixture of the Montclairs and the Baltimores was, for me, the indicator of the deep divide between my two lives: one was my official life, the Montclair Goldman life, and the other was secret, the Baltimore Goldman life. I took the initial of my middle name, Philip, and on my homework and school notebooks I wrote *Marcus P. Goldman*. Then I added a loop to the P, which made it Marcus B. Goldman. I was the P that sometimes became a B. And as if to prove me right, life played funny tricks on me: alone in Baltimore, I felt like one of *them*. As I wandered around the neighborhood with Hillel and Woody, the officers in the patrol cars would greet us and call us by name. But when I went with my parents to Baltimore for Thanksgiving, I remember how ashamed I felt the moment we drove into Oak Park in our old car, as if it was written on the bumper that we didn't belong to the dynasty of Goldmans who lived there. If we met one of the security guards, I made the secret sign of the initiated, and my mother, who didn't know what was going on, scolded me: "Markie, would you stop acting the clown, making those stupid gestures at the officer?"

The most horrible thing was if we got lost in Oak Park: the streets were circular and you could easily become confused. My mother got annoyed, my father stopped in the middle of an intersection, and they would argue about which way to go until a security guard showed up to see what was going on with that beat-up, obviously suspicious, old car. My father explained why we were there, while I made the sign of the secret brotherhood so the guard wouldn't think there was any relation between those two strangers and myself. Sometimes the guard would simply point us in the right direction, but other times, if he was suspicious, he would escort us to the Goldman house to make sure our intentions were honorable. When Uncle Saul saw us arrive he immediately came out.

"Evening Mr Goldman," said the security guard, "sorry to bother you, just wanted to make sure you're expecting these folks at your place."

"Thank you, Matt," (or whatever other name happened to be on the badge; my uncle always called people by the name on their badge – at restaurants, the movie theater, the freeway toll booth). "Yes, everything's in order, thank you, everything's fine."

He said, everything's fine. He didn't say, Matt, you oaf, how could you act suspicious of my own blood, the flesh of my flesh, my dear brother? The tsar would impale any guards who treated a member of his family like this. But in Oak Park Uncle Saul congratulated Matt like the good guard dog you reward for barking, to make sure he'll go on barking. And once the guard had left, my mother said, "Yeah, that's right, go ahead, you can leave now, now that you know we're not bandits," while my father begged her to be quiet and not call attention to herself. We were only guests.

In the Baltimore heritage, there was only one place that was free of Montclair contamination: the vacation home in the Hamptons. My parents had shown good taste by refraining from ever going there – at least with me. For those who don't know how the Hamptons have changed since the 1980s: this used to be a quiet, modest place by the ocean, right outside New York City, and now it's been transformed into one of the most upscale resorts on the east coast. The house in the Hamptons had also led several lives in succession, and Uncle Saul never tired of telling how when he had bought the little wooden house in East Hampton for a song everyone had made fun of him, affirming it was the worst investment he could have made. They hadn't reckoned with the Wall Street boom in the 1980s, which heralded the beginning of a golden age for a generation of traders: new fortunes had taken the Hamptons by storm, the region was gentrified overnight and the value of real estate skyrocketed.

I was too young to remember, but they told me that every time Uncle Saul won a case, the house would undergo some slight improvement, until one day it was knocked down altogether to make room for a new house that was magnificent, full of charm and comfort. Roomy, luminous, cleverly covered in ivy, and at the back, a patio surrounded by blue and white hydrangea bushes, a swimming pool, and a gazebo covered with birthwort where we had our meals.

After Baltimore and Miami, the Hamptons was the conclusion of the Goldman Gang's yearly geographical triptych. Every year, my parents allowed me to spend the entire month of July there. That was where, in my uncle and aunt's vacation house, I spent the happiest summers of my youth, together with Woody and Hillel. That was also where the seeds of the tragedy were planted. In spite of everything, my memory of my time there is still one of absolute happiness. I recall blissful summer days, all alike, drifting with a perfume of immortality. How did we spend our time? Living out our triumphant youth. We were going to conquer the ocean. We went chasing girls as if they were butterflies. We went fishing. We went looking for rocks so we could jump into the ocean and measure ourselves against life.

The place we liked best of all was the property of this adorable couple called Seth and Jane Clark, relatively elderly, with no children, very wealthy – I think he owned an investment fund in New York – whom Uncle Saul and Aunt Anita had befriended over the years. Their estate, called *Paradise on Earth*, was a mile from the Baltimores'. It was a fabulous place: I remember the luxuriant garden, the Judas trees, the borders of rose bushes, the cascading fountain. Behind the house a swimming pool overlooked a private white sand beach. The Clarks gave us the run of the place, and we were over there all the time, jumping in the pool, or swimming in the ocean. There was even a little dinghy moored to a wooden dock which we used to explore the bay from time to time. To thank the Clarks for their kindness, we frequently did odd jobs for them, mostly gardening, something we were very good at for reasons I'll explain further on.

In the Hamptons we lost track of dates and days. Maybe that was what deceived me: that impression that it would all last forever. That we would last forever, as if in that magical place, in those streets and houses, people could escape time and its ravages.

I remember the table on the patio where Uncle Saul set up what he called his "office". Right next to the swimming pool. After breakfast, he would bring out his files, along with the telephone, and work at least until midday. Without betraying professional secrecy, he told us about the cases he was working on. I was fascinated by his explanations. We asked him how he planned to win and he replied, "I will win because I must. Goldmans never lose." He asked us what we would do in his place. So we pictured ourselves, the three of us, as great men of the law, and we shouted out all the ideas that went through our heads. He smiled and said we'd make very good lawyers, and that we could all work for his firm one day. Just the thought of it set me dreaming.

A few months later, on a visit to Baltimore, I came upon some press clippings Aunt Anita had preciously saved describing the trials he'd prepared in the Hamptons. Uncle Saul had won. All the papers talked about him. I even remember some of the headlines:

UNBEATABLE GOLDMAN

SAUL GOLDMAN, THE LAWYER WHO NEVER LOSES

GOLDMAN STRIKES AGAIN

He practically never lost a case. And my discovery of his victories reinforced the passion I felt for him. He was the greatest uncle, and the greatest lawyer.

*   *   *

Early in the evening I woke Duke from his nap to take him home. He liked it at my place and didn't really feel like moving. I had to drag him out to the car parked in front of the house then lift him into the back. Leo was watching, amused, from his porch. "Good luck, Marcus, I'm sure that if she doesn't want to see you anymore it means she likes you." I drove to Kevin Legendre's house and rang the bell on the interphone.

3

Coconut Grove, Florida
June 2010. Six years after the tragedy.

It was dawn. I was sitting out on the terrace of the house where my uncle now lived, in Coconut Grove. He'd moved there four years earlier.

He came out without making a sound and I gave a start when he said, "Already up?"

"Morning, Uncle Saul."

He was holding two cups of coffee and set one down before me. He noticed my pages covered in writing.

"What's your new novel about, Markie?"

"I can't tell you, Uncle Saul. You already asked me yesterday."

He smiled. Watched me writing for a moment. Then, before he turned away, stuffing his shirt tail into his slacks and tightening his belt, he asked me solemnly, "Some day I'll be in one of your books, huh?"

"Of course," I answered.

My uncle left Baltimore in 2006, to come and live in this elegant little house in Coconut Grove, south of Miami. There was a little patio in front surrounded by mango and avocado trees; every year there was more fruit, and when there were heat waves, their cool shade was refreshing.

The success of my novels gave me the freedom to come to see my uncle as often as I liked. Most of the time, I came by car. I would leave New York on a sudden impulse; sometimes I would decide that very morning, throw a few things into a bag I tossed onto the back seat and off I'd drive. I would take highway I-95 as far as Baltimore, then keep heading south to Florida. It would take two whole days, with a stop halfway in Beaufort, South Carolina, at a hotel I began to stay at regularly. If it was winter, I would leave a New York City swept with polar winds, my car covered in snow and me wearing a thick sweater with a steaming coffee in one hand and the steering wheel in the other. By the time I'd get to Miami it would be eighty-five degrees with people walking around in T-shirts, enjoying the dazzling sunshine of a tropical winter.

Sometimes I took the plane and rented a car at Miami airport. This meant the trip took a tenth the time, but the powerful feeling that otherwise came over me when I reached Uncle Saul's place was somehow diminished. The plane restricted my freedom with its schedules, airline company rules, the endless lines and pointless waiting incurred as a result of the security procedures the airports had been forced to take since 9/11. On the other hand, a virtually total feeling of freedom came over me if, the previous morning, I had decided simply to get in the car and drive due south. I left when I wanted, I stopped when I wanted. I was master of rhythm and of time. As the hundreds of miles of freeway I now knew by heart went by, I never tired of the beauty of the landscape, and could never stop marveling at the size of the country; it seemed endless. Finally I reached Florida, then Miami, then Coconut Grove, then Uncle Saul's street. When I pulled up outside his house I found him out on the porch. He was always expecting me. I wouldn't even tell me I was coming, but there he would be, waiting. Faithfully.

On this occasion, I had been in Coconut Grove for two days. I had come, like every time, without warning, and when he saw me, Uncle Saul had been overjoyed that I had come to put an end to his solitude, and he gave me a big hug. I held him close, this man defeated by life. With my fingertips I caressed the cloth of his cheap shirt, and I closed my eyes and breathed in his pleasant smell, which was the only thing that hadn't changed. And on finding that smell again, I pictured myself back on the patio of his luxurious Baltimore house, back in the glory days. I pictured my magnificent Aunt Anita beside him, and Woody and Hillel, my wonderful cousins. Just a single whiff of his smell took me back, deep into memory, into the neighborhood of Oak Park, and once again for the space of a moment I relived the happiness of having known them.

In Coconut Grove I spent my days writing. It was there I found the quiet I needed to be able to work. I realized that while I might live in New York, I never really wrote there. I always needed to go somewhere else and shut myself off. I worked out on the patio when the weather was mild, and if it was too hot, in the cool air-conditioned study Saul had set up especially for me in the guest room.

As a rule I took a break at the end of the morning and went to the supermarket to say hi. He liked for me to come and see him at the supermarket. In the beginning I found it difficult: I was embarrassed. But I knew how glad it made him when I came to the store. The minute I got there, I always felt a little twinge in my heart. One morning, the sliding doors opened in front of me and I saw him there, at the checkout, busy filling customers' bags with their purchases, sorting by weight and how perishable they were. He wore the green employee apron, with a pin that said his name, *Saul.* I heard the customers say, "Thank you, Saul. Have a nice day." He was always jovial, in a good mood. I waited until he wasn't busy to indicate my presence and I saw his face light up. "Markie!" he cried, joyfully, every time, as if it were my first visit.

To the check-out clerk next to him he said, "Look, Lindsay, it's my nephew Marcus."

She looked at me as if I were a strange beast and said, "Are you the famous writer?"

"That's him!" said my uncle in my place, as if I were the president of the United States.

She made a sort of curtsy and promised to read my work.

The supermarket employees liked my uncle, and whenever I showed up, he always found someone to fill in for him. Then he would take me up and down the aisles to meet his co-workers, one by one. "Everyone wants to say hello, Markie. Some of them have brought their book so you'll sign it. You don't mind, do you?" I always did so gladly, then we finished our visit at the juice and coffee bar: my uncle had grown fond of a young black man who worked there; he was as tall as a mountain and gentle as a lamb, and his name was Sycomorus.

Sycomorus was roughly my age. He had dreams of becoming a singer, and while waiting for glory he pressed revitalizing vegetables into the juicer on request. Whenever he could he would shut himself in the employee lounge and film himself with his cell phone, singing the latest tunes and snapping his fingers, then he'd share his videos on social networks to let the rest of the world know he had talent. He dreamt of taking part in a T.V. talent show called "Sing!" that was broadcast nationwide, where singers hoping to break through and become famous competed.

Early that month of June 2010, Uncle Saul was helping him fill out application forms to audition as a candidate for the show by means of a video recording. There were some questions about disclaimers and image rights that Sycomorus didn't understand. His parents wanted him to become famous. As it was clear they had nothing better to do, they spent their days coming to visit their son at his place of work to fret about his future. They were glued to the juice counter and between two customers the father berated his son and the mother tried to act the mediator.

The father was a failed tennis player. The mother had dreamt of becoming an actress. The father had wanted Sycomorus to become a tennis champion. And the mother wanted him to be a great actor. At the age of six, Sycomorus was a slave to the tennis court, and had starred in a commercial for yogurt. By the time he was eight he couldn't stand tennis anymore and swore never to pick up a racket again in his life. He had started doing the rounds of all the casting sessions with his mother, in search of the role that would launch his career as a child star. But the role never came, and now, with no diploma or training, he was squeezing juice.

"The more I think about your T.V. show stuff, the more I think it's a total waste of time," the father said.

"You don't get it, Dad. This show is going to launch my career."

"Yeah, right. All it'll do is make you look ridiculous. What good can it do you to make a spectacle of yourself on television? You never liked singing. You should have been a tennis player. You had everything it takes. It's a real pity your mother made you lazy."

"But Dad," Sycomorus implored, desperately seeking his father's recognition, "everyone talks about this show."

"Leave him alone, George, if that's his dream," his mother interrupted, gently.

"Yes, Dad! Singing is my life!"

"You put vegetables in a blender, that's your life. You could've been a tennis star. You ruined everything."

As a rule, Sycomorus ended up in tears. To calm down, he would reach under the counter for the binder he brought from home to the supermarket every day and which contained the collection of articles about Alexandra Neville he had lovingly collected and sorted, compiling every fact about her that he considered worthy of interest. Alexandra was Sycomorus's role model, his obsession. Where music was concerned, he was in her hands. Her career, her songs, the way she reinterpreted them during her concerts: in his opinion, she was perfection personified. He followed every one of her tours, and came back with souvenir T-shirts designed for teenage girls, which he wore. "If I learn everything there is to know about her, maybe I'll be able to have a career like hers," he said. Most of what he knew about her came from the tabloids he read avidly, cutting out articles during his free time.

Sycomorus consoled himself, turning the pages of his binder, imagining that one day he too would be a star. His mother was brokenhearted, but she encouraged him: "Look at your binder, sweetheart, it does you good."

Sycomorus ran his hands admiringly over the plastic-covered pages.

"Mom, I'll be like her someday . . ."

"She's blond, and she's white," his father said, annoyed. "You want to be a white girl?"

"No, Dad, I want to be famous."

"That's just the problem, you don't want to be a singer, you want to be famous."

Sycomorus's father had a point. There was a time when astronauts and scientists were the stars. Nowadays our stars are people who do nothing and spend their time taking selfies or pictures of their dinner. While the father was trying to make his son see reason, the people waiting in line for revitalizing juice were getting impatient. Finally the mother tugged on her husband's sleeve:

"Be quiet now, George," she scolded. "He'll get fired the way you go making a scene. You want your son to lose his job because of you?"

The father clung to the counter in a gesture of despair and murmured one last request to his son, as if he didn't have the proof there before him:

"Just promise me one thing. Whatever happens, please, don't ever become gay."

"Promise, Dad."

And the parents went off to walk around the store.

During that same period, Alexandra Neville was in the middle of a concert tour. Notably, she was performing at the American Airlines Arena in Miami, and everyone in the supermarket knew about it because Sycomorus had managed to get a ticket, and in the employee lounge he had posted a countdown of the days until the concert; he had renamed the day of the concert "Alexandra Day".

A few days before the concert we were enjoying a balmy early evening out on the patio at the house in Coconut Grove, and Uncle Saul turned to me:

"Marcus, do you think you could set up a meeting between Sycomorus and Alexandra?"

"No way."

"Are you still angry with each other?"

"We haven't spoken in years. Even if I wanted to, I wouldn't know how to get hold of her."

"I have to show you what I found while I was tidying up," Uncle Saul said, getting up from his chair.

He vanished for a moment and came back with a photograph in his hand. "It was stuck in a book that belonged to Hillel," he explained. It was the famous photograph of Woody, Hillel, Alexandra and me as teenagers in Oak Park.

"What happened between Alexandra and you?" asked Uncle Saul.

"It's not important," I said.

"Markie, you know how much I like having you here. But sometimes I worry. You should get out more, have some fun. Get a girlfriend."

"Don't worry about me, Uncle Saul."

I held out the photograph to give it back to him.

"No, keep it," he said. "There's something written on the back."

I turned it over and recognized her handwriting. She had written:

I LOVE YOU GOLDMAN BOYS

4

That month of March 2012 in Boca Raton, when I found Alexandra again, I started stealing her dog Duke every morning. I brought him home, he spent the day with me, and in the evening I took him back to Kevin Legendre's house.

The dog liked it so much at my place that he began waiting for me by the fence at Kevin's. I would come in the early morning and there he'd be, sitting and watching out for me. As soon as I got out of the car he would bound up to me, showing how happy he was by trying to lick my face while I bent down to pat him. I opened the back, he jumped in eagerly and off we went to spend the day at my place. And then he couldn't help it, he started coming all on his own. Every morning at six o'clock Duke would announce his presence, barking outside my door, with the kind of precision human beings will never have.

We had a good time together. I bought him all the happy dog paraphernalia: rubber balls, toys to chew on, food, bowls, snacks, blankets to make him comfortable. At the end of the day I took him home, and both of us were overjoyed to see Alexandra again.

In the beginning our meetings were brief. She thanked me, apologized for the bother, and sent me home again, without even inviting me in.

Then one time she wasn't there. It was that muscular pain in the neck of a Kevin who greeted me and took Duke in. "Alex isn't here," he said in a friendly tone. I asked him to say hello to her for me and was turning to go when he invited me to stay for supper. I accepted. And I have to admit we had a very pleasant evening. There was something eminently likable about him. He was the kindly fatherly type, about to retire at the age of thirty-seven, with a few million dollars in his bank account. The sort who would take the children to school, train their soccer team, organize barbecues for birthdays. The laid-back type, that was Kevin.

And that very evening Kevin explained how he had hurt his shoulder and the team had given him some time off. During the day he was doing physiotherapy, and in the evening he cooked steaks, watched television, and slept. He couldn't help but gloat that Alexandra gave him divine massages, which made him feel a lot better. Then he made a list of all the movements that hurt and described all his physiotherapy exercises. He was a simple man in the literal sense of the term, and I began to wonder what Alexandra saw in him.

While the steaks were cooking, he suggested we inspect the hedge to find out how Duke was getting out. He went down one side of the hedge, I took care of the other. I soon found an enormous hole Duke had dug in the lawn to get to the other side of the fence, and obviously I didn't point it out to Kevin. I told him that my half of the hedge was intact (which wasn't a lie), and he confirmed that his was too, and we went to eat our steak. Duke's escapes puzzled him.

"I don't understand why he's doing this. It's the first time. This dog means the world to her. I'm afraid he'll get run over."

"How old is he?"

"Eight. That's already old for a dog this size."

I did some quick math in my head. Eight years – that meant she bought Duke just after the tragedy.

We drank a few beers. Rather, he did, mainly. I was careful to empty mine discreetly onto the lawn to get him to drink more. I needed to soften him up. I eventually brought up the subject of Alexandra, and with the help of the alcohol he confided in me.

He told me they'd been together for four years. They began their affair at the end of 2007.

"In those days I was playing for the Nashville Predators, and she was living in Nashville. We had a mutual friend, and I had been trying to win this woman over for some time. And then on New Year's Eve we were at the same party, at that same friend's house, and that's when it all began."

I felt like throwing up, just imagining their first embrace on a boozy New Year's Eve.

"Love at first sight, then," I said, acting the fool.

"No, it was tough at first," Kevin replied, touching in his sincerity.

"Really?"

"Yeah. Apparently, I was her first relationship since she'd broken up with her previous boyfriend. She never wanted to talk about him. Something major, serious, happened. But I don't know what. I don't want to push her. Some day, when she's ready, she'll tell me."

"Did she love him?"

"The previous guy? More than anything, I think. I thought I'd never manage to make her forget him. I never talk about it. Everything is great between us now and I'd rather not open up old wounds."

"You're right. The guy must have been a real jerk."

"I don't know. I don't like to judge people I don't know."

Kevin was so nice he was annoying. He took a sip of beer and eventually I asked him the question that had been bugging me more than anything.

"Have you and Alexandra talked about getting married?"

"I proposed. Two years ago. She cried. Not for joy, if you see what I mean. I understood that it meant 'not for the time being.'"

"Sorry to hear that, Kevin."

He put a thick friendly hand on my arm.

"I love that girl," he said.

"I can see that."

Suddenly I felt ashamed that I was trying to get involved in Alexandra's life like this. She'd asked me to stay away, and I had rushed to tame her boyfriend and befriend her dog.

I went home before she got back.

Just as I was turning the key in the lock, I heard Leo's voice; he was out on his porch, hidden in the darkness.

"You missed our chess game, Marcus," he said.

I remembered I had promised we would play when I got back from Kevin's, never dreaming I'd stay for dinner.

"I'm sorry, Leo, I completely forgot."

"It's no big deal."

"Want a drink?"

"I'd love one."

He came over and we settled out on the patio; I poured some scotch. It was very mild out; frogs in the lake filled the night with song.

"You can't stop thinking about that girl, can you?" Leo said.

I nodded. "It's that obvious?"

"Yes. I did some research."

"About what?"

"About you and Alexandra. And, well, I found something very interesting: there's nothing. And believe me, I spend my days on Google, and it's just when there's nothing that you have to dig. What's going on, Marcus?"

"I'm not even sure myself."

"I didn't know you went out with that movie actress Lydia Gloor. That's on the Internet."

"Briefly."

"Isn't she the one who is in the adaptation of your first book?"

"She is."

"Was that before or after Alexandra?"

"After."

Leo gave me a cautious look.

"You cheated on Alexandra with that actress, didn't you? You had been happy together. But success went to your head a little, you saw that actress in raptures in front of you and you slipped up, just for one torrid night. Am I right?"

I smiled, amused by his imagination.

"No, Leo."

"Oh, Marcus, don't keep me in suspense like this, please! What happened between you and Alexandra? And what happened with your cousins?"

When he asked me those questions, Leo didn't realize they were connected. I didn't know where to begin. Who should I speak about first? Alexandra, or the Goldman Gang?

I decided to start with my cousins, because to speak about Alexandra, I had to speak about them first.

* * *

I'll tell you about Hillel to start with, because he was the first. We were born the same year and he was like a brother to me, his genius a mixture of wild intelligence and an innate sense of provocation. He was very thin, but his physical appearance was counterbalanced by a formidable spirit, along with exceptional nerve. His frail body hid a huge soul and above all a rock-solid sense of justice. I still remember how he took my defense, when we were only eight years old – in those days, Woody hadn't shown up in our lives yet – at an outdoor sports camp in Reading, Pennsylvania, where Uncle Saul and Aunt Anita had sent him for spring vacation to help him develop physically; I went along too, out of a sense of brotherly obligation. In addition to the pleasure of his company, I think I went to Reading to protect Hillel from any bullies we might find among the participants; at school, Hillel was the usual scapegoat for the other pupils because he was so small. But I didn't realize that the camp in Reading actually was for children who were weak, underdeveloped, or convalescent, and I found myself looking like a Greek god among all the atrophied, myopic kids, so I was automatically chosen every time by the camp counselors to start the exercises when everyone else was staring at their shoes.

The second day was devoted to exercises on the gymnastics apparatus. The counselor brought us together by the rings, balance beams, parallel bars, and tall vertical poles. "We're going to begin with the first basic exercise: climbing the pole." He pointed to the row of poles at least twenty-four feet high. "Right, you're going to go up one by one, then once you're up there, if you feel like you can do it, move over to the next pole, then slide down, like a fireman. Who wants to start?"

He probably thought we would all rush over to the poles, but we didn't move.

"Maybe you have a question?" he asked.

"Yes," said Hillel, raising his hand.

"Go ahead."

"You really want us to climb up there?"

"Absolutely."

"And if we don't want to?"

"You have to."

"Why?"

"Because I said so."

"And why do you decide?"

"Because that's just how it is. I'm the camp counselor, and I decide."

"Did you know that our parents pay to send us here?"

"Yes, and what of it?"

"Well, then, technically you are our employee and you have to obey us, completely. So we could even ask you to cut our toenails if we wanted to."

The counselor gave Hillel a funny look. He tried to regain control of the lesson: struggling to sound authoritarian, he barked, "Come on, now! Someone get a move on, we're wasting time."

"That looks like a really long way up," continued Hillel. "How far is it, twenty-five, thirty feet?"

"I suppose," said the counselor.

"What do you mean, you suppose?" said Hillel indignantly. "Don't you even know your own equipment?"

"Quiet, now, please. And since no-one wants to volunteer, I will pick one of you."

Of course, the counselor pointed at me. I protested that I was always the one who had to go first, but the counselor didn't want to know.

"Go ahead," he ordered. "Climb up that pole."

"And why don't you climb up it yourself?" said Hillel again.

"What?"

"You go first yourself."

"I have no intention of letting myself be ordered around by a kid," said the counselor.

"Are you afraid to go up there?" asked Hillel. "I'd be afraid, in your shoes. Those bars look really dangerous. You know, I'm not exactly a hypochondriac, but I read somewhere that a fall of ten feet is enough to break your back and you can end up paralyzed for life. Who wants to be paralyzed for life?" he asked, looking around at everyone.

"Not me!" we shouted in unison.

"Be quiet!" screamed the counselor.

"Are you sure you have a gym teacher's diploma?" asked Hillel, yet again.

"Of course I do! Now stop it!"

"I think we'd all feel better if we saw your diploma," continued Hillel.

"For heaven's sake, I don't have it here!" said the counselor, whose self-confidence was vanishing into thin air.

"You don't have it here, or you don't have it at all?" replied Hillel.

"Di-plo-ma! Di-plo-ma!" we all began to shout.

We kept chanting the word until the counselor, at his wits' end, jumped like a monkey onto the pole and shimmied up to show us what he was capable of. It was surely to impress us that he began to make all sorts of useless movements, and what was bound to happen, happened: his hands slipped and he fell from the top of the pole, in other words from a height of twenty-three feet, to be precise. He crashed to the floor and let out a terrible cry. We did our best to console him, but the doctors in the ambulance explained that he had broken both legs and we wouldn't see him again for the length of our stay. Hillel was sent home from the sports camp, and so was I. Aunt Anita and Uncle Saul came to get us and took us to the county hospital so that we could apologize to the poor counselor in person.

It was one year after this episode that Hillel met Woody. He was nine, now, and still very short and thin, still the butt of his schoolmates' taunting; they called him Shrimpie. The other children bullied him so much that in two years he changed schools three times. But every time he was just as unhappy in the new place as at the old ones. All he wanted was a normal life, to have friends in the neighborhood and get on like other kids his age. He had one absolute passion: basketball. He loved it. On the weekend, sometimes he'd call some kids from class. "Hi. It's Hillel . . . Hillel. Hillel Goldman." He'd have to repeat his name over and over until finally he said, "Shrimpie." And the kid on the end of the line, not always with malicious intent, got it at last. "I wondered if you were going to the playing field this afternoon." And the answer came, no, not at all. But Hillel knew they were lying. He would hang up politely, and an hour later he would say to his parents, "I'm going out to play basketball with my friends." He'd climb on his bike and set off for the day. He always went to the playing field: his friends, who were not supposed to be there, actually were, of course. He didn't blame them, he'd just sit on a bench and hope they would let him play, too. But no-one ever wanted Shrimpie on their team. He would come home, downcast, trying to look happy all the same. He didn't want his parents to worry about him. When they sat down at the dinner table, he would be wearing his Michael Jordan jersey, his arms sticking out of the sleeves like two twigs.

"So did you play some today?" Uncle Saul asked one evening.

Hillel shrugged.

"Not really. The others say I'm not very good."

"I'm sure you play like a champion."

"No, I really am pretty lousy. But if no-one gives me a chance, how do they want me to get better?"

It was hard for my aunt and uncle to find the right balance between being overprotective and letting him learn that the world was a tough place. In the end they decided to send him to a prestigious private school, Oak Tree, which was not far from home.

They liked the school right away. They met with the headmaster, Mr Hennings, who took them on a tour of the campus while he explained how exceptional his establishment was: "Oak Tree School is one of the best in the country. We have first-rate classes, taught by professors hired from all over the country, and a tailor-made curriculum." The school encouraged creativity: they had an art studio, music classes, pottery workshops, and they were proud of the weekly newspaper that was written and edited entirely by pupils in a state-of-the-art office. Then Mr Hennings convinced Uncle Saul and Aunt Anita once and for all by intoning the opening notes of his miraculous symphony for desperate parents: "Happy children, motivation, guidance, sense of responsibility, reputation, quality, body and mind, all kinds of sports, breeding ground for champion equestrians."

I don't know how Hillel managed to antagonize all his classmates at Oak Tree in the space of only a few days. As if bolstered by this exploit, he then went on to alienate a majority of the faculty by finding typos in the exercise books, correcting one teacher on his pronunciation of a Latin word, and asking questions that were considered inappropriate for his age.

"We'll be teaching you that in ninth grade," the teacher said.

"And why not now, since I asked you?"

"Because that's just the way it is. It's not on the curriculum, and the curriculum is the curriculum."

"Maybe your curriculum isn't suitable for the class."

"Maybe you're the one who's not suitable for the class, Hillel."

In the school corridors, he stood out. He habitually wore a plaid shirt buttoned all the way up to his neck to hide the basketball jersey he always wore underneath, in the hopes of one day fulfilling his dream: to unbutton his shirt and appear as the invincible athlete, scoring baskets to the cheers of the other students. His backpack was heavy with the books he had borrowed from the library, and he could never be parted from his basketball.

It took only one week at Oak Tree for his everyday life to become hell. The class bully took an immediate dislike to him – a squat, obese boy called Vincent, whom his classmates had nicknamed Porky.

It is hard to say when the hostilities began. Porky, by virtue of his nickname alone, was the target of the other children's mockery. In the playground they all shouted at him, holding their noses: "If it stinks of shit, Porky did it!" Porky would jump on them to beat them up, but they'd all flee like a herd of terrified zebras – all except the weakest one, Hillel; Porky would catch up with him, and Hillel would pay for the others. As a rule, Porky stopped at merely twisting his arm, for fear of being caught by a teacher, and he'd say, "See you later, Shrimpie. Make yourself look nice, you got it coming to you!" After class, Porky would hurry to the basketball court next to the school, where Hillel went to practice shooting hoops, and he would gleefully beat him up while all the pupils in the class watched. Porky would grab Hillel by the neck, drag him along the ground and punch him, encouraged by bursts of applause.

As he always managed to catch Hillel, Porky began systematically torturing him. Every day, as soon he got to school, he latched onto him and would not let go. And the other pupils saw him as a pariah. After only three weeks, Hillel was begging his mother to let him leave Oak Tree, but Aunt Anita asked him to make an effort. "Hillel, sweetie, we can't keep changing your school. If it goes on like this and you can't get used to being in a school environment, we'll have to send you to a school for children with special needs." She said this with great tenderness and a touch of fatalism. Hillel, who didn't want to upset his mother or, worst of all, end up in a special needs school, had to resign himself to his daily after-school drubbings.

I know that Aunt Anita took him shopping and tried to draw inspiration from the boys his age she knew in order to get him to dress in a more conventional way. When she dropped him off at school in the morning she would beg him: "Try not to attract attention, O.K.? And make some friends." Once, she gave him muffins for his snack so that he could hand them out and make himself liked. He said, "You can't buy friends with muffins, Mom." She looked at him, somewhat disarmed. At recess, Porky emptied Hillel's backpack out onto the ground, took the muffins and shoved them all down Hillel's throat. In the evening, Aunt Anita asked, "Did your friends like the muffins?" "Yeah, Mom, they loved them." The next morning she added even more, unaware she was condemning her son to extremes of buccal elasticity. The muffin show soon became a huge success: pupils clustered in the playground to watch Porky stuffing half a dozen little cakes down Hillel's throat. They shouted in unison, "Eat! Eat! Eat! Eat!" The teacher heard that something was going on and gave Hillel a demerit, and wrote on his report card, "*He has a certain showmanship, but doesn't know how to share.*"

Aunt Anita voiced her concern to Hillel's pediatrician.

"He says he doesn't like school. He sleeps poorly at night and doesn't eat. I can tell he isn't happy."

The doctor turned to Hillel.

"Is it true what your mom says, Hillel?"

"Yes."

"Why don't you like school?"

"It's not school, it's more like the other kids."

Aunt Anita sighed:

"It's always the same story. He says it's the other kids. But we've changed schools several times already."

"Don't you realize if you don't make an effort to fit in, you'll have to go to a school for special needs, Hillel?"

"Not a *special school* … I don't want to."

"Why not?"

"I want to go to a normal school."

"Then the ball is in your court, Hillel."

"I know, Doctor, I know."

Porky beat him, stole from him, humiliated him. He made him drink bottles filled with a yellowish liquid and slurp up puddles of stagnant water; he smeared his face with mud. He lifted him up as if he were a twig, shook him like a maraca and shouted, "You're just a shrimp, a piece of dog shit, a blockhead!" And when eventually he ran out of vocabulary, he punched him in the stomach so hard that Hillel couldn't breathe. Hillel was scarily thin, and Porky made him fly through the air like a paper airplane; he slammed him with his school bag; he pounded his head, twisted his arm every which way, and in the end he said, "I'll only stop if you lick my shoes." So to make him stop, Hillel complied. In front of everyone he got down on all fours and licked the soles of Porky's shoes, and Porky seized the opportunity to kick him in the face a few times. Half of the pupils were laughing and the other half, in a surge of popular fever, rushed over to take their turn to beat him up. They jumped on him, crushed his hands, pulled his hair. They all had only one goal in mind: saving their own skin. As long as Porky had Hillel to keep him busy, he would leave them alone.

Once the show was over, they all left. "If you squeal on us, you're toast!" Porky hissed, gratifying him with one final spit in the eyes. "Yeah, we'll roast you alive!" echoed the choir of followers. Hillel stayed on the ground, like a scarab turned upside down, then once the commotion had died down, he got back to his feet, picked up his ball, and went at last to the deserted basketball court. He shot hoops, played imaginary games, then went home in time for dinner. When Aunt Anita saw his battered body and torn clothes she cried, horrified, "Hillel, My God, what happened?" And with a dazzling smile, hiding his pain so he wouldn't cause his mother any, he said, "Oh, nothing. It was just a hell of a game, that's all, Mom."

Twenty miles away, in East Baltimore, Woody was a boarder in a home for troubled children. The director, Artie Crawford, was an old friend of Uncle Saul and Aunt Anita's. They were active volunteers at the home: Aunt Anita arranged free medical visits, while Uncle Saul had set up a legal advice service to help the boarders and their families with various administrative procedures.

Woody was our age, but he was the exact opposite of Hillel: he was physically much more mature and developed, and he looked considerably older. A far cry from placid Oak Park, the neighborhoods in East Baltimore were riddled with explosive crime, drug trafficking, and violence. The home had a hard time keeping the children in school; they were easily swayed by the bad company they kept, and the possibility of rebuilding their missing family unit within a gang held great appeal. Woody belonged to this category: a boy who liked to fight, but who was not bad at heart, easily influenced and in the grip of an older boy, Devon – a tattooed, part-time drug dealer, never without a gun in his waistband that he liked to show off in the shelter of a back street.

Uncle Saul knew Woody because he had acted on his behalf on several occasions. He was a polite, likeable kid, but since he got into so many fights, the police picked him up on a regular basis. Uncle Saul liked him a lot because he always fought for a noble cause: an old lady who had been insulted, a friend who was in trouble, a buddy from the home who was younger and who had been shoved around or bullied into giving money – along came Woody, restoring justice with his fists. Whenever he had had to intervene in his favor, Uncle Saul had managed to convince the police to let Woody go without filing charges. Until fairly late one evening when Artie Crawford, the director of the home, called to tell him that Woody was in trouble again, and this time it was serious: he had struck a policeman.

Uncle Saul immediately went down to the police station on Eastern Avenue where Woody was being held. On the way, he even went to the trouble of disturbing the police chief's assistant, a man he knew well, in order to prepare the terrain: he might need a helping hand from someone higher up to prevent any zealous judge from getting a hold of the file. When he got to the station, he found Woody not in a cell or handcuffed to a bench but comfortably installed in an interrogation room reading a comic book and drinking hot chocolate.

"Woody, is everything alright?" Uncle Saul asked as he came into the room.

"Good evening, Mr Goldman," the boy replied. "I'm sorry you're going to all this bother for me. Everything's fine, the policemen are really nice."

He was not even ten years old but he had the build of a boy of thirteen or fourteen: prominent muscles already, and tough-boy bruises on his face. And now he had been warming the hearts of the neighborhood cops, who had made him a nice little hot chocolate.

"And is that how you thank them?" replied Uncle Saul, slightly annoyed. "By punching them in the face? Woody, for God's sake, what got into you? Hitting a policeman? Do you know what that means?"

"I didn't know he was a policeman, Mr Goldman, I swear. He wasn't in uniform."

Woody explained that he been drawn into a fight with three guys twice his age: just as he was about to send them flying, a policeman in civilian clothes stepped in to separate them and in the process received a punch that knocked him to the ground.

Just then, an inspector came into the room; he had a huge black eye.

Woody stood up and gave him a friendly hug.

"Like I said, I'm so sorry, Inspector Johns, I thought you were one of the bad guys."

"Sheesh, these things happen. Let's drop it. Hey, if ever you need help one day, you can always give me a call."

The inspector handed him his business card.

"Does this mean I can leave now, Inspector?"

"Yes. But next time you see a fight, you call the police, you don't go sorting it out yourself."

"Promise."

"Do you want another hot chocolate?" asked the inspector.

"No, he doesn't want another hot chocolate," barked Uncle Saul. "Honestly, Inspector, show some dignity: he punched you!"

He led Woody out of the room and started lecturing him:

"Woody, you'd better realize you're going to end up in deep trouble. There won't always be nice cops and nice lawyers to help you when you're up shit creek. You could end up in prison, don't you see?"

"Yes, Mr Goldman. I know."

"So why do you go on behaving like this?"

"I think it's like a gift. I have a gift for fighting."

"Well then, find another gift, please. Besides, a kid your age has no business being out at night. You should be asleep."

"I can't sleep. I don't like it at that home. I felt like going for a walk."

They had reached the reception area, where Artie Crawford was waiting for them.

Woody thanked Uncle Saul again:

"You're my savior, Mr Goldman."

"I wasn't very useful this time."

"But you have always been there for me."

Woody took seven dollars out of his pocket and handed it to him.

"What's this?" asked Uncle Saul.

"It's all the money I have. It's to pay you. To thank you for helping me out 'cause I got up shit creek."

"Don't say shit. And you don't need to pay me."

"You said shit, just now."

"I shouldn't have. I'm sorry."

"Mr Crawford says you should always pay people back one way or another for the favors they do you."

"Woody, would you like to pay me?"

"Yes, Mr Goldman. I really would."

"Then stop getting yourself arrested. That would be the biggest pay for me, the best salary I've ever had. To see you ten years from now and know that you're at a good university. To see a fine, accomplished young man and not a delinquent who has already spent half his life in a juvenile prison."

"I'll do that, Mr Goldman. You'll be proud of me."

"And for heavens' sake, stop calling me Mr Goldman. Call me Saul."

"Yes, Mr Goldman."

"Right, get going now, and start becoming a good person."

But Woody had a sense of honor. He absolutely wanted to thank my uncle for his help, and the next morning he showed up at his office.

"Why aren't you in school?" Uncle Saul said irritably, when he saw him come in the office.

"I wanted to see you. There must be something I can do for you, Mr Goldman. You've been so good to me."

"Just think of it as life nudging you in the right direction."

"I could mow your lawn if you want."

"I don't need someone to mow my lawn."

"No, but I'll do a really fine job. You'll have an amazing lawn."

"My lawn is fine as it is. Why aren't you at school?"

"Because of your lawn, Mr Goldman. I'd be really glad to mow your lawn to thank you for being so kind to me."

"Don't trouble yourself with that, son."

"I'd really like to, Mr Goldman."

"Woodrow, raise your right hand, please, and repeat after me."

"Yes, Mr Goldman."

He raised his right hand and Uncle Saul declared, "I, Woodrow

Marshall Finn, hereby swear never to get myself up shit creek again."

"I, Woodrow Marshall Finn, hereby swear never to . . . you told me not to say shit anymore, Mr Goldman."

"O.K. Fine. Then say, I swear not to get into trouble."

"I swear not to get into trouble."

"O.K., you've paid me. We're even. Now you can go back to school. Off you go."

Woody grumbled, resigned. He didn't feel like going back to school, he wanted to mow Uncle Saul's lawn. He headed toward the door, dragging his feet, until he noticed some photographs on a piece of furniture.

"Is that your family?" he asked.

"Yes. This is my wife, Anita, and my son, Hillel."

Woody picked up one of the frames and observed the faces on the photograph.

"They look nice. You're lucky."

Just then the door opened and Aunt Anita rushed in, too upset to notice Woody.

"Saul!" she cried, her eyes red with tears. "He got beat up at school again! He says he doesn't want to go back. I don't know what to do."

"What happened?"

"He says all the other kids make fun of him. He says he doesn't want to go anywhere anymore."

"We just changed schools in May," sighed Uncle Saul. "Then again in the summer to put him in this school. We can't change again. This is unbearable."

"I know . . . Oh, Saul! I'm at my wits' end . . . "

5

My dinner with Kevin in Boca Raton in early March 2012 brought me a little closer to Alexandra.

In the days that followed, whenever I took Duke home after he had run away to my place, she started letting me into the house, then she even offered me something to drink. As a rule it was a bottle of water or a can of soda that I drank standing up in the kitchen, but that was already something.

"Thank you for the other night," she said late one afternoon when we were alone. "I don't know what you did to Kevin, but he likes you a lot now."

"I just acted myself."

She smiled.

"Thank you for not saying anything to him about the two of us. I'm really fond of Kevin, and I don't want him thinking there are still any emotional ties between you and me."

I felt a twinge of sorrow at her words.

"Kevin told me you turned down his marriage proposal."

"That's none of your business, Marcus."

"Kevin is a nice guy, but he's not your type."

I instantly regretted my words. What business was it of mine indeed? She merely shrugged then blurted, "You have Lydia."

"How do you know about Lydia?" I asked.

"I read about it in one of those stupid magazines."

"You're talking about something that happened over four years ago. We haven't been together in a long time. Just a passing fling."

I wanted to change the subject so I decided to show Alexandra the photograph I had brought with me.

"Do you remember this picture?"

She gave a nostalgic smile and stroked the picture with her fingertips.

"Who would have imagined back then that you would become a famous writer," she said.

"And you a famous singer."

"I wouldn't have without you."

"Stop it."

There was a moment of silence. Suddenly she said my name the way she used to, before:

"Markie," she murmured, "I've been missing you for eight years."

"Same here. I've followed your entire career."

"I read your novels."

"Did you like them?"

"Yes. A lot. I often re-read passages from your first novel. I can see your cousins in it. And the Goldman Gang."

I smiled. I looked again at the picture I was holding.

"You seem fascinated by that picture," she said.

"I don't know whether I'm fascinated or haunted."

I put the picture in my pocket and left.

That day as I drove out Kevin's gate, I didn't notice the black van parked in the street, or the man at the wheel who was watching me.

I continued on my way home, and he followed me.

* * *

Baltimore, Maryland
November 1989

Woody's urge to mow their lawn, ever since he had shared it with him, had been running through Uncle Saul's head. Particularly when Artie came to dinner and told them he was having a hard time with Woody, trying to get him to fit in.

"At least he likes school," Artie said. "He likes to learn, and he has a quick mind. But the minute class is over, he gets into mischief, and we can't keep watching him all the time."

"And his parents?" asked Uncle Saul.

"The mother vanished from the scene a long time ago."

"A junkie?"

"Not even. She just disappeared. She was young. The father, too. He thought he could bring the kid up, but the day he found a real girlfriend, all hell broke loose at home. The boy was hopping mad, lashing out at everyone. The social worker got involved, and the family judge. He was placed in the home, supposedly temporarily, then the dad's girlfriend got transferred to Salt Lake City and the dad used it as a pretext to follow her across the country, marry her, and have children with her. Woodrow stayed behind in Baltimore, he doesn't want to know about Salt Lake City. They speak on the phone from time to time. Occasionally the dad writes. What worries me about Woodrow is that he hangs around with this kid Devon, a small-time delinquent who smokes crack and plays around with a gun."

It occurred to Uncle Saul that if Woody were busy mowing lawns after school he wouldn't have time to hang around in the street. He talked it over with Dennis Bunk, an old gardener who had a virtual monopoly on garden maintenance in Oak Park.

"I'm not hiring, Mr Goldman. Specially not any little bastard delinquents."

"He's a good kid."

"He's a delinquent."

"You need help, you're having trouble keeping up with your workload as it is."

What Uncle Saul said was true: Bunk couldn't cope, and he was too cheap to pay for an employee.

"Who'll pay his salary?" Bunk wanted to know, sounding defeated.

"I will," said Uncle Saul. "Five dollars an hour for him and two for you, for training him."

After one last hesitation, Bunk agreed, pointing a threatening finger at Uncle Saul.

"I warn you. If that little jerk breaks any of my equipment or steals from me, you'll be the one to pay."

But Woody did no such thing. He was thrilled by Uncle Saul's proposal that he work for Bunk.

"Will I be taking care of your garden too, Mr Goldman?"

"Maybe, sometimes. But you have to help Mr Bunk. And do what he says."

"I promise I'll work hard."

After school and on the weekends, Woody jumped in the local bus and came to Oak Park. Bunk was waiting for him in his pickup in a street near the bus stop and they did the round of gardens.

It turned out that Woody was a diligent, devoted assistant. A few weeks went by, and fall came to Maryland. The century-old trees in Oak Park turned red and yellow, then showered their dead leaves onto the lanes. The lawns needed raking, plants had to be readied for winter, and swimming pools had to be covered.

In the meantime, at Oak Tree School, Porky went on tormenting Hillel. He threw pine cones and stones at him, tied him up and forced him to eat dirt, along with sandwiches he found in the trash. "Eat! Eat! Eat!" the other children gaily chanted, while Porky pinched Hillel's nose to force open his mouth so he could ram the food in. When he had the strength to scoff at him, Hillel would thank him warmly: "Thank you for the good food, I didn't have enough to eat at lunch." And the blows rained down harder than ever. Porky emptied Hillel's school bag out onto the ground and threw the textbooks and notebooks into the garbage can. In his spare time, Hillel had started a poetry notebook, and inevitably it fell into Porky's hands; he made him eat certain pages while he read others out loud, then burned what was left. Hillel was able to save one poem from his auto-da-fé, a poem written for Helena, his secret love, a cute little blond girl who didn't miss a single one of Porky's displays. Hillel saw it as a sign, and taking his courage in both hands he gave his poem to Helena. She made photocopies and posted them around the school. When Mrs Chariot, who was in charge of the student paper, found it, she congratulated little Helena on her talent as a poetess, gave her a bonus point and published the text in the school newspaper under Helena's name.

The list of Hillel's visits to the doctor – particularly for repeated infections of the mouth – was growing alarmingly, and Aunt Anita eventually went to see the headmaster.

"Mr Hennings, I think my son is being mistreated at your school," she said.

"No, no, no-one is mistreated at Oak Tree, we have supervisors, rules, we have a charter for getting along. This school is all about happiness."

"Hillel comes home every day with his clothes torn and his note-books damaged or missing altogether."

"He has to learn to take care of his belongings. You know if he neglects his notebooks he will have a demerit on his report card."

"Mr Hennings, he's not neglecting anything. I think he has become someone's scapegoat. I don't know what's going on here, but we're not paying $20,000 a year to see our son come home from school with his mouth full of bacteria. There is something wrong, don't you think?"

"Does he wash his hands properly?"

"Yes, Mr Hennings, he washes his hands."

"Because you know boys at that age can be real pigs . . . "

Aunt Anita, annoyed, could see the conversation was going around in circles, so eventually she said, "Mr Hennings, my son has bruises on his face, all the time. I don't know what to do anymore. Force him to fit in, or put him in a special institution? Because to be perfectly frank with you, there are mornings I wonder what is going to happen if I keep sending him to your school."

She burst into tears, and as Mr Hennings didn't want any trouble at Oak Tree, he consoled her, and promised to remedy the situation. He sent for Hillel, to try to get to the bottom of the matter.

"Look, Hillel," he began, "are you having trouble in school?"

"Let's just say for some reason after class people pick quarrels with me on the basketball court behind school."

"Ha! And how would you describe it? Would you say they're teasing you?"

"I'd say they're assaulting me."

"Assaulting? No, no. There's no assault at Oak Street. They might get a bit rowdy. You know, it's normal to get kind of rowdy when you're a boy. Boys like to play a bit rough."

Hillel shrugged.

"I really don't know, Mr Hennings. All I want is to play basketball without being bothered."

The headmaster scratched his head, looked closely at the skinny kid, who nevertheless had plenty of composure, and suggested, "Maybe you could be on the school basketball team, what do you think of that?"

Hennings figured that this way the boy could play ball but under the protection of an adult. Hillel liked the idea, and the headmaster immediately took him to see the head of the phys. ed. department.

"Shawn," Mr Hennings said to the phys. ed. teacher, "can we put this young champ on the basketball team?"

Shawn surveyed the boy with his tiny skeleton and pleading eyes.

"No way," he said.

"And why not?"

Shawn leaned closer to the headmaster's ear and murmured, "Frank, we're a basketball team, not a home for the disabled."

"Hey, I'm not disabled!" Hillel protested.

"No, but you're real skinny," Shawn said. "You'll be a burden on us."

"Why don't you just try him out?" the headmaster suggested.

The gym teacher leaned closer again and said, "Frank, the team is full. And there's a waiting list as long as your arm. If we make an exception for this boy here, it will upset the other pupils' parents. And I don't want any fuss. I tell you: the minute I put him on the court we'll lose. And one more thing, we're already not on top this year. Our basketball results overall are not great, but if I—"

Hennings nodded and turned to Hillel, inventing some articles of house rules to explain in great detail why they couldn't change the make-up of the basketball team in the middle of the year. A horde of children suddenly rushed into the room for a training session, and Hillel and the headmaster sat down on the bench at the bottom of the bleachers.

"So what should I do, Mr Hennings?" Hillel asked, finally.

"Give me the name of the kids who've been bothering you. I'll call them in to talk things over. And we'll organize a good behavior workshop."

"No, that will only make things worse! And you know it, too."

"So why don't you just avoid those guys?" Hennings said, getting annoyed. "Just don't go to the basketball court if you don't want to be harassed, it's as simple as that."

"I won't give up going to play basketball."

"Stubbornness is an ugly trait, son."

"I'm not stubborn. I'm resisting fascists."

Hennings went completely white.

"Where did you pick up that strange word? I hope you haven't been learning words like that in class? At Oak Tree school, we don't teach words like that."

"No, I read it in a book."

"What book?"

Hillel opened his bag and took out a history book.

"What sort of horrible thing is this?" said Hennings, aghast.

"A book I borrowed from the library."

"The school library?"

"No, the local library."

"Well, I ask you not to bring this book to school and to keep that sort of comment to yourself. I don't want any trouble. But I see that you are well-informed. You should use that strength to defend yourself."

"But I don't have any strength. That's the whole problem."

"Your strength is your intelligence. You're a particularly intelligent little boy. And in fairy tales, intelligence always triumphs over physical strength."

The headmaster's suggestion left its mark. That same afternoon, sitting in the school newspaper office, Hillel wrote a text that he then gave to Mrs Chariot to be published in the next issue of the newspaper. It told the story of a little boy, a pupil at a private school for rich kids. At every recess he was tied to a tree and subjected to all sorts of torture by his classmates, who displayed an inventiveness as insidious as it was disgusting, and the young hero ended up with terrible infections in his mouth. None of the adults noticed that he was being made into a martyr, least of all the headmaster, for he was busy with the phys. ed. teacher sucking up to the pupils' parents. At the end of the story the pupils set fire to the tree and the little boy, and began dancing around the pyre singing an ode of thanks to the school faculty for making it so easy for them to beat up those were weaker than them.

When she read the text, Mrs Chariot at once alerted the headmaster; he forbade its publication and summoned Hillel to his office.

"Do you realize that your story is full of words we don't allow here?" Hennings thundered. "And I haven't even started on the content of this ridiculous story, or your insolence in criticizing the faculty!"

"What you're doing is called censorship," Hillel protested, "and that's something else the fascists did, I read about it in my book."

"I don't want to hear your stories about fascism, do you understand? It's not censorship, just common sense! We have a moral charter at Oak Tree, and you have violated it."

"And what about my letter to Helena, which was published in the previous issue?"

"As I already explained, Mrs Chariot thought it was a poem that Helena herself had written."

"But as soon as the newspaper was published, I told her that I was the one who wrote the poem!"

"You did right to let her know."

"Then she should have stopped the distribution of the newspaper!"

"And why is that?"

"Because the publication of that letter was terribly humiliating for me."

"Please, Hillel, enough of this capricious behavior. The poem was very pretty, unlike this text which is just a jumble of abominable vulgarity."

Hennings sent Hillel to see the school psychologist.

"I read your story," said the psychologist, "and I found it very interesting."

"Well, you're the only one."

"Mr Hennings tells me you read books about fascism."

"I borrowed one from the library."

"Is it what inspired your tale?"

"No, what inspired it was how useless this school is."

"Maybe you shouldn't read those books."

"Or maybe the others should."

As for Uncle Saul and Aunt Anita, they begged their son to make an effort: "Hillel, you haven't even been there three months. You really have to try to learn to live in harmony with other people."

Finally there was a session in the amphitheater with all the pupils on the topic of "Misbehavior and bad language." Hennings spoke at length about Oak Tree's moral and ethical values, and explained why the school charter allowed neither rowdy behavior nor bad words. Then the children learned a slogan, "Bad words, my ear hurts!" which they were supposed to chant if they caught a classmate swearing. Then the pupils could ask questions about anything that was bothering them.

"Ask me whatever you like," Hennings declared, before shooting a derisive wink at Hillel and adding, "there's no censorship."

A forest of hands went up in the auditorium.

"Playing ball in the schoolyard – is that bad behavior?"

"No, it's exercise," Hennings said. "On condition you don't throw the ball straight at your friend's head."

"The other day I saw a spider in the cafeteria and I shouted because I was afraid," one girl confessed, somewhat sheepishly. "Was that rowdy behavior?"

"No, shouting because you're afraid is allowed. But shouting to make a racket and irritate your classmates is bad behavior."

"But what if someone shouts because they want to misbehave then makes everyone believe he saw a spider so he won't be punished?" asked one pupil who was worried that there would be ways to get around the rule.

"That would be dishonest. And it's not good to be dishonest."

"What does that mean, to be dishonest?"

"Take this example: if you pretend to be sick so you don't have to go to school, you're being very dishonest. Next question?"

One little boy raised his hand and Hennings nodded to him to speak.

"Is *sex* a bad word?"

Everyone in the ampitheater held their breath and Hennings felt a moment of awkwardness.

"Sex isn't a bad word, but it is, shall we say, an unnecessary word."

There was a sudden commotion in the room. If sex wasn't a bad word, could they use it without violating the Oak Tree charter?

Hennings banged on the lectern to restore calm, aware that this was a perfect example of rowdy behavior, and everyone immediately fell silent.

"Sex is a word you mustn't say. It's a forbidden word, that's what it is."

"Why is it forbidden if it's not a bad word?"

"Sex is a bad thing, that's all there is to it. It's like drugs, something terrible."

When Aunt Anita heard about Hillel's story from Hennings, she was distraught. She had reached a point where she no longer knew whether Hillel was an innocent victim or was paying the price of his own provocative behavior: she was aware that his tone could sometimes be annoying or perceived as arrogant. He grasped things more quickly than other children did: in class he got bored very quickly, he was impatient. This riled the other children. So what if basically Hillel was no more than the victim of bad behavior that he himself had instigated, as Hennings said? Once again she said to her husband, "If someone ends up antagonizing everyone, isn't it because they aren't behaving in a friendly enough way?"

. She decided to sensitize Hillel's schoolmates to the problem of bullying and to explain to them that sometimes if a child wants to belong too badly, they end up antagonizing everyone. She went around Oak Park to speak to the parents of her son's schoolmates, and explained to the children at length that "sometimes you think that teasing behavior is just a game and you don't realize that you're hurting your schoolmate." It was more or less on this basis that she went to speak to Mr and Mrs Reddan, the parents of little Vincent, otherwise known as Porky. The Reddans lived in a magnificent house not far from the Baltimore Goldmans' home. Porky listened attentively to Aunt Anita and as soon as she had finished speaking, he performed an extraordinary number: sobbing and weeping he said, "Why didn't my friend Hillel ever tell me that he felt rejected at school, that's really terrible! We all love him so much, I can't understand why he feels left out." Aunt Anita explained that Hillel was a bit different, and Porky hiccupped, blew his nose, then as a grand finale solemnly invited Hillel to his birthday party, the following Saturday.

At the party, the moment the Reddan parents had their backs turned, Hillel got his arm twisted, his face soaped with icing from the birthday cake, and was thrown fully clothed into the swimming pool. When she heard the sound of splashing and the children's laughter, Mrs Reddan came running, and scolded Hillel briskly for going into the pool without prior permission. Then she saw the destruction wrought on the layer cake, and her son, in tears, explained that Hillel wanted to eat the cake without sharing it with anyone, before he, Porky, had even blown out the candles. She called Aunt Anita and told her to come and fetch her son right away. When she arrived at the Reddans' gate, Aunt Anita found the mother holding Hillel firmly by the arm, and next to her Porky, in tears, giving an Oscar-winning performance, explaining between sobs that Hillel had completely ruined the party. On the way home Aunt Anita shot her son a disapproving glance. "Why do you always have to attract attention, Hillel? Don't you even want to make a few friends?"

Hillel got his revenge by writing a new story. This time it was out of the question to try to use the school newspaper. He decided to publish and photocopy this new tale himself. The day the school newspaper came out, he replaced the official issue in the display racks with his own. When she discovered the swap, Mrs Chariot hurried to Mr Hennings' office with all the copies of the pamphlet she was able to find. "Frank, Frank! Look what Hillel Goldman has done now. He's published a pirate newspaper with the most awful story!" Hennings grabbed the copy that Mrs Chariot was holding out to him, read it, and nearly choked. He immediately summoned Uncle Saul, Aunt Anita, and Hillel.

The story was entitled *The Little Pig*. Hillel told the story of an obese pupil called Porky who took malicious pleasure in terrorizing his schoolmates. In the end, fed up, they killed him in the school toilets, hacked him to pieces and put him in the meat locker in the cafeteria, mixing him up with the cuts of meat that had just been delivered. The boy's absence gives rise to a police search. The next day at lunch the police come to the cafeteria to question the pupils. "We simply must find my little lamb," moans Porky's mother, with all the characteristics of an utter imbecile. An inspector interrogates the pupils one after the other as they are cheerfully dining on roast pork. "You haven't seen your schoolmate?" he asks. "Haven't seen him, Inspector," the pupils reply in unison, their mouths full.

"Mr and Mrs Goldman," Hennings said calmly to Uncle Saul and Aunt Anita, "once again your son has written a story that we cannot tolerate. This is a glorification of violence, and it is completely unacceptable to have this type of publication going around Oak Tree."

"What about the freedom to write, the freedom of opinion!" Hillel wanted to know.

"That's enough now!" Hennings barked. "Stop comparing us to a fascist state."

Hennings then looked somewhat embarrassed and explained to Uncle Saul and Aunt Anita that he could not keep Hillel in the school much longer if the boy made no effort to fit in. At the behest of his parents, Hillel promised not to publish any more leaflets. They also agreed he would write a letter of apology that would be posted throughout the school.

By replacing the school newspaper with his own creation, Hillel had deprived the pupils of their usual issue. To spare Hillel, the headmaster asked the teachers not to divulge the reason why. The issue would be reprinted before the end of the day. But Mrs Chariot, who was oversensitive and was now exasperated by the complaints of pupils who could not understand why the paper was not ready at the usual time, eventually lost her temper and screamed at the protesters pounding on the door of the newspaper office, which was usually so quiet: "Because of a certain pupil who thinks he's better than everyone else, there won't be any newspaper this week! That's why! The issue is simply canceled! Canceled, do you hear me? Canceled! Those pupils who went to the trouble of writing articles will never see them published. Never, ever! You all have Goldman to thank." Ever compliant, the pupils thanked Hillel by kicking him and slamming him with their notebooks. Porky, after punching him, shoved him into the middle of a ring of his schoolmates, then ordered, "Take your pants down." Hillel, wiping his bloody nose, trembling with fear, did as he was told and the others laughed. "You have the skinniest legs I've ever seen," Porky said. And everyone laughed even louder. Then he told Hillel to hand over his pants and he tossed them up into the highest branches of a tree. "Go home now. Everyone has to see your skinny legs." It was a neighbor driving by who saw Hillel half naked in the street and took him home. He told his mother that a dog had chased him and made off with his pants.

"A dog? Hillel . . . "

"Yes, Mom, I swear. He was holding on to my pants so tight that he ended up tearing them, and then he ran off with them."

"Hillel, darling, what is going on?"

"Nothing, Mom."

"Are they ganging up on you at school?"

"No, Mom, I swear."

Hillel, deeply humiliated, decided he had to take revenge on the revenge of the revenge. The opportunity came along a few days later when Porky was out of school for two days due to a bad cold. At least, that was the real reason behind his absence. His classmates had no way of knowing, of course. When a note appeared in each of their lockers saying PORKY IS OFF SICK WITH CHRONIC WIND, the pupils took it at face value, and when he returned, they mocked him mercilessly. After a morning of constant taunts and people walking past him with their noses pinched, or pretending to be sick, Porky's temper was completely frayed.

"It's a lie!" he bellowed for the umpteenth time. "I don't have chronic wind!"

At recess, he ransacked every locker, determined to destroy every last note.

"Who wrote these?" he demanded. "Someone made this up – who was it?"

No-one would admit to the crime, and nobody had any further

evidence, even when Porky went round to every member of the class in turn, waving the notes at them and shouting at them to reveal the culprit. The case might have been closed there and then, but for one crucial final witness.

"You know," said little Helena, Hillel's former flame, squinting at one of the notes. "If you look closely, that handwriting kind of looks like Hillel Goldman's . . ."

She barely had time to finish her sentence. With a roar of rage, Porky launched himself at Hillel's vanishing figure as he shot away down the corridor.

They were seen leaving the school through an emergency exit, crossing the playground, then the basketball court, before heading into the Oak Park neighborhood: Hillel's stick-like figure galloping just ahead of Porky charging like a wild beast, and a bit further behind them a group of pupils following so they wouldn't miss the show.

"I'll kill you!" screamed Porky. "I'll kill you for good!"

Hillel was running as fast as he could, but he could hear Porky's footsteps getting closer: he had nearly caught up. Hillel was headed for his house. With a bit of luck he could get there in time and be safe. But just before reaching his home, he tripped on a kid's bike abandoned at the entrance to the alley and went flying.

6

Baltimore
November 1989

Hillel, with Porky just behind him, caught his foot in the bike and lay sprawled on the sidewalk. He knew he could no longer escape a beating, and he rolled up in a ball to protect himself. Porky leapt on him, and began kicking him repeatedly in the sides, before grabbing him by the hair and jerking his head up. Suddenly a voice rang out.

"Let him go!"

Porky turned around. Behind him was a boy he had never seen before; the hood of his sweater pulled up over his head made him look threatening. "Let him go," the boy said again. Porky shoved Hillel back on the sidewalk and started over to the boy, determined to pick a fight. He hadn't gone three steps when he received a punch right in the face, which knocked him to the ground. He rolled over holding his nose, and burst into tears.

"My nose!" he cried. "You broke my nose!" Just then the other pupils who'd been in on the chase came running up.

"Come and see," shouted one of them. "Porky is crying like a girl!"

"It really hurts!" sobbed Porky.

"Who are you?" one of the kids asked Woody.

"I'm Hillel's bodyguard. And if you bother him, I'll smash every last one of you in the nose."

They raised their palms in peace.

"We all like Hillel," said one of them, without getting off his bike.

"We don't want any trouble for him. Do we, Hillel? And besides, if you want us to, we can go and beat up Porky."

"It's not nice to beat up people," said Hillel, still on the ground.

Woody helped Porky to his feet and said: "Get away from here, lardass, go put some ice on your nose." Porky disappeared without further ado, still sobbing, and Woody helped Hillel to his feet.

"Thanks, old man," said Hillel. "You really got me out of a tight corner."

"No problem. I'm Woody."

"How did you know who I am?"

"There are pictures with your face all over your dad's office."

"You know my dad?"

"He helped me get out of shit creek once or twice."

"You're not supposed to say shit."

Woody smiled.

"You really are Mr Goldman's son."

"And how do you know my name?"

"I heard your parents talking in your dad's office the other day."

"My parents? You know my mother too?"

"Like I said, I know your father. Thanks to him I'm working for Mr Bunk, the gardener. I was busy mowing lawns when I saw that fat boy chasing you. And I know that everyone pesters you, because when I was in your father's office the other day, I saw your mother come in – and hey, she's really pretty – and—"

"Yuck, don't be gross! Don't talk about my mother like that!"

"Yeah, well anyway, your mother came in your dad's office and she said she was worried because everyone at school wants to smash your face in. So as a result I was really glad that lardass was beating you up, that way I could defend you, 'cos I have to thank your dad for defending me."

"I don't know what you're talking about. When did my dad defend you, what for?"

"I ran into some trouble, got into some fights, and every time he helped me."

"Fights?"

"Yeah, I get into a lot of fights."

"Maybe you could teach me how to fight,"Hillel said. "How long would it take me to be as strong as you?"

Woody made a face.

"Well, you don't look too hot when it comes to fighting. So I'd say it'll probably take you all your life. But I could go to school with you. That way no-one would dare to bother you anymore."

"You would do that?"

"Sure I would."

From the day he met Woody, Hillel had no more trouble at school. Every morning when he left the house, he found Woody at the stop for the school bus. They would both climb on board, then at school Woody would escort him along the corridors, blending into the crowd with the other pupils. Porky kept his distance. He didn't want any trouble with Woody.

After class, Woody would be there again. The two of them often went to the basketball courts together and played a few games, then Woody took Hillel home.

"I have to rush, Bunk thinks I'm pruning plants at your neighbors'. If he sees me with you, I've had it."

"How come you're here all the time?" asked Hillel. "Don't you go to school?"

"I do, but I finish early. I have time to get here."

"Where do you live?"

"In a group home in East Baltimore."

"Don't you have parents?"

"My mom doesn't have time to look after me."

"And your father?"

"He lives in Utah. He has a new wife. He's real busy."

When they were outside the Goldman house, Woody said goodbye to Hillel and vanished, even though Hillel always invited him to stay for supper.

"I can't," Woody replied.

"Why not?"

"I have to go and work for Bunk."

"Just come when you're finished and then have supper with us."

"No. I'm too embarrassed."

"What's embarrassing about it?"

"Your parents. I mean, not them, not *your* parents. Just adults."

"My parents are cool."

"Yeah, I know."

"Wood, why are you protecting me?"

"I'm not protecting you. It's just I like hanging around with you."

"I think you're protecting me."

"Then you're protecting me, too."

"What am I protecting you from? I'm a wuss."

"You protect me from being all alone."

And what started out as the reimbursement of the debt Woody owed Uncle Saul turned into an unshakable friendship between Woody and Hillel. Every day Woody came all the way to Oak Park. On weekdays, he played his role as bodyguard. On Saturdays, it was Hillel who joined him where he worked for Bunk, and on Sundays they spent the day together in the public garden or at the basketball court. Woody would be already standing there on the sidewalk at dawn, in the cold and dark, waiting for Hillel. "Why don't you come in and have a hot chocolate?" Hillel insisted. "You're going to freeze out there." But Woody always refused.

One Saturday morning when Woody showed up in the dark outside the Baltimore Goldmans' gate, he found Uncle Saul drinking his coffee. He nodded to him.

"Woodrow Finn. Well, well! So you are the one who is making my son so happy."

"I haven't done anything wrong, Mr Goldman, I swear."

Uncle Saul smiled.

"I know you haven't. Come on, come inside."

"I'd rather stay outside."

"You can't stay outside, it's freezing. Come in."

Woody followed him timidly into the house.

"Have you had breakfast?"

"No, Mr Goldman."

"Why not? You have to eat in the morning. It's important. Especially if you're gardening afterwards."

"I know."

"How are things at the home?"

"O.K."

Uncle Saul made him sit down at the kitchen counter and prepared him some hot chocolate and pancakes. Everyone else was still asleep.

"You know that thanks to you Hillel is all smiles again?" Uncle Saul said.

Woody shrugged. "If you say so, Mr Goldman."

Uncle Saul smiled at him. "Thank you, Woody."

Woody shrugged again. "It's nothing."

"How can I thank you properly?"

"You can't. You don't owe me anything, Mr Goldman. In the beginning I came to see you because I owed you a favor. And now I've met Hillel and we're friends."

"Well, you can think of me as your friend now, too. And if you need anything at all, just ask. What's more, I want you to come for breakfast every weekend. I don't like you going to play basketball on an empty stomach."

While he eventually agreed to come into the house on Saturday and Sunday mornings, Woody always refused to stay for supper in the evening. Aunt Anita had to resort to boundless patience to tame him. Initially she waited outside the house for them to come back from the basketball court. She said hello to Woody, who often blushed on seeing her and rushed off like a wild animal. Hillel got annoyed: "Mom, why do you do that! Can't you see you scare him?" She burst out laughing. Then she started waiting with cookies and milk, and before Woody had time to run away she'd offer him a snack. She took advantage of one rainy day to convince him to come inside. She called him "the famous Woody". He blushed to the roots of his hair, went all purple and stammered. He thought she was very beautiful. One afternoon she said, "Tell me, famous Woody: would you like to stay for supper tonight?"

"I can't, I have to go and help Mr Bunk plant some bulbs."

"Just come afterwards."

"I'd better go back to the home afterwards. They'll be worried if I don't come back, and I'll get in trouble."

"I can call Artie Crawford and ask permission, if you want. Then I'll drive you back to the home."

Woody agreed for Aunt Anita to telephone and he was granted permission to stay for supper. After the meal he said to Hillel, "Your parents are really nice."

"I told you so. They're really laid-back, you can come here as much as you want."

"I thought it was really cool the way your mother called Crawford to tell him I was staying for supper. Nobody has ever made me feel like that."

"Feel like what?"

"Important."

In the Baltimore Goldmans Woody found the family he had never had, and before long he had earned a place among them in his own right. On weekends he would arrive early in the morning. Uncle Saul let him in and he sat at the breakfast table; Hillel joined him soon afterwards. Then the two of them went off to help Dennis Bunk. In the evening, Woody regularly stayed for dinner. He insisted on making himself useful: he insisted on helping prepare the meals, setting and clearing the table, doing the dishes, and taking out the garbage. One morning when he was watching Woody busily cleaning up the kitchen, Hillel said, "It's morning. Relax. You don't have to do this."

"I want to do it, I want to. I don't want your parents to go thinking I'm taking advantage."

"Look, come and sit down, finish your cereal and read the newspaper. Read it, otherwise you'll never learn a thing."

Hillel forced him to take an interest in everything. He talked to him about the books he had read, or the documentaries he watched on television. Every weekend, come rain or shine, they hung out on the basketball court. They made a fantastic pair. Just the two of them confronted all the N.B.A. teams without a quiver. They took the legendary Chicago Bulls to the cleaners.

One day Aunt Anita explained to me that she realized Woody was truly part of the family the day she took Hillel to the supermarket and saw him put a packet of cereal with marshmallows in the cart. "I thought you didn't like marshmallows," she said. And Hillel replied with the tenderness of a brother, "No, I can't stand them, but they're for Woody. They're his favorite."

Before long Woody's presence at the Baltimores' came to seem perfectly natural. With Artie Crawford's consent, he now showed up for pizza evenings on Tuesdays, movies on Saturdays, not to mention the trips to the aquarium, a place Hillel couldn't get enough of, and excursions to Washington, where they even visited the White House.

On evenings when he'd had dinner at the Goldman's, Woody insisted on taking the bus back to the group home. He was afraid that if they fussed over him too much, the Goldmans would eventually tire of him and ask him to leave. But Aunt Anita would not allow him to go home alone. It was dangerous. She drove him back, and as she was about to drop him off outside the austere building she said, "Are you sure you'll be O.K.?"

"Don't worry about me, Mrs Goldman."

"But I do worry."

"You shouldn't go out of your way for me, Mrs Goldman. You're already so kind."

One Friday evening, when they stopped outside the decrepit home, she felt her heart sink. She said, "Woody, maybe you should sleep at our place tonight."

"I don't want to be a bother, Mrs Goldman."

"You're not a bother, Woody, for anyone. The house is big enough for everybody."

That was the first time he slept at the Goldmans'.

One Sunday morning he showed up at the house very early, in the midst of a terrible downpour. Uncle Saul found him soaked and freezing. They decided to give Woody a key to the house. From that day on, he came even earlier, setting the table, making toast and orange juice and coffee. Uncle Saul was the first one to come downstairs. They'd sit side by side and eat breakfast together, sharing the newspaper. Then came Aunt Anita, who always greeted him with a ruffle of his hair, and if Hillel was slow to appear, Woody would go up to his room to wake him up.

One Monday morning in January 1990, on his way to the bus stop, Hillel found Woody hiding in the bushes, in tears.

"Woody, what's going on?"

"At the home they don't want me to come here anymore."

"Why not?"

Woody looked down.

"I've been skipping school for a while."

"What? Why?"

"I feel better here. I wanted to be with you, Hill! Artie is furious. He called your father. He says I can't work for Bunk anymore."

"But he let you come here now?"

"I ran away! I don't want to go back there. I want to stay with you!"

"No-one can stop us seeing each other, Wood. I'll find a solution."

The solution was to move Woody that very day into the Baltimores' pool house. No-one would disturb him there until summer; no-one ever went there. Hillel gave him some blankets and food, and a walkie-talkie to communicate.

That evening, Artie Crawford stopped by the Baltimores' to tell them Woody had disappeared.

"What do you mean, *disappeared*?" Aunt Anita asked.

"He didn't come back to the home. We found out he's been skipping class for weeks."

Uncle Saul turned to Hillel.

"Have you seen Woody today?"

"No, Dad."

"Sure?"

"Yes . . . "

"Do you have any idea where he could be?" asked Artie.

"No, I'm sorry."

"Hillel, I know that you and Woody are very close. If you know anything, you have to tell us, it's very important."

"There is something . . . He talked about going to Utah, to find his dad. He wanted to take the bus to Salt Lake City."

That night, they spoke through the walkie-talkie. Hillel whispered, hidden under his blankets, to make sure his parents couldn't hear him.

"Woody? Are you O.K.? Over."

"Everything's fine, Hill. Over."

"Crawford came to the house tonight."

"What did he want?"

"He was looking for you."

"What did you tell him?"

"That you were in Utah."

"Good thinking. Thanks. Over."

"You're welcome, pal."

Woody went on hiding in the pool house for the next three days. On the morning of the fourth day, he crept out at dawn and hid in the street to wait for Hillel, to walk him to school.

"You're crazy," Hillel said. "If someone sees you, you're finished!"

"I'm going crazy in the pool house. I need to stretch my legs. And if Porky doesn't see me at the school, he'll go after you again."

Woody walked Hillel as far as the schoolyard, where he mingled with the crowd of pupils. But that morning, the headmaster noticed a boy he had never seen before, and he knew immediately he could not be a pupil at the school. He notified the police. A few minutes later a patrol car pulled up outside the school. Woody saw it right away and tried to make his escape but ran straight into Hennings.

"And who are you, young man?" Hennings said, his tone severe, as he slapped up a firm hand on Woody's shoulder to hold him back.

"Run, Woody!" Hillel shouted. "Get away!"

Woody slipped out of Hennings' grasp and was making a break for it, but the police caught up with him. Hillel ran up, shouting, "Leave him alone! Leave him alone! You have no right!" He wanted to push the policeman away, but Hennings stepped in and restrained Hillel. The boy burst into tears. "Leave him alone!" he cried again, as the policemen took Woody away. "He didn't do anything! He didn't do anything!"

All the pupils in the schoolyard were watching, transfixed, as Woody was shoved into the police car, until Hennings and the teachers dispersed them, telling them to get back to their classrooms.

Hillel spent the morning in the infirmary, in tears. At lunchtime, Hennings went to see him.

"Come on, son, go to class now."

"Why did you do that?"

"The director of Woody's home notified me that I would probably find him here. Your friend ran away – do you know what that means? It's very serious."

With a heavy heart, Hillel went back to the classroom for the afternoon lessons. Porky was waiting impatiently. "Time for my revenge, Shrimpie," he said. "Now that your little friend Woody isn't here anymore, I'll deal with you as soon as class is over. I have a delicious dog turd waiting for you. Have you ever eaten dog turd? No? You can have it for dessert. And you'll gobble down every last bite. Yum, yum!"

When the bell rang at the end of the day, Hillel ran out of the classroom with Porky hot on his heels. "Catch Shrimpie!" Porky shrieked. "Catch him, we're going to beat the living daylights out of him." Hillel galloped down the corridors, then just as he was about to go out onto the basketball court, he took advantage of his small stature in order to weave his way back through the flow of children coming down the stairs from their classrooms. He went up to the second floor then down the deserted corridors until he found the caretaker's storage room. He hid there for a long time, holding his breath. The blood was pounding in his temples, and he could hear his heart pounding in his ears. When at last he dared to go out, night had fallen. The corridors were dark and deserted. He moved on tiptoe, looking for the way out, and soon he saw he was in the corridor leading to the newspaper office. As he went by, he saw that the door was ajar and he heard a strange noise. He stood still and listened. He recognized Mrs Chariot's voice. Then he heard the sound of low murmuring, followed by a giggle. He looked in through the narrow gap in the doorway and saw Mr Hennings sitting on a chair with Mrs Chariot in his lap with her arms around his neck. Her hair had come loose and her blouse was undone.

"Oh Adeline," Mr Hennings said.

"Herbert," she echoed breathlessly.

"Have you been a naughty little bitch?" asked Hennings.

Hillel, who did not know what on earth was going on, pushed the door open and cried, "Bad words, my ear hurts!"

Mrs Chariot stood up abruptly and shrieked.

"Hillel?" stammered Hennings, while Mrs Chariot clutched at her blouse and dashed out.

"What are you doing?" asked Hillel.

"We were just playing," Hennings said. "We were . . . it was . . . And what are you doing here?"

"I was hiding because the other kids want to hit me and make me eat a dog turd," Hillel explained to the headmaster, who was no longer listening but looking for Mrs Chariot in the corridor.

"That's great," Hennings said. "Adeline? Adeline, are you there?"

"Can I go on hiding?" Hillel asked. "I'm really afraid of what Porky might do."

"Yes, yes, that's fine, son. Have you seen Mrs Chariot?"

"She left."

"Left where?"

"I don't know, she went that way."

"O.K., find something to do, I'll be right back."

Hennings went up and down the corridor calling, "Adeline? Adeline, where are you?" He found her hiding in a corner.

"Don't worry, Adeline," he said, "the kid didn't see a thing."

"He saw everything!" she squawked.

"No, no. I assure you."

"Really?" she asked, her voice trembling.

"Certain. Everything's fine, no need to worry. And besides, he's not the sort to make a fuss. Don't be anxious, I'll speak to him."

But when he got back to the newspaper office, Hennings saw that Hillel had vanished. He found him one hour later, at the door to his own home, ringing the bell.

"Hello, Mr Hennings."

"Hillel? What are you doing here?"

"I think I have something that belongs to you," said Hillel, removing a pair of women's panties from his schoolbag.

Hennings' eyes went as round as saucers, and he flapped his hands frantically in the air.

"Put those filthy things away!" he ordered. "I don't know what you're talking about!"

"I think these belong to Mrs Chariot. I think she left them in the newspaper office, when she was in there with you just now."

"Shut up and get out of here!" hissed Hennings.

From the living room Mrs Hennings called out to inquire who was at the door.

"Nobody, darling," said Hennings in a syrupy voice. "Just a pupil with a problem."

"Maybe we should ask your wife if these belong to her?" suggested Hillel.

Hennings attempted awkwardly to grab the panties, but to no avail, so he called out to his wife, "Honey, I'm going out for short walk!"

He stepped out on the sidewalk in his slippers and dragged Hillel with him.

"Are you crazy, showing up like this?"

"There's a place over there that sells ice cream," Hillel said.

"I'm not going to buy you any ice cream. It's suppertime. Besides, how did you get here?"

"Does Mrs Chariot like ice cream?"

"Yes, she – I mean, how should I know?"

"Why did she take her blouse and panties off in the newspaper office?"

"We were playing a game."

"I've never heard of a game like that."

"No, well, it's just a game for grown-ups."

"And you were using a bad word. You said we shouldn't use words like that."

Hennings gulped for a moment, then he said quickly, "It's part – it's part of the game."

"The game for grown-ups?"

"Something like that."

"That's really weird."

"You know, son, adults can be weird."

"I know."

"And so why do you play the grown-up game with Mrs Chariot? Is it 'cos you don't love your wife anymore?"

"On the contrary, I love my wife. I love her very much. You know, sometimes men have needs. And they have to fulfill them. But that doesn't mean they don't love their wives. Shutting myself inside the newspaper office with Mrs Chariot is one way of staying with my wife. And I love my wife. I wouldn't want her to be sad. She would be sad if she heard about this. Do you understand? I'm sure you do."

"Yes, I understand. But you are Mrs Chariot's boss, so that's going to cause a lot of trouble, for sure. And besides, I'm sure the parents would be disappointed if they found out . . ."

"Enough! I get it! What do you want?"

"I want a free place at the school for my friend Woody."

"Are you out of your mind? You think I can pull $20,000 out of my hat?"

"You're the one who's in charge of the budget. I'm sure you'll know how to manage. All you have to do is add a chair at the back of the class. That's not very complicated. And besides, that way you can go on loving your wife and playing games with Mrs Chariot."

The next day, Mr Hennings contacted Artie Crawford to inform him that the Oak Tree School P.T.A. would be very happy to grant Woody a scholarship. After discussing it with my aunt and uncle they suggested, to Hillel's delight, that Woody should move in with them to be near the school. The evening after Woody was enrolled at Oak Tree, Mr Hennings wrote in his logbook: *Decided today to grant an exceptional scholarship to a strange kid, Woodrow Finn. Little Hillel Goldman seems to be under his spell. We'll see if the arrival of this new pupil will allow him to reveal his potential, as I've long been hoping.*

That was how Woody came into the Baltimore Goldmans' lives. He moved into one of the guest bedrooms, which had been rearranged to make him feel at home. Uncle Saul and Aunt Anita had never known Hillel to be as happy as he was in the years that followed. Woody and Hillel went to school together and came home together. They had lunch together, went to detention together, did their homework together, and on the playing field, despite their difference in size, they had to be on the same team. It was the beginning of a period of tranquility and absolute happiness.

Woody joined the school basketball team, and was instrumental in their winning of the championship for the first time. As for Hillel, he developed the school newspaper in a spectacular way: he added a whole section devoted to the basketball team, and put the issues on sale the evening of a game. The money the paper earned went to fund the new "Parent-Teacher Scholarship Association". He earned the teachers' admiration and his schoolmates' respect: in his log Hennings wrote about Hillel: *A fantastic kid, exceptionally intelligent. He's an undeniable asset to the school. He has managed to bring his schoolmates together around the newspaper project and he arranged for the mayor to visit the school for a conference on politics. In a word: excellent.*

Before long the playing field behind the school was no longer enough for Woody and Hillel. They needed something bigger, they needed a place equal to their ambitions. After class, they went to daydream in the gym at Roosevelt High, near their school. They would get there before the basketball team's training session, make their way stealthily down to the floor, and pretend they were at the Los Angeles Forum or Madison Square Garden, with a delirious crowd chanting their names. Hillel climbed up the bleachers, Woody went to stand at one end of the gym.

Hillel pretended he was holding a microphone: "Two seconds to the end of the game, the Bulls are two points behind. But if their wing, Woodrow Finn, scores a basket, they will win the playoffs!" Woody, in a moment of grace, his eyes half-closed, muscles taut, took aim. His body left the floor, his arms extended, the ball shot through the room in absolute silence and went to land in the basket. Hillel let out a scream of joy: "Viiic-tory for the Chicago Balls, with this decisive basket scored by the miiiighty Woooooodrow Finn!" They threw their arms around each other, ran a lap of honor, then scampered off, afraid they might get caught.

Sometimes Woody would go to see Aunt Anita and ask her in a whisper, "Mrs Goldman, I . . . I would like to try and call my father. I'd like to give him some news."

"Of course, sweetheart. Use the phone whenever you want."

"Mrs Goldman, it's just that . . . I don't want Hillel to know. I don't really want to talk about that with him."

"Go up to our bedroom. The telephone is next to the bed. Call your father whenever you want and as often as you want. You don't need to ask, sweetheart. Go upstairs, I'll take care of distracting Hillel."

Woody slipped discreetly into Uncle Saul and Aunt Anita's room. He reached for the telephone and sat on the carpet. He took a piece of paper out of his pocket, and dialed the number on it. No-one answered. The answering machine picked up and he left a message: "*Hi, Dad, it's Woody. I'm leaving you a message because . . . I just wanted to let you know, I'm living with the Goldmans now, they're really nice to me. I'm on the basketball team at my new school. I'll try to call you again tomorrow.*"

* * *

A few months later, just before Christmas vacation, 1990, when Uncle Saul and Aunt Anita invited Woody to go with them to Miami, his first reaction was to say no. He thought the Goldmans were generous enough with him as it was, and that a trip like that would cost a lot of money.

"Come with us, we'll have fun," insisted Hillel. "What else are you going to do? Spend your vacation at the group home?" But Woody would not give in. One evening Aunt Anita went to see him in his room. She sat on the edge of his bed.

"Woody, why don't you want to come to Florida?"

"I just don't, that's all."

"It would make us so happy to have you with us."

He burst into tears. She put her arms around him and gave him a hug.

"Woody, honey, what's wrong?"

She ran her hand through his hair.

"It's just that . . . no-one has ever cared for me like you do. No-one has ever taken me to somewhere like Miami."

"We're glad to do it, Woody. You're a great kid, we're very fond of you."

"Mrs Goldman, I stole . . . oh, I'm really sorry, I don't deserve to live with you."

"What did you steal?"

"The other day, when I went up into your room, there was this photo of you on the dresser . . . "

He got up from his bed, swallowing his tears, then he opened his backpack, took out a family photograph, and handed it to Aunt Anita.

"I'm sorry," he sobbed. "I didn't want to steal, but I wanted a picture of you. I'm afraid that one day you'll leave me behind."

She stroked his hair.

"No-one is going to leave you behind, Woody. Besides, you were right to mention the picture to me: there's someone missing on it."

The following weekend, the Baltimore Goldmans, now four instead of three, went to the shopping mall to have some family photographs taken.

Back at home, Woody called his father. Once again he got the answering machine and he left a new message: "*Hey, Dad, it's Woody. I'm going to send you a photograph, you'll see, it's great! It's me with the Goldmans. We're all going to Florida at the end of the week. I'll try to call you from there.*"

I remember it well, that winter of 1990 in Florida, when Woody came into my life for the first time. There was an immediate camaraderie between the three of us, and that was when the great adventure of the Goldman Gang began. I think it was when I met Woody that I truly began to love Florida; before then, it just seemed kind of boring. Like Hillel, I too was bowled over by that strong, charming boy.

At the end of their first year together at Oak Tree, just as they were about to have their yearbook pictures taken, Hillel brought Woody a package.

"This is for me?"

"Yes. It's for tomorrow."

Woody unwrapped the package: it was a yellow T-shirt with the logo *Friends for Life*.

"Thanks, Hill!"

"I found it at the mall. I got one, too. That way, we'll have the same T-shirt on the picture. I mean, if you want. I hope you don't think it's really lame."

"No, it's not lame at all!"

Alphabetical order meant that Woodrow Marshall Finn came just before Hillel Goldman. And in the yearbook for 1990–1991 at Oak Tree School, where their photographs are featured side by side, it's hard to say who of the two looks more like the true Goldman.

7

Until I met Duke in 2012, I had never been aware of the intense connection that was possible between man and dog. Given all the time I spent with him, I inevitably became attached. It was impossible not to succumb to his mischievous charm, the tenderness of his head on your lap begging for a caress, his pleading gaze every time you opened the fridge.

I had noticed that as my ties to Duke became stronger, the situation with Alexandra seemed to grow calmer. She had lowered her guard somewhat. She occasionally called me Markie, like before. Once again I saw her sweetness, her gentleness, the way she burst out laughing at my stupid jokes. Stolen moments with Alexandra filled me with a joy I hadn't felt in a long time. I realized I had only ever wanted her, and those moments when I took Duke back to Kevin's house were the happiest in my day. I don't know if it was my overactive imagination playing tricks, but I had the impression that she fixed things so that we would be more or less alone. If Kevin was exercising out on the patio, she'd lead me into the kitchen. If he was in the kitchen fixing protein shakes or marinating steaks, she would take me out on the patio. There were gestures, brief touches, gazes, and smiles that made my heart beat faster. For a brief moment it would be as though we were in harmony once again. And when I climbed back into my car I was all flustered. I wanted so badly to invite her out to dinner. To spend an entire evening just the two of us, without her hockey player, who kept on treating me to detailed accounts of his physiotherapy sessions. But I didn't dare take the initiative; I did not want to spoil things.

Out of a fear of jeopardizing what I had, only once did I send Duke home again. It was one morning when I woke up feeling guilty, and I had a gut feeling that I was about to be unmasked. When Duke started barking at six o'clock sharp, I opened the door; he went into a moving display of puppy love, and I crouched down next to him. "You can't stay," I said, rubbing his head. "It'll arouse suspicion. You have to go home."

He gave me his sad look and lay down on the porch, ears low. I forced myself to stick to my decision. I closed the door and sat down behind it, feeling as unhappy as he was.

I hardly worked that day. I missed Duke. I needed him, I needed to hear him chewing on his plastic toys, or snoring on my sofa.

That evening, when Leo came over to play chess, he noticed my crestfallen expression.

"Did someone die?" he said when I opened the door.

"I didn't see Duke today."

"He didn't come?"

"He did, but I sent him home. I'm afraid of being caught out."

He give me a funny look.

"Aren't you maybe getting a little deranged?"

The next day, by the time Duke barked at 6 a.m. I had already fixed him some prime meat. As I had to go to the post office, I took him with me. I couldn't resist the urge to go for a walk in town; I took him to the dog salon and then we went to eat pistachio ice cream in a little artisan place I like to go to. We were sitting out on the patio and I was holding his waffle cone, which he was licking with passion, when I heard a man calling to me.

"Marcus?"

I turned around, terrified at the thought of who might have caught me red-handed. It was Leo.

"Leo, for Christ's sake, you scared me!"

"Marcus, are you completely nuts? What are you doing?"

"Eating ice cream."

"You're walking around town with this dog, for everyone to see. Do you want Alexandra to find out what's been going on?"

Leo was right, and I knew it. Maybe deep down that was what I wanted: for Alexandra to find out. For something to happen. I wanted more than our stolen moments. I realized I wanted everything to be as it had been before. But eight years had gone by and she had a new life.

Leo told me in no uncertain terms to take Duke back to Alexandra before I got the urge to take him to the movies or do some other idiotic thing. I did as he said. When I got home, I found him outside his house, gazing at his notebook. I thought he'd been sitting out there to watch out for my return.

"Well?" I said, nodding toward his notebook, as blank as ever. "How are you getting on with your novel?"

"Not bad. I figured I could write the story of an old guy who sees his young neighbor showing his love for a woman through her dog."

I sighed and sat down next to him.

"I don't know what to do, Leo."

"Think how it was with that dog. You should let yourself be chosen. The problem with people who get a dog is that often they don't understand that you can't choose a dog, it's the other way around: it's the dog who decides who he likes. It's the dog who adopts you, and pretends to obey all your rules so you won't be unhappy. If there's no real bond, it's fucked. I'll give you an example, with this horrible true story of something that happened in Georgia: there was this single mother, a complete lost cause who, to brighten up her life, and that of her two children, bought a dachshund with multicolored eyes she called Whisky. But to her great misfortune, Whisky was not at all the right match, and cohabitation became untenable. As she didn't manage to get rid of him, the woman decided to bring out the big guns: she sat him down outside her house, poured gasoline all over him and set fire to him. The poor mutt, ablaze, howling like a wolf, started racing around like the Devil himself and eventually ended up inside the house where the two kids were sprawled in front of the television. The whole house went up in flames, and Whisky and the kids along with it, and the firemen found nothing but ashes. Now you understand why you always have to let the dog choose you."

"I'm afraid I don't get your story, Leo."

"You have to go about it the same way with Alexandra."

"You mean I have to burn her alive?"

"No, you imbecile. Stop playing at bashful lovers: fix it so she chooses you."

I shrugged.

"Anyway, I think she's going back to Los Angeles soon. The idea was to stay as long as Kevin was convalescent, and he's more or less recovered."

"So what, you're just going to let it happen? Do something so she stays! And anyway, are you going to tell me what happened between you two, in the end? You still haven't told me how you met."

I stood up.

"Next time, Leo. I promise."

The next morning, my buddy Duke got caught while trying to escape. He barked as usual outside my house at six in the morning, but when I opened the door, I saw Alexandra behind him, half-amused, half-incredulous, wearing what looked like her pajamas.

"There's a hole at the end of the garden," she said. "I found it this morning. He goes under the hedge and comes straight here. Can you believe it!"

She burst out laughing. She was still just as beautiful, even in pajamas with no makeup.

"Would you like to come in for a coffee?" I offered.

"Sure."

I suddenly realized that Duke's toys were scattered all over the living room.

"Give me a minute, I have to put on some pants."

"You're already wearing pants," she pointed out.

I didn't say anything and just closed the door, asking her to be patient for a moment. I rushed around the house picking up all Duke's toys, his bowls, his blanket, and I threw them into my room.

I went straight back to open the front door, and Alexandra shot me an amused look. As I closed the door behind her, I failed to notice the man watching us from his car, taking photographs.

8

In keeping with an unchanging calendar, every four years Thanksgiving is preceded by a presidential election. In 1992 the Goldman Gang campaigned for Bill Clinton.

Uncle Saul was a staunch Democrat, which was the cause of constant tension during the winter vacation in Florida in early 1992. My mother maintained that Grandfather had always voted Republican, but now that the Great Saul was a liberal, Grandfather would align his vote with his. Whatever the case, Uncle Saul gave us our first lesson in citizenship by encouraging us to rally to the Clinton cause. We were almost twelve and were in the thick of the Goldman Gang saga. Just the thought of campaigning together with them – it hardly mattered who it was for – filled me with joy.

Woody and Hillel were still working for Mr Bunk. Not only did they enjoy it, but it supplemented their allowance. They worked quickly and well, and some Oak Park residents, annoyed by how slow Mr Bunk was, contacted them directly to do their gardens. When this happened, they deducted twenty percent of their earnings, which they gave back to Bunk without him realizing – depositing the money in his jacket pocket, or in the glove compartment of his pickup. Whenever I went to Baltimore, I had a great time helping them, above all when they were working for their own clients. They had built up a faithful little clientele, and they wore T-shirts they'd had made at the local haberdashery: stitched just over the heart was *Goldman Gardeners, est. 1980*. They made me one, too, and I never felt prouder than when I was wandering through Oak Park with my two cousins, the three of us wearing our magnificent uniforms.

I was in awe of their enterprising spirit and very proud to be earning a little money by the sweat of my brow. This had been an ambition of mine ever since I had discovered the talents of the self-made man in one of my Montclair schoolmates, Steven Adam. Steven was very nice to me: he often invited me over for the afternoon and would ask me to stay to supper. But there were times when, as soon as we sat down to eat, he flew into a terrible rage. If the least little thing bothered him he would start insulting his mother; it scared the living daylights out of me. All it took was for him to not like the dinner and suddenly he would pound his fist and send his plate flying, screaming, "I don't want any of your gross garbage juice!" His father would immediately get to his feet: the first time I witnessed this, I thought he was about to give his son an almighty slap, but to my great surprise, he went and got a plastic piggy bank from the dresser. It was always the same rigmarole. The father would go running after Steven, whining, "The swear jar piggy bank! Three bad words, seventy-five cents!" "Shove it up your ass, your son-of-a-bitch piggy bank!" answered Steven, running across the living room waving his middle finger. "Swear jar! Swear jar!" ordered his father, his voice trembling.

Like in a fairytale, the end was always the same. The father would grow weary and cease his grotesque ballet. To save face, he would say in a self-important tone, "Well, I'll advance you the money, but I'll take it out of your allowance!" He'd take a five dollar bill from his pocket and slip it into the pig's behind before he sat back down at the table, looking chastened. Then Steven returned to his place with no-one scolding him; he'd eat his dessert, burp and then run off again, grabbing the piggy bank on the way and locking himself in his room to hide the booty while his mother took me home and I said to her, "Thank you very much for the delicious meal, Mrs Adam."

Steven had a head for business. It wasn't enough to collect the money his own bad language produced, he also supplemented his income by hiding his father's car keys and holding them to ransom. One such morning, when his father realized the keys were missing he came and begged at Steven's door: "Steven, give me back my keys. I'm going to be late for work. You know what will happen if I'm late again, I'll be fired. My boss told me I would." The mother came to the rescue, banging on the door like a fury.

"Open up, Steven! In the name of God, open at once, do you hear me? Do you want your father to lose his job? Do you want to be out on the street?"

"I don't care! It'll cost you $20 if you want your rotten keys!"

"Alright," the father said. "Alright."

"Slide the money under the door," Steven ordered.

The father did as he was told, then the door opened abruptly and the keys flew into his face.

"Thanks, fat-ass!" shouted Steven before slamming the door.

Every week at school, Steven showed us the wads of bills, which grew ever thicker, and with which he generously took us out for ice cream. It was like a fashion phenomenon: the trendsetter is often imitated but rarely equaled. I know that my friend Lewis tried the trick of making money by insulting his father, but the only salary he got was a smack in the face that made his head spin, and he never tried again. So I was proud to go back to Montclair loaded with the dollars I earned working as a gardener, because it allowed me, too, to invite everyone for ice cream, and to impress my friends.

Mr Bunk was always reticent to pay me a salary. When he saw me coming, he immediately started grumbling that he wouldn't pay me, that Hillel and Woody cost him enough already, but my cousins always split the day's earnings with me. Even though all he did was complain, we liked Bunk. He called us his "little scumbags", and we called him Skunk, because he smelled. He was uncommonly vulgar, and every time we said his name wrong he would spew out a heap of insults, to our great delight: "My name is Bunk! Bunk! Is that so hard? You little shitheads! Bunk with a B! B like Bitch! Or Boot your ass!"

In February 1992, even though he didn't win the New Hampshire primary, Bill Clinton remained a serious contender for the Democratic nomination. We got hold of some bumper stickers which we stuck on letterboxes and on the bumpers of Bunk's clients' cars, as well as on his pickup. That spring the country was seething with unrest after the acquittal of four police officers accused of savagely beating a black citizen at the end of a car chase; a passerby had filmed the beating, and the country was in an uproar. This was the beginning of what became known around the world as the Rodney King affair.

"I don't get it," Woody said with his mouth full. "What does this mean, *recuse*?"

"Woody dear, finish your mouthful before you speak," scolded Aunt Anita gently.

Hillel began to explain.

"The prosecutor said the jury is biased and has to be replaced. Either in full or in part. That's what it means, recuse."

"But why?" asked Woody, who had hurried to finish swallowing so he wouldn't miss any of the conversation.

"Because they're black. And Rodney King is black, too. The prosecutor said that with a jury made up of African-Americans the verdict would not be unbiased. So he asked to recuse the jurors."

"Yes, but by the same token, a jury made up of whites will be on the cops' side!"

"Exactly! That's the whole problem. The white jury acquitted the white policemen for beating up a black guy. That's why they're having riots."

There was only one thing people could talk about at the Baltimore Goldman dinner table: the Rodney King affair. Hillel and Woody followed the events passionately. The affair stimulated Woody's interest in politics, and a few months later, in the fall of 1992, he and Hillel began quite naturally spending every weekend campaigning for Bill Clinton, manning the stand for the local Democratic party on the supermarket parking lot in Oak Park. They were far and away the youngest campaigners in the group, and one day a local television crew noticed them and interviewed them as part of a news report.

"Why are you campaigning for Clinton?" the reporter asked Woody.

"Because my friend Hillel said it's the right thing to do."

The reporter, somewhat embarrassed, then turned to Hillel.

"And do you think Clinton is going to win?"

Then he listened, dumbfounded, to what the twelve-year-old boy had to say.

"You have to have a clear picture of things. It's a difficult election. George Bush has achieved a lot during his term, and even just a few months ago I would have said he was going to win. But now there's a recession, unemployment is soaring, and the recent riots after the Rodney King affair didn't make things easier for Bush."

The electoral period coincided with the arrival of a new pupil in Woody and Hillel's class: Scott Neville, a boy who had cystic fibrosis and a physiognomy that was even more stunted than Hillel's.

Mr Hennings came to explain to the children what cystic fibrosis was. All they retained of his explanation was that Scott had great difficulty breathing, and this earned him the nickname "Half-Lung".

Scott had trouble running, which meant he couldn't run away, so he became Porky's new victim of choice. But this lasted only a few days, because the moment Woody realized what was going on, he threatened to smash Porky's face in, and that made him stop at once.

Woody watched over Scott the way he had watched over Hillel, and the three boys soon discovered they had a lot in common.

Before long they told me about Scott, and I have to confess I was sort of jealous to see my cousins forming a trio with someone besides me: Scott went with them on their trips to the aquarium, and to the public garden, and on election night while I sat bored in Montclair, Hillel and Woody, along with Uncle Saul, Scott, and Scott's father, Patrick, went to watch the election at Democratic headquarters in Baltimore. They were ecstatic when the results were announced, then poured out onto the street to celebrate. At midnight they stopped at the Dairy Shack in Oak Park, where they ordered enormous banana milkshakes. On the night of November 3, 1992, my Baltimore cousins had witnessed the election of the new president first-hand. I had spent the evening cleaning out my room.

That night, it was past two o'clock in the morning by the time they eventually went to bed. Hillel collapsed like a log, but Woody couldn't fall asleep. He listened all around him: everything seemed to indicate that Uncle Saul and Aunt Anita were asleep. He opened the door quietly and tiptoed down to Uncle Saul's study. He reached for the telephone and dialed the number he knew by heart. It was three hours earlier in Utah. He felt a tug of joy when the phone was picked up.

"Hello?"

"Hi, Dad. It's Woody!"

"Oh, Woody . . . Woody who?"

"Uh . . . Woody Finn."

"Oh, Woody! Jesus, sorry, son! You know with the noise of the phone I didn't recognize you. How are you, son?"

"I'm fine. Really fine. Dad, I haven't talked to you in so long! Why don't you ever pick up? Did you get my messages on the answering machine?"

"Woody, when you call, it's mid-afternoon here and nobody's home. We're at work, you know. And then I tried to call you back, but at the group home they told me you're never there."

"That's because I'm living with the Goldmans, now. Like I told you."

"Of course, the Goldmans. Ha-ha, so tell me, champ, how are you?"

"Oh, Dad, we were campaigning for Clinton, it's been great. And tonight we celebrated the victory with Hillel and his dad. Hillel said it was partly because of us. You don't know how many weekends we spent in the parking lot at the shopping center handing out bumper stickers to people."

"Bah," said the father, "don't waste your time on that bullshit, son. Politicians are all rotten."

"But you're proud of me all the same, right Dad?"

"Of course! Of course, son! I'm real proud."

"Because you said that politicians are rotten . . ."

"Well, if you like it, that's fine."

"What do you like, Dad? Maybe we could like the same thing?"

"I like football, kid. I like the Dallas Cowboys! They're a real team. Do you ever watch football, son?"

"Not really. But I will now! And say, will you come and see me here, Dad? I could introduce you to the Goldmans. They are really super nice."

"Sure thing, son. I'll come soon, I promise."

After he hung up, Woody sat for a long time in Uncle Saul's swivel chair with the receiver in his hand.

Overnight, Woody lost all interest in basketball. He didn't want to play anymore, and neither Jordan nor the Bulls could revive his passion. He swore by the Dallas Cowboys. He continued playing on the school basketball team, but his heart was not in it. His shots became careless, even though they ended up in the basket anyway. When, one Saturday morning, he informed Hillel he didn't want to go to play basketball anymore, and that he would probably never play again, Hillel lost his temper. This was their first real argument.

"What's this sudden obsession of yours?" Hillel said, irritated, at a loss to understand. "We like basketball, don't we?"

"What do you care? I like football, that's all."

"And why Dallas? Why not the Washington Redskins?"

"Because I like what I want to like."

"You're so weird! You've been weird all week!"

"And you've been an asshole all week."

"Hey, don't get mad! I just think that football is stupid, that's all. I like basketball better."

"Then play by yourself, dorkface, if you don't like football."

Woody ran off, and even though Hillel called out after him, he didn't stop. Hillel waited for a moment, hoping he'd come back. And when he didn't, he went looking for him. On the playing fields, at the Dairy Shack, in the public gardens, along the streets where they usually hung out together. Then he hurried back to tell his parents.

"What do you mean, you got into a fight?" Aunt Anita said.

"He's obsessed with football, Mom. I asked him why, and he got mad."

"These things happen, sweetheart. Don't worry. Friends sometimes get into arguments. He won't have gone far."

But when Woody didn't come home, they drove around the neighborhood looking for him. In vain. Uncle Saul came home from the office and also scoured Oak Park, but Woody was nowhere to be seen. Aunt Anita informed Artie Crawford of the situation. By dinner time, as there was still no sign of Woody, Artie called his contact in the Baltimore police to report him missing.

Uncle Saul spent the rest of the evening outside looking for Woody. When he got back, at around midnight, they still had no news. Aunt Anita sent Hillel to bed. When she tucked him in, she tried to reassure him: "I'm sure he's fine. Tomorrow you'll have forgotten all about it."

Uncle Saul stayed up part of the night. He fell asleep on the sofa until the phone woke him at around three o'clock in the morning. "Mr Saul Goldman? It's the Baltimore police here. It's about your son, Woodrow."

Half an hour after the police called, Uncle Saul was at the hospital where Woody had been taken.

"Are you his father?" asked the receptionist.

"Not exactly."

A policeman came to get him at the reception.

"What happened?" asked Uncle Saul, following the policeman down the corridor.

"Nothing serious. We picked him up in the street in a neighborhood to the south. He has a few bruises. He's a really sturdy little guy. You can take him home. Who are you, anyway? His father?"

"Not exactly."

Woody had crossed Baltimore by bus without a penny. His initial plan had been to take a Greyhound all the way to Utah. He wanted to get to the bus station, but he took the wrong city bus twice, so then he continued on foot and found himself in a rough neighborhood, where he ended up getting into a fight with a gang who wanted the money he didn't have. He messed up one of the guys in the gang, but the others had laid into him, and thoroughly.

Uncle Saul went into the room and found Woody crying, his face swollen. He put his arms around him.

"I'm sorry, Saul," sobbed Woody. "I'm sorry I've been so much trouble. I . . . I didn't know what to say. I said you were my father. I just wanted someone to come and get me."

"You did the right thing."

"Saul . . . I think I don't have any parents."

"Don't say that."

"And I got into an argument with Hillel. He must hate me."

"Not at all. It happens, friends argue. It's normal. Come on, let me take you home. To our house."

Artie Crawford had to intervene before the policemen agreed to let Woody leave with Uncle Saul.

In the autumnal night, the Goldman house was the only one in the neighborhood with its lights on. They opened the door and Aunt Anita and Hillel, who were waiting in the living room with worried faces, rushed up to them.

"My God, Woody!" exclaimed Aunt Anita when she saw the boy's face.

She took Woody into the bathroom; she put ointment on his injuries and checked the bandage on his eyebrow: he'd had a few stitches.

"Does it hurt?" she asked gently.

"No."

"Honestly, Woody, what got into you? You could've been killed!"

"I'm sorry. If you all hate me, I'll understand."

She pulled him close.

"Oh, sweetheart, honestly . . . how could you think such a thing! What makes you think anyone could hate you? We love you like a son. You must never doubt that for a moment."

She held him tight, touched his battered face again, and led him to his room. He lay down, and she lay next to him and stroked his hair until he fell asleep.

Life went back to normal at the Baltimore Goldman's. But now in the morning Hillel took a football with him. After class, Woody and Hillel no longer went to the basketball court at Roosevelt High, but to the playing field where the football team usually practiced. They crossed the field and planned decisive game strategies. Scott, who was a huge football fan, went with them and acted as referee and commentator, until he was too out of breath to speak. "Victorious touchdown in the last seconds of the championship final!" he cried, his hands cupped around his mouth, while Woody and Hillel, their arms in the air, went to wave to the empty bleachers, where the delirious crowd was chanting their names, about to invade the pitch and lift up the invincible twosome in triumph. Then they went to celebrate the victory in the locker room, where Scott pretended to be a recruiter from the N.F.L., and he had them sign their math homework sheets as if they were phenomenal contracts. Typically, when the janitor heard the noise he came down to the deserted locker rooms, so the boys fled without further ado, Woody in front, Hillel next, and Scott trailing behind, wheezing and spitting.

Over vacation the following spring, Woody went to Salt Lake City to see his father. Hillel gave him his football so he'd be able to play there, with his father and his twin sisters, whom he hadn't met.

The week in Utah was a disaster. Woody did not fit in with the Salt Lake City Finns. It wasn't that his stepmother was mean, she was just too busy with the twins. The day he arrived she said, "You look like a kid who knows how to manage on his own. Make yourself at home. Help yourself to whatever you want from the fridge. Everybody eats when they feel like it, the girls can't stand sitting down for dinner, they have no patience." On Sunday, his father suggested they watch some football on television. They spent the afternoon together. But no-one was allowed to speak during the game, and at half-time, his father rushed into the kitchen to make nachos and popcorn. By the end of the day, his father was in a foul mood: all the teams he had bet on had lost. He had work to prepare for the next day so he left for the office, just when Woody thought he might take him out to supper somewhere.

The next day, when he came back from walking around the neighborhood, Woody opened the front door and came upon his father, who was getting ready to go out jogging. His father looked at him, surprised, and said, "What's the idea, Woody, don't you ring the bell before you walk into someone's house?"

Woody felt like a stranger at his father's home. He was deeply hurt. His true family was in Baltimore. His brother was Hillel. Suddenly he needed to hear his voice and he called him.

"I don't get along with him, I don't like them, everything is horrible here!" he complained.

"What about your sisters?" asked Hillel.

"I hate them."

Hillel could hear a woman's voice in the background: "Woody, are you on the phone again? I hope it's not a long-distance call. Do you know how much that costs?"

"Hillel, I gotta go. They tell me off all the time here, anyway."

"O.K., pal. Hang in there."

"I'll try. Hill?"

"Yes?"

"I want to come home."

"I know, pal. Soon."

The day before his return to Baltimore, Woody made his father promise they would have supper together, just the two of them. During his entire stay he hadn't had one moment alone with his father. At five o'clock Woody stood outside the house. At eight o'clock, his stepmother brought him a soda and some chips. At eleven o'clock, his father came home.

"Woody?" he said, sensing a presence in the dark. "What are you doing outside at this time of night?"

"Waiting for you. We were supposed to have supper together, remember?"

His father walked toward him and the sensor lights switched on. Woody saw his face, flushed with drink.

"Sorry, kiddo, I didn't see the time."

Woody shrugged and handed him an envelope.

"Here, this is for you. You see, deep down I knew it would end like this."

His father opened the envelope and took out a sheet of paper: on it was written *FINN*.

"What's this?" he asked.

"It's your name. I'm giving it back to you. I don't want it anymore. I know who I am now."

"And who are you?"

"A Goldman."

Woody got to his feet and went into the house without saying another word.

"Wait!" shouted his father.

"Bye, Ted," said Woody, not even looking at him.

Woody was glum when he came home from his visit to Salt Lake City. On the playing field at Roosevelt High he explained to Hillel and Scott, "I wanted to play football to be like my father, but my father is just a jerk who went off and abandoned me. So now I don't know if I really like football."

"Woody, you have to do something else, something that makes you happy."

"Yes, but I don't know what makes me happy."

"What's your passion in life?"

"Well, that's just what I don't know."

"What do you want to do later on?"

"Well . . . I want to do whatever you're doing."

Hillel grabbed him by the shoulders and shook him like a tree.

"What is your dream in life, Wood? When you close your eyes and dream, how do you see yourself?"

Woody gave a big smile.

"I want to be a football star."

"Well, there you go!"

On the playing field at Roosevelt High, where the janitor chased after them relentlessly, they resumed their lives as football players, more determined than ever. They went there every day after school and on weekends. On days when there were games, they would sit up in the bleachers and watch the game noisily, and once it was over, they would replay all the moves until the janitor showed up again in a huff to chase them out. Scott was finding it harder and harder to run, even over a short distance. Ever since he had almost passed out after one janitor-evading sprint, Woody never went anywhere with him without a big wheelbarrow he'd borrowed from Skunk, and into which Scott would clamber the moment they had to make a getaway.

"Ah, it's you again!" shrieked the janitor, raising his fist in a rage. "You have no right to be here! Give me your names! I'm going to call your parents!"

"Jump in the wheelbarrow!" shouted Woody to Scott; Hillel helped him in, while Woody picked up the handles.

"Stop!" yelled the old man, scurrying as fast as he could.

With his powerful arms Woody drove the convoy at full tilt; Hillel ran ahead to guide him, and they went tearing through Oak Park. The residents soon got used to the sight of this strange convoy of three boys with one of them, thin and pale but radiant with joy, sitting deep inside a wheelbarrow.

At the beginning of the following school year, Aunt Anita signed Woody up for the local Oak Park football team. Twice a week she came to get him after school and drove him to practice. Hillel always went along, and watched Woody's exploits from the bleachers. It was 1993. Eleven years before the tragedy: the countdown had begun.

9

One evening in mid-March 2012, I took my courage in both hands. Kevin was away, and after dropping Duke off, I turned the car around and rang at the gate to the house.

"Did you forget something?" Alexandra said over the interphone.

"I have to talk to you."

A moment later, she opened the gate and stepped outside. I didn't get out of the car, but merely rolled down the window.

"I'd like to take you somewhere."

All she said was, "What am I supposed to tell Kevin?"

"Don't tell him anything. Or tell him what you want."

She locked up the house and got into the passenger seat.

"Where are we going?" she asked.

"You'll see."

I turned the ignition and left her neighborhood to take the freeway to Miami. Night was falling. Lights from the buildings along the ocean twinkled all around us. The car radio was playing the latest hits. I could smell her perfume in the car. I saw myself as I had been ten years earlier, with her, driving across the country with her first demos to try to convince radio stations to play them. Then, as if destiny was playing with our hearts, the station we were listening to in the car played her first hit song. I saw tears on her cheeks.

"You remember when we heard this song on the radio for the first time?" she said.

"Yes."

"It was thanks to you, Marcus, all that. You were the one who encouraged me to go after my dreams."

"It was thanks to you yourself. And no-one else."

"You know that's not true."

She was crying. I didn't know what to do. I put a hand on her knee and she took it, and squeezed it hard.

We drove to Coconut Grove in silence. I went through the residential streets and she said nothing. Then at last we arrived outside my uncle's house. I pulled over and switched off the engine.

"Where are we?" asked Alexandra.

"This is where the story of the Baltimore Goldmans came to an end."

"Who lived here, Marcus?"

"Uncle Saul. He spent the last five years of his life here."

"When . . . when did he die?"

"November. Nearly four months ago."

"I'm sorry, Marcus. Why didn't you say anything the other day?"

"I didn't feel like talking about it."

We got out of the car and sat down in front of the house. I felt good.

"What was your uncle doing in Florida?" she asked.

"He had to get away from Baltimore."

Night had fallen over the quiet street. The twilight was conducive to sharing secrets. The gloom prevented me from seeing her eyes, but I could tell she was looking at me.

"I've been missing you for eight years, Marcus."

"Me too."

"I just want to be happy."

"Aren't you happy with Kevin?"

"I'd like to be happy with him the way I was happy with you."

"Couldn't you and I—"

"No, Marcus. You hurt me too badly. You left me."

"I left because you should have told me what you knew, Alexandra."

She wiped her eyes with the back of her hand.

"Stop it, Marcus. Stop behaving as if it were all my fault. What would it have changed if I had told you? Do you think they would still be alive? Don't you get it – you couldn't have saved your cousins?"

She burst into tears.

"We were supposed to spend our life together, Marcus."

"You have Kevin now."

She felt that I was blaming her.

"What did you expect me to do, Marcus? Wait for you all my life? I waited long enough for you. I waited so long. I waited for years. Years, you hear me? Initially, I replaced you with the dog. Why do you think I got Duke? To fill my solitude, hoping you'd come back. After you left, I spent three years hoping every day I'd see you again. I told myself you were upset, that you needed time—"

"And I never stopped thinking about you, all those years," I said.

"That's bullshit, Markie! If you had really wanted to see me again, you would have. You preferred to go and shag that second-rate actress."

"That was three years after we split up! And it didn't count."

My relationship with Lydia Gloor started because of a misunderstanding. It happened in the fall of 2007, in New York. The rights to my first novel, *G for Goldstein*, had been sold to Paramount, and shooting was scheduled to start the following summer in Wilmington, North Carolina. One evening I was invited to go and see an adaptation of *Cat on a Hot Tin Roof* on Broadway that was playing to sold-out houses. Playing Maggie was Lydia Gloor, a young movie actress who was all the rage just then, directors were fighting over her. Apparently Lydia Gloor's Maggie was the revelation of the year. Critics were unanimous, and everyone who was anyone in New York was rushing to see her. My own opinion after I'd seen the play was that Lydia Gloor was lousy: she was good for the first twenty minutes. Her Southern accent was perfect. The problem was that she gradually lost it and by the end of the performance she sounded almost German.

The whole story would have ended there if pure coincidence had not arranged things so that the next morning I ran into her at the café I go to every day downstairs from my apartment. I was sitting at a table reading the paper and quietly drinking my coffee. I only noticed her when she came over.

"Hi, Marcus," she said.

We had never met and I was surprised she knew my name.

"Hello, Lydia. A pleasure to meet you."

She pointed to the empty chair in front of her.

"May I join you?"

"Of course."

She sat down. She seemed embarrassed. She began fiddling with her coffee cup.

"Apparently you were at the play last night."

"Yes, it was great."

"Marcus, I would like . . . I would like to thank you."

"Thank me? What for?"

"For letting me be in the film. It's terrific you agreed. I . . . I loved the book, I've never had a chance to tell you."

"Hey, wait a minute: what film are you talking about?"

"Well, uh, *G for Goldstein.*"

That was how I found out that she would be playing Alicia (Alexandra, in fact). I didn't understand what was going on. The casting process was finished, I had approved every one of the actors. She had not been cast as Alicia. This was impossible.

"There must be a misunderstanding," I said awkwardly. "They'll be shooting the film next summer, but you're definitely not in the cast. You must be confusing it with something else."

"Confusing it? No way. I signed a contract. I thought you knew . . . Well, I thought you'd given your consent."

"No. As I said, there must be some misunderstanding. I did indeed approve the cast and you were not chosen to play the part of Alicia."

She said again that she was absolutely sure of what she was saying. That she had spoken to her agent that very morning. That she'd read my book twice, that she really liked it. As she spoke, she went on nervously playing with her coffee cup, and eventually it tipped over and the hot liquid splashed across the table and onto me. She rushed over to mop up my shirt with paper napkins and even her silk scarf, apologizing over and over, completely panicked, and I was probably beside myself, because I blurted out words which I would soon regret:

"Listen, you cannot play Alicia. For a start, you don't look anything like her. And then I saw you in the play last night, and I'm not at all convinced."

"What do you mean, *not at all convinced*?" she gasped.

I don't know what came over me. I said, "I don't think you're talented enough to play in my film. That's all there is to it. I don't want you in the film. I don't want you in my life."

Obviously, this was completely tactless of me, words uttered in a moment of irritation, no doubt. Their impact was immediate: Lydia burst into tears. The flavor of the month was weeping at my table in the café. I could hear customers murmuring all around me, and some started taking photographs. I tried to console her, apologizing over and over again. I told her I had gotten carried away, but it was too late. She went on crying, and I didn't know what to do. Eventually I got out of there and hurried home.

I knew I had landed myself in a mess, and the consequences came quickly: a few hours after the incident, I was summoned by Roy, an influential individual in the movie business, one of the producers of the film adaptation of *G for Goldstein*, who happened to be in New York that week. He met with me in his office high up in a skyscraper on Lexington Avenue.

"You writers are nothing but a bunch of neurotic mental retards!" he bellowed, scarlet, perspiring, liable to burst out of his too-tight shirt.

"You reduced the biggest rising star in the country to tears in a sidewalk café? What sort of beast are you, Goldman? Some sort of pervert? A maniac?"

"Listen, Roy," I stammered, "there's been a mistake—"

"Goldman," he interrupted, "you are the youngest, most promising writer I know, but you are also a never-ending source of hassle!"

The first photographs of Lydia and me the café customers had taken were up on the Internet. The rumor machine was humming away: what did writer Marcus Goldman say to Lydia Gloor to make her cry? When she left the café in Soho, she called her agent, who called a bigwig at Paramount, who called Roy, who summoned me then and there to read me the riot act, something he excelled at. His assistant, Marisa, searched the Internet for all the posts regarding the "mistake", and whenever a new one popped up, she would print it out and burst into the office – which meant at regular intervals – shouting in her shrill voice, "Another article, Roy!"

"Read it to us, Marisa, read us the latest news about the Goldman fiasco so I can evaluate the extent of the disaster."

"This one is from the *Today in America* website: '*What is going on between successful author Marcus Goldman and actress Lydia Gloor? Several witnesses were present at a terrible argument between the two young stars. We will keep you posted.*' There are already some comments."

"Read them, Marisa," shouted Roy. "Read them!"

"Lisa F. in Colorado says, '*That Marcus Goldman is a real creep.*'"

"Hear that, Goldman? Every woman in America hates you!"

"What? Come on, Roy, it's just one internet troll."

"Beware of women, Goldman, they're like a herd of buffalo: if you hurt one of them, all the others will come to her rescue and trample you to death."

"Roy, I swear, I have nothing to do with that woman."

"I know that, you confounded idiot! That's the whole problem. Look, I'm doing everything I can for your career, I'm putting together the film of the century, and you go and screw everything up. You know, Goldman, you're going to end up killing me with your knack of ruining everything. And what will you do when I'm dead, huh? You will come and cry on my grave because there'll be no-one left to help you. Did you have to go and say such horrible things to that young woman, an actress everyone adores? When you reduce an actress everyone adores to tears, well, then you set everyone against you! And if everyone is against you, no-one will go and see the film based on your book! Do you want everyone to hate you? Look, it's already all over the Internet: big bad Marcus and sweet little Lydia."

"But she's the one who came and told me she was in the cast," I said, trying to justify myself. "All I did was tell her she was mistaken."

"But she is in the cast, you amazing genius! She is the lead actress in the film."

"Come on, Roy, we went over the cast together. We approved the choice of actors together. What happened to that actress we cast initially?"

"She's out!"

"Out?"

"You heard me. O-u-t."

"But why?"

"During the break, on her last film set, she overdid the donuts."

"Oh, come on Roy, don't give me that bullshit!"

"It's the truth. I called her agent and I said, hey, you, get rid of that fat sow and get out of here! This is a film set, not a pig farm."

"Enough! Why is Lydia Gloor in this film?"

"Paramount changed the cast."

"But why? What right do they have to do that?"

"There weren't enough bankable actors. Lydia Gloor is very bankable. Much more so than any of the crummy actors you chose, straight out of the New York gutters."

"Bankable?"

"Yes, sir. It matters, the relation between the salary the production pays an actor and the money the film goes on to make. Little Miss Gloor seems very bankable: if she's in the film, more people will want to see it. It means more money for you, for me, for them, for everyone."

"I know what bankable means."

"No, you don't. Because if you did, you would be licking the soles of my shoes to thank me for hiring her."

"But why in hell are you giving in to every one of Paramount's desires? I refuse to have her play Alicia, that's all there is to it."

"Oh, Marcus, you cannot refuse a thing. You really want me to show you all the tiny, incomprehensible clauses that you signed? We let you in on the casting to keep you happy. You'll see, it will be a huge hit. She's costing us a fortune. What's expensive is good. Everyone will rush to see the film. As for you, if you want to go on playing the heartbreaker, you can expect some radical feminists to start burning your books in the public arena and demonstrating outside your house."

"Roy, they don't make them worse than you."

"Is this how you thank me for looking out for your future?"

"My future is in books," I said. "Not in your stupid film."

"Oh, please, stop singing your little revolutionary anthems no-one believes in anymore. Books are history, kid."

"How can you say that?"

"Come now, don't be sad, Mr Goldman. In twenty years nobody will be reading anymore. That's the way it is. They'll all be too busy playing with their cell phones. You know, Goldman, publishing is finished. Your children's children will be curious about books the way we are about the pharaohs' hieroglyphics. They'll say, 'Granddad, what were books for?' And you'll say, 'For daydreaming. Or for cutting down trees, can't say I really know.' By then it will be too late to wake up: the stupidity of humanity will have reached a critical threshold and we will kill each other off because of our congenital stupidity (which is more or less what we're doing already). There's no future in books, Goldman."

"Oh, really? So where is our future, Roy?"

"In movies, Goldman. In movies!"

"Movies?"

"Movies, Goldman, they're the future! People want images now.

People don't want to have to think anymore, they want to be led! They are enslaved from morning to night, and when they go home, they're lost: their boss and master, the kindly hand that feeds them, is no longer there to beat them and guide them. Thank God for television. People turn it on, bow down before it, and hand over their destiny. 'What shall I eat, Master?' they ask their television. 'Frozen lasagna!' order the ads. They hurry to the microwave with their disgusting little dinner. Then they're down on their knees asking, 'And what should I drink, Master?' 'Ultra-sweet Coca-Cola!' blares the television. And once again it orders, 'Eat, you pig, eat! May your flesh become fat and flabby.' And the people obey. They stuff their faces. Then after their meal, the television gets mad and changes its advertising tune: 'You're too fat! You're too ugly! Go and work out! Be beautiful!' And you have to buy electrodes to sculpt your body, creams to firm up your muscles while you sleep, magic pills that will do that workout for you because you don't feel like it, you're too busy digesting your pizza. That's what a life cycle is, Goldman. Man is weak. He is gregarious by instinct and likes to crowd together with others in dark rooms known as movie theaters. And wham! Along come the ads, the popcorn, the music, free magazines, trailers before your film that tell you, 'You klutz, you got the wrong film, go see this one instead, it's much better!' Yes, but the problem is, you already paid for your tickets, you're stuck! So you'll have to come back to see that other film, and another trailer will show you that once again you're just a schlemiel, and so, unhappy and depressed, you'll go drink your soda and gobble down your chocolate ice cream you paid an exorbitant amount for to forget how miserable you are. Maybe there will just be you, Goldman, and a handful of die-hards holding out in the last bookstore in the country, but you won't be able to go on fighting indefinitely: the nation of zombies and slaves will triumph, sooner or later."

I collapsed in an armchair, disgusted.

"You're out of your mind, Roy. You are joking, aren't you?"

In lieu of an answer, he looked at his watch and tapped the face.

"Go on, get going now, Goldman, you're going to be late."

"Late?"

"For your dinner with Lydia Gloor. Stop by your house, squirt on some aftershave and put on a suit, it's a very chic restaurant."

"Oh, Roy, for Pete's sake! Now what have you done?"

"She just got the bouquet of flowers, and a very kind note in your handwriting."

"But I never sent her a thing!"

"I know you didn't. If I had to wait for you to feel like moving your ass, we'd be here until tomorrow morning. All I ask of you is to have dinner with her. In a public place. So everyone can see that you are a kind man."

"No way, Roy."

"There is no 'no way'. That girl is our gold nugget. We are going to look after her. We have to cherish her!"

"You don't understand. I have nothing to say to her."

"You are incorrigible, Goldman: you're young, you're rich, you're handsome, you're a famous writer and what you do? You whine. You complain! Stop playing the wailing Greek chorus, will you?"

That memorable evening, Lydia and I had dinner at the Pierre. I thought it was merely a dinner to calm things down. But Roy had orchestrated the whole thing: there were paparazzi waiting in ambush, and already first thing the next morning, on the Internet, there were photographs depicting a so-called romance between the two of us, and everyone believed it.

"I read a magazine article about the two of you," said Alexandra, after listening to my story on the porch of my uncle's house. "All the tabloids talked about it."

"It was nothing. I was set up."

She looked away.

"The day I saw the article was the day I decided to move on. Until then I had waited for you, Marcus. I thought you were going to come back. You broke my heart."

* * *

Nashville, Tennessee
November 2007

It was nine o'clock in the evening when Samantha, one of her close friends, showed up. Samantha had been trying to call her all day long, to no avail. Since no-one answered the interphone, Samantha climbed over the fence and headed toward the house. She pounded on the door.

"Alex? Open up. It's Sam. I've been trying to reach you all day." No answer. "Alex, I know you're in there, your car is parked out front."

There was the sound of a lock turning and Alexandra opened the door. She looked haggard, her eyes swollen with tears.

"Alex, my God! What's going on?"

"Oh, Sam . . . "

Alexandra collapsed in her arms and burst into tears. She could not say a single word. Samantha had her sit down in the living room and went to the kitchen to make some tea. Then she saw the tabloids spread across the table. She picked one up at random and read the headline.

LYDIA GLOOR DATING WRITER MARCUS GOLDMAN

Alex joined her in the kitchen, followed by Duke.

"He's with her. He's going out with Lydia Gloor," Alexandra choked.

"Oh, sweetie . . . I'm so sorry. Why didn't you say anything?"

"I wanted to be alone."

"Oh, Alex. You mustn't be alone. I don't know what happened with that Marcus, but you have to forget him. You have everything going for you! You're beautiful, intelligent, the world is your oyster."

Alexandra shrugged.

"I don't even know how to flirt anymore."

"Oh, stop it, please!"

"It's true!"

Samantha was married to one of the star players from the Nashville Predators hockey team.

"Listen, Alex," she said. "There's this hockey player, Kevin Legendre. He's really nice, and he's crazy about you. He's been nagging me for months to set up a meeting. Come have supper with us on Friday. I'll invite him too. It can't hurt to try, can it?"

* * *

"I went to dinner," Alexandra said. "I had to forget you. And I did."

"But I wasn't even with Lydia then!" I protested. "I was waiting for you, too, Alexandra! When those pictures came out, absolutely nothing had happened between us."

"But the two of you did have a relationship, didn't you?"

"That was after!"

"After what?"

"After I saw the photos of you and Kevin in the tabloids. I was devastated. So Lydia was a shoulder to cry on. It didn't last very long. Because I could never forget you, Alexandra."

She gave me a sad look. I saw a tear welling in the corner of her eye then spill down her cheek.

"What have we done to each other, Marcus?"

128

10

Coconut Grove, Florida
June 2010. Six years after the tragedy.

Every day when I got to Coconut Grove I went by the supermarket to have lunch with Uncle Saul. We would go and sit on one of the benches outside in front of the supermarket, and we'd have either a sandwich or a chicken salad with mayo, along with a Dr Pepper.

Faith Connors, the manager at Whole Foods, often came out to greet me. She was a lovely woman. Single, in her fifties, and as far as I could tell, she had a soft spot for Uncle Saul. Sometimes she would sit with us to smoke a cigarette. Sometimes, in honor of my presence in Florida, she would give my uncle the day off so we could make the most of being together. And that's what she did, that day.

"Get out of here, the pair of you," she said as she walked up to the bench.

"You sure?" asked Uncle Saul.

"Positive."

We did not hesitate. I gave Faith a kiss on both cheeks and she laughed as she watched us walk away.

We crossed the parking lot to go back to our cars. Uncle Saul stopped at his, an old rattletrap Honda Civic that he bought on the cheap.

"I'm parked over there," I said.

"We can go for a walk, if you want."

"I'd love to. What you feel like doing?"

"Why don't we go to Bal Harbor? It will remind me of when we used to go for walks with your aunt."

"Fine with me. I'll meet you at the house. That way we can leave my car."

Before climbing into his old Honda Civic, he banged on the roof with a smile.

"Remember, Markie? Your mother had the same one."

He started up and I watched him pull away before I turned to go to my black Range Rover. It was worth – I had worked it out – five times his annual salary.

At the height of their glory, the Baltimore Goldmans liked to go to Bal Harbor, a fancy suburb to the north of Miami. There was an open-air shopping mall that consisted solely of luxury boutiques. My parents couldn't stand the place, but they let me go there with my aunt and uncle and cousins. When I crept into the back seat of their car, I found again that sensation of insolent happiness I only ever felt when I was with them. I felt good, I felt like a Baltimore.

"You remember when we used to come here?" said Uncle Saul when we reached the parking lot of the shopping mall.

"Of course."

We wandered past the pools on the ground floor, which were swimming with aquatic turtles and enormous Chinese carp; they used to fascinate us, back then, Hillel, Woody and me.

We got some coffee to go and sat down on a bench to watch people strolling by. Staring at the pool in front of us I reminded Uncle Saul of the time when Hillel, Woody and I had gotten it into our heads to try and catch a turtle and we'd ended up in the water. My story made him laugh, and his laughter did me good. It was his old laugh. A strong, solid, happy laugh. I saw him as he'd been fifteen years earlier, in his expensive clothes, wandering through the boutiques in the same shopping mall with Aunt Anita on his arm, while the three of us, the Goldman Gang, climbed around on the artificial rocks by the pools. Every time I go back there, I can see my aunt Anita, her sublime beauty, her wonderful kindness. I hear her voice, feel the way she would ruffle my hair. I can see her sparkling eyes, her fine lips. The loving way she would hold Uncle Saul's hand, her gestures full of affection, the discreet kisses she gave him on the cheek.

Would I, as a child, have wanted to swap my parents for Saul and Anita Goldman? Yes. This thought was, in fact, the first act of violence I ever committed against my parents. For a long time I thought I had been the most considerate of sons. And yes, my behavior toward them became violent whenever they made me feel ashamed. Such moments came only too soon: during the winter of 1993, when we were spending our customary vacation in Florida, I became truly aware of just how superior my Uncle Saul really was. It was right after our Goldman grandparents had moved out of their apartment in Miami to go and live in a retirement home in Aventura. Once they had sold their old place, there would be no more campsite for all-the-Goldmans-together. When my mother told me, at first I thought this meant we would never go back to Florida. But she reassured me: "Markie, sweetie, we'll stay in a hotel. It won't change a thing." In fact, it changed everything.

For a time, we had been the right age to enjoy staying at the complex where the Goldman grandparents had their apartment. For several years, all we knew was camping out in the living room, chasing each other up and down the stairs, the rather dirty swimming pool, the grimy little restaurant, and we were perfectly happy. We had only to cross the street to go to the beach, and just next to it there was a huge shopping center that offered plenty of things to do on rainy days. It was more than enough. All that mattered to Hillel, Woody and me was to be together.

After my grandparents moved, we had to get reorganized. Uncle Saul had been prospering in recent years: people paid top dollar for his advice. He bought an apartment in an upscale residence on West Country Club Drive called the Buenavista, and this would confuse all my points of reference. The Buenavista was private, and the only way in was through a gate that was kept locked twenty-four hours a day, and which opened only when you had shown your credentials to the security guard armed with a club, sitting in a sentry box.

I was fascinated by the place. I discovered a marvelous world where we could move around in perfect freedom, from the apartment on the 26th floor to the swimming pool with its slides, or the gym, where Woody worked out. A single day at the Buenavista swept away with one stroke all the time we'd spent in Florida up to then. Obviously, the conditions of our stay were governed by my parents' limited budget, and suffered from the comparison. They found a nearby motel, the Dolph'Inn. I hated everything about it: the grimy old rooms, the break-fast in a narrow space next to the reception area, where they set out plastic tables every morning, or the kidney-shaped swimming pool at the back of the building, where the water was so full of chlorine that all you had to do was walk along the edge of it for your eyes and throat to start stinging. What was more, to save money my parents took only one room: they slept in the double bed, and I had the spare bed next to them. I remember my mother's hesitation, every winter we stayed there, just as we were about to enter the room. She would open the door and pause for a moment, because she must have thought, as I did, how gloomy the room was, then she'd instantly get hold of herself, put her suitcase down, switch on the light and declare, beating the cushions on the bed as they gave off clouds of dust, "Isn't it great to be here?" No, it was not great to be there. Not because of the hotel, or the spare bed, or my parents. But because of the Baltimore Goldmans.

After our daily visit to our grandparents' retirement home, we all went to the Buenavista. Hillel, Woody and I hurried up to the apartment to put on our swimming trunks, then we went back down to splash around in the waterfalls in the swimming pool, where we stayed until evening.

As a rule, my parents didn't hang around. Just time for lunch, then they left. I knew they wanted to leave because they had this weird habit of standing by the bar shack, trying to catch my attention. They would wait for me to see them, and I always acted as if I hadn't. Then finally I resigned myself and swam over to them. "Markie, we're going to get going," my mom said. "We've got some shopping to do. You can come with us, or you can stay here and have fun with your cousins if you'd rather." I always chose to stay. For nothing on earth would I have forfeited even one hour away from there.

It took me a long time to figure out why my parents were so eager to leave the Buenavista. They only came back at the end of the day. Sometimes we all stayed for dinner at my aunt and uncle's place, sometimes we all went out. But sometimes my parents wanted to have dinner just the three of us. My mother would say, "Marcus, do you want to come and have a pizza with us?" I wanted to be with the other Goldmans. So I would look over at Woody and Hillel, and my mother would instantly understand and say, "Stay here and have fun, we'll come and get you at around eleven." I was lying, looking at Hillel and Woody: it was really Uncle Saul and Aunt Anita I was looking at. Because I would rather have stayed with them than go with my parents. And yet I felt like a traitor. Like on those mornings when my mother wanted to go to the shopping mall, and I asked them to drop me off first at the Buenavista. I wanted to get there as quickly as I could, because if I got there early, I could have breakfast with Uncle Saul and not at the Dolph'Inn. Breakfast at the Dolph'Inn meant being crammed together by the entrance, eating soggy donuts heated up in the microwave, off paper plates. The Baltimores had breakfast on the glass table on their balcony, and even if I showed up without warning, there was always a place set for me. As if they had been expecting me. The Baltimore Goldmans and the survivor from Montclair.

Sometimes I convinced my parents to drop me off early at the Buenavista. Woody and Hillel would still be sleeping, Uncle Saul drinking his coffee and going through his files while Aunt Anita sat next to him, reading the newspaper. I was always fascinated by how calm she was, how she could run the whole house in addition to her job. As for Uncle Saul, in spite of his files, his appointments, and the fact that he often came home late during the week, he did everything he could so that Hillel and Woody wouldn't notice how busy he was. For nothing on earth would he have missed a visit with them to the Baltimore aquarium, and at the Buenavista it was the same thing. He was available, present, relaxed, in spite of the neverending calls and faxes from his office, and the long stretches he spent between one and three o'clock in the morning revising his notes and preparing his memos.

In my spare bed at the Dolph'Inn, as I struggled to fall asleep, while my parents snored with gusto, I liked to picture the Baltimores in their apartment, all asleep except for Uncle Saul, who was still working. In my mind, his study was the only room with a light on in the entire tall building. The warm wind of the Florida night came in through the open window. If I'd been staying there, I would have crept up to the door to the study and stood there all night admiring him.

What was so fabulous about the Buenavista? Everything. It was both amazing and painful to me, because unlike at the Hamptons, where I could feel like a Baltimore Goldman, my parents' presence in Florida kept me trapped in the skin of a Montclair Goldman. It was thanks to, or because of this, that I realized for the first time something I had failed to see in the Hamptons: the social gap had widened within the Goldman family, and it was going take me a long time to understand just what repercussions this could have. The most obvious sign to me was the deference with which the security guard at the entrance to the residence greeted the Baltimore Goldmans, having opened the gate for them ahead of time as soon as he saw them coming. Whenever we Montclair Goldmans drove up he always asked, even though he knew who we were, "Can I help you?"

"We're here to see Saul Goldman in apartment 2609."

He asked for an I.D., typed on his computer, picked up his telephone, and rang the apartment. "Mr Goldman? There is a certain Mr Goldman at the gate to see you . . . Fine, thank you, I'll let him in." He opened the latch to the gate and said, "Go on in," with a magnanimous nod of his head.

My days at the Buenavista with the Baltimores were bathed in sunshine and happiness. But every evening, my parents ruined my marvelous Baltimore existence, even though they had no idea of their guilt. Their crime? Coming to get me. As on every other evening, I would sit in the back seat of the rented car, a sullen expression on my face. And as usual, my mother would ask, "So, did you have fun, dear?" I wished I had the courage to list out loud all the questions beginning with "why" that I was dying to ask every time I left the Baltimores to go back to the Montclairs. Why didn't we have a summer house, like Uncle Saul? Why didn't we have an apartment in Florida? Why could Woody and Hillel sleep in the room at the Buenavista, whilst I had to sleep in that folding cot in a crummy room at the Dolph'Inn? Why had Woody been chosen? Lucky Woody, who had managed to swap his useless parents for Uncle Saul and Aunt Anita. Why hadn't it been me? But instead of any of that, I merely went on being a nice little Montclair Goldman, and stifled the question that tormented me more than any other: why couldn't we be Baltimore Goldmans, too?

In the car, my mother would begin to lecture me: "You mustn't forget to call Aunt Anita and Uncle Saul when we get back to Montclair. As always, they have been so nice to you." I didn't need a reminder to thank them. I called them every time I got back from vacation. Because I was polite, and also because I was nostalgic. I would say, "Thank you for everything, Uncle Saul," and he'd reply, "Oh, it's nothing, nothing at all. You don't need to keep thanking me all the time. I'm the one who has to thank you for being such a good kid, and for making us glad to spend time with you." And when it was Aunt Anita who picked up the phone, she would say, "Markie my kitten, it's perfectly natural, you're a member of the family." I blushed when she called me "kitten". Just as I blushed when she saw me and complimented me, "You are becoming such a handsome boy," or when she felt my arm and exclaimed, "Say, you're getting some muscles, aren't you!" And on the days that followed I would look at myself in the mirror with a proud, blissful smile. Was I, an adolescent, falling in love with my aunt Anita? I probably was. A little bit more every time I saw her.

Years later, the winter following the success of my first novel, in other words roughly three years after the tragedy, I indulged in a luxurious Christmas vacation at a fashionable hotel in South Beach. It was the first time I'd been back to Miami since the Buenavista. I stopped my car outside the gate.

The security guard peered out of his sentry box.

"Morning, sir. Can I help you?"

"Yes, I'd just like to come in for a moment, if I may."

"Are you a resident here?"

"No, but I've come here often. I knew people who used to live here."

"Sorry, sir, if you're not a resident or a guest I have to ask you to leave."

"They lived on the 26th floor, apartment 2609. The Goldman family."

"There's no Goldman on my register, sir."

"Who lives in apartment 2609 now?"

"Sorry sir, I'm not authorized to give out that information."

"I'd just like to come in for ten minutes. Just to go and look at the swimming pool. To see if it's changed."

"Sir, I have to ask you to leave now. This is private property. Otherwise I'll have to call the police."

11

One warm Tuesday morning Alexandra showed up at my place in Boca Raton, on the pretext that her dog, as usual, had run off.

"Why would your dog be at my place?"

"I don't know."

"If I'd seen him, I would have brought him back to you."

"True. Sorry I bothered you."

She looked as if she were about to leave.

"Wait. Would you like to have a coffee?"

She smiled.

"Sure, why not."

"Just give me a few minutes, please. It's a real mess inside."

"It doesn't matter, Markie."

I felt a shiver when she called me Markie. But I knew I mustn't get distracted.

"No, it's a disgrace to invite people in when it's such a mess. Give me a minute."

I hurried out onto the rear patio. The really warm weather had just begun and Duke was lolling in a kid's inflatable swimming pool I had bought for him.

I tipped it out to empty it, and Duke along with it. He looked unhappy. "Sorry, buddy, you have to get out of here." He sat down and stared at me. "Go on! Scram! Your boss is at the front door!" As he still didn't move, I threw his rubber ball as far as I could. It landed in the lake, and Duke bounded after it.

I hurried to usher Alexandra into the house. We sat down in the kitchen, I put some coffee in the machine, and as she was looking out the window, she saw her dog swimming in the lake.

"What the—" she exclaimed. "Duke is down there."

We went and got Duke out of the water, with the ball in his mouth. She removed it. "The stuff people throw in this lake," I said.

She stayed at my house for a long time. When she had to leave I gave Duke a friendly pat. She looked at me for a long time without speaking: I think she was about to kiss me. Suddenly she turned her head and walked away.

I watched her go down the front steps and back to her car. She drove off. It was then that I noticed a black van parked in the street: there was a man behind the wheel, watching me. When he saw me looking at him, he turned the ignition. I rushed out, but he drove off in a hurry. I ran after him, waving at him to stop. He had disappeared before I had the presence of mind to write down the license number.

Hearing the noise, Leo came out on his porch.

"Everything alright, Marcus?"

"There was this strange guy in a van," I said, breathlessly. "He looked really weird."

Leo joined me in the street.

"A black van?" he said.

"Yes."

"I've seen it a few times. I thought it belonged to a neighbor."

"He was anything but a neighbor."

"Do you think he's threatening you?"

"I – I don't really know, Leo."

I decided to call the police. The patrol car showed up ten minutes later. Unfortunately, I had no lead to give them. All I could tell them was that I'd seen a black van. The police told me to call them if I noticed anything strange, and they promised to drive up and down the street a few times during the night.

* * *

The Goldman Gang was always a threesome. But I would be at a loss to say whether I was a founding element or whether, in fact, the gang only existed because of the friendship between Hillel and Woody, with the third element grafted on. The year of the Buenavista was when Scott Neville assumed a more prominent position in my cousins' life, so much so that I began to get the impression he'd been rewarded not only with their friendship but also the third spot in the Goldman Gang.

Scott was funny, knew everything there was to know about football, and more than once when I called them, my cousins said, "You'll never guess what Scott did at school today."

I was horribly jealous of him: because I had met him, I knew he was a very likable person. Moreover, because of his illness, he really deserved all the kindness he received. The worst was when I imagined him in the wheelbarrow, propelled along by Woody and Hillel, on display like an African king in his sedan chair.

When we got back from Christmas vacation he even managed to infiltrate the *Goldman Gardeners* team, following an incident that left Bunk unable to work for some time.

During the winter, Skunk shoveled the snow on his customers' sidewalks and driveways. It was hard, physical work, particularly during those winters when it snowed repeatedly, which meant constant shoveling.

One Saturday morning, when Woody and Hillel were removing piles of snow from in front of a customer's garage, Skunk arrived, furious.

"Hurry up, you scumbags! Haven't you finished here yet?"

"We're doing what we can, Mr Skunk," said Hillel.

"Then do more! And the name is Bunk! Bunk! Not Skunk!"

As he often did, he waved a shovel in front of them, as if threatening to hit them.

"I had Mrs Balding on the phone. She said you didn't go to her place last week and she almost couldn't get out of her house."

"We were on vacation," Woody pleaded.

"I don't care, scumbags! Hurry up!"

"Don't worry, Mr Skunk," Hillel reassured him. "We'll work hard."

Bunk turned purple.

"Bunk!" he screamed. "MY NAME IS BUNK! BUNK! BUNK! How many times do I have to tell you? Bunk with a B! B as in … as in—"

"B as in Bunk, maybe?" Hillel suggested.

"B as in Bash-your-goddam-face-in-for-Christ's-sake!" exploded Skunk, before suddenly collapsing on the ground.

Woody and Hillel ran over. He was twisting this way and that, like a worm. "My back!" he croaked, as if paralyzed. "My back, for fuck's sake!" Poor Skunk had shouted so loud he'd thrown his back out. Hillel and Woody helped him back to their place. Aunt Anita settled him on the sofa in the living room and examined him. Apparently, it was a trapped nerve. Nothing serious, but complete rest was imperative. She prescribed painkillers and drove Skunk home, while Uncle Saul, Woody, and Hillel followed her in the gardener's pickup truck they had rescued from the next street over. Once Skunk was in bed, Aunt Anita and Uncle Saul went to buy medicine and do some shopping, while Woody and Hillel kept him company. Sitting on the edge of his bed, they suddenly saw a tear form in his eye and roll down a wrinkle in his wizened, weather-beaten skin.

"Don't cry, Mr Skunk," Woody said kindly.

"I'm going to lose my customers. If I can't work, I'll lose all my customers."

"Don't you worry about that, Mr Skunk. We'll take care of everything."

"You little scumbags, promise me you'll take good care of my customers."

"We promise, poor Mr Skunk."

The evening of the incident, when my cousins explained what had happened, I declared I was ready to come to Baltimore right away to help them out. The Goldman Gang had an unfailing sense of honor: we had only our word, and we intended to keep it.

But when I asked my mother for permission to miss school to go to Baltimore and help my cousins shovel snow outside the garages of Oak Park, of course she wouldn't give it to me. And since my cousins needed help, it was Scott who won the honor of joining the team of Goldman Gardeners.

He shoveled enthusiastically, which meant frequent stops to catch his breath. His parents, Patrick and Gillian Neville, were worried to see him outside all the time. They came looking for Woody and Hillel at the Baltimore house, to tell them they had to be extra careful because of Scott's health.

Woody and Hillel promised to look after him. When the fine weather returned and there was talk of getting the gardens ready for the springtime, Gillian Neville was very nervous of having her son go on working with the Gang. Patrick, on the contrary, found that his son was flourishing from his contact with the two boys. He took Woody and Hillel for a milkshake at the Dairy Shack and explained the situation.

"Scott's mom is a little worried to see him gardening. It makes him tired, and exposes him to a lot of dust and dirt. But Scott likes being with you. It's good for his morale, and that's important, too."

"Don't you worry, Mr Neville," said Hillel reassuringly. "We'll take special care of Scott."

"He has to drink a lot of water, and take regular breaks to rest, and wash his hands every time he's been touching tools."

"We'll watch out for all that, Mr Neville. Promise."

That year I went to Baltimore for spring vacation. I could understand why my cousins liked Scott's company so much: he was a most endearing boy. One afternoon we all went to his house; his father had asked us to help him with his plants. This was the first time I met the Nevilles. Patrick was the same age as Uncle Saul and Aunt Anita. He was a good-looking man, athletic and very affable. His wife Gillian wasn't a classic beauty, but there was still something very appealing about her. Scott had a sister, whom my cousins had never met. I think it was their first time at the Nevilles' too.

Patrick took us down to the end of his garden: from outside, his house was like the Baltimores', just a bit more modern. On the western side, two rows of scrawny hydrangea were baking in the sun. A few drab rosebushes languished nearby.

Woody looked at the plants with an expert eye.

"I don't know who planted those flowers for you, but the hydrangea are facing the wrong way. They don't really like the sun, you know. And they look thirsty. Is your automatic sprinkler connected?"

"I think so . . . "

Woody sent Hillel to check the sprinkler, then he examined the leaves on the roses.

"Your rose is sick," was his diagnosis. "You have to treat it."

"Can you do that?"

"Sure."

Hillel came back.

"There's a leak in one of the hoses. It will have to be changed."

Woody agreed.

"In my opinion," he added, "you should think about moving the hydrangea to the other side. But we'll have to check with Mr Bunk to see what he thinks."

Patrick Neville looked at us, amused.

"I told you they were good, Dad," said Scott.

It was hot and Patrick offered us something to drink; we eagerly accepted. As his shoes were covered with dirt, he peered through one of the French doors and called, "Alexandra, can you bring some water for the boys, please?"

"Who's Alexandra?" Hillel said.

"My sister."

She arrived a few seconds later, carrying a tray with little bottles of spring water.

We were speechless. She was a perfect beauty. Her eyes slightly slanting, blond hair rippling in the sun, a delicate face and elegant nose. In her ears she wore sparkling little diamonds, and her fingernails were painted red. She gave us a smile, revealing her straight, very white teeth, and our hearts began beating faster. And as the three of us had always shared everything, we decided we would all love this girl with the laughing eyes.

"Hi, guys," she said. "So you're the ones Scott's always talking about?"

After stammering for a moment, we introduced ourselves one after the other.

"Are you brothers?" she asked.

"Cousins," Woody said. "We're the three Goldman cousins."

She gave us another ravishing smile.

"Well, Goldman cousins, very pleased to meet you."

She kissed her father on the cheek, told him she was going out for a moment, and vanished, leaving nothing but a trace of apricot-scented shampoo.

Scott thought it was gross that we all had a crush on his sister. We couldn't help it. Alexandra had just conquered our hearts once and for all.

The day after that first meeting with her, we went to the post office in Oak Park, at Aunt Anita's request, to buy some stamps. On our way out, Woody suggested we stop at the Dairy Shack for a milkshake. Just as we were sitting down at a table with our orders, in she came. She saw us, must have noticed how enthralled and incredulous we were, then she gave a peal of laughter and sat down at our table, greeting each of us by name.

That is one quality she has never lost: everyone will tell you how kind, sweet, and marvelous she is. In spite of her worldwide success, the glory and money and everything that goes with it, she is still that authentic, gentle, delightful person who set us dreaming when we were only thirteen years old.

"So you live in the neighborhood," she said, reaching for a straw, which she then dipped into our milkshakes to taste them.

"We live on Willowick Road," Hillel said.

She smiled. And when she smiled, her slanting eyes made her look mischievous.

"I live in Montclair, New Jersey," I said, feeling obliged to point this out.

"You're cousins, you said?"

"My father and his father are brothers," Hillel explained.

"And you?" she asked Woody.

"I live with Hillel and his parents. We're like brothers."

"So that means we're all cousins," I concluded.

Again that ringing laughter. That was how she came into our lives, the girl we'd grow to love so much, all three of us. *A-lex-and-ra*. A handful of letters, four little syllables that would turn our entire world upside down.

12

Baltimore, Maryland
Spring – Fall, 1994

For the two next years, she lit up our lives.

My beloved cousins, if you were still here, we would tell again the story of how she conquered us.

In the summer of 1994 I begged my parents to let me spend two weeks in Baltimore after my stay in the Hamptons. To be with her.

She had grown fond of us and we were over at her house all the time. As a rule, big sisters and little brothers don't get along, or at least that is what I had observed among my friends in Montclair. They called each other names and played dirty tricks. But at the Nevilles', things were different, surely because of Scott's illness.

Alexandra enjoyed our company. She even sought us out. And Scott loved having his sister around. She called him "pumpkin" and covered him with tender gestures. When I saw her teasing him, putting her arm around him, stroking his shoulder, or kissing his cheek, I suddenly began to wish that I had cystic fibrosis, too. Having always been fussed over as much as a Montclair deserved, I was fascinated now by how much attention a child could get.

I promised the heavens a thousand wonders in exchange for a whopping case of cystic fibrosis. To accelerate the divine process, when no-one was looking I licked Scott's forks and drank out of his glass. When he had a coughing fit, I tried to inhale some toxic fumes.

I went to the doctor's, who found that, unfortunately, I was in great shape.

"I have cystic fibrosis," I declared, to help him with his diagnosis.

He burst out laughing.

"Hey!" I protested. "Show some respect for a sick person."

"You don't have cystic fibrosis, Marcus."

"How do you know?"

"I know because I'm your doctor. You're in fine health."

Weekends in Baltimore always meant Alexandra too, now. She was everything we could have dreamt of: funny, intelligent, beautiful, sweet, and dreamy. What fascinated us most was her musical talent. We were her first real audience: she had us come over and she would pick up her guitar and play for us. We listened, spellbound.

She could play for hours, and we never tired of listening. She shared her compositions with us, and asked for our opinions. It took only a few months for Aunt Anita to agree to sign Hillel and Woody up for guitar lessons, whereas back in Montclair my mother refused, with a fearsome argument: "Guitar lessons? What for?" I don't think she would have seen anything wrong with me taking violin or the harp. She could have imagined me becoming a virtuoso, or an opera singer. But when I told her I wanted to be a rock star, she pictured me as some grimy rocker with long dirty hair.

Alexandra became the first and only a female member of the Goldman Gang. In an instant she belonged to our group, so much so that we wondered how we could have lived so long without her. She joined in our pizza parties with the Baltimores, she came with us to the old people's home to visit Aunt Anita's father, and she even won our prestigious inter-Goldman trophy for wheelchair racing. She could drink as much Dr Pepper in one go as the three of us could, and burp just as loud.

I genuinely liked all the Neville family. It was beginning to seem as if the entire population of Baltimore had been granted superior genes. This was borne out by the fact that all the Nevilles were as good-looking and attractive as the Goldmans. Patrick worked for a bank, and Gillian was a trader. They had come from Pennsylvania a few years earlier, but were originally from New York. They were extremely kind to us. We were always welcome at their place.

Alexandra's presence in Baltimore – that is, once I had become aware of the Neville family – increased both my excitement at the thought of going there, and my distress at having to leave. Mingled with my sadness was a sensation I had hitherto never felt toward my cousins: jealousy. Alone in Montclair, I fell prey to absurd fantasies: I imagined Woody and Hillel coming home from school and stopping off at her place. I imagined her rubbing up against them and I would go wild with anger. I ranted and raved as I pictured Alexandra hanging on Hillel's every word as if he were some genius, or eyeing Woody for his athlete's muscles. And who was I, after all? Not really an athlete, nor really all that smart; I was just a Montclair. In a moment of deep dismay during my geography class I even wrote her a letter to tell her how sorry I was not to live in Baltimore, too. I copied the letter out on elegant stationery, rewrote it three times so that every word would be perfect, and sent it certified Express Mail to be sure she got it. But she never answered. I called the post office over a dozen times to give my reference number, to make sure the letter had been delivered to Alexandra Neville, Hanson Crescent, Oak Park, Maryland. She had received it. She had signed the acknowledgement of receipt. Why didn't she answer? Had her mother intercepted the letter? Or did she have feelings she didn't dare confess and which, consequently, prevented her from writing back? When I finally returned to Baltimore, the first thing I asked her when I saw her was whether she had gotten my letter. She said, "Yes, Markie-moo. Thank you, by the way." I had written her a beautiful letter, and all she could say was *Thank you, Markie-moo*. Hillel and Woody burst out laughing when they heard the nickname she had just made up for me.

"Markie-moo," Woody spluttered.

"A letter about what?" Hillel asked, mockingly.

"None of your business," I said.

But Alexandra said, "A very nice letter where he tells me he wishes he lived in Baltimore, too."

Hillel and Woody began laughing like imbeciles and I stood there mortified, crimson with shame. I began thinking there really must be something between Alexandra and one of my cousins, and from signs I observed, everything seemed to indicate it was Woody, which would hardly have surprised me since all the girls and even all the women went into raptures over him – he was handsome and muscular, brooding and mysterious. I wished I'd been abandoned by my parents the way he had, if it meant I could have ended up handsome and strong and living in the Baltimore Goldmans' house.

When the weekend was nearly over and I heard her say a last, "'Bye, Markie-moo", I felt my heart sink. She said, "Are you coming back next weekend?"

"No."

"Oh, what a pity! When are you coming back?"

"I don't know right now."

At moments like that, I almost got the impression I meant something special to her, but then my two cousins immediately cackled like monkeys and said, "Don't worry, Alexandra, you'll be getting a *loooove* letter soon." She laughed, too, and I left, sheepish.

Aunt Anita drove me to the station. On the platform, an ugly, dirty little boy was waiting for me. I had to take off my clothes in front of him and give him back the magnificent Baltimore fleece, while he handed me a garbage bag containing the stinking, filthy Montclair suit. I put it back on, kissed my aunt and got on the train. Once I was on board, I could no longer hold back my tears. And in spite of all my prayers, and of all the hurricanes, tornadoes, snowstorms and other cataclysms that swept through the United States those years, not a single one had the bright idea of unleashing its fury while I was still in Baltimore to enable me to prolong my stay. Right until the last moment, I hoped for a sudden natural disaster, or some major breakdown on the railroad which would stop the train from leaving. Anything, just so I could rush back to my aunt and back to Oak Park where Uncle Saul was waiting, along with my cousins and Alexandra. But the train always left the station and took me with it, back to New Jersey.

* * *

Fall 1994 was our first year of high school, and Hillel and Woody left private school to go to Buckerey High, which had a renowned football team. Uncle Saul and Aunt Anita would probably never have dreamt of putting Hillel in public high school if the coach from the Buckerey team hadn't come in person to recruit Woody. It all happened a few months earlier, before the end of their last year at Oak Tree, when a visitor rang the bell at the Baltimore Goldmans'. The man was no stranger to Woody, who had just opened the door. But even though his face looked familiar, he couldn't remember where he'd seen him.

"You're Woodrow, aren't you?" said the man at the door.

"Everybody calls me Woody."

"I'm Augustus Bendham, the football coach at Buckerey High. Are your parents here? I'd like to speak to all three of you."

Aunt Anita, Uncle Saul, Woody and Hillel sat down in the kitchen to talk to Bendham.

"So," he began, playing nervously with his glass of water, "forgive me for showing up unannounced, but I'm here to make you a somewhat unusual proposal. I've been watching Woodrow play with his football team for a while now. He's talented, really talented. He has immense potential. I'd like to have him on the high school team. I know your kids are in private school and that Buckerey is a public high school, but my team is top this year, and I think that with a player of Woody's caliber we have every chance of winning the title. Moreover, he'll only stagnate on the local team, whereas if he plays in the school championship, he'll make real progress. I think this is an opportunity both for Buckerey and for Woody. As a rule I never normally go so far as to ask parents to enroll their kid at Buckerey just to have one more talent on the team. I make do with who's there, that's part of my job. But this time it's different. I cannot recall ever having seen someone his age play like this. I'd really like to see Woodrow on the team as soon as school starts."

"Buckerey isn't the nearest high school to where we live," Aunt Anita pointed out.

"True, but you don't have to worry about that. We can find the space for Woodrow. If your boy wants to go to Buckerey, then he will."

Uncle Saul turned to Woody.

"What do you think?"

He paused, thinking for a moment, then asked the coach: "Why me? Why are you so eager to have me at your school?"

"Because I've seen you play. And I've never seen anything like it in my entire career. You're strong and heavy, and yet you run at the speed of light. You alone are worth two or three of my usual players. I'm not saying that just to give you a big head. You haven't reached your full potential, far from it. You'll have to work like a dog. To give of yourself the way you never have. I'll personally make sure you do. I have no doubt that thanks to football you'll be able to get a scholarship to any college in the country. But I think you may not have time to go to college."

"What do you mean?" asked Uncle Saul.

"Just that I think this kid here will become an N.F.L. star. Believe me, as a rule I'm not in the habit of doling out compliments. But what I've seen on the playing field these last few months …"

Bendham's proposal was the only topic of conversation at the Baltimore Goldman dinner table over the days that followed. They all had their own reasons to think that the possibility of Woody joining the Buckerey football team was great news. Uncle Saul and Aunt Anita, pragmatic, thought that this was a unique opportunity for Woody to be able to go on to a good college afterwards. Hillel and Scott – who had immediately been informed of the coach's predictions – foresaw money and glory. "Do you know how much a professional football player makes?" said Hillel, excitedly. "Millions! They earn millions of dollars. Wood, this is huge!"

They looked into it: Buckerey High was a good, demanding school, and its football team was indeed renowned. When Bendham came back to see the Baltimores to obtain their final verdict, he found Woody, Hillel, and Scott waiting for him outside the house. "I'll come and play football for Buckerey if you fix it so my friends Hillel and Scott can be transferred to the same school," Woody said.

Then they had to convince Scott's parents to let their son go to a public high school, and they were not at all sure. Aunt Anita invited them to dinner one evening without their son.

"Boys, we really appreciate what you've been doing for Scott," Mrs Neville said to Woody and Hillel. "But you have to understand that the situation is complicated. Scott is not well."

"We know he's not well, but he has to go to school, doesn't he?" said Woody.

"Boys," Aunt Anita began, gently, "Scott might be better off in a private school."

"But Scott wants to come to Buckerey with us," Hillel said. "It's not fair, not to let him."

"He really has to be treated with great care," Gillian said. "I know you don't mean any harm, but all this football business . . . "

"Don't worry, Mrs Neville," Hillel said, "he doesn't have to run. We put him in a wheelbarrow and Woody pushes him."

"Boys, he's not used to so much excitement."

"But he's happy with us, Mrs Neville."

"The other children will make fun of him. In a private school, he would be better protected."

"If the pupils make fun of him, we'll smash their faces in," Woody promised.

"No-one is going to smash anyone's face in!" Uncle Saul said, starting to get annoyed.

"I'm sorry, Saul," Woody said. "I only wanted to help."

"It's not helping at all."

Patrick took his wife's hand.

"Gil, Scott is so happy with them. We've never seen him like this. He's come alive, at last."

In the end, Patrick and Gillian allowed Scott to enroll at Buckerey High, and he started, with Hillel and Woody, in the fall of 1994. But their fears were justified: in the privileged world of Oak Tree, their son had been sheltered; now, already on his first day at high school, his sickly appearance made him the target of other pupils. They stared and made fun of him. That same first day, disoriented in the huge corridors of an unfamiliar building, Scott asked directions to the classroom from a girl whose boyfriend was a big kid in senior year; at the end of the day the boy cornered him, twisted his arm in front of everyone, then jammed his head into a locker. Woody and Hillel found him there, sobbing. "Don't tell my parents," Scott pleaded. "If they find out, they'll make me change schools."

They had to do something for Scott. After a brief discussion, Hillel and Woody decided that Woody would beat up the boyfriend first thing the next day, so that all the other pupils would be well aware of the consequences if anyone tried to mess with their friend.

The hefty boy – Rick was his name – practiced martial arts, but this did not impress Woody, nor would it prove any use to the poor kid. As agreed, the next morning during recess, Woody went and found Rick and floored him with one sudden punch to the nose. While Rick lay sprawled on the ground, Hillel poured orange juice onto his head and Scott danced around his body, his arms raised, shouting in victory. Rick was taken to the infirmary and the three other boys to the office of Mr Burdon, the principal; Uncle Saul and Aunt Anita, Patrick and Gillian Neville, and coach Bendham were also urgently summoned.

"Well done, you three," said the principal. "Second day of school, your first year here, and already you're beating up your fellow students."

"Have you gone crazy?" said Bendham reproachfully.

"Have you gone crazy?" said the Nevilles.

"Have you gone crazy?" said Uncle Saul and Aunt Anita.

"Don't worry, Mr Burdon," Hillel explained, "we're not thugs. This was preventive warfare. That kid Rick really enjoys terrorizing kids who are weaker than him. But he'll behave now. You have my word as a Goldman."

"Silence, for heaven's sake!" shouted Burdon, annoyed. "In my entire career I have never seen a kid take back so much. Two days after school starts and you're already punching your schoolmates in the face? You've broken the record! I want nothing more to do with you! Do you understand? As for you, Woody, your behavior is unworthy of a member of the football team. Any more tricks like this and I will take you off the team."

At Buckerey no-one ever bothered Scott again. As for Woody, his reputation had been made. In the school corridors he was respected, and he quickly earned respect on the football field, too, where he played brilliantly for the Buckerey Wildcats. Every day after class he went to practice, accompanied by Hillel and Scott who, with Bendham's consent, sat on the trainer's bench and watched the team.

Scott was passionate about football. He commented on the players' moves and explained the rules to Hillel at length, and before long Hillel could go on about it forever. At the same time he discovered an unsuspected talent: he was a good coach. He had a good vision of the game, and could immediately detect a player's weakness. He sometimes shouted instructions to the players from the bench, and Bendham found this highly amusing. He said, "Hey, Goldman, you're going to steal my job if this keeps up!" Hillel smiled, although he did not notice that when the coach said Goldman, Woody instinctively turned his head, too.

13

In Boca Raton, after I had spotted the man at the wheel of the black van, Leo and I spent two nights hidden in my kitchen keeping watch on the street. We peered into the darkness for the slightest suspicious movement. But other than a neighbor who went jogging in the middle of the night, a patrol car cruising by at regular intervals, and raccoons that came to pillage the garbage cans, we saw nothing.

Leo was taking notes.

"What are you writing?" I asked him in a whisper.

"Why are you whispering?"

"I don't know. What are you writing?"

"I'm writing down any suspicious activity. That crazy woman jogging, the raccoons . . ."

"Add the police car, while you're at it."

"I did. You know, often it's the cop who's guilty. That would make a good novel. Who knows where this will lead?"

It didn't lead anywhere. There was no further sign of the van or its driver. My main concern was to know what he was looking for. Was he trying to get at Alexandra? Should I warn her?

But I would find out soon enough.

It happened at the end of March 2012, roughly a month and a half after I moved to Boca Raton.

*   *   *

As the season progressed, Hillel and Scott got more and more involved with the Wildcats. They went to every practice, changed in the locker room with the regular players to put on a football jersey, and then went out to their observation bench. On days when they went to an away game, they rode on the team's bus, wearing a suit and tie like all the others. Their constant presence among the team made them fully-fledged members in no time. Bendham was touched by their commitment and wanted to give them a more official role, so he placed them in charge of the equipment. But the trial lasted no more than a quarter of an hour: Hillel was too weak to carry much of anything, and Scott was quickly out of breath.

The coach had them sit on his bench and suggested they call out advice to the players. Which is what they did, analyzing each one's game with remarkable precision. Then they called the guys over one by one, who consulted them as if they were the oracle at Delphi. "You're wasting your energy galloping like a horse when you don't need to. Maintain your position and don't move until the action comes to you." Every one of the helmeted giants listened attentively. Hillel and Scott became the first and only students in the history of Buckerey High School to wear the orange and black Wildcat jersey even though they didn't officially belong to the team. And when, at the end of practice, Bendham shouted, "Good work, Goldman," Woody and Hillel both turned around at the same time and replied in unison, "Thanks, Coach."

At the Baltimore Goldman dinner table the sole topic now was football. When they came home from practice, Woody and Hillel related the day's exploits in great detail.

"And what about your schoolwork?" asked Aunt Anita. "Is that going well?"

"It's O.K.," said Woody. "Could be better, Hillel is giving me a hand. He doesn't need to work, he understands everything straight off the bat."

"I'm kind of bored, Dad," Hillel said, more than once. "High school isn't really the way I imagined."

"How did you imagine it?"

"I don't know. Maybe more stimulating. But at least there's football."

That year, the Buckerey Wildcats made it to the championship quarter-finals. When they came back from Christmas vacation, the football season was over, so Woody, Hillel, and Scott began looking for something new to do. Scott liked drama. And it turned out it was a good activity for him, to work on his breathing. They signed up for a drama class with Ms Anderson, their English teacher, a very kind young woman.

Hillel had a natural talent for leadership. On the football field, he was a coach. On stage, he became a director. He suggested to Ms Anderson that they produce an adaptation of *Of Mice and Men*, and she agreed enthusiastically. And that was the start of a whole new set of problems.

After rigging an audition among the participants in the class Hillel decided on the cast. Scott, to his delight, got the part of George, and Woody was chosen to play Lennie.

"You're playing the bozo," Hillel explained to Woody.

"Hey, I don't want to play some bozo . . . Ms Anderson, can't you find someone else? Besides, I'm no good at this sort of thing. What I know how to do is play football."

"Shut up, Lennie," Hillel ordered. "Go get your script, let's do a run-through. Go on, everybody, take your place."

But after the first rehearsal, several of the students' parents complained to the principal about the text the students were being asked to perform. Burdon took their side and asked Ms Anderson to choose a more appropriate text. Furious, Hillel went to Burdon's office to demand an explanation.

"Why won't you let us perform *Of Mice and Men* with Ms Anderson?"

"Some of the parents complained about the play and I think they were right."

"I'd be curious to know what they complained about."

"It's full of bad words, you know that very well. Come on, Hillel, do you really want this performance, which is supposed to do the school proud, to be nothing but a vulgar, blasphemous heap of slang?"

"But it's John Steinbeck! Are you completely crazy, Mr Burdon?"

Burdon looked daggers at him.

"You're the one who's crazy, Hillel – don't you dare speak to me in that tone of voice. I will do you a favor and pretend I didn't hear you."

"But for crying out loud, you can't outlaw a text by John Steinbeck!"

"I don't care if it's Steinbeck or not, I refuse to allow that awful, provocative book to be read in this school."

"Well, then this school is useless!"

Furious, Hillel decided to give up drama class. He was angry with Mr Burdon, with what he represented, with the high school. He suddenly began wearing the dejected look of the worst days at Oak Tree, and he felt depressed. His performance at school was catastrophic and Ms Anderson summoned his parents. Aunt Anita and Uncle Saul, taken by surprise, discovered a side of Hillel that was very different from the enlightened boy they knew he could be. He lost all interest in school, he was insolent with his professors, and he was racking up one bad grade after another.

"I think he's stopped paying attention because he's not motivated," Ms Anderson told them.

"But then what should we do?"

"Hillel is really very bright. He's interested in so many things. He knows so much more about just about everything than any of his schoolmates. Last week, I tried with great difficulty to explain the basis of federalism to the class, along with the functioning of the American state. Hillel already knows politics like the back of his hand and he was making comparisons with ancient Greece."

"Yes, he's passionate about ancient history," Aunt Anita said ruefully.

"Mr and Mrs Goldman, Hillel is fourteen years old and he reads books about Roman law."

"What are you trying to tell us?" Uncle Saul said.

"That maybe Hillel would be happier in a private school. With an appropriate curriculum. He would find it so much more stimulating."

"But he just left private school. And he'll never agree to be separated from Woody."

Uncle Saul and Aunt Anita tried to speak to him, to get at the bottom of the matter.

"The problem is that I think I'm useless," Hillel said.

"But how can you say such a thing?"

"Because I can't finish anything. I can't concentrate at all. Even if I wanted to, I couldn't. I don't understand anything in class, I'm completely lost."

"What do you mean, *you don't understand anything*? Hillel, listen, you're such a bright boy! You have to give yourself the means to succeed."

"I promise I'll try and make an effort."

Aunt Anita and Uncle Saul also asked for an appointment with Mr Burdon.

"Hillel may be bored in class," the principal said, "but more than anything, he complains about everything, he doesn't like it when things don't go his way. He started drama class and then suddenly dropped it all."

"He dropped it because you censored his play."

"*Censored*?" Burdon snorted. "Listen, Mr Goldman, an apple never falls far from the tree, you sound just like your son. Steinbeck or no Steinbeck, we cannot have bad language in our high school performance. It's obvious you're not the ones who will have the parents on your back as a result. Hillel should have chosen a more appropriate play. Who at the age of fourteen wants to put on a play by Steinbeck?"

"Maybe Hillel is advanced for his age," Aunt Anita said.

"Yeah, yeah, yeah," Burdon said with a sigh, "It's always the same old story, 'my child is so intelligent but you think he's a simpleton'. I hear it

159

all the time, you know. 'My child is very special, yadda yadda yadda', and 'he needs attention, bla bla bla'. The truth is we are in a public high school, Mr and Mrs Goldman, and in a public high school everybody is in the same boat. We can't start imposing special conditions for so-and-so, even for very good reasons. Can you imagine if every student had to have their own little program because they are 'special'? I already have enough problems with the cafeteria, with all the fussy Hindus, Jews, and Muslims who aren't prepared to eat the same food as everyone else."

"So what do you suggest?" Uncle Saul said.

"Well, maybe Hillel should simply work a little harder. If you knew how many kids I've had in the school whose parents thought they were geniuses, and then you run into them a few years later at the cash register of some gas station."

"What's wrong with people who work at gas stations?" asked Uncle Saul.

"Nothing! Nothing! For Pete's sake, can't a man even say what he thinks! You are so refractory in this family! All I'm saying is that maybe Hillel needs to work instead of thinking he already knows everything and that he's smarter than all his teachers combined. If he's getting bad grades, it's because he's not working hard enough, that's all there is to it."

"Well, obviously he's not working hard enough, Mr Burdon," said Aunt Anita. "That's the whole problem, and that's why we're here. He's not working because he's bored. He needs stimulation. He needs to be pushed. Encouraged. He's wasting his potential."

"Mr and Mrs Goldman, I have taken a close look at his grades. I realize this might be hard to accept, but as a rule, when a student has bad grades, it means he's not very bright."

"You know I can hear what you're saying, Mr Burdon," said Hillel, who was listening in on the conversation.

"And there he goes again, the insolent kid. He always has to have his mouth open, doesn't he? I'm having a discussion with your parents just now, Hillel. You know, if this is the way you behave with your teachers, it's not surprising they all dislike you. As for you, Mr and Mrs Goldman, I heard your line about 'my child has bad grades because he's exceptional', but I'm sorry to tell you that this is called denial. Exceptional students – why, we don't even see them go through here, and by the age of twelve they already have a degree from Harvard."

Woody decided to take things in hand and to re-motivate Hillel by letting him do what he did best: coach the football team. There was no regular team practice off-season; league regulations didn't allow it. But there was nothing to stop players from getting together among themselves for collective work-outs. So, at Woody's request, the entire team began meeting twice a week to practice, under Hillel's orders and seconded by Scott. The purpose of this preparation was to win the championship the following fall, and as the weeks went by, the players pictured themselves lifting up the trophy all together, Scott included. One day he had said to Hillel, "Hill, I want to play. I don't like being a coach. I want to play football. I want to be on the playing field next year. On the team."

Hillel looked at him ruefully.

"But Scott, your parents will never allow it."

Scott look devastated. He sat down on the lawn and tugged at tufts of grass. Hillel sat next to him and put an arm around his shoulders.

"Don't worry," he said. "We'll fix it. You just have to be careful, your father said so. Drink a lot of water, take frequent rests, and wash your hands."

And so Scott officially joined the unofficial Wildcat team. He warmed up as best he could, and took part in some of the exercises. But he got out of breath quickly. He dreamt of playing wing: to catch the ball at the 50-yard line, make a spectacular sprint, make it through all the opponents' defense and mark a touchdown; to be borne triumphantly in the air by the rest of the team, and hear the stadium screaming his name. Hillel gave him a wing position, but it was obvious he could not run more than ten yards. So they figured out a new way to go about it: they'd put Scott in a wheelbarrow and roll him as far as the goal line, and there the player pushing him would tip the wheelbarrow over and Scott along with it. And when he made contact with the ground with the ball in his arms, he'd score a touchdown. This new combination, called "a wheelbarrow", was a resounding success with everyone on the team. Part of practice was now devoted to sessions of pushing fellow team members in the wheelbarrow, and this had the effect of spectacularly increasing the players' sprinting abilities, because as soon as they set off without their wheelbarrow, they turned into regular rockets.

I never got the chance to see a "wheelbarrow" with my own eyes. But there must have been something gripping about the sight, because before long hosts of Buckerey students were flocking to practice sessions, normally only followed by a few groupies. Hillel would order his players to practice certain plays, then suddenly, when he gave the signal, shooting out of nowhere, one of the most robust players – often it was Woody – would career across the playing field with Scott sitting regally in his wheelbarrow. The quarterback would send him the ball from the far end of the field: it required exceptional agility and strength on the part of the pusher to get it to where Scott could catch the ball, then they had to make it to the goal line, zigzagging, avoiding fullbacks who did everything they could to violently intercept Woody, the wheelbarrow, and Scott. But when the wheelbarrow made it to the goal line and Scott hurled himself to the ground and scored, the spectators would scream with joy. And everyone shouted, "Wheelbarrow! Wheelbarrow!" as Scott got back up, his teammates congratulating him, and he'd go to greet his cohort of fans, which was growing by the day, to celebrate his goal. Finally, he always remembered to drink, catch his breath, and wash his hands.

These few months of practice were the happiest of the newly-constituted Goldman Gang's time at school. Woody, Hillel, and Scott were the stars of the football team and the glory of Buckerey High. Until one day in spring, not long after Easter, when Gillian Neville, who was waiting for her son on the high school parking lot, heard the cheers coming from the crowd. Scott had just made a touchdown. Gillian walked over to the playing field to see what was going on, and found her son wearing the uniform of a football player, hurtling across the playing field in a wheelbarrow. And she screamed, "Scott, in the name of Heaven! Scott, what are you doing?"

Woody stopped short. All the players froze, the spectators stopped shouting. There was a deathly silence.

"Mom?" Scott said, removing his helmet.

"Scott! You told me you were going to chess class."

Scott lowered his head and climbed out of the wheelbarrow.

"I lied to you, Mom. I'm sorry."

She hurried over to her son and put her arms around him, stifling a sob.

"Don't do this to me, Scott. Don't do this, please. You know how afraid I am for you."

"I know, I don't want you to worry. We weren't doing anything wrong, really."

Gillian Neville raised her head and saw Hillel with a note pad in his hand and a whistle around his neck.

"Hillel," she shouted, heading over to him. "You promised!"

Suddenly she lost all composure and rushed at him, and gave him a resounding slap.

"Do you know you are going to kill Scott with your insane behavior?"

Hillel was reeling from the blow.

"Where is the coach?" Gillian screamed. "Where is Bendham? Does he at least know what you are doing?"

A scandal erupted. Mr Burdon was informed, and a complaint was filed with the Maryland school board. Burdon summoned the coach, Scott and his parents, Hillel, Uncle Saul, and Aunt Anita to his office.

"Did you know your players were organizing practice?" the principal asked the coach.

"I did," Bendham said.

"And you didn't think it might be wise to put a stop to it?"

"Why should I? My players are making progress. You know the rules, Mr Burdon: coaches aren't supposed to have any contact with players off season. To have Hillel organizing group practice is manna from Heaven and perfectly within the rules."

Burdon gave a sigh and turned to Hillel.

"Did no-one ever tell you not to put a sick kid in a wheelbarrow? This is humiliating!"

"Mr Burdon," Scott said, "it's not what you think! On the contrary, I've never been as happy as these last few months."

"So these boys take you for a ride in a wheelbarrow and you're happy?"

"Yes, Mr Burdon."

"What the— For the love of heaven, this is a high school, not a circus!"

Burdon dismissed the coach, Scott, and his parents, to speak with the Goldmans in private.

"Hillel," he said, "you're a smart kid. Haven't you seen what sort of state little Scott Neville is in? Exercise is very dangerous for him."

"Actually, I think a little bit of exercise does him a world of good."

"Are you a doctor?" asked Burdon.

"No."

"Then keep your opinions to yourself. You're impertinent. I'm not asking you for a favor, I'm giving you an order. Stop putting this sick little boy in a wheelbarrow, or making him do any sort of gymnastics. It's very important."

"Alright."

"I want more than that. I want you to give me your word."

"I promise."

"Good. Fine. Now, your clandestine practice is over. You are no longer a member of the team, you will have nothing more to do with them, I don't want to see you in their bus, in their locker room, or anywhere else. I don't want to have anything more to do with you."

"First drama, and now football. You're taking everything away from me!" Hillel said, indignantly.

"I'm not taking anything away from you, I'm simply applying the rules necessary for the smooth functioning of this establishment."

"I didn't break any rules, Mr Burdon. There is nothing stopping me from coaching the team off-season."

"I forbid you."

"On what legal basis?"

"Hillel, do you want to be expelled from this high school?"

"No, but tell me what is wrong with me training the team off-season?"

"Training the team? You call this training? Putting a child with cystic fibrosis in a wheelbarrow to push him across the playing field – you call that training?"

"I've read the rules, you know. There's nothing in there that says it's forbidden for one player to transport another while he is holding the ball."

"Alright, Hillel," Burdon stormed, losing all his composure, "you want to play the lawyer, is that it? Are you the lawyer for sick kids in wheelbarrows?"

"I just wish you wouldn't be so . . . averse to change."

The principal put on a contrite air then turned to Uncle Saul and Aunt Anita and declared: "Mr and Mrs Goldman, Hillel is a good kid. But this is the public school system. If you're not happy with the way things are, you have to put him back in private school."

"May I remind you that it is Buckerey High School that came to get us," Hillel protested.

"Came to get Woody, yes. But with you it's different: you are here because Woody wanted you to go with him, and we agreed. But feel free to change schools if that's what you want."

"It's really not nice to say that. It means you don't give a damn about me!"

"What do you mean? That's not true at all. I think you're a good kid,

I enjoy having you in the school, but you're a student like all the others. You want to stay in public high school, you have to abide by the rules. That's the way the system here works."

"You are mediocre, Mr Burdon. Your high school is mediocre. Is sending people to private school your answer for everything? You reduce everything to the lowest common denominator! You won't have Steinbeck because there are three bad words in the text, but you're incapable of recognizing the significance of his work! And you hide behind obscure rules to justify your lack of intellectual curiosity. So don't go talking to me about how a system works, because this school system is totally dysfunctional and you know it. And a country with a dysfunctional school system is neither a democracy nor a state that respects the rule of law!"

There was a long silence. The principal sighed and eventually asked, "Hillel, how old are you?"

"I'm fourteen, Mr Burdon."

"Fourteen. So why aren't you out there skateboarding with your friends, instead of wondering whether the rule of law depends on the quality of a country's school system?"

Burdon stood up and went to open his office door, to signal that the meeting was over. Woody, who was waiting on a chair in the corridor, heard the principal say to Uncle Saul and Aunt Anita as he shook their hands: "I don't think that your boy Hillel will ever fit in here."

Hillel burst into tears. "No, no, you just don't understand! I spent an hour talking to you and you didn't even have the decency to listen to me." He turned to his parents. "Mom, Dad, I just want someone to listen to me! I want some consideration!'

To calm everyone down, all four Baltimores went to drink a milkshake at the Dairy Shack in Oak Tree. Sitting opposite each other in a booth, they were unusually quiet.

"Hillel, kitten," Aunt Anita said eventually, "your father and I have spent a lot of time discussing the situation. There is a special alternate school . . ."

166

"No, no special schools!" Hillel shouted. "Not one of those, please! You mustn't split us up, Woody and me!"

Aunt Anita took a brochure from her bag and put it down on the table.

"At least take a look at it. It's a place called Blueberry Hill. I think you'd like it there. I cannot stand seeing you so unhappy in this high school."

Reluctantly, Hillel leafed through the document.

"Besides, it's sixty miles away!" he complained. "No way! I'm not going a hundred and twenty miles round trip every day!"

"Hillel, darling, angel . . . you would sleep there."

"What? No, no! I don't want to!"

"Kitten, you would come home every weekend. You could learn so much that way. You're bored at school now."

"No, Mom, I don't want to! I don't want to! Why should I go there?"

That evening, Woody and Hillel read the leaflet about Blueberry Hill together.

"Wood, you have to help me!" Hillel begged, completely panicked. "I don't want to go there. I don't want us to be apart."

"Neither do I. But I don't know what to do: you're the one who's good at school, in principle. Try to stop standing out. Do you think you can do that? You got President Clinton elected! You know everything about everything! Make an effort. Don't let that stupid Burdon run you down. Go on, don't worry, Hill, I won't let you leave."

Hillel, terrified at the thought he might be sent to a special school, no longer felt like doing anything. On Friday evening, Aunt Anita went into Woody's bedroom. He was at his desk doing homework.

"Woody, Mr Bendham called. He said you left him a note saying you were quitting the football team. Is that true?"

Woody lowered his head.

"What's the point of it, anyway?" he murmured.

"What do you mean, treasure?" she said, crouching down to have her eyes level with his.

"If he goes to a special school, that will mean I can't live with you anymore, right?"

"No, Woody, of course not. It doesn't change anything, this is your home. We love you like a son, you know. The special school is a place for Hillel, where he can flourish. It's for his good. You will always have a home here."

A tear ran down his cheek. She put her arms around him and hugged him tight.

On Sunday, just before lunch, Bendham stopped by at the Baltimore Goldmans' unannounced. He invited Woody to go out to lunch and took him for a hamburger at one of his regular diners.

"I'm sorry about the note, Coach," Woody apologized once they were sitting down. "I didn't really want to leave the team. I was angry because of all the trouble they're making for Hillel."

"You know, kid, I'm sixty years old. I've been training football teams for nigh on forty years, and in my entire career I've never been out for lunch with a single one of my boys. I have my rules, and this is one of them. So why would I do it now? I've had a fair share of guys who decided they wanted to drop the team. They felt they would rather go hang out with girls than run with a ball in their arms. It was a sign, it meant they weren't serious. I didn't waste any time trying to get them back. Why waste time with guys who don't want to play when I had others who are lining up to join the team?"

"I'm serious, Coach. I promise you!"

"I know, son. That's why I'm here."

The waiter brought them their order. The coach waited for him to leave before he continued.

"Listen, Woody, I know there's a good reason why you wrote me that note. I want you to tell me what's going on."

Woody explained the problems Hillel was having – the principal who wouldn't listen, the threat of a special school hovering over him.

"He doesn't have any trouble paying attention," Woody said.

"I know that, son," the coach said. "You just have to hear him speak. In his head he's a hell of a lot more developed than most of the teachers."

"Hillel needs a challenge! He needs to feel the pull of something higher. He's happy with you. He's happy on the playing field."

"You want him back on the team? But what are we going to do with him? He's the skinniest kid I've ever seen in my entire life."

"No, Coach, it wasn't exactly a playing position I was thinking of. I have an idea, but you're going to have to trust me."

Bendham listened attentively, nodding to signify that he approved of Woody's proposal. When they had finished lunch, Bendham drove to a nearby residential neighborhood. He stopped outside a little one-story house, where an R.V. was parked.

"You see, kid, this is my house. And that R.V. belongs to me. I bought it last year, but I haven't really used it yet. It was a good bargain, I bought it for my retirement."

"Why are you telling me this, Coach?"

"Because in three years I'm going to retire. That will correspond to the end of your high school. You know what would make me happy? To finish by winning the cup and sending the best player I've ever had to the N.F.L. So I'll go along with your idea. In exchange, I want you to promise you'll come back to practice and work as hard as you have up to now. I want to see you in the N.F.L. one day, kid. And I'll take my R.V. and work my way up and down the East Coast so I won't miss a single one of your games. I'll watch you from the bleachers and tell the guys sitting next to me: I know that kid, I was his coach in high school. Promise me, Woodrow. Promise me this is just the beginning of a great adventure between you and football."

"I promise, Mr Bentham."

The coach smiled.

"O.K., then, let's go tell Hillel."

Twenty minutes later, in the Baltimore Goldmans' kitchen, Hillel,

Uncle Saul, and Aunt Anita sat listening to the coach, dumbfounded.

"You want me to be your assistant, Coach?" Hillel repeated, incredulously.

"Precisely. Starting next fall. My official assistant. I have the right to hire you, Burdon can't stop me. Besides, you'll make a terrific assistant: you know the guys, you have a good vision of the game, and I know you keep records about the other teams."

"Did Wood tell you that?"

"Never mind who did. What's important is that we've got three major seasons up ahead, I'm not young anymore, and I could really do with a helping hand."

"Oh, my God! Yes! Yes! I would love to."

"There's just one condition: to be on the team you have to have good grades. That's in the rules. Members of the football team have to pass in all their subjects, and that is valid for you, too. So if you want to be on the team, you'll have to get back up to scratch in the classroom, right away."

Hillel gave his word. For him, this was a resurrection.

14

On the morning of March 26, 2012, I was awoken by the phone ringing. It was five o'clock in the morning. It was my agent calling from New York.

"It's in the press, Marcus."

"What are you talking about?"

"You and Alexandra. You're on the front page of the most popular rag in the country."

I hurried to the nearest supermarket, open twenty-four hours a day. They were just unloading a wooden pallet with stacks of magazines wrapped in cellophane.

I grabbed one, tore off the plastic, took out a magazine and read, to my horror:

WHAT'S THE SCOOP ON
ALEXANDRA NEVILLE AND MARCUS GOLDMAN?
Secret escapade in Florida

The guy in the black van was a photographer. He had spent several days spying on us and trailing us, then sprang it on everyone when he sold his exclusive story to a magazine.

He'd been there right from the start: he saw me stealing Duke, saw Alexandra and me in Coconut Grove, Alexandra coming to my house. It all looked very much as if we were having an affair.

I called my agent back.

"We have to stop it," I told him.

"It's impossible. They've been very clever. There have been no leaks, no advance press on the Internet. All the photographs were taken in public places without any direct intrusion into your privacy. It's all been brilliantly put together."

"I didn't do anything with her."

"You can do what you like."

"I said there's nothing between us! There must be some way we can block the sale of this magazine."

"It's all just conjecture, Marcus. That's not illegal."

"Does she know about it?"

"I expect she does. And if she doesn't now, she soon will."

I waited for an hour before going to ring at the gate to Kevin's house. I saw the camera and the interphone light up, which meant that someone had seen me, but the gate remained closed. I rang again, and finally the front door to the house opened. It was Alexandra. She came down to the gate, but she stayed on the other side.

"You stole my dog?" she said, her gaze furious. "Is that why he was always over at your place?"

"I did it once. Or twice. After that he came on his own, I swear."

"I don't know if I should believe you, Marcus. Are you the one who tipped off the press?"

"What? Why the hell would I do that?"

"I don't know. So I would break up with Kevin, maybe."

"Alexandra! Don't tell me that's what you think!"

"You had your chance, Marcus. Eight years ago. Don't come ruining my life. Leave me alone. My lawyers will be in touch to obtain your formal denial."

* * *

Baltimore, Maryland
Spring–Summer, 1995

I was feeling more and more isolated in Montclair.

While I was stuck in New Jersey, Paradise awaited me with open arms in Oak Park. Not one but two wonderful families, the Baltimores and the

Nevilles, who had become good friends on top of it. Uncle Saul and Patrick Neville were tennis partners. Aunt Anita invited Gillian Neville to join in volunteer activities at Artie Crawford's children's home. Hillel, Woody, and Scott were doing stuff together all the time.

One day at the beginning of April, Hillel, who read the *Baltimore Sun* every day, found an article about a music contest a national radio station was organizing. Participants were invited to audition by performing two of their own compositions, which they submitted as audio or as a video. The winner would be able to record five tracks in a professional studio, and one of them would be played on that radio station for six months. Naturally, Uncle Saul had the latest high-tech movie camera, and naturally he offered to lend it to Hillel and Woody. And from my prison in New Jersey I got excited calls from my cousins every day to tell me that their project was progressing nicely. For an entire week, Alexandra spent all her late afternoons rehearsing at the Goldman's, and on the weekend, Hillel and Woody filmed her. I was dying of jealousy.

But, contest or a no contest, the three of us – Woody, Hillel, and me – were nosed out before long because one day Alexandra showed up at the Baltimores' with Austin, her boyfriend. It was bound to happen: Alexandra, seventeen years old, as beautiful as a goddess, was not going to set her sights on some fifteen-year-old gardeners. She preferred a guy from her high school, a daddy's boy who was handsome as Adonis and as strong as Hercules, but about as smart as a bowl of Jello. He would go down into the basement, sprawl on the sofa, and not even listen to Alexandra's compositions. He couldn't care less about music, whereas music was her whole life, something that imbecile Austin could not grasp.

There were two months to go before they would announce the results of the contest. In the meantime, Alexandra got her driver's license, and on weekends, in the evening, when Austin left her in the lurch to go out with his buddies, she came and picked us up at the Baltimores'. We went for milkshakes at the Dairy Shack, then we parked in a quiet street and stretched out on a lawn gazing up at the night sky and listening to the music coming through the open doors from the car radio. Alexandra would sing along to the music and we imagined one of her songs being played over and over on the radio.

At times like that, we felt as if she belonged to us. We would talk for hours. Austin was often the topic of the conversation. Hillel eventually dared to come out with the question all three of us had been dying to ask: "What are you doing with such a jerk?"

"He is anything but a jerk. He might be kind of abrupt, but he's a nice boy."

"Yeah sure," Woody joked. "Then it must be his convertible that makes hims such an airhead."

"No, seriously," Alexandra said, defending him, "you should get to know him."

"I still think he's a jerk," Hillel said, decisively.

And Alexandra concluded: "I love him. That's the way it is."

When she said "I love him", she broke our hearts.

Alexandra did not win the contest. All she got was a curt letter telling her that her application had not been successful. Austin told her that if she had not won, it was because she was no good.

To be perfectly frank, when Woody and Hillel called me to tell me the news, part of me was relieved: it would have hurt me to see her career launched thanks to some contest Hillel had dug up and a video that had been produced exclusively by the Baltimores. Still, I felt really sorry for her, because I knew how much the contest meant to her. I got her phone number from the operator, took my courage in two hands, and called her, something I had never dared to do in spite of the urge that had been gnawing away at me for months. To my great relief, she was the one who answered, but the phone call didn't get off to a good start.

"Hi, Alexandra, it's Marcus."

"Marcus who?"

"Marcus Goldman."

"Who?"

"Marcus, Woody and Hillel's cousin."

"Oh, Marcus the cousin! Hi, Marcus, how are you?"

I told her I was calling about the contest, that I was sorry she hadn't won, and as we went on talking, she began to cry.

"Nobody believes in me," she said. "I feel so alone. Nobody gives a damn."

"I do, I give a damn," I said. "If they didn't choose you, it means it's a stupid contest. They don't deserve you! Don't let them get you down! Keep on going. Make another demo."

After hanging up, I collected all the savings I had, put them in an envelope, and sent them to her so she could record a professional demo.

A few days later, I got a delivery notice slip from the post office. My mother questioned me at length, concerned that this meant I had been buying porn videos.

"No, Mom."

"Promise me."

"I promise. If I were, I'd have had them sent somewhere else."

"Where?"

"Mom, I was joking. I didn't order any porn videos."

"Then what is it?"

"I don't know."

Although I protested, she insisted on going with me to the post office to pick up the letter and she waited next to me at the counter.

"Where was the letter sent from?" she asked the postal employee.

"Baltimore," he replied, handing me an envelope.

"Are you expecting something from your cousins?" she asked me.

"No, Mom."

She ordered me to open it and I finally said, "Mom, I think it's personal."

Now that her terror of pornography had passed, her face lit up.

"Have you got a girlfriend in Baltimore?"

I looked at her without answering and she finally spared me by going to wait in the car. I found a corner off to myself in the post office and carefully opened the envelope.

Dear Markie-moo,

I'm so mad at myself: I never thanked you for writing to tell me you would have liked to live in Baltimore. I was very touched. Maybe someday you'll move here, who knows?

Thank you for your letter and the money. I can't accept the money but you convinced me to stick with it and use my savings to record a demo.

You're really a very special person. I'm lucky to know you. Thank you for encouraging me to become a singer; you're the only one who believes in me. I'll never forget this.

I hope I'll see you soon in Baltimore.
With love,

Alexandra

P.S. it would be better if you don't tell your cousins I wrote to you.

I read and re-read the letter ten times. I held it over my heart. I was dancing across the concrete floor at the post office. Alexandra had written to me. *To me.* I could feel my gut contract with emotion. I went to join my mother in the car and didn't say a word the whole way home. Then when we were pulling up the drive, I said to her, "I'm really glad I don't have cystic fibrosis, Mom."

"That's good, sweetheart. That's good."

15

On March 26, 2012, the day the magazine article came out, I stayed at home, doors locked.

My phone was ringing off the hook. I didn't answer. It was pointless: everyone wanted to know if it was true. Were Alexandra Neville and I an item?

I knew it wouldn't take long for the paparazzi to descend upon my door. I decided to go and stock up with enough shopping so I wouldn't need to go out for a fair amount of time. When I came back from the supermarket, with the trunk of my car filled with bags of food, Leo, who was gardening outside his house, asked me if I was preparing for a siege.

"Well, didn't you hear?"

"No."

I showed him a copy of the magazine.

"Who took these photos?" he asked.

"The guy in the van. He was a paparazzo."

"You wanted to be famous, Marcus. But now your life doesn't belong to you anymore. You need a hand with all this?"

"No thanks, Leo."

Suddenly we heard barking behind us.

It was Duke.

"What are you doing here?" I said.

The dog stared at me with his black eyes.

"Go away," I ordered.

I went to drop off the first load on my porch and the dog followed me.

"Go away!" I shouted.

He looked at me, not budging.

"Go. Away!"

He did not move.

Just then I heard the sound of an engine. Brakes squealing. It was Kevin. He was beside himself. He jumped out of the car and headed straight for me, raring for a fight.

"You son of a bitch!" he screamed in my face.

I backed up.

"Nothing happened, Kevin! Those pictures are a lie! It's you Alexandra cares about!"

He kept his distance.

"You really took me for a ride."

"I didn't take anyone for a ride."

"Why didn't you tell me you two had a relationship?"

"It wasn't up to me to tell you about it."

He held a threatening finger out toward me.

"Get out of our lives, Marcus."

He grabbed Duke by the collar to drag him to the car. The dog tried to get loose. "You come here!" he bellowed, shaking him.

Duke yelped. Kevin shouted at him to shut up and shoved him into the trunk of his S.U.V. Climbing back into his car he said, threateningly, "Don't you ever go near her again, Goldman. Not her, or this dog, or anybody. Sell this house and move far away. You no longer exist as far as she's concerned. You hear me? You don't exist!"

He drove off, tires squealing.

Duke looked longingly at me through the rear window and barked a message I could not interpret.

* * *

Baltimore
Fall, 1995

When we went back to school that fall it meant starting the football season again. In no time the Buckerey High Wildcats were the talk of the town. They made a triumphant start to the championship season. The whole school was passionately following the team and it soon got a reputation for being invincible. What could have happened in the space of a few months for the Wildcats to have changed so much?

The Buckerey stadium was full at every game. And when it was an away game, cohorts of devoted, noisy fans went with them. That was all it took for the local press to rename the team "The Invincible Buckerey Wildcats".

The team's success filled Hillel with immense pride. As the coach's assistant, he had found his place among the Wildcats.

Scott's health, on the other hand, had deteriorated. He'd had several close calls at the end of the summer. He looked terrible and often had to have an oxygen bottle with him. All he could do now was follow the games from the bleachers. Whenever he stood up to celebrate a touchdown, he was overcome with sadness at not being down on the field. His morale was in free-fall and his parents were distraught.

One cold September Sunday morning, the day after a game the Wildcats had won hands down, he snuck out of the house and went to the Buckerey stadium. It was deserted. The air was very damp; the lawn was covered with an opaque mist. He stood at one end of the playing field and began to run across it, imagining that he was carrying the ball. He closed his eyes and saw himself as a powerful wing: he too was an Invincible. Nothing could stop him. He thought he could hear the crowd cheering him on, chanting his name. He was playing for the Wildcats and was about to score the final point. Thanks to him they would win the championship. On and on he ran, he felt the ball in his arms even though he didn't have it. He ran until he was out of breath, until he collapsed on the wet grass, motionless.

Thanks to the quick response of a man walking his dog, Scott was saved. He was taken by ambulance to Johns Hopkins Hospital, where he underwent a series of tests. His condition had taken a turn for the worse.

Aunt Anita went to tell Hillel and Woody what had happened.

"What was he doing on the playing field?" Hillel said.

"We have no idea. He went out without telling anyone."

"How long will he be in the hospital?"

"At least two weeks."

They went to see Scott every day.

"I want to do what you're doing," he told Woody. "I want to be on the playing field. I don't want to be sick anymore."

At last Scott was able to go home. He had to have complete rest. Every day, after practice, Woody and Hillel went to see him. Sometimes the entire team joined them. The Wildcats crowded into Scott's bedroom, telling him about the day's exploits. Everyone said they were going to win the trophy. To this day, not a single team from the high school league has bettered the records the Wildcats set during the 1995–1996 season.

One Saturday afternoon in mid-October, the Wildcats played a major game at the Buckerey stadium. Before they went off to join the team, Woody and Hillel stopped off at the Neville's. Scott was in bed, and very dejected.

"All I want is to be with you guys," he said. "I want to go gardening with you, and play football with you. Like we did before."

"Can't you come and watch the game?"

"My mom won't let me. She wants me to rest, but all I ever do is rest."

Once Hillel and Woody had left, Scott was overwhelmed with despair. He went down to the kitchen: the house was deserted. His sister was away, his father was at a meeting and his mother had gone shopping. Then it occurred to him: he could run away and be with the Wildcats. There was no-one there to stop him.

Scott climbed on his old bicycle. It was too small for him, but it still worked, that was the main thing. He headed for the high school, stopping at regular intervals to catch his breath.

*

Gillian Neville came home. She called out to Scott, but he didn't answer. She went upstairs, and when she opened the door to his bedroom, she saw he was asleep in his bed. She didn't disturb him; let him get his rest.

Scott arrived at the stadium at the end of the first quarter. The Wildcats were already well ahead. He left his bike against the fence and slipped into the locker room.

He could hear Bendham's voice giving instructions and he hid in the shower. He didn't want to be a spectator. He wanted to play. He waited until the next quarter. He had to speak to Hillel.

A strange premonition compelled Gillian Neville to go and wake her son. She pushed open the door to his room. He was still asleep. She went closer to the bed and when she touched the sheets she realized there was no-one beneath them: instead of her son, she found nothing but pillows, the perfect illusion of a boy sleeping.

During the third quarter, Scott managed to attract Hillel's attention; he hurried into the shower.

"What are you doing here?"

"I want to play!"

"Are you crazy? No way."

"Please. I just want to play in a game, just once."

Gillian Neville drove all over Oak Park. She tried to reach Patrick, who didn't pick up the phone. She went to the Goldmans', but no-one came to the door: they were all at the game.

At the end of the third quarter, Hillel spoke to Woody and explained the situation. He told him his idea. Woody took advantage of some down time to talk it over with the other players. Then he gestured to Ryan, a wing with a light build, to come over, and he explained in detail what he had to do.

*

Gillian went back home. Still no-one. She felt the panic rising and she burst into tears.

There were only five minutes left in the game.

Ryan asked to leave the playing field.

"I have to go to the toilet, Coach."

"Can't it wait?"

"Sorry, I really need to go."

"Hurry up!"

Ryan went into the locker room and handed his jersey and helmet to Scott, who was waiting.

There were only two minutes of play left. The coach railed against Ryan when he finally came out of the locker room, and ordered him to get back in position. Bendham was so focused that he did not notice anything unusual. Play began. Ryan walked kind of funny, and his position was all wrong. The coach shouted orders at him, but he didn't react. Suddenly, it was the entire team that went crazy, moving into a triangular formation. "What the hell are you doing, for Christ's sake!" he shouted.

Then Hillel cried, "Now!" He saw Woody run to the wing's position and stand next to Ryan. The Wildcats had the ball again and Woody grabbed it. All the players got in a circle around Ryan, Ryan received the ball and started running across the field, escorted by all the other players, who were protecting him.

For a moment there was not a sound in the stadium. The players on the opposing team were completely thrown off their bearings, and watched dumbfounded as the compact formation crossed the field. Scott went over the goal line and set the ball on the ground. Then he raised his arms up to the sky, pulled off his helmet, and the entire stadium began screaming with joy.

"*Tooooooouchdooooown for the Buckerey Wildcats! They've won the game!*" shouted the sportscaster over the loudspeakers.

"This is the greatest day of my life!" Scott said exultantly, dancing in celebration. On the field, all the players clustered around him and lifted him up triumphantly. Bendham stood there for a moment, stunned, not knowing how to react, and then he burst out laughing and joined in the cheers as everyone chanted Scott's name and called for a tour of the stadium. Scott eagerly responded, blowing kisses to the crowd and waving left and right. He began to cross the playing field, feeling his heart pounding fit to burst. It was harder and harder to breathe, he tried to remain calm but he felt as if he were suffocating. Then suddenly he collapsed.

16

On March 28, 2012, Alexandra went back to Los Angeles.

The day she left, she dropped an envelope off at my house. Leo happened to see her, and came to knock at my door.

"You just missed your girlfriend."

"She's not my girlfriend."

"A big black S.U.V. just stopped outside your house and she left this envelope."

He handed it to me. On it was written:

To Markie-moo

"I don't know who this Markie-moo is," I said.

"I think it's you," Leo said.

"No. It's some mistake."

"Well, in that case, I'll open it."

"Don't you dare."

"I thought the letter wasn't for you."

"Give it to me!"

I took the envelope from him and opened it. On the paper inside was a telephone number.

555-543-3984
A.

"Why would she give me her telephone number? And above all, why would she leave it outside my door when she knows that any old journalist could come by here and see her, or even take the envelope?"

"Poor old Markie-moo," Leo said, "you're such a spoilsport."

"Don't call me Markie-moo. And I'm not a spoilsport."

"Of course you are. Here's this woman, cute as can be, who is completely lost because she's dying of love for you, but she doesn't know how to tell you."

"She doesn't love me. That was before."

"Oh, for crying out loud, are you doing this on purpose? You show up in her life, which had been all calm and comfortable, you make a monumental stir, she decides to run away, but in spite of everything, when it's time to leave, she tells you how to get in touch with her. Do you need a diagram, or what? I'm worried about you, Marcus. It looks as if you really are absolutely useless when it comes to the emotional stuff."

I looked at the sheet of paper, then I asked Leo, "So what am I supposed to do, Doctor Lonely Hearts?"

"Call her, you numbskull!"

It took me a long time to get up the nerve to call her. When I finally did, the phone was switched off. She was probably on the plane to California. I tried again a few hours later: it was late in Florida, which meant early evening in Los Angeles. She did not answer. She was the one who called me back. I picked up but she did not speak. We stayed on the line for a long time, in silence. Finally she said, "Do you remember, after my brother died . . . it was you I called. I needed your presence, so we'd stay on the phone for hours, hardly speaking. Just so you'd keep me company." I didn't say anything. We were silent. Eventually she hung up.

* * *

Baltimore, Maryland
October 1995

The paramedics couldn't get Scott's heart beating again, and they declared him dead there on the grass, on the Buckerey playing field. Classes at Buckerey High were canceled the next day, and a crisis center was set up. As the students gradually drifted in, they were sent to the auditorium, while the principal's message was played repeatedly over the loudspeakers: "Due to yesterday evening's tragic event, all today's classes have been canceled. Students are requested to head to the auditorium." At the foot of Scott's locker were piles of flowers, candles, and stuffed animals.

Scott was buried in a cemetery in the outskirts of New York, where the Nevilles were from originally. We all went, Woody, Hillel, and I, together with Uncle Saul and Aunt Anita.

Before the ceremony I looked for Alexandra. I couldn't see her anywhere. Eventually I found her alone in one of the rooms in the funeral parlor. She was crying. She was dressed in black. She had even put black polish on her nails. I sat down next to her. I took her hand. I thought she was so beautiful that I had a kind of erotic urge to kiss her palm. So I did. And as she didn't pull her hand away, I did it again. I kissed the back of her hand, and every one of her fingers. She nestled close against me and murmured into my ear, "Don't let go of my hand, Markie, please."

The ceremony was tough. I had never had to deal with such a situation. Uncle Saul and Aunt Anita had prepared us, but it was something else to go through it. Alexandra was inconsolable: I could see the black tears from her mascara smudged across our hands. I didn't know whether I should talk to her and reassure her. I would have liked to wipe her eyes, but I was afraid of being clumsy. So I just went on holding her hand as tight as I could.

But what was difficult was not so much the sadness of the occasion as the tension we could sense between Patrick and Gillian. I thought the speech Patrick made for his son was very beautiful. He entitled it "The Resignation of a Sickly Child's Father". He paid homage to Woody and Hillel and thanked them for the happiness they had brought Scott. He said things more or less along these lines:

"Are we truly happy, we affluent people of Oak Park or New York? Who here can truly say they are completely happy?

"My son Scott was happy. And thanks to two young fellows, who got him out of the house.

"I saw what my son was like before Woody and Hillel came along, and I saw him afterwards.

"Thank you, both of you. You put a smile on his face, a smile I had never seen. You gave him a strength I had never seen.

"Who, even at the end of a long life, can truly claim to have made one of their fellow human beings happy? Hillel and Woody, you can. You can."

Patrick's speech triggered a very awkward and embarrassing altercation with his wife during the meal that followed the funeral. We were all in the living room in Gillian's sister's house, eating petits fours, when we heard the sound of raised voices coming from the kitchen. "You *thanked* them?" Gillian was shouting. "They killed our son, and you say thank you?"

The scene was unbearable. I suddenly recalled all the times I had hated Scott, when I been jealous of his illness and wished that I too could have cystic fibrosis. I felt like crying, but didn't want to in front of Alexandra. I went out into the garden. I called myself a bastard. Bastard! Bastard! Then I felt a hand on my shoulder. I turned around: it was Uncle Saul. He hugged me and I burst into tears.

I'll never forget the way he hugged me that day.

The weeks that followed were filled with sadness.

Hillel and Woody felt guilty. And it didn't make things any easier, the fact that Mr Burdon was calling for sanctions. He summoned Hillel and Bendham to his office. Woody was pacing back and forth outside the door, worried. At last the door opened and Hillel came out, in tears.

"They've thrown me off the team!" he cried.

"What? What do you mean?"

Hillel didn't answer but ran off down the hall. Then Woody saw Bendham come out of the office in turn, looking shattered.

"Coach, tell me it isn't true!" Woody cried. "Coach, what is going on?"

"What happened was very serious. Hillel has to leave the team. I'm really sorry . . . there's nothing I can do."

Woody, furious, went into Burdon's office without knocking.

"Mr Burdon, you can't take Hillel off the football team!"

"What business is it of yours, Woodrow? And who gave you permission to burst into my office like this?"

"Is it revenge? Is that it?"

"Woodrow, I won't say it again: get out of my office."

"Don't you even want to tell me why you fired Hillel?"

"I didn't fire him. Technically he was never part of the team. No student can be in charge of other students. Mr Bendham should never have offered him a position as assistant. And besides, Woody, do I have to remind you that he killed a student? If it weren't for his harebrained idea, Scott Neville would still be alive!"

"He didn't kill anybody. It was all Scott ever dreamt of, to play!"

"I don't like your tone one bit, Woodrow. What do you expect: your little friend has been complaining that I'm not doing my job properly. So I'm going to do my job. You'll see. Now get out of here."

"You have no right to do this to Hillel!"

"I have every right. I am the principal of this high school. You are only students. Students and nothing else. Do you understand that?"

"You'll pay for it!"

"Is that a threat?"

"No, it's a promise."

There was nothing to be done. It was the end of football for Hillel.

In the middle of the following night, Woody crept out of the Goldman house and rode his bike to Burdon's place. Under cover of darkness he stole across the garden, took a spray can from his bag, and in huge letters across the façade of the house he wrote: *BURDON PILE OF SHIT*. No sooner had he finished spraying the last word than he felt a halo of light on the back of his neck. He turned around but, blinded by the flashlight, could see nothing. "What are you doing there?" a man's voice asked firmly. And Woody saw that it was two policemen.

Uncle Saul and Aunt Anita were woken by a call from the police station, summoning them to come and get Woody.

"*Burdon pile of shit?*" said Aunt Anita despairingly. "Couldn't you have found another way? Oh, Woody, what came over you to do such a thing?"

He hung his head in shame and murmured, "I wanted revenge for what he did to Hillel."

"But you can't take revenge!" Uncle Saul said, in an even tone. "That's not the way things work, and you know that very well."

"What's going to happen to me now?" Woody said.

"That depends whether or not Burdon presses charges."

"Will I be expelled?"

"We don't know. You did a very foolish thing, a very serious foolish thing, Woody, and your fate is no longer in your own hands."

Woody was expelled from Buckerey High School.

Bendham did all he could to stick up for him against Burdon; there was a violent altercation when Burdon refused to go back on his decision to expel the boy.

"Why are you so rigid, Steve?" Bendham exploded.

"Because there are rules, Coach, and they have to be respected. Did you see what that little hooligan did to my house?"

"But that's just the prank of a kid! You should have made him sweep out the school toilets for six months, but you don't do this, you don't go crushing those two kids the way you have."

"Augustus, that's just the way it is."

"Dammit, Steve, you're running a school, it's a school, for fuck's sake! You're here to build these kids' lives, not destroy them!"

"Exactly. I'm running a school. And you don't seem to realize what that means in the way of responsibilities. We are here so that these kids will adapt to our society and not the other way around. They have to learn that there are rules and if they don't respect them there will be consequences. Call me cruel if you like, I know that I'm doing it for their sake and that one day they will thank me for it. Kids like that end up in prison if no-one takes them in hand."

"Kids like these two, Steve, end up N.F.L. stars and Nobel prize laureates! You'll see, ten years from now there will be cameras in this schoolyard filming the glory of the Goldmans."

"Phooey! The glory of the Goldmans! Don't tell me you believe all that crap."

"And when the reporters hand you the microphone for you to say a few words, you'll stammer pathetically how they were your favorite students, the best ones in your school, and you never doubted their talent for even a moment!"

"That's it, Coach, you've gone too far. I've heard enough."

"You know what, Steve, I'm the one who's heard enough: go fuck yourself."

"Excuse me? Are you completely out of your mind? I'll file a report, Augustus. You'll have to answer for this, too."

"File all the goddamn reports you like. I'm out of here! I will not be a part of your shit system, because all it knows how to do is deprive two kids of their dreams. I'm out of here, you won't see me again."

He went out, slamming the door as hard as he could. He resigned from his position with immediate effect, and put in a request for early retirement.

The following weekend, Woody went to Bendham's place and found him loading his things into his R.V.

"Don't go, Coach . . . the team needs you."

"There is no more team, Woody," Bendham said, without stopping what he was doing. "I should have retired a long time ago."

"Coach, I came to ask for your forgiveness. It's all my fault."

Bendham put a box down on the grass.

"No, Woody, not at all. It's the fault of the bullshit system. Of those rotten teachers. I'm the one who should ask you for forgiveness, Woody. I didn't know how to stick up for you and Hillel the way I should have."

"So, are you running away?"

"No, I'm retiring. I'm going to drive across the country, and I'll be in Alaska between now and summer."

"You're going off to Alaska in your fucking R.V. so you won't have to deal with reality, Coach."

"Not at all. I've always wanted to take this trip."

"But you have your entire life to go to fucking Alaska!"

"Life is not that long, son."

"It's long enough for you to stay here a little longer."

Bendham put his hands on Woody's shoulders.

"Go on playing football, kid. Not for me, not for Burdon, not for anyone but yourself."

"I don't give a fuck, Coach! I don't give a fuck about any of that crap!"

"No, you do give a fuck! Football is your whole life!"

* * *

Patrick and Gillian's marriage did not survive Scott's death.

Gillian could not forgive her husband for encouraging Scott to play football. She needed to think, she needed space. Above all, she didn't want to go on living in the house in Oak Park. One month after Scott's funeral, she decided to move back to New York, and she rented an apartment in Manhattan. Alexandra went with her. They left in November 1995.

My parents gave me permission to go and spend the weekend of their departure in Oak Park, to say goodbye to Alexandra. Those were the saddest days I ever spent in Baltimore.

"Is that the girl who wrote to you?" my mother said, when she dropped me off at Newark Station.

"Yes."

"You'll see her again some day," she told me.

"I doubt it."

"I'm sure you will. Don't be so sad, Markie."

I tried to convince myself that my mother was right and that if Alexandra really mattered to me, it would be our fate to cross paths again, but all the way to Baltimore my heart was heavy. And in my aunt's car, I tried to keep my head down and didn't even feel like waving to the security guards.

Alexandra left the next morning – it was a Saturday – in her mother's car, in what was like a funeral procession, made up of two moving vans. We spent our last hours together in her bedroom, which was empty. There was nothing left to show she had ever been there except for the thumbtacks that had held up the posters of her favorite singers. Even her guitar was gone.

"I can't believe I'm leaving," Alexandra murmured.

"Neither can we," Hillel said, with a catch in his throat.

She opened her arms wide and Woody, Hillel and I snuggled into her embrace. There was that delicious perfume on her skin, and her hair smelled of apricot. All three of us closed our eyes and stayed like that for a moment. Until Patrick's voice called up from downstairs.

"Alexandra, are you up there? It's time to go, the movers are waiting."

She went down the stairs and we followed, hanging our heads.

Outside the house she asked to take a photograph of all four of us. Her father immortalized us there in front of what used to be their house. "I'll send it to you," she promised. "We'll write."

She embraced us one last time, one after the other.

"Goodbye, my little Goldmans. I'll never forget you."

"You'll always be a member of the Gang," Woody said.

I saw a tear pearling on Hillel's cheek and I wiped it off with the end of my thumb.

We watched her climb into her mother's car, and we formed a guard of honor. Then the car started up and went slowly down the drive. She waved to us for a long time. She was crying too.

With one last burst of passion, we jumped on our bikes and escorted the car through the neighborhood. We saw her reach for a piece of paper in the car and on it she wrote a few words. Then she stuck it against the rear window and we could read:

I LOVE YOU GOLDMAN BOYS

17

I have never told anyone what happened in November 1995, after Alexandra and her mother moved away to New York.

In the period following Scott's funeral we called each other all the time. She was asking for me and I felt really proud. She said she couldn't go to sleep without someone nearby, so we would call each other and leave the receiver next to our heads on the pillow while we slept. Sometimes we were still on the line in the morning.

When my mother got the telephone bill she had a fit.

"What do you talk about for hours and hours?"

"It's because of Scott," I explained.

"Oh," she said, disconcerted.

I was about to find out that Scott could go on being a fantastic friend even from beyond the grave. Just saying his name had a magical effect.

"What's with this bad grade?" "It's because of Scott."

"Why did you cut class?" "Because of Scott."

"I want pizza for supper tonight . . ." "Oh, no, not again." "Please, it reminds me of Scott."

Scott opened all the doors for me to go and see Alexandra in New York as often as I liked. Because what had started off as just a little crush over the phone evolved, after she moved, into a true relationship. Manhattan was only half an hour by train from Montclair, and I began meeting her several times a week in Manhattan, in a café near her school. I took the train, my heart racing at the prospect of having her all to myself. In the beginning, we did no more than continue our endless phone conversations, but now we were face-to-face, with my gaze lost in hers. It was one day when I was sitting next to her that I took her hand and took the plunge, doing what I had dreamt of for so long: I kissed her, and she returned my kiss, a long deep kiss. That was the beginning of a year when the Goldman Gang interested me less, and she became my sole obsession. Several times a week I went to meet her at the café in New York. What a joy to see her, hear her, touch her, talk to her, caress her, kiss her. We wandered down the streets, exchanging kisses in the shelter of a square. Whenever I saw her coming, my heart immediately began to pound in my chest. I felt alive, more alive than I ever had. Without daring to admit it, I knew this was a feeling that went beyond what I felt for the Baltimores.

She said that I was helping her to overcome her grief. She felt different when I was with her. We sought each other out, and before long our relationship blossomed.

I felt as if I were sprouting wings, so much so that one day, feeling somewhat overconfident, I decided to surprise her when she came out of school. I saw her leave the building, surrounded by a group of girl-friends, and I rushed up to hug her. When she saw me, she recoiled, kept me at a distance and acted very coolly before walking away. I went back to Montclair, feeling sheepish and disconcerted. That evening she called me.

"Hey, Marcus."

"Do we know each other?" I said, annoyed.

"Markie, please don't be angry with me."

"I suppose you have a good explanation for the way you behaved this afternoon."

"Marcus, you're two years younger than me."

"So?"

"So, it's embarrassing."

"What's embarrassing about it?"

"I really like you, but you're two years younger, that's all!"

"So what's the problem?"

"Oh my poor little baby Marcus, you're so naïve, it makes you even cuter. It's, like, kind of shameful."

"Just don't tell anyone."

"People are bound to find out."

"Not if you don't tell them."

"Oh, just drop it, baby Marcus! If you want to see me, nobody must know."

I relented. We went on meeting at the café. Sometimes she came to Montclair, where she didn't know anyone, so she didn't risk anything. Blessed be Montclair, a little suburban town inhabited by strangers.

Before long my passion for Alexandra began to have a dramatic effect on my schoolwork. In class, all I could think of was her, and I hardly heard a thing. She was dancing in my head, dancing on my notebooks, dancing at the blackboard, dancing with the science teacher and murmuring, "Marcus . . . Marcus . . ." and I got to my feet to dance with her. "Marcus!" shouted the science teacher. "Have you lost your mind? Go back to your desk if you don't want me to put you in detention." My homeroom teacher called my parents because she was worried about my plummeting results at school. It was my second year of high school and my mother, thinking that maybe I had undetected mental shortcomings, wept during the entire interview, finding consolation between sobs as she recalled – something almost all mothers do when they learn their child is having difficulty at school – that even Einstein had a really hard time with math. Einstein or no Einstein, for me the consequence was that not only was I grounded, but I also had to take intensive remedial lessons at home. I refused, I pleaded, rolled on the ground, promised to get good grades again, but there was nothing for it: every day after school, someone would be coming to coach me with my homework. So I swore I would be insolent, sullen, distracted, and fart the entire time.

On the verge of despair, I eventually told Alexandra, explaining that we were doomed to see each other less often. That very evening she called my mother. She explained that my math teacher had contacted her about coaching me in math. My mother told her she had already found someone, but when Alexandra told her that the lessons would be paid for by the Montclair high school, my mother relented and hired her. This was the sort of magic trick Alexandra could pull off.

I will never forget the day she rang the doorbell at our house. Alexandra, the goddess of the Goldman Gang, was showing up at the Montclairs.

To the girl I loved the first thing my mother said was, "You'll see, I tidied up his room. It was such a mess, you can't concentrate when it's messy. I also took the opportunity to put all his old toys in the cupboard."

Alexandra burst out laughing, and I went crimson with shame.

"Mom!" I cried.

"Oh, Markie," my mother said, "it's no secret to anyone that you leave your dirty underwear all over the place."

"Thank you for being so thorough, Mrs Goldman," said Alexandra. "We'll go to Marcus's room now. He has homework to do. I'll make him work hard."

I led her up to my room.

"That's so cute your mom calls you Markie," she said.

"Don't you dare call me that."

"And I can't wait for you to show me your toys."

My homework with Alexandra was to put my tongue in her mouth and fondle her breasts. I was both terrified and excited at the thought that at any moment my mother might burst into the room with cookies. But she never did. At the time I thought it was chance giving me a helping hand, but today I realize that I probably underestimated my mother: she was no fool, and she had no intention of disrupting her son's youthful discovery of the joys of love.

Alexandra charmed my mother. My results at school skyrocketed and my freedom was restored to me.

Soon I was spending every weekend in New York. When her mother wasn't there, Alexandra invited me to her place. I stood outside the house with my heart pounding, she opened the door, took me by the hand, and led me to her room.

For a long time I associated the rapper Tupac with Alexandra. On the wall above her bed she had a huge poster of him. We would fling ourselves onto the mattress, she got undressed, and I saw Tupac watching us and suddenly, he gave me the thumbs up, like a blessing. Nowadays all it takes is one of his songs on the radio to trigger an extraordinary Pavlovian reflex in me where I picture myself naked in the bed with Alexandra. She was the one who taught me how to make love, and I have to say I managed pretty well. I grew more and more confident. I would go into her room, greet Mr Tupac, we'd tear off our clothes and start making love. After sex, we would lie there and talk for a long time. She put on an oversized T-shirt and rolled a joint that she went to smoke by the window. Yes, because you have to know that she was also the first person who taught me how to smoke a joint. When I got back to Montclair for dinner with my parents, exhausted and still high, my mother would ask with a knowing smile, "How is little Alexandra doing?"

I'll never know whether I was the first member of the Goldman Gang to experience the joys of love. I couldn't talk to Woody and Hillel about Alexandra. I felt as if I was betraying them. And in any case, I had to respect Alexandra's wish not to tell anyone about our relationship.

Sometimes I saw her talking with older boys when she got out of class. I was sick with jealousy. When I met her at the café I asked her, "Who are those jerks hanging around you?"

She laughed.

"Nobody. Just friends. No-one important. No-one as important as you are."

"Couldn't we go out together with your friends one time?" I pleaded.

"No. You mustn't talk about us."

"But why not? We've been together almost four months now. Are you ashamed of me or what?"

"Stop freaking out about this, Markie-moo. We're just better off if no-one knows about us."

"How do you know I haven't told anyone?"

"I just do. Because you're different. You're a decent guy, Markie-moo. You're different from other boys and that's why you're precious."

"Stop calling me Markie-moo!"

She smiled.

"Alright, Markie-moo."

*   *   *

In the late spring of 1996 Patrick Neville, who for several months had been looking for a way to move to New York to be closer to his daughter and to try to save his marriage, landed an important position in an investment fund based in Manhattan, and he in turn left Oak Park. He moved into a nice apartment on 16th Avenue, not far from Gillian's place. Alexandra suddenly had two homes and two bedrooms, which greatly enhanced the possibilities for my stays in New York. And when Patrick and Gillian went out to dinner in their efforts to re-connect, we no longer knew which way to turn, or which apartment to meet at.

I was constantly at her place, but I also wanted her to come and stay over in Montclair for a change. For the weekend of my birthday, I pulled off the extraordinary feat of getting my parents to go away. I decided to invite Alexandra to Montclair for the night. In an effort to be romantic, I decided to go to Alexandra's high school and when I located what I thought was her locker, I slipped a card through the door inviting her to join me two days later. On the appointed evening, I prepared a romantic dinner with candles, flowers, and subdued lighting. I had invited her for seven o'clock; at eight o'clock, as I had no news, I called her mother's place, and her mother told me she wasn't there. Same story from her father. At ten o'clock, I blew out the candles. At eleven, I threw the dinner into the garbage. At eleven thirty, I opened a bottle of wine I had stolen from my father and drank it all by myself. Drunk and alone, I sang a pathetic happy birthday to myself and blew out my own candles. I went to bed with my head spinning and the feeling that I hated her. For two days I ignored her. I did not go to New York and I didn't answer her calls. Finally she was the one who came to find me in Montclair and caught me on my way out of school.

"Marcus, are you going to tell me what's going on?"

"What's going on? You've gotta be joking! How could you play such a mean trick on me?"

"What are you talking about?"

"My birthday!"

"What do you mean, your birthday?"

"You stood me up on the evening of my birthday. I invited you to my place and you didn't come."

"How do you expect me to know it's your birthday if you don't tell me anything?"

"I left you a card in your locker."

"I never got it."

"Oh," I said, thrown by her answer.

I'd left it in the wrong locker . . .

"Besides, Markie, isn't it a bit lame to play treasure hunt instead of picking up the phone to get the information across? When you're in a couple, you have to communicate."

"Ha! Because we're a couple?"

"What do you think we are, Markie-moo!"

She looked me right in the eye and I felt overwhelmed by a huge wave of happiness. We were a couple. She grabbed hold of me, and in front of everyone she put her tongue in my mouth, then she pushed me back and said, "Now, get lost."

I was part of a couple. I couldn't get over it. Another thing I couldn't get over was that the following weekend Alexandra came by car to Montclair to get me and took me for a drive. At first I didn't know where we were going until we were in the Lincoln tunnel.

"Are we going to Manhattan?"

"Yes, angel."

Then I realized we would be spending the night there when she stopped outside the Waldorf Astoria.

"The Waldorf?"

"Yes."

"We're going to stay at the hotel?"

"Yes."

"But I don't have any overnight things," I protested.

"I'm sure we can find you a toothbrush and a shirt. They do have that sort of thing in New York, you know."

"I didn't even tell my parents."

"In this hotel they have special machines they call telephones and you can use them to get in touch with the outside world. Markie-moo, you're going to call your mother and tell her you're sleeping over at a friend's. It's time to start taking risks in life. You don't want to be a Montclair for the rest of your life, do you?"

"What did you just say?"

"I said, you don't want to be in Montclair for the rest of your life, do you?"

I had never set foot in a hotel like that. With phenomenal nerve, Alexandra waved a fake I.D. at the reception which said she was twenty-two years old, paid with a credit card she unearthed from God knows where, then told the receptionist, "The young man here forgot his belongings. If you can put all the necessary toiletries in the room, he will be eternally grateful." My eyes were as big as saucers. This was the first time I'd ever been out with someone as part of a couple, the first time I would be making love in a hotel, and the first time I'd ever lied shamelessly to my mother to go and spend the night in a girl's arms – and what a girl!

That evening she took me to a café in the West Village that had a small stage for intimate gigs. She went onto the stage where a guitar was waiting and played her compositions for over an hour. Everyone in the café was watching her, but she was looking at me. It was one of the first warm spring evenings. When her gig was over, we wandered around the neighborhood for a long time. She said this was where she imagined she would live someday, in an apartment with a huge patio, where she could spend her evenings looking out at the city. She talked, and I drank in her words.

Back at the Waldorf Astoria, while my mother thought I was at my friend Ed's, we made love for a long time. There was a huge mirror on the wall, and I could see myself between her thighs. Observing our nakedness and our movements in the mirror, I thought we made a very handsome couple: and we did. When I was above her, for all that I was only sixteen years old, I felt as strong as a man. Sure of myself, brave, I moved at a cadence I knew she liked, and which made her arch her back more and more, as she asked for more and clung to my back until she felt the discharge of pleasure that made her moan one last time, leaving her mark on my skin with the tips of her delicately polished nails. A complicit silence invaded the room. With her hand she lifted up her hair then collapsed breathless on the pile of pillows, offering me the vision of her breasts pearling with sweat.

It was Alexandra who compelled me to dare to live my life. When she was getting ready to do something slightly taboo and she sensed my reticence, she would grab me by the hand, look at me with her fiery gaze and say, "Are you afraid, Markie? What are you afraid of?" Then she squeezed my hand again and led me into her world. I called it Alexandra's world. One day I ended up saying to her, "Maybe I'm a little bit in love with you."

She took my face between her hands and looked deep in my eyes.

"Markie-moo, there are certain things you shouldn't say to a girl."

"I was joking," I said, extricating myself from her arms.

"Sure."

Before confiding in you here, I had never told anyone about the absolute love Alexandra Neville and I shared in 1995 and 1996. Nor did I ever tell anyone how she broke my heart after ten months of being together. She had made me so happy, it was inevitable that one day she would end up hurting me.

At the end of the summer in 1996, she went off to college in Connecticut. She came to see me in Montclair to tell me she was leaving – bravely, the day before she left, while we were walking around my neighborhood.

"Connecticut isn't all that far," I said. "And besides, I'm getting my driver's license."

Her gaze was full of sadness.

"Markie-moo . . ."

Just the way she had said my name, I understood.

"So, you're done with me."

"Markie, it's not that . . . it's college. It's a new phase for me, I want to be free. You . . . you're still in high school."

I pressed my lips together not to burst into tears.

"Well, bye then," I said, simply.

She took my hand, I pulled away. She could see my eyes were shining.

"Markie-moo, you're not going to cry now, are you?"

She hugged me.

"Why would I cry?" I said.

For a long time my mother asked for news of "little Alexandra". And when one of her friends told her that her son needed private lessons she lamented, "Such a shame. Little Alexandra was really good. Your son Gary would have really liked her."

For years that was my mother's refrain: "What ever became of little Alexandra?" And I would reply, "I don't know." "You never heard from her again?" "Never." "What a pity," my mother would say, visibly disappointed.

For a long time she believed that I had never seen her again.

18

There was something almost apocalyptic about that summer I broke up with Alexandra, the summer of 1996.

She left me just before I left for the Hamptons, and for the first time in my life I went out there with a heavy heart. When I arrived I discovered that everyone in the Goldman Gang was in a glum mood. The entire year had been difficult: after Scott's death, my cousins' peaceful routine had been disrupted.

In the space of a few months Hillel and Woody had been separated not once but twice. First of all in October, when Woody was expelled from Buckerey. Then in January, when Hillel was sent to the special school, after a disastrous end to his semester. He was only home at Oak Park on weekends.

I felt as if everything were falling apart. And there were more blows to come: the day I arrived, my cousins and I went to Paradise on Earth to say hello to our kindly neighbors, the Clarks. And the first thing we saw was a FOR SALE sign stuck in the lawn outside the house.

Jane opened the door; she looked downcast. In the living room, Seth was in a wheelchair. He'd had a stroke and was in very poor health. He couldn't do anything anymore. And the house, with its steps and stairways, was no longer suitable. Jane wanted to sell it as quickly as possible. She knew she would have neither the time nor the energy to keep it up, and she wanted to part with it while it was in good condition. She was prepared to sell it for a very good price: for a buyer, it was the chance of a lifetime. Some even said it was the deal of the century.

Already all the real estate agents in the region were talking about it when Uncle Saul and Aunt Anita started thinking about buying it. Jane Clark, out of friendship for them, even gave them a first option on the sale. We talked about it all the time. At every meal we asked Uncle Saul where he stood with his deliberations.

"Are you going to buy Paradise on Earth?"

"We don't know yet," said Uncle Saul, a faint smile on his lips.

He hardly left his summer study out in the gazebo. I saw him deal first with his legal files, then the financial plans for the house, and he juggled easily between calls to the bank and calls from his office in Baltimore. He seemed to me more and more impressive as the years went by.

*　*　*

The days in the Hamptons spent fishing and swimming from the Clarks' jetty did us good. Being the Goldman Gang, all together again, helped banish our melancholy. We devoted ourselves to giving a hand to Jane Clark, because we felt a great deal of affection for her: we helped her with the shopping, or to carry Seth out onto the patio in his chair so he could enjoy sitting there in the shade of a parasol.

Every morning Woody went out running. I went with him nearly every day. I loved being alone with him at that time, how we could talk as we ran.

I could tell he was finding it hard not to be with Hillel anymore. He now had the status of only son at the Baltimores'. He got up on his own, took the bus on his own, and ate lunch on his own. He was nostalgic, and sometimes he went into Hillel's room to mope, sprawling on the bed and throwing a baseball into the air. Uncle Saul had taught him how to drive. He got his license quickly. On Tuesdays he was alone now with Aunt Anita for their traditional pizza evening. They would order the food and settle in front of the television, side-by-side on the sofa.

To motivate him for football practice, Uncle Saul had bought him a season ticket for the Washington Redskins games. The three of them went together like a family, wearing identical Redskins caps. Aunt Anita sat between her two men and they devoured popcorn and hotdogs. But in spite of my aunt and uncle's efforts, Woody had become somewhat antisocial again, and I think he tried not to spend too much time at the house. At high school he practiced at the stadium after class with the other team members so he would be in peak condition when football season started up in the fall. Aunt Anita also came to watch him. She was a little bit worried about him. One evening, she sat in the bleachers and cheered him on. Once practice was over, she waited for him outside the locker room. At last he would appear, freshly showered, muscles gleaming, magnificent.

"Saul made a reservation at the steak house you like. You want to join us there?" she said, threading her arm through his.

"No, thanks. That's really nice of you, but we're going out to eat with the team."

"O.K., have fun then, and be careful on your way home. Do you have your keys?"

"Yes, thanks."

"And some money?"

He smiled.

"Yes, thanks."

He watched her walk away to her car. His teammates came out of the locker room one by one. There was always one of them who would gratify him with a friendly slap on the back.

"Hey dude, your mom is really gorgeous."

"Shut up, Danny, or I'll smash your face in."

"Take it easy, just joking. Are you coming to eat with the team?"

"No thanks, I'm already busy. See you tomorrow, same time?"

"Yeah, O.K., see you tomorrow."

He left the stadium on his own and headed out to the parking lot. He made sure that Aunt Anita had left, then he got in the car that Uncle Saul had lent him and drove off.

It took forty-five minutes to drive to Blueberry Hill. He switched on the car radio and put the volume up as loud as his ears could stand. As always, he left the freeway one exit too soon to stop at a fast food drive-in. He ordered two cheeseburgers, French fries, onion rings, two cokes, and some vanilla donuts. Then once he'd been served, he continued along the freeway toward Blueberry school.

To be sure he wouldn't be noticed, he switched off the headlights before reaching the deserted school parking lot. He parked as far as possible from the first building. As always, Hillel was already waiting for him. He rushed over to the car and opened the passenger door.

"Hey, old man," he said, settling in his seat, "I thought you'd never get here."

"Sorry, practice went on longer."

"You feel good?"

"Sure!"

Hillel burst out laughing.

"You're too much, Wood. Wait and see, you'll end up in the N.F.L."

He put his hand in the paper bag Woody held out to him and took out a cheeseburger. He felt around inside the bag and smiled.

"You even got fried onion rings? You're the best! What would I do without you!"

They wolfed down their meal.

Then without consulting each other, as if by tacit agreement, they got out of the car and sat on the hood. Woody reached in his pocket for a pack of cigarettes, took one out, then handed the pack to Hillel, who helped himself. Two incandescent spots in the night were the only signs of their presence.

"I cannot believe you went to the Redskins games. Dad would never let us get a season ticket to the Bullets!"

"Well, maybe it's because you weren't old enough then. You should ask him now."

"Nah, I don't care now."

"Here, I got you a cap from the team. Aren't you going to eat your onion rings?"

"I'm not hungry anymore."

"Aw, don't be mad, Hill. It's only a few stupid football games. Next time you're there, we'll go see a game together."

"Nah, like I said, I don't care."

Once they had finished their cigarettes, it was time to say goodbye. Hillel would get back in the building the way he had come out: through the kitchen window. Once he was inside, he would creep back to his room. Before saying goodbye, they gave each other a hug.

"Take care, old man."

"You too. I miss you. Life's not the same without you."

"I know. Same here. It's just a shit time, we'll be together again. Nothing can keep us apart, Wood, nothing."

"You're my brother forever, Hill."

"You too. Drive safely."

Hillel vanished into the night and Woody drove away. On the road back to Baltimore, in the intermittent sweeping light from the other cars on the road, he noticed that his biceps had gotten even bigger. They were bursting out of the sleeves of his sweater. He was working out as if there were no tomorrow. He took stock of the other things in his life: he wasn't really interested in his classes, or in girls, or in making friends. All his time and energy were devoted to football. He was on the playing field one hour before the beginning of practice to work by himself on his kicks and the length of his passes. He went running twice a day, five days a week. Seven miles in the morning and four in the evening. Sometimes he went running in the middle of the night, when Uncle Saul and Aunt Anita were asleep.

It was only toward the end of our stay, after they had deliberated for a month, that Uncle Saul and Aunt Anita gave up the idea of buying Paradise on Earth. For a house of that caliber with a private beach, given the way real estate prices were skyrocketing in the region, the "deal of the century" still cost several million dollars.

This was the first time I ever saw my uncle Saul come up against a barrier he could not surmount. In spite of his financial ease, he could not afford the six million dollars they wanted for the house. Even if they had sold their own vacation house, he would have ended up with a second mortgage, since he hadn't finished paying off the Buenavista. Added to that were the maintenance costs for the Paradise, which would be considerably higher than anything he'd spent up to now. It wasn't reasonable, and he decided it was wiser not to put in a bid.

I know all this because I overheard a conversation he had with Aunt Anita after a visit from the agent handling the sale of the house, at the end of which Aunt Anita said, holding him close, "You are a wise and cautious man, and that's why I love you. We are fine in this house. Above all, we are happy. We don't need anything more."

When we left the Hamptons, Paradise on Earth had not yet found a buyer. Little did we imagine the surprise in store the following summer.

* * *

During the interim, I was finding it very hard to get over the break-up with Alexandra. I could not accept the fact she did not want me, and that the year we had spent together did not matter as much to her as it had mattered to me. For several months I hung around New York and the places where we had loved. I wandered around her high school, near the café we used to go to; I went back to the music stores where we would spend hours browsing, and the bar where she used to play. Neither the owner of the music store nor the manager of the bar had news of her.

"The girl with the guitar," I said. "You remember her?"

"Sure I remember," each of them replied, "but I haven't seen her in a long time."

I stood around waiting outside the buildings where her parents lived. And I soon realized that neither Patrick nor Gillian lived in their respective apartments anymore.

Puzzled, I started looking for them. I found no trace of Gillian. Patrick Neville, on the other hand, had done extremely well for himself in New York. His fund was performing extraordinarily well. I had not realized he was really somebody in the world of finance: he had written several books on economics and I found out he even taught at Madison University in Connecticut. I eventually found his new address: an elegant building on E. 65th St. a few blocks from Central Park, with a doorman, a canvas canopy and a carpet on the sidewalk.

I went there several times, especially on weekends, hoping to run into Alexandra on her way out of the building. But to no avail.

I did see her father several times, however. Eventually I went up to him one day as he was about to go into his building.

"Marcus?" he said. "How nice to see you! How are you?"

"I'm O.K."

"What are you doing in this neck of the woods?"

"I was just going this way and I saw you get out of the taxi."

"Well, what a small world."

"How is Alexandra?"

"She's fine."

"Is she still playing her music?"

"I don't know. That's a strange question."

"She hasn't been back to the music store, or to the bar where she used to sing."

"She doesn't live in New York anymore, you know."

"I know, but doesn't she come back here for visits?"

"Yes, regularly."

"Then why doesn't she go to sing at the bar anymore? Or to the guitar store. I think she must've stopped her music."

He shrugged.

"She's busy with her studies."

"Her studies are pointless. In her soul she's a musician."

"You know, she went through a tough period. She lost her brother. And then her mother and I are getting a divorce. I guess she hasn't got the heart to sing her little songs."

"They weren't little songs, Patrick. Music is her dream."

"Well, maybe she'll get back to it."

He shook my hand in a kindly way to end our conversation.

"She should never have gone to college."

"Oh, really? And where should she have gone?"

"Nashville, Tennessee," I said, straight off the bat.

"Nashville, Tennessee? Why?"

"Because that's the city for real musicians. She could have become a star vocalist. She's a terrific musician and you can't see that."

I don't know why I brought up Nashville. Maybe because I dreamt of going far away with Alexandra. For a long time, I dreamt she did not go to Madison University. For a long time I dreamt that the day she came to Montclair to break up with me, she really only came so that I would take her to Nashville. In my dream she blows the horn and I come out of the house, carrying my bag. She's driving an old convertible, she's wearing sunglasses, and on her lips she has that dark red lipstick she puts on when she's happy. I jump into the car without even opening the door, she starts up and off we go. We are leaving for a better world, the world of our dreams. We drive for two days, through New Jersey, Pennsylvania, Maryland, Virginia. We spend the night in Roanoke. The next morning we're in Tennessee, at last.

19

At the beginning of spring 2012, after the first article about Alexandra and me, there were more articles in other magazines. It was a hot topic. Other than the handful of pirated photographs, which the magazines sold on to each other, the tabloids had nothing concrete to fuel the articles the readers wanted. Their solution was to question former classmates who were glad of their fifteen minutes of fame and who agreed to provide testimonies about us that had nothing to do with the main topic.

They found Nino Alvarez, for example, a nice kid who had been in my class when I was eleven. They asked him: "Have you ever seen Alexandra and Marcus together?"

"No," Alvarez said, solemnly.

Which the media translated as:

MARCUS FRIEND ASSERTS
HE NEVER SAW HIM WITH ALEXANDRA

Neighbors and casual paparazzi drove by my place on a regular basis to take pictures of the house. I couldn't go out and chase them away without them taking my picture as well, so as a result, I was constantly calling the police to get rid of them. Over time, I even befriended an entire squadron of cops who came out to my place one Sunday for a barbecue.

I had moved to Boca Raton for peace and quiet, and I had never been pestered so much in my life, including by my own friends, with whom

I could share none of my deepest emotions, for fear they might not keep them to themselves. I was in search of the privacy I had forfeited in my pursuit of fame. I couldn't have everything.

I eventually got into the habit of going to Uncle Saul's house, in Coconut Grove. It felt strange to be there without him. That was why I had bought a house in Boca Raton so soon after his death. I wanted to be in Florida, but I couldn't go to his place anymore. I didn't have the courage.

But now because I had started going there again, I got used to the house. I found the courage to start going through Uncle Saul's boxes. It was hard to sort through them, to envisage getting rid of some of his things. It forced to me to face a reality I found even harder to accept: the Baltimores were no more.

I missed Woody and Hillel. I realized that Alexandra was right: a part of me still believed I could have saved them.

* * *

The Hamptons, New York
1997

Without a doubt, the roots of the tragedy are to be found in that last summer I spent with Hillel and Woody in the Hamptons. The enchanted childhood of the Goldman Gang could not last forever: we were seventeen years old, seniors in high school – our last year. Soon we'd be starting college.

I remember the day I arrived. I had taken the Jitney, and I knew the route by heart. Every bend, every town we went through, every stop was familiar. After three hours I came to the main street in East Hampton, where Hillel and Woody were waiting impatiently. The bus hadn't even stopped before they were shouting my name, as excited as ever, bowing down in front of the Jitney as it maneuvered, the better to greet me. I put my face up to the window of the bus and they banged on the window to urge me to hurry up, as if they could wait no longer.

I can still see the two of them as if they were here before me. We had grown. They were as dissimilar physically as they were close emotionally. Hillel was still very skinny and looked younger than his age, and he still wore braces on his teeth. Woody, given his height and build, seemed much older: tall, handsome, muscular and radiant with health.

I jumped out of the bus and we flung our arms around each other. And for a long while we hugged as tight as we could, making one solid mass of muscle, flesh, and heart.

"Fucking A Marcus Goldman!" Woody shouted, his eyes shining with joy.

"The Goldman Gang is together again!" Hillel said exultantly.

All three of us had our driver's license now. They had come to get me in Uncle Saul's car. Woody grabbed my suitcase and tossed it into the trunk. Then we climbed in the car to drive down the triumphant road of our final vacation.

During the twenty minutes the trip lasted, all the way to the house, they told me insatiably what the summer held in store, raising their voices above the sound of warm air rushing in through the open windows. Woody was driving, wearing dark glasses, a cigarette dangling from his lips; I was in the passenger seat and Hillel, in the back, put his head between the two front seats, the better to participate in the conversation. We reached the coast, drove along the ocean, to the charming neighborhood where the house was. Woody made the tires squeal on the gravel and blew the horn to signal our arrival.

I found Uncle Saul and Aunt Anita just where I had left them a year earlier: comfortably settled on the porch, reading. The same classical music wafted through the open window of the living room. It was as if we had never left one another, as if East Hampton would last forever. Again I see myself going up to them, and when I recall the moment when

I kissed them and hugged them – which was basically the only tangible proof that we had ever really been apart – I remember how I loved to feel their arms around me. My aunt made me feel like a man, my uncle made me feel proud. I remember all the odors, too: their skin smelling of soap, their clothes of the laundry room in the Baltimore house, Aunt Anita of shampoo and Uncle Saul of aftershave. Each time, life tricked me a little bit more by making me believe that the cycle of our meetings would be eternal.

On the table in the shelter of the awning I found the usual pile of book review sections from the *New York Times* which Uncle Saul had not finished reading and was plowing through in dubious chronological order. I also noticed a few brochures from various universities. And our precious notebook where we wrote down our forecasts for the coming season, for all the sports: baseball, football, basketball, and hockey. We did not restrict ourselves to playing Sunday fortune tellers by decreeing who would win the Super Bowl or the Stanley Cup. We went much further: the winners of each Conference, the final scores, the best players, the best scorers and transfers. We wrote down our names and just next to them, our predictions. And the following year we would take up the notebook to see which one of us had the best intuition. That was one of my uncle's occupations: as the seasons went by, to keep tabs on the various sports results and then compare them with our prophecies. If one of us got something right, or close, he was amazed. And he'd say, "Well, whaddya know! Whaddya know! How'd you guess that?"

To do things in a brotherly way, at the age of around ten or twelve we had decided on a neutral, acceptable choice of teams for the Goldman Gang to support officially. This compromise was based on our geographical affinities. For baseball, it had to be the Baltimore Orioles (Woody and Hillel's choice). For basketball, the Miami Heat (in honor of the Goldman grandparents). For football, the Dallas Cowboys, and finally, for hockey, the Montreal Canadiens, probably because back then, when we came up with our choices, they had just won the Stanley Cup, and that was enough to convince us.

That year, because of all that had happened with the football team at Woody and Hillel's high school, we decided to drop football from our catalog of predictions. Only Uncle Saul still talked about the football season as if nothing had happened. I know he did it for Woody's sake. He wanted to reconcile him with the sport.

"Are you glad you'll be starting the season again, Woody?" he said.

Woody's only response was to shrug.

"Come on, Wood, you're super strong now on top of it," Hillel said encouragingly. "Mom says that if you go on like that, you're bound to get a scholarship for college."

He shrugged again. Aunt Anita had gone into the kitchen to get some iced tea and now she came back and caught the end of our conversation.

"Leave him alone," she said, running her hand tenderly through his hair and joining us on the bench.

Like all the kids our age who were about to start their senior year, choosing a college was an all-engrossing topic. The best establishments took only the best students, and this important part of our future would depend on our performance in school that year.

"Students should be chosen for their potential, not their ability to learn by heart and rehash like morons everything they're supposed to stuff into their heads," Hillel said suddenly, as if he had read our thoughts.

Woody waved his hand in the air, as if he wanted to banish any bad thoughts; he suggested we go to the beach. He didn't have to say it again. In the blink of an eye we were already in our swimsuits and in the car, the radio on full blast, on our way to a little beach we liked just outside East Hampton.

Most of the people on the beach were our age. When we arrived we were greeted by a group of girls who had obviously been waiting for Hillel and Woody. Especially Woody. Wherever he went, there was always a little cluster of girls, most of them beautiful or at least with good figures. They were lolling on their beach towels, warmed by the sun. Some of them were much older than us – this we knew because they could buy beer legally, and they kept us supplied – but that did not stop them looking at Woody with a fiery gaze.

I was the first one to dive in. I ran out to the end of a wooden jetty and flung myself into the waves. Woody and Hillel were straight behind me. First Hillel, with his stick-like build; then Woody, bursting with strength and vitality, hewn from stone. Before it was his turn to jump, he stood on the jetty and offered his prominent chest muscles to the sun, flashed his healthy, white teeth in a brilliant smile and cried, "The Goldman Gang is back!" His muscles contracted into a formidable armor and I saw him execute a prodigious somersault before he disappeared into the water.

Although we never confessed as much to each other, Hillel and I wished we looked more like Woody. He was a god of an athlete, the best I had ever seen. He could have had a successful career in any sport: he was a dauntless boxer, a swift runner, he excelled at basketball and worshiped football. From one summer to the next I saw his body develop. He was something else, that was for sure. I had noticed already when I saw him in his T-shirt at the bus stop, and I had felt it when he hugged me, and now that he was there before me – chest bared, splashing around in the cold water – I could see it clearly.

Treading water, we surveyed our territory. The air was so clear that in the distance we could see the little private beach at Paradise on Earth.

Hillel told me the house had finally been sold.

"Who to?" I said.

"No idea," Hillel said. "Dad talked to one of the guys who does the maintenance and he said the owner is coming at the end of the week."

"It was really cool when the Clarks were there. I wonder who bought the place," said Woody. "Maybe the new owners will let us use the beach from time to time in exchange for some gardening."

"Not if they're old fuddy-duddies," I said.

"I found a dead skunk in the road. We could always go get it and throw it into their garden."

We laughed.

Woody picked up a pebble and with an agile gesture sent it skipping across the surface of the water. His biceps hardened into an impressive knot.

"What the hell have you been doing all year?" I said, measuring the circumference of his arm with my hands. "You're huge!"

"Dunno. I just did what I had to do: I worked out, a lot."

"And the college recruiters?"

"They're interested. But you know, Markie, I'm sick of football. Life was better before. When we were together, Hillel and me. Before they sent him to that fucking special school."

For the second year in a row, Woody and Hillel had been apart. Woody skipped another pebble into the distance, casually. As if anything to do with college was of no importance, in the end. It was almost true: all we wanted at that moment was to live our youth to the fullest, and the call of the Hamptons was powerful. The town was pretty, and there was a heat wave that summer. Climatically and psychologically, there was probably never a finer summer for the good American people than that month of July 1997. We were the golden youth of an ever-strengthening, peaceful country.

That evening after supper we took Uncle Saul's car and went off into the countryside on our own. It was a cloudless night and we lay in the grass to gaze at the stars. Woody and I were smoking, but Hillel was choking on his cigarette. "Quit smoking, Hill," Woody said. "It hurts to listen to you."

"Marcus," Hillel eventually said, "you have to come and see one of Woody's games. It's a scream."

"What do you mean, what's so funny?" Woody said, offended.

"The way you smash the other players' faces in."

"That's my technique. I'm an offensive player."

"Offensive? You should see him, Markie, he's a regular bulldozer. He sends guys from the other team flying, with just a nudge of his shoulder. You don't even have time to breathe a sigh of relief and his team has already scored. They won nearly all their games last season."

"You should go into boxing," I said. "I'm sure you could become a pro."

"Whaaa? Not on your life! Boxing? I don't want my nose broken. What girl would marry me if I smash my schnozz in?"

Woody didn't have to worry about finding a girl to marry him. All the girls loved Woody. They were all crazy about him.

Hillel suddenly turned serious.

"Guys, this is probably our last summer for a long time. Soon we'll be in college and we'll have other things to worry about."

"Yup," Woody agreed, a touch of nostalgia in his voice.

At the end of our first week, while we were having breakfast on the patio, Uncle Saul came back from an errand in town and told us he'd seen a car parked outside Paradise on Earth. The new owners had arrived.

Driven by curiosity, Woody, Hillel and I gobbled down the rest of our cereal and rushed over to find out what the new owners were like, and to offer them a few hours of gardening in exchange for use of the jetty and the beach. We put on our Goldman gardener T-shirts (regularly updated for size) to give us a semblance of credibility. We rang the doorbell and when the door opened we were knocked speechless: there stood Alexandra.

20

The Hamptons
July 1997

We found Alexandra again, there in the Hamptons, as if we had never been apart. Once the moment of astonishment had passed, she let out an enthusiastic shout. "The Goldman Gang!" she cried, hugging each one of us in turn. "I can't believe it!" She embraced me with disconcerting spontaneity and a magnificent smile.

Then her father came over, wondering what all the ruckus was about, and he greeted us warmly. We later told Aunt Anita and Uncle Saul, who went in turn to welcome the new residents. "Well, whaddya know!" Uncle Saul exclaimed, hugging Patrick. "So you're the one who bought Paradise?"

My cousins were radiantly happy to be with Alexandra again. I could sense, from their gestures and excitement, what they felt for her. The last time they had seen her, all four of us had been crying our eyes out: she was moving from Oak Park to New York. But for me, nothing could be the way it had been.

Aunt Anita invited Alexandra and Patrick for dinner that very evening and all seven of us were reunited under the gazebo covered with birthwort. Patrick Neville explained that he had been looking for a house in the region for a long time and that Paradise on Earth had been an absolutely unique opportunity. I wasn't really listening to the conversation; I was devouring Alexandra with my eyes. I think she was avoiding my gaze.

After the meal, while Uncle Saul, Aunt Anita and Patrick Neville were having an after-dinner drink by the swimming pool, I went for a walk along the road with Alexandra and my cousins. It was dark out, but there was a pleasant lingering warmth. We talked about whatever came into our heads. Alexandra described student life at Madison University. She didn't really know what she wanted to do yet.

"And your music?" Woody said. "Are you still playing?"

"Not as much as before. I don't really have time."

"That's a pity," I said.

"I have to admit I miss it."

Seeing her again was heartbreaking. I was still so attached to her voice, her face, her smile, her smell. Basically, I didn't really feel like seeing her. But she was our neighbor and I didn't see how I could avoid her. Particularly as both my cousins couldn't get enough of her and there was no way I could tell them what had happened between the two of us.

The next day she invited us to come swimming at her place. I went along with Woody and Hillel, reluctantly. The ocean was cold and we spent the afternoon by the swimming pool, which was much bigger than the Baltimores'. At one point she arranged things so I would come and help her with the drinks in the kitchen, so we'd be alone for a moment.

"'Markie-moo, I just wanted to tell you . . . I'm glad to see you again. I hope you don't feel awkward, because I don't. I'm glad to see that we can still be friends."

I put on a sullen expression. No-one had said anything about being friends.

"Why did you never get in touch again?" I asked, in a tone of outrage.

"Get in touch?"

"I often went by your father's place, in New York."

"My father's place? But Marcus, what do you expect from me?"

"Nothing."

"Don't say anything, I can tell you're mad at me. Are you mad because I went away?"

"Maybe."

She sighed to show she was irritated.

"Marcus, you are a terrific boy. But we're not together anymore. I'm glad to see you, you and your cousins, but if it's too hard for you to see me without digging up the past, then I'd rather we avoided each other."

I lied to her and told her that I wasn't digging up anything, that our affair had hardly meant a thing to me, that I could scarcely remember it. I took a few cans of Dr Pepper and went back out to my cousins. I had found Alexandra again, but she wasn't the same Alexandra. The last time I had seen her, she had still been mine. And now here she was a young woman who was very much at one with the world, a student at a prestigious university, whereas I was still stuck in my little world in Montclair. I knew I ought to forget her, but when I saw her by the swimming pool, in her swimsuit, her reflection in the water became her reflection in the mirror at the Waldorf Astoria, and images of our past came back to haunt me.

We spent our entire time in the Hamptons at the Nevilles'. We were welcome to go there whenever we wanted, and we could not resist the sublime, powerful pull of the Paradise. This was the first time, for me, that something belonging to the Baltimores had been outclassed: in comparison with the house Patrick Neville had bought, my aunt and uncle's summer place was like Montclair in the Hamptons.

Patrick had redesigned the kitchen, installed a steam bath in the basement, and furnished the interior in the best possible way. The tiles in the swimming pool had been changed. But he had preserved that dream-inducing fountain, and the flagstone path that wound its way among the hydrangea bushes down to the white sand beach, lapped by deep blue waves.

Ever since he had moved to New York, Patrick Neville had had phenomenal success with his investment fund. He had literally made a fortune.

For all that we were dazzled by the beauty of the Paradise, the reason for our constant presence there was the Nevilles themselves. Alexandra, of course, but also her father, who was growing fond of us. In Oak Park he had always been very kind toward us. He was a truly good person. But in the Hamptons we discovered another side of him: charismatic, cultivated, a man who liked to enjoy himself. We were surprised to find ourselves seeking out his company.

Occasionally when he opened the door to us, Patrick told us that Alexandra had gone out but wouldn't be long. And then he would invite us into the kitchen and offer us a beer. "You're not too young," he declared, as if to ward off any possible protest. "Basically, you're men already. It makes me proud to know you." He'd flip the caps off the bottles one after the other and hand them out, then drink to our health.

I realized there was something about the Gang that was a little bit out of the ordinary, and he was impressed. He enjoyed talking with us. One day he asked us what we were passionate about. We all started shouting at once, off the top of our heads, how we loved sports and girls, and anything else that came to mind. Hillel mentioned politics and Patrick grew even more enthusiastic.

"I've always been fascinated by politics, too," he said. "And history. Literature, too. "The empty vessel makes the loudest sound."

"Shakespeare," Hillel said.

"Exactly," Neville said, his face lighting up. "How did you know that?"

"That little runt knows everything," said Woody with pride. "He's a genius."

Patrick Neville looked at us with a smile, happy to see us there.

"You're good kids," he said. "Your parents must be really proud of you."

"My parents are real jerks," Woody said amiably.

"Yeah," Hillel confirmed. "They're so bad I had to lend him mine."

Neville made a funny face, then burst out laughing.

"Oh, you really are good kids! Another beer?"

We made ourselves at home at the Paradise. As if it weren't enough to hang out there all day long, we now started spending our evenings there too. But I soon realized that Alexandra's presence among the Goldman Gang was affecting my complicity with Woody and Hillel. I had trouble keeping her at a distance: I had to reckon with Woody and Hillel, whose hormones were boiling over; they gazed at her hungrily. I was much too jealous to leave them alone with her. At the swimming pool I spied on them. I watched as they made her laugh, I watched Woody grabbing her with his muscular arms and throwing her in the water, I looked at her eyes and tried to detect whether they shone brighter whenever she looked at either of my cousins.

With each passing day my jealousy increased. I was jealous of Hillel, his charisma, his knowledge, his ease. I could see how she looked at him, I could see how she rubbed against him, and it drove me crazy.

It was the first time Woody ever annoyed me: here was this guy I had always liked so much, and now I began to hate him – when he was in a sweat and took his T-shirt off, and revealed his perfectly formed body: she could not help but look at him and sometimes she even complimented him. I could see how she looked at him, how she brushed against him, and it drove me crazy.

I began keeping an eye on them. If one of them went off to look for a missing tool, I became wary. I imagined secret trysts and embraces. In the evening when we got back to the Goldman house and had dinner out on the patio, Uncle Saul said, "Are you alright, kids? You're not saying much."

225

"We're O.K.," one of us would say.

"Is everything alright over at the Nevilles'? Is there something I ought to know?"

"Everything's fine, we're just tired."

What Uncle Saul could sense was tension among the members of the Gang, and it was becoming difficult to hide. For the first time in our life together, all three of us wanted something that we could not share.

21

During the month of April 2012, as I went through Uncle Saul's things, memories of the Goldman Gang danced through my mind. The weather was particularly stifling. An unusual heat wave had Florida in its grip and there was one thunderstorm after another.

It was during one torrential downpour that I finally decided to call Alexandra. I was sitting out under the awning, sheltered from the driving rain. I took out her note, which had not left the back pocket of my jeans, and slowly tapped in the number.

She picked up on the third ring.

"Hello?"

"It's Marcus."

There was a moment's silence. I didn't know if she was embarrassed or happy to hear me, and I almost hung up. But eventually she said, "Markie, I'm glad you called."

"I'm really sorry about the photographs and that whole fuck-up. Are you still in Los Angeles?"

"Yes. And you? Did you go back to New York? What's that noise I can hear?"

"I'm still in Florida. It's the rain. I'm at my uncle's house. I'm going through his things."

"What happened to your uncle, Marcus?"

"The same thing as to all the Baltimores."

There was an awkward silence.

"I can't stay on the line too long. Kevin is here."

"We haven't done anything wrong."

"Yes and no, Markie."

When she called me Markie it meant all was not lost. And it was precisely because all was not lost that it was wrong. She said, "I had managed to put us behind me. To regain a certain stability. And now everything is all mixed up again. Don't do this to me, Markie. Don't do this to me if you don't believe in us."

"I never stopped believing in us."

She did not say anything.

The rain was coming down harder than ever. We stayed on the line, not talking. I stretched out on the bench: I saw myself again as a teenager, with the old telephone on a cord, lying on my bed in Montclair, while she lay on hers in New York, the two of us starting up a conversation that would probably last for hours.

*   *   *

The Hamptons
1997

That summer, Patrick Neville's presence had a decisive influence on our choice of college. He talked about Madison, where he taught, more than once.

"In my opinion, it's one of the best universities, given the prospects it offers. Regardless of career choice."

Hillel said he wanted to study law.

"Madison doesn't have a law faculty," Patrick said, "but it does have an excellent degree course. Moreover, you have time to change your minds along the way. By the time you finish the first four years of college, you might have discovered another vocation. Ask Alexandra, she'll tell you she's delighted with the place. And it would be great if you were all together again."

Woody wanted to be able to play football at college level. There too, Patrick considered Madison a good choice.

"The Madison Titans are an ace team. Several players in the current N.F.L. Championship got their start there."

"Really?"

"Really. The university has a good athletic scholarship program."

Patrick, as he told us, was a football fanatic, and had played in college. An old friend he had kept in touch with was a sports director for the New York Giants.

"We love the Giants," Woody said. "Do you go to their games?"

"Whenever I can. I even got the chance to visit the locker rooms."

We couldn't get over it.

"Did you meet the players?" Hillel asked.

"I know Danny Kanell quite well," he told us.

"No way," said Woody.

Patrick went out of the room for a moment and came back with two frames in which there were photographs of himself with Giants players on the lawn at their stadium in East Rutherford, New Jersey.

That evening, at the Baltimore dinner table, Woody told Uncle Saul and Aunt Anita about our discussion with Patrick Neville about college football. He hoped that Patrick could help him get a scholarship.

Woody wanted to secure a place on a college team not so much to finance his studies, but above all because it was the gateway to the N.F.L. He was training relentlessly, for that sole purpose. He got up in the morning before we did and went on long runs. Sometimes I went with him. He was much heavier than me, and yet he ran faster, and for longer. I admired him while he did his push-ups and pull-ups, lifting the weight of his own body as if it were nothing. A few mornings earlier he had told me, while we were jogging along the ocean, that to him football was the most important thing in the world.

"Before football, I was nothing. I didn't exist. Since I began playing, people know me, they respect me."

"It's not true you didn't exist before football," I said.

"The Baltimores have given me their love. Or lent it to me. They can take it away again. I'm not their son. I'm just some kid they felt sorry for. Who knows, someday they might turn their backs on me."

"How can you even think such a thing! You're like a son to them."

"Goldman isn't my name, not by law or by blood. I'm just Woody, the kid who hangs around with you guys. I have to build my own identity and to do that, football is all I have. You know, when Hillel got thrown off the Buckerey team, I wanted to stop football, too. To support him. Saul convinced me not to. He told me I shouldn't act on impulse. He and Anita found me a new high school and a new team. I let them convince me. But nowadays I feel bad about the way I behaved. I feel as if I didn't assume my responsibilities. It was unfair that Hillel had to pick up the pieces."

"Hillel was an assistant trainer. He should have stopped Scott from going out on the playing field. He knew he was sick. It was his responsibility as a trainer. What I mean is, you can't compare yourself to him. He liked to be with all of you on the playing field and shout at guys who were bigger than him, that's all. For you football is your life. It may even become your career."

He made a face.

"But I still feel bad."

"There's no reason to."

Uncle Saul was not as convinced about Madison as we were. At dinner, after Woody talked to him about the various opportunities the place offered, Uncle Saul said, "I'm not saying it's not a good college, I'm just saying you have to choose depending on what you want to do there."

"For football, in any case, it's great," Woody said again.

"It may be great for football, but if you want to study law, for example, you have to start your degree course at a university that has a law faculty. It just makes more sense. Georgetown, for example, is a good school. And besides, it's not far from home."

"Patrick Neville said not to limit our possibilities," Hillel said.

Uncle Saul rolled his eyes.

"Well, if Patrick Neville said so . . ."

Sometimes I got the impression that Patrick annoyed Uncle Saul. I remember one evening when we were all invited to dinner at the Paradise. Patrick had done things on a grand scale: he had hired a chef to do the cooking, and staff to serve. When we got home that night, Aunt Anita praised the meal. This triggered an argument with Uncle Saul, not a major or lasting one, but at the time it made me uncomfortable because it was the first time I had ever seen my aunt and uncle argue.

"Of course it was good," Uncle Saul said. "He hired a cook. He could've had a barbecue, it would've been more informal."

"But, Saul, he's a man on his own, he doesn't like to cook. In any case, the house is magnificent."

"Too flashy."

"You didn't say that when the Clarks lived there."

"When the Clarks lived there, it was charming. He redecorated everything, it's nouveau riche."

"Does it bother you that he makes a lot of money?" asked Aunt Anita.

"I'm very happy for his sake."

"That's not the impression I get."

"I don't like people who are nouveau riche."

"And so we are not?"

"We have better taste than that guy, that's for sure."

"Oh, Saul, don't be petty."

"Petty? Honestly, you think that guy has taste?"

"Yes. I like the way he's redone the house, I like the way he dresses. And stop calling him *that guy*. His name is Patrick."

"The way he dresses is ridiculous: he wants to look young and hip, but all he looks is like some aging beau with a facelift. I'm not sure New York is good for him."

"I don't think he had a facelift."

"Come on, Anita, the skin on his face is as smooth as a baby's bottom."

I didn't like it when my uncle and aunt called themselves by their first names. They only did it when they were mad. The rest of the time, they used endearments and tender little nicknames that made it look as if they were as much in love as on the first day.

From hearing Patrick Neville go on about the place, I began mulling over the possibility of going to Madison University myself. Not so much for the school itself but because I wanted to be near Alexandra. The thought of having her close made me realize how happy I was when she was around. I could picture the two of us on campus, our intimacy restored. I got up the courage to share my plans with her one week before the end of our stay at the Hamptons. We were about to leave the Paradise after spending the day by the pool, and I gave my cousins some excuse that I'd forgotten something at the Nevilles' to go back into the house. I went in without knocking, with a firm step, and found her on her own, still by the pool.

"I could come and study at Madison," I said.

She pulled down her dark glasses and gave me a disapproving look.

"Don't do that, Marcus."

"Why not?"

"Don't do it, that's all. Forget that stupid idea."

I didn't see what was stupid about my idea but I had the tact not to answer back, and I walked away. I could not understand why she was so pleasant around my cousins and so mean to me. I couldn't tell whether I loved her or hated her.

Our stay was due to end the last week of July 1997. The night before, we went to the Paradise to say goodbye to the Nevilles. Alexandra wasn't there, only Patrick. He gave us each a beer and handed out his business card: "It's been great getting to know you three fantastic guys. If one of you wants to apply to Madison, be sure to get in touch. I'll endorse your application."

Still early that evening, just after dinner, Alexandra dropped by Uncle Saul and Aunt Anita's. I was alone on the porch, reading. When I saw her, my heart began to pound.

"Hey, Markie-moo," she said, sitting down next to me.

"Hey, Alexandra."

"Were you going to leave without saying goodbye?"

"We stopped by earlier, but you weren't there."

She smiled and stared at me with her slanting gray-green eyes.

"I was thinking we could go out tonight," she suggested.

A powerful rush of euphoria went all through me.

"Sure," I said, finding it hard to hide my excitement.

I looked deep in her eyes, and it seemed as if she was about to tell me something very important. But all she said was, "Are you going to go and get Woody and Hillel, or are we going to sit here all night?"

We went out to a bar on the main street that had an open mic where local musicians came to perform. All you had to do was sign up at the bar, and the master of ceremonies would call participants up on stage one after the other.

Since we had left the house Hillel had been playing Mister-Know-it-All to impress Alexandra. He was dressed up to the nines and was swamping us with words and knowledge. I felt like slapping him and was only too delighted when the music from the bar drowned him out and he was obliged to shut up.

We listened to a first group. Then a boy was called up on stage and he played a few pop numbers, accompanying himself on the piano. A group of three rowdy boys sitting at a table behind us booed his performance.

"Hey, show some respect," Alexandra told them.

Their only response was to insult her. Woody turned around: "What did you say, asshole?" he roared.

"You have a problem with that?" one of them asked.

That was all it took: despite Alexandra's pleas, Woody got up and grabbed the arm of one of the boys and gave it a sharp twist.

"You want to take care of this outside?" Woody growled.

He was so classy when he fought. Like a lion.

"Let go of him," Alexandra ordered, rushing over to Woody and pushing him with both hands.

Woody let the boy go; he moaned with pain and the three would-be aggressors fled without further ado. The pianist had finished his last number and the name of the next performer came over the loudspeakers.

"Alexandra Neville. Next up is Alexandra Neville."

Alexandra froze and went pale.

"Which one of you three was stupid enough to do this?" she said.

It was me.

"I thought you'd be glad," I said.

"Glad? Marcus, are you out of your mind?"

I saw her eyes fill with tears. She looked at each one of us in turn and said, "Why do you all have to behave like idiots? Why do you have to spoil everything? You, Hillel, why do you act like some performing monkey? You're better when you're yourself. And you, Woody, why do you have to get mixed up in things that don't concern you? You think I can't take care of myself? You had to attack those guys who didn't do anything to you? As for you Marcus, I've had enough of your hare-brained ideas. Why did you do that? To humiliate me? If so, well then, you sure did."

She burst into tears and rushed out of the bar. I ran after her and caught up with her down the street. I held her arm. I blew up.

"I did it because the Alexandra I used to know wouldn't have run away: she would have got up on stage and wowed her audience. You know what, I'm glad I saw you again, because now I know I don't love you anymore. The girl I used to know filled me with dreams."

I started to head back to the bar.

"I quit music!" she cried, in a flood of tears.

"But why? It was your passion."

"Because no-one believes in me."

"But I believe in you!"

She wiped her eyes with the back of her hand. Her voice was trembling.

"That's your problem, Marcus, you're all dreams. Life isn't a dream."

"We have only one life, Alexandra! One little teeny tiny life! Wouldn't you rather spend it going after your dreams than rotting in that stupid college? You have to dream, and dream big! Only the biggest dreams survive. The other ones – they dissolve in the rain, vanish in the wind."

She gave me one last, lost look with her big eyes before she ran off into the night. I shouted, at the top of my lungs, "I know I'll see you back on stage, Alexandra. I believe in you!" It was the echo of the night that answered: she had vanished.

I went back to the bar, where there was a sudden commotion. I heard shouting: a fight had just broken out. The three boys had come back with three more friends to deal with Woody. I saw my two cousins in the middle of six strangers and I hurried into the crowd. I was screaming like a condemned man: "The Goldman Gang never loses! The Goldman Gang never loses!" We fought bravely. Woody and I quickly stunned four of them. He was incredibly strong, and I was a good boxer. The other two were in the process of flooring Hillel and we leapt on them and pummelled them until they ran off, leaving their friends moaning on the ground. There was the sound of sirens. "The cops! The cops!" came a shout. Someone had called the police. We ran away. We ran through the night as if the Devil were on our heels. Down the small back streets of East Hampton and we kept on running until we were sure we were safe. Breathless, bent double trying to fill our lungs, we looked at each other: we hadn't only been fighting with a bunch of hooligans, but with each other. We knew that the feelings we all had for Alexandra made us rivals.

"We have to make a pact," Hillel declared.

Woody and I instantly understood what he was referring to.

In the secrecy of the night, we joined our hands together and, in the name of the Goldman Gang, so we would never be rivals, we swore we would give Alexandra up; every last one of us.

* * *

Fifteen years later, the oath of the Goldman Gang still resonated inside me. After many long minutes of silence, while I lay there on the porch of my uncle's house in Coconut Grove, I eventually began to speak again.

"We made a pact, Alexandra. That last summer in the Hamptons, Woody, Hillel, and I made a promise to each other."

"Marcus, you will only begin to truly live when you stop stirring up the past."

There was a moment of silence. Then she murmured, "And what if it was a sign, Marcus? And what if it wasn't a coincidence that we met again?"

Everything begins the way everything ends, and books often begin with the end.

I don't know whether the chapter of our youth was closed the moment we finished high school or just one year before, at the end of July 1997, at the end of that summer in the Hamptons which witnessed the moment the seal of our friendship, our promise of eternal loyalty, was broken, a promise that was unable to withstand the adult life we were about to embrace.

Part Two

THE BOOK OF THE LOST BROTHERHOOD
1998–2001

22

If you happened to visit Madison University in Connecticut between 2000 and 2010, you were bound to see the football stadium: during that decade it was known as the Saul Goldman Stadium.

I have always associated Madison University with the grandeur of the Goldmans. That was why I could not understand why my uncle Saul called me at home in New York at the end of August 2011, to ask me to do what he thought was an important favor: he wanted me to be there at the removal of his name from the facade of the stadium, scheduled to take place the next day. This was three months before his death, and six months before I saw Alexandra again.

I was not aware at the time of my uncle's situation. He had been behaving strangely for a while, but I had no way of knowing that these were the last months of his life.

"Why do you want me to be there so badly?" I said.

"From New York it only takes an hour by car—"

"But honestly, Uncle Saul, that's not the point. I don't understand why you think it's so important."

"Please, just do it, that's all."

I have never been able to say no to him, so I agreed.

Uncle Saul had organized everything, so the president of the university was waiting for me, standing to attention in the stadium parking lot as I arrived. "It's an honor to meet you, Mr Goldman," he said. "I didn't know Saul was your uncle. Don't worry, we waited for you, in keeping with your uncle's request."

He started walking solemnly toward the stadium, toward the entrance where stainless steel letters set in concrete had proclaimed my uncle's renown:

SAUL GOLDMAN STADIUM

On a boom lift with an articulated arm, two workers conscientiously unscrewed each letter, then let them crash to the ground with a metallic clang.

UL GOLDMAN STADIUM
GOLDMAN STADIUM
MAN STADIUM
ADIUM

Then the workers set about fixing to the bare wall a luminous sign, belonging to a company that mass-produced breaded chicken, which would be ensuring the stadium's financing for the next ten years.

"That's it," the president said. "Please thank your uncle once again on behalf of the University. He has been very generous."

"I'll be sure to do that."

The president was about to leave, but I held him back. There was something I was dying to ask him.

"Why did he do this?"

He turned around.

"Do what?"

"Why did my uncle finance the maintenance of the stadium for ten years?"

"Because he was generous."

"There must be something else. He is generous, but it was not like him to put himself in the limelight like this."

The president shrugged.

"I have no idea. You'll have to ask him."

"And how much did he donate?"

"That's confidential, Mr Goldman."

"Oh, come on . . ."

After a brief hesitation he said: "Six million dollars."

I was flabbergasted.

"My uncle donated six million dollars to have his name on the stadium for ten years?"

"Yes. Naturally, his name will be added to the wall, along with the other major donors, at the entrance to the administrative building."

I stood for a moment looking at the sign representing a smiling chicken as it was being attached to the facade of the stadium. Back then, my uncle had certainly been a relatively wealthy man, but unless he had a source of money I did not know about, I found it hard to imagine how he could have made a donation of six million dollars to the university. Where could he have found that kind of money?

I called him when I got back to the parking lot.

"That's it, Uncle Saul, it's done."

"How did it go?"

"They unscrewed the letters and put a sign up in their place."

"Who is going to be financing the stadium?"

"A company that makes breaded chicken."

I could hear the smile in his voice.

"You see, Marcus, where your ego can lead you. One day you have your name on a stadium, and the next day you're wiped off the surface of the planet to make room for breaded chicken breasts."

"No-one wiped you off the surface of the planet, Uncle Saul. They were just metal letters screwed into concrete."

"You're a good boy, nephew. Are you going back to New York now?"

"Yes."

"Thank you for doing that, Marcus. It means a lot to me."

But my doubts lingered. My uncle, now a supermarket employee, had paid six million dollars ten years ago to have his name on a stadium. I felt sure that even back then he did not have that kind of money. That had been the asking price for the Clarks' house in the Hamptons, and Saul had insisted he could not afford it. How could he have come up with such a colossal sum four years later? Where had he found the money?

I got back in my car and drove off. That was the last time I went to Madison.

Thirteen years had gone by since we started college. That was in 1998, and in those days Madison, to me, seemed like a temple of glory. I had kept my promise to Alexandra not to go and study there, choosing rather the humanities department of a little college in Massachusetts. Hillel and Woody, on the other hand, who'd been smart enough not to commit to anything, could not resist their desire to re-create the Goldman Gang with Alexandra, and Patrick Neville encouraged them: they had stayed in touch with him following our vacation in the Hamptons.

According to custom, during winter vacation in our senior year we had applied to several different schools; notably, we all sent applications to Burrows College in Massachusetts. It almost worked out, the three of us going there together. Four months later, at around Easter, I received a letter informing me that I had been accepted. A few days later, my cousins called to tell me their news: they were screaming so loud into the receiver that it took me a while to understand. They had been admitted to Burrows, too. We were going to be reunited.

But my excitement did not last for long: two days later, they each got a letter from Madison University. They had both been accepted there, too. Thanks to Patrick Neville's connections, Woody had been granted a sports scholarship so he could play on their team, the Titans. This was the door opening onto a professional career, particularly given Patrick's contacts with the New York Giants. Woody accepted the offer from Madison and Hillel decided to follow him. So in the fall of 1998, while I left New Jersey for Massachusetts, a little car registered in the state of Maryland chugged its way for the first time through Connecticut and along the Atlantic coast to the small town of Madison. The countryside was wearing the colors of an Indian summer: maples and sycamores were ablaze with red and yellow leaves. The car went through Madison and down the main drag, bright with the colors of the Titans, for the team was the pride of the town and the scourge of every other college in the league. Before long they came to the first red brick buildings.

"Stop the car here!" Hillel shouted.

"Here?"

"Yes, here! Stop!"

Woody pulled over onto the shoulder. They got out; dazzled, they admired the campus there before them. They looked at each other, laughed with joy, and leapt into each other's arms. "Madison University!" they cried in unison. "We did it, bro! We did it!"

It looked as if friendship, stronger than anything, had triumphed once again, and that after the year and a half Hillel had spent in the special school, they had chosen Madison to be together again. On the drive up they had promised to share a room, to sign up for the same classes, to eat together and study together. But with hindsight I would come to realize that the choice of Madison had been made for one single, bad, reason. And the reason came walking toward them across the campus lawn, the first morning of class: Alexandra.

"The Goldmans!" she cried, rushing into their arms.

"You didn't expect to see us here, did you?" Hillel said with a smile.

She burst out laughing: "You're so cute, you two big dorks! I knew perfectly well that you were coming."

"Really?"

"My father can't stop talking about you. You're his latest obsession."

And that was how our college lives began. And just as they had always done, my Baltimore cousins shone brightest.

Hillel started growing a beard, and it suited him: the skinny little boy, the unpleasant intellectual from Oak Tree School had become a fairly good-looking young man, full of drive and charisma, tastefully dressed, admired for his dazzling intelligence and clever way with words. His professors singled him out in no time, and he made himself indispensable to the editorial committee of the college newspaper.

Woody, more manly than ever, ripe with strength and testosterone, had become as handsome as a Greek god. He had let his hair grow and wore it brushed back. He had a devastating smile, his teeth were a radiant white, his body was as if sculpted from stone. I would not have been surprised to see him, at the height of his career as a football player, on one of those huge advertising posters for clothes or aftershave that cover whole walls in Manhattan six storeys high.

I went regularly to Madison to attend Woody's games in what was still called the Burger-Shake stadium, with a capacity of 30,000 seats, always full, and where I heard tens of thousands of spectators chanting Woody's name. I could not help but notice the bond between the three of them; it was obvious they were happy, and I can confess here that I was filled with envy, not to be a part of their group anymore. I missed them. The Goldman Gang now consisted of the three of them, and Madison was their territory. My cousins had given the third spot in the gang to Alexandra, and only years later would I understand that this third spot at the heart of the gang was not a permanent position; I had occupied it, as had Scott, and now it was Alexandra's turn.

Already by Thanksgiving of our freshman year in college, in November 1998, I was dazzled by what they had accomplished. I got the impression that in just a few months everything had changed. The joy of seeing them again in Baltimore was unaltered, but the pride of belonging to the Baltimores which had galvanized me as a child was gone. Up until then it was my parents who were outclassed by Uncle Saul and Aunt Anita, but now it was my turn to see my cousins outshine me.

Woody, the invincible Viking of the stadium, was like the sun at the center of a universe of football, radiating with strength. As for Hillel, he wrote for the college paper and was attracting a lot of attention. One of his professors, a regular contributor to the *New Yorker*, told him to submit one of his pieces to the prestigious magazine. I looked at them, sitting there at the magnificent Thanksgiving table, in that luxurious house, and I admired their arrogance and pictured their destinies: Hillel, defender of great causes, would become an even more eminent lawyer than his father – who was, moreover, ready and waiting for his son to move into the office next to his, already reserved for him. *Goldman & Goldman, Father & Son, Law Offices.* Woody would join the Baltimore Ravens football team, founded two years earlier and already achieving exceptional results thanks to a remarkable campaign to recruit young talent. Uncle Saul said he had access to people high up – which didn't surprise anyone – and assured Woody that he would be in the spotlight. I could picture them a few years down the road, neighbors in Oak Park, where they would buy their own magnificent, mansions.

My mother must have sensed how distraught I was, and when it was time for dessert she suddenly felt obliged to emphasize my own achievements: she looked around the table and declared, "Markie is writing a book!"

I turned crimson and begged her to stop.

"What's it about?" Uncle Saul said.

"It's a novel," my mother said.

"It's just an idea," I stammered, "we'll see if anything comes of it."

"He's already written a few short stories," my mother went on. "They're really good. Two of them were published in the college paper."

"I'd like to read them," Aunt Anita said kindly.

My mother promised to send them, and I made her promise to be quiet. I got the impression that Woody and Hillel were scoffing at me. I felt stupid with my insipid short stories next to what they had become – in my eyes, half-gods, half-lions, half-eagles, ready to take flight toward the sun, while I was still the same impressionable little adolescent, light years away from their self-assured brilliance.

That year the Thanksgiving dinner seemed to surpass previous years. Uncle Saul had become younger. Aunt Anita was even more beautiful. Was it really like that, or was I too busy admiring them all to realize that the Baltimores were, in fact, losing their grip? My uncle, my aunt, my two cousins: I thought they were perpetually ascending; they were in free-fall, halfway down. I only understood this years later.

In spite of everything I imagined for them, when my cousins returned to Baltimore after college, it would be neither as hotshot lawyer nor as star of the Ravens.

How could I ever have suspected what lay in store?

23

At my college in Massachusetts I was feeling somewhat left out, so I was all the more annoyed to discover that in Madison – as had been the case in Baltimore with Scott – the Goldman Gang could be expanded to include the Nevilles. After Alexandra, it was Patrick Neville's turn to be granted a privileged spot among them.

Every Tuesday Patrick went to the university to teach his weekly class. According to rumor, you could tell what sort of mood he was in depending on his means of transport: on days when he was in a good mood, he would arrive at the wheel of a black Ferrari, speeding through New England like an arrow. If he was in a bad mood, he drove a Yukon S.U.V. with tinted windows. He was very well known on campus and any number of students claimed to be his followers.

Whenever he went to Madison, he always made a point of seeing Woody and Hillel: before long they had grown close.

On Tuesday evenings he took them, with Alexandra, for dinner to a restaurant on the main drag. When he had time, he attended the Titans' practice, wearing a cap with the team's colors jammed tight on his head. He went to all the home games and sometimes even away games, despite the fact that it meant several hours on the road. He always invited Hillel to go along with him.

I think Patrick enjoyed Woody and Hillel's company because when he was with them, it was a way of being with Scott again.

With Hillel and Woody Patrick could do what he wished he could have done with his son. During the second semester at Madison, as football season was over, he regularly invited them to spend the weekend at his place in New York. Full of awe, they described the luxury of his apartment: the view, the Jacuzzi out on the terrace, a television in every room. They soon felt at home, admiring his artwork, smoking his cigars, drinking his Scotch.

During spring vacation 1999, he invited them to the Hamptons. The week after the end of exams they came to see me in Montclair, driving Patrick's black Ferrari, which he had lent them. I suggested we go have dinner somewhere, but since the car had only two seats, I had to take my mother's old Honda Civic, while they roared through town ahead of me in their speed machine. During the meal, I learned they had changed their career plans somewhat. New York had superseded Baltimore; economics had triumphed over law.

"You have to be in finance," Hillel said. "If you knew the kind of life Patrick leads . . ."

"We had lunch with the Giants' sporting director," Woody said. "We even got to go and visit the stadium in New Jersey. He said he'll send a scout to watch me play next year."

They showed me photographs of themselves on the lawn outside Giants Stadium. I imagined them several years later, at the same spot, celebrating the Giants' victory at the Super Bowl, with Woody the star quarterback and his adoptive brother Hillel, the new golden boy all of Wall Street would be fighting over.

Something happened at the beginning of their second year in college. One evening as he was driving back to campus along Route 5, about five miles after crossing the bridge near Lebanon, Woody almost ran over a young woman walking on the side of the road. It was pitch black out. He immediately stopped and sprang out of the car.

"Are you alright?" he said.

She was in tears.

"I'm fine, thank you," she said, wiping her eyes.

"It's dangerous to walk along this road."

"I'll be careful."

"Get in, I can give you a lift," Woody offered.

"No, thank you."

"Get in, I said."

In the end the girl accepted his offer. In the light in the car Woody thought he recognized her. She was a pretty girl with short hair. Her face was familiar.

"Are you a student at Madison?"

"No."

"Are you sure you're okay?"

"I'm sure. I don't feel like talking."

He drove in silence and dropped her off where she asked him to, next to a deserted gas station at the entrance to Madison.

Her name was Colleen. Woody read it on her badge the very next day, when he saw her behind the counter at the gas station where he had left her the night before.

"I knew I'd seen you somewhere," he said. "When I dropped you off here, it came back to me."

"Please, don't talk about that. Did you get gas?"

"Full tank, pump number three. And these chocolate bars. I'm Woody."

"Thank you for yesterday, Woody. Please, don't talk about it anymore. That'll be twenty-two dollars."

He handed her the money.

"Colleen, is everything alright?"

"Everything is fine."

A customer came in, and she asked Woody to leave.

He complied. She disconcerted him.

Colleen was the only employee at the gas station. She spent her days alone there. She couldn't be any older than twenty-two, she hadn't gone beyond high school and was already married to a guy from Madison, a truck driver who spent several days a week on the road. She had a sad gaze. A shy way of not looking her customers in the eye.

The gas station was her only horizon. It was probably the reason why she took such pride in looking after the place. The adjacent shop was clean and always well-stocked. There were even a few tables where people passing through could stop for a coffee or an industrial-sized sandwich that Colleen heated up in a microwave. When the customers went away again, they always left a small tip on the table, and she would slip it into her pocket without mentioning it to her husband. As soon as the weather was fine, she would put the tables and chairs out on the strip of lawn next to the building.

There were not many places to go out in Madison, and students always gathered in the same places. When they wanted to be alone, Woody and Hillel went to the gas station.

Troubled by his nocturnal encounter with Colleen, Woody began hanging out at the gas station. Sometimes it was on the pretext of buying chewing gum or windshield wash. More often than not he dragged Hillel along with him.

"Why do you absolutely have to go all the way out there?" Hillel eventually asked.

"There's something not right. I want to figure it out."

"Why don't you just admit you have the hots for her?"

"Hill, that girl was walking in the dark, by the side of the road, crying her eyes out."

"Maybe her car broke down."

"She was scared. She was afraid."

"Afraid of who?"

"I don't know."

"Wood, you can't protect everyone."

Because they spent a lot of time there, they eventually managed to get to know Colleen a bit better. She was not as shy, and she even would stop and chat with them from time to time. She sold them beer even though they were under age. Colleen said she didn't risk anything selling them alcohol because Luke's father – Luke was her husband – was the local chief of police. And this Luke, it turned out, was a strange bird, according to my cousins. He seemed ornery and was always rather unpleasant. Woody sometimes ran into him at the gas station and he didn't like him. He said he got a weird feeling when he saw him. When Luke was in town, Colleen behaved differently. She seemed happier when he was away.

I also had the opportunity to go to the gas station during my visits to Madison. I noticed at once that Colleen liked Woody. She had a special way of looking at him. She almost never smiled, except when she was talking to him. It was a clumsy, spontaneous smile, which she quickly forced herself to hide.

At first I thought Woody was getting soft on Colleen. But then I soon realized he was not. Because both my cousins liked one and the same girl: Alexandra.

Alexandra was in her fourth and final year of college. Then she would be gone. They thought about no-one else. It didn't take me long to figure out that their indestructible friendship was not enough. Their life together on campus, their times out together, their football games did not fully satisfy them. They wanted more. They wanted her love. I became absolutely convinced of this when I saw how they reacted once it became obvious she was seeing someone: one weekend when Patrick Neville invited them over, they took the opportunity to search her room. They told me about it at Thanksgiving, and Hillel showed me what he had found in one of her desk drawers. A cardboard drawing of a red heart.

"You searched her room?" I said, stunned.

"Yes," Hillel said.

"Are you guys completely crazy?"

Hillel was furious with her.

"Why didn't she tell us she had a boyfriend?"

"And what makes you think she's seeing someone now?" I answered. "Maybe this drawing is old."

"There are two toothbrushes in the bathroom next to her room," Woody said.

"You even went into her bathroom?"

"Why shouldn't we! I thought she was our friend, and friends tell each other everything."

"Well, good for her if she has a boyfriend," I said.

"Yeah sure, good for her."

"Sounds like it annoys you."

"We're her friends, and I think she ought to tell us."

The friendship that legitimized their threesome concealed much deeper feelings, in spite of the pact that we had made in the Hamptons.

In the months that followed they became obsessed with the idea that Alexandra had a lover. They wanted to find out who he was, at any cost. When they asked her, she swore she was not seeing anyone. That drove them even crazier. On campus they followed her, to spy on her. They tried to listen to her telephone conversations using Hillel's old recording device, which he had brought from Baltimore for the purpose. They even questioned Patrick, who did not have a clue.

At the end of May 2000, we all went to Alexandra's graduation.

After the official part, during a moment when everyone was standing around waiting, Alexandra slipped out. She didn't notice that Woody was following her.

She headed straight to the science building where I was waiting for her. When she saw me, she leapt into my arms and gave me a long kiss.

Just then Woody appeared; dumbfounded, he shouted, "So it's you, Marcus? You've been her guy all along?"

24

On that day in May 2000, I had no choice but to explain myself to Woody and tell him everything.

He was the only person who knew about my wonderful relationship with Alexandra.

It had all started up again between Alexandra and me that fall, just after our last vacation in the Hamptons. I had gone back to Montclair feeling somewhat sorry that I had seen her again, only to find out that I was still in love with her. And then a few weeks later, as I was leaving the high school, I saw her sitting on the hood of her little car. I could not hide my excitement.

"Alexandra, what are you doing here?"

She was wearing a sullen, pouty expression.

"I wanted to see you again."

"I thought you didn't go out with little kids."

"Get in, stupid."

"Where are we going?"

"I don't know yet."

Where were we going? Down the road of life. From that day on, when I sat in the passenger seat of her car, we were in the grip of an inseparable, passionate love. We called and wrote all the time, and she sent me parcels. She came to Montclair on the weekend, and sometimes I borrowed my mother's old car and drove to New York or Madison, radio on full blast. We had my parents' blessing, and Patrick Neville's, and they promised not to tell anyone. Because it seemed preferable for my cousins not to find out. And so I broke the oath of the Goldman Gang, the promise never to make Alexandra my own.

The following year, when I started at the faculty of arts at Burrows College, we were only one hour apart. My roommate Jared let me have the room to myself on weekends, and Alexandra would join me. And I did something to my cousins that I had never done: I lied to them. I lied so I could go and be with Alexandra. I said I was in Boston, or Montclair, when in fact I was in New York with her. And when they were in New York with Patrick Neville, I was snug in her bed in Madison.

I still felt jealous from time to time, in spite of everything, knowing that the three of them were together at college, and I envied that special closeness she had with them. One day she eventually said, "Are you jealous of your cousins, Marcus? You're completely crazy! All three of you are completely crazy, in fact." She was right. I was not possessive by nature, and I did not fear rivals, but I dreaded the other members of the Goldman Gang. Then she came out with this odd, innocuous remark that to me was like a dagger in the heart: "You won, Markie. You won, you got me. What more do you want? You're not going to cause a scene just because I go and have hamburgers with your cousins?"

I was the one who got her into music again. I was the one who encouraged her to pursue her dream. Who made her go back to playing in bars in New York, and persevere with her composition in her student room at Madison. She was determined now, once she finished her studies, to take control of her destiny, and she was about to sign with a New York producer and launch her career.

After I had confessed everything, Woody promised not to say anything to Hillel.

He did not judge me. He simply said, "You're lucky to have her, Markie," and he honored me with a friendly slap on the shoulder.

We started our third year in college in the fall of 2000, and Woody began devoting more time to football and to Colleen, with whom he had become quite close. We were twenty years old.

I think he was very sad because of Alexandra. But he never said anything to Hillel, and he turned to sports for consolation. He was forever training. Sometimes he went running twice a day, the way he used to in the special school days. He became the Titans' star player. The team was chalking up one victory after the other, while Woody added to his star performances. He was on the front page of the college magazine's fall issue.

He went to see Colleen at the gas station every day. I think he needed someone to look after him. When he brought her the college magazine, she told him she was proud of him. But two days later he found her with marks on her neck. He saw red.

"What happened?" he said.

"Go away, Woody."

"Colleen, did Luke do that? Is your husband beating you?"

She begged him to go away and he obeyed. For three days running, each time he came to the gas station she motioned to him discreetly to indicate that he had to leave. The fourth day, she was waiting for him outside. He got out of the car and went up to her. She didn't say a word but took him by the hand and led him into the storeroom. Then she sought his lips and kissed him.

"Colleen . . . you have to tell me what's going on," Woody murmured.

"It's Luke . . . he found the college magazine in the drawer by the counter. He went ballistic."

"Did he hit you?"

"It's not the first time."

"Bastard. Where is he?"

She could tell that Woody would like nothing better than to go after him.

"He left this morning, for Maine. He'll be back tomorrow night. But don't do anything, Woody, please. You'd only make things worse."

"So I'm supposed to just stand here with my arms crossed while he beats you up?"

"We'll find a solution."

"And in the meanwhile?"

"In the meanwhile, just love me," she murmured. "Love me the way I've never been loved."

He kissed her again, then took her, tenderly, there in the storeroom. He felt good with her.

Their emotional connection grew stronger every time Luke went away. For part of the week, when Woody was in Madison, she was his. Ever since Luke had found the magazine, he was on his guard. He watched her constantly, controlled her more than ever. Woody couldn't go near her. He kept watch from a distance, both at the gas station and at their house.

Then Luke drove off in his truck. And it was a liberation for Colleen. Once she finished work at the gas station, she went into her garden and out the back, met Woody in a nearby street, and they went off together. He took her with him on campus; she wouldn't see anyone she knew there. She felt safe.

One evening, in the bed in the room Hillel had lent them, as she was curled up against him after lovemaking, he noticed bruises on her naked back.

"Why don't you file a complaint? He'll end up killing you."

"His father is chief of police in Madison and his brother is deputy," Colleen reminded him. "There's nothing I can do."

"I suppose Luke was too stupid to become a cop."

"He wanted to. But he has a police record, for assault."

"Then why don't you go file a complaint someplace else?"

"Because it's all the Madison jurisdiction. And besides, I don't want to."

"I don't know if I can do this, watch you being mistreated like this."

"Finish your studies, Woody. Then you'll come for me, and take me far away from here."

*

But they could not go on like that for very long. Luke suspected something was up and began making sure she was at home. Colleen had to call him the minute she left the gas station, then again from the house. Then he would call her back, without warning, to make sure she was really there. It was not in her interest to miss a call. She paid a heavy price one evening when she went next door to help with a leak in her neighbor's kitchen.

When Luke went away and Woody was able to see her again, he got the impression she'd been in a tornado. But even those moments were becoming less frequent.

Luke's brother began stopping off at the gas station on a regular basis to see who might be lurking around. Then he began waiting for her at the end of the day to escort her home. "I just want to make sure you get home safely," he said. "You never know who might be hanging around the street these days."

The situation was getting serious. Woody kept an eye on Colleen from a distance. To go any closer would be dangerous. Hillel often went with him. The two of them would sit hiding in the car. They watched the gas station, or the house. Sometimes, with Hillel acting as lookout, Woody ventured inside and spent a few minutes with Colleen.

One evening when they were driving in the vicinity of the house, a police car flagged them down. Woody pulled over onto the shoulder and Luke's father got out of the squad car. He went up to him, checked on their identity then said to Woody:

"Listen carefully, bud. Stick to football and watch where you put your dick. Above all, don't go making trouble. Got it?"

"How did you know I play football?" Woody said.

The father gave him an insincere smile.

"I like to know who I'm dealing with."

The boys drove off, back to campus.

"You better be careful, Wood," Hillel said. "This whole business is starting to get out of hand."

"I know. But what am I supposed to do? Knock her husband flying once and for all?"

Hillel shook his head, helpless.

"I don't want anything to happen to you, Woody. And I have to admit this whole business is making me nervous."

*　*　*

That year, for the first time, I wasn't with my cousins on Thanksgiving. Two days earlier, they had informed me that Patrick Neville had invited them to a party some Giants players would be attending. I decided to go to Baltimore all the same. As I had done all through childhood, I went the day before, by train. But in Baltimore, to my utter disappointment, no-one was waiting for me on the platform. I took a taxi to Oak Park. As we pulled up outside the Baltimore house, I saw Aunt Anita coming out.

"Good God, Markie!" she said when she saw me. "I had completely forgotten you were coming this evening."

"It's no big deal. I'm here now."

"You know your cousins aren't here."

"I know."

"Markie, I am so terribly sorry. I'm on duty tonight at the hospital. I have to go. Your uncle will be pleased to see you. There's some food ready in the fridge."

She gave me a hug. And as she did, I felt that something had changed. She seemed tired, and sad. I no longer saw in her that brilliant light that had so often caused my childish, then adolescent, heart to sing.

I went in. I found Uncle Saul in front of the television. Like Aunt Anita, he welcomed me with a mixture of warmth and sadness. I went upstairs to leave my things in one of the guestrooms, and I wondered what was the point of all these rooms if they were empty. I walked down the endless hallways, and into the huge bathrooms. I went through each of the three living rooms, all in darkness. No fire in the hearth, no television on, no books or newspapers lying open, waiting for an impatient reader to pick them up again. I found Uncle Saul fixing our dinner. He had set two places at the bar. There had been a time, not that long ago, when sitting at that same bar Hillel, Woody, Saul and I, noisily champing at the bit, would hand our plates across to Aunt Anita, and she would bestow her radiant smile on her little troop, then turn back to the Teflon griddle where she was cooking gargantuan amounts of pancakes, eggs, and turkey bacon.

We didn't say much while we ate supper. Saul didn't seem very hungry. The only thing he talked about was the Baltimore Ravens.

"Don't you want to come and see a game for once? I have tickets, but no-one is interested. They're having a great season, you know. I told you I know quite a few people in the Ravens' ownership group?"

"Yes, Uncle Saul."

"Then come and see a game. Tell your cousins. I have free tickets, in a box and everything."

After the meal, I went for a walk through the neighborhood. I gave a friendly wave to neighbors walking their dogs, as if I knew them. When I passed a security guard in his patrol car I made the secret sign and he responded. But the gesture was pointless: the blessed days of our childhood were lost forever, impossible to recover. The Baltimore Goldmans belonged to the past now.

* * *

That same evening, while I was in Baltimore and my cousins were in New York, Colleen came home late. She got out of the car and ran toward the house. She turned the knob, but the door was locked. He had already left. She looked at her watch: it was seven twenty-two. She could have cried. She opened the door with her key and went into the dark house. She knew that when he got back he would punish her.

She wasn't supposed to get home late from the gas station. She knew this, Luke had told her so. She closed at seven, and at seven fifteen she had to be home. If she wasn't, Luke would go out. He'd spend some time in a bar he liked, and when he came home, he'd deal with her.

That night she waited until eleven o'clock. She wished she could have called Woody, but she didn't want to get him involved. She knew it would end badly. At times like this she felt like running away. But where would she go?

Luke came into the house and slammed the door. She jumped. He was standing on the threshold to the living room.

"I'm sorry," she moaned at once, to appease his anger.

"What the fuck were you doing? Huh? Huh? You finish at seven. Seven! Why do you make me wait around like a fuckin' asshole? You think I'm stupid, right?"

"Please forgive me, Luke. Some customers arrived at seven, and the time it took to close, it made me five minutes late."

"You finish at seven, I want you home at seven fifteen! Is that so hard to understand? But you always want to act smart."

"But Luke, it takes time to close everything."

"Quit moaning, will you? Go get your ass in my car."

"Luke, no!" she begged.

He held up a threatening finger.

"You better do what I say."

She went out and climbed into his pickup. He joined her and started the car.

"Forgive me, Luke, forgive me," she said nervously. "I won't be late again."

But he wasn't listening. He heaped insults upon her. She burst into tears. They left Madison, and Luke headed down route 5, dead straight. He drove over the Lebanon bridge and kept on going. She begged him to turn around and go home. He sniggered. "What, you don't like being with me?" Then suddenly he stopped in the middle of nowhere.

"End of the line, everyone out," he said, in a tone that brooked no protest.

In vain she protested: "Luke, please, don't do this."

"Get out!" he shouted.

The moment he shouted, she knew she had to obey. She climbed out of the car and he drove away at once, abandoning her eight miles from home. This was her punishment: to walk home in the middle of the night, all the way to Madison. She vanished into the damp mist, wearing as usual only a short dress and thin pantyhose. The dark swallowed her up.

The first time, she had protested. When Luke, yelling until he turned crimson, had ordered her to get out, she had rebelled. She told him that no-one treated their wife like this. He got out of the car.

"Come on then, angel, come here," he had said, almost tenderly.

"What for?"

"Because I'm going to punish you. I'm going to beat you so that you'll understand that when I give you an order you have to obey."

She immediately apologized: "I'm sorry, I didn't mean to make you angry. I'll go, I'll do what you want. Forgive me, Luke. I didn't mean to make you mad."

So she got out of the car and headed off down the road, but she hadn't gone five yards before Luke's voice caught up with her.

"You didn't get what I said, did you? Maybe we don't speak the same language?"

"Yes, Luke. You told me to leave, so I'm leaving."

"That was before! Now the orders have changed. What did I say, huh?"

She burst into tears, terrified.

"I don't know, Luke. Forgive me, I don't understand anything anymore."

"I told you to come over here so I can punish you. Or did you forget?"

She felt her legs begin to buckle.

"Forgive me, Luke, I've learned my lesson. I promise I won't disobey anymore."

"Come here!" he screamed, not moving. "When I tell you to come here, you do what I say! Why do you always try and act so smart, huh?"

"I'm sorry, Luke, I was an idiot, I won't do it again."

"Come here, for fuck's sake. Come here or I'll give you a double dose."

"No, Luke, please!"

"Get over here!"

She went closer, terrified, and stood before him.

"Five nice slaps now, O.K.?"

"I . . ."

"O.K.?"

"Yes, Luke."

"I want you to count them."

She stood in front of him, and he raised his hand. She closed her eyes, weeping uncontrollably. He gave her a colossal slap that knocked her to the ground. She screamed.

"I said, count!"

She was sobbing, on her knees on the damp asphalt.

"One . . ." she muttered, between two sobs.

"Good! Now, on your feet!"

She got back up. He slapped her again. She bent double, her hands on her cheeks.

"Two!" she screamed.

"Good. Now go on, get back in position."

She obeyed, he straightened her head and slapped her again as hard as he could.

"Three!"

She fell over backwards.

"Come on, come on, don't stay there, get up. And I didn't hear you count."

"Four," she sobbed.

"You see, we're nearly done. Come on, come stand in front of me, nice and straight."

When he'd finished hitting her, he ordered her to get out of his sight and she fled. She had already walked for an hour when she reached the bridge by Lebanon. It was not even half-way to Madison. She had taken off her heels, which hurt and slowed her down, and she walked on the cold, rough asphalt in her bare feet. Suddenly headlights lit up the road. A car was coming. The driver only noticed her at the last moment and nearly hit her. He stopped at once. She had already seen the boy at the gas station. That was the night she had met Woody.

Ever since, if she came home late from work, Luke left her out on the deserted road and forced her to walk home. That night when she arrived home at last, she found Luke had locked the door from the inside. She lay down on the little sofa on the porch and fell asleep, shivering from the cold.

Woody was increasingly worried. Hillel shared his concerns with me in the early days of 2001.

"I don't know why he suddenly got so fond of that girl. But for six months now all he can think of is saving her. I think he's changed. Do you know anything?"

"No."

I was lying. I knew that Woody was trying to forget Alexandra by taking care of Colleen. He wanted to save himself by saving her. I also realized that when Hillel joined Woody on his nighttime surveillance of Colleen's house, it was not for the sake of his company but to keep watch on Woody himself; he wanted to stop him from doing something stupid.

He was not able to prevent a confrontation between Luke and Woody that February, in a bar in Madison.

* * *

Madison, Connecticut
February 2001

Woody was driving down the Main Street in Madison when he noticed Luke's pickup parked outside a bar. He slammed on the brakes and pulled in next to him. Luke had not been on any delivery runs for ten days now. Ten days during which Woody had not seen Colleen. Ten days when he had been forced to observe her from a distance. One evening, a few days earlier, he had heard shouts coming from their house, but Hillel managed to keep him from getting out of the car to intervene. It was time for this to stop.

He went in and found Luke at the bar counter. He headed straight for him.

"Well, well, if it isn't our football player!" Luke said. He had already had one too many.

"You better watch it, Luke," Woody said.

Luke was at least ten years older than him. He was sturdier, with a broader build, thick hands, and a cantankerous expression.

"You got a problem, football player?" asked Luke, standing up straight.

"I have a problem with you. I want you to leave Colleen alone."

"Oh, yeah? You want to tell me how I'm supposed to take care of my own wife?"

"Exactly. Stop taking care of her, period. She doesn't love you."

"You think you can talk to me like that, asshole? You got two seconds to get out of here."

"If you so much as lay a finger on her—"

"Yeah, and then what!"

"I'll kill you."

"Fucking asshole!" Luke shouted, grabbing hold of Woody. "You're just a fucking asshole!"

Woody shook him off, pushed him away, then landed him a right in the face. Luke punched him back and some of the patrons in the bar rushed over to pull them apart. There was a moment of confusion, then the sound of sirens in the distance. Luke's father and brother strode into the bar to calm things down. They arrested Woody and shoved him into the police car. They left town and took him to a deserted quarry, where they clubbed him until he passed out.

He came to a few hours later, his face swollen, one shoulder dislocated. He dragged himself to the road and waited for a passing car.

Eventually one stopped and drove him to the hospital in Madison, where Hillel went to find him. His injuries were only superficial, but he would have to be careful with his shoulder.

"What happened, Woody? I looked for you half the night."

"Nothing."

"Woody, you got off easy this time. Any more and you'd never be able to play football again. Is that what you want? To completely fuck up your career?"

Colleen, too, paid a heavy price for Woody's intervention.

When he saw her one week later at the gas station, she had a black eye and a torn lip.

"What did you do, Woody?"

"I wanted to stick up for you."

"It's better if we don't see each other anymore."

"But Colleen—"

"I asked you to stay away."

"I wanted to protect you."

"We mustn't see each other anymore. It's better like this. Please, just go away!"

He did as she asked.

Spring vacation came a few weeks later. Hillel and I made the most of it to get Woody away from Madison, to get his mind on other things: we took him to spend ten days at the Buenavista.

The stay in Florida coincided with a sudden, serious deterioration in Grandfather Goldman's health. He contracted pneumonia and it left him feeling very weak. When we left Florida, Grandfather was still in the hospital. Aunt Anita said he wouldn't survive much longer. He was able to leave the hospital and go back to the residence, but he was bedridden. We went to visit him every morning, early: after a night's rest, he felt like talking. He may not have had much strength left, but he had all his wits about him. One day while we were talking, Woody said, "Actually, Grandfather, I just realized I don't even know what you did in life."

Grandfather gave him a luminous smile.

"I was the C.E.O. of Goldman and Company."

"What was that?"

"A small firm manufacturing medical equipment. I founded it myself. It was my life's adventure. Can you imagine, Goldman and Company existed for over forty years. I used to like going to the office: we were in a nice red brick building you could see from the road, and you could read, in big capital letters: GOLDMAN. I was very proud of it."

"But where was it? In Baltimore?"

"No, in New York state. And we lived a few miles away, in Secaucus, New Jersey."

"Whatever happened to Goldman and Company?" Woody said.

"We sold it. Marcus, you were already born but you wouldn't remember. It was in the mid-1980s."

Grandfather had aroused Woody's curiosity, and he asked if there were any photographs from the Goldman and Company era. Grandmother dug out a shoebox where all sorts of photographs were stowed, higgledy-piggledy. Most of them had been taken recently: there were a lot of unfamiliar faces – friends of theirs from Florida – and a few snaps of Grandfather and Grandmother together. Then finally we found a photograph of Grandfather outside the famous Goldman and Company building, and we gazed at it for a long time. There were also a few pictures of Hillel, Woody, and myself as adolescents, taken during one of our stays in Florida.

"The Goldman Gang," Grandfather said, waving the picture, and we all burst out laughing.

May the memory of our grandfather Max Goldman be honored. He died six weeks later. What I have kept of those last moments with him is the image of his vivacity and sense of humor, even at the threshold to his final dwelling.

I can still remember his gentle laughter. And I remember his demanding nature. The way he walked, and his invariable elegance. There is not a single ceremony or awards event or important meeting that does not, when the time comes for me to put a tie around my neck, make me think of him, always impeccably dressed.

Glory to you, oh my beloved grandfather. I hope you know how much I miss you here on earth. I like to think you're looking down on me from up there, and that you have been following my career with a mixture of amusement and emotion. So you will know that my digestion is excellent and I do not suffer from irritable bowel syndrome. Perhaps I owe it to the masses of All-Bran you made me consume in Florida, while you looked on with a kindly gaze. I want you to know, too, that I thank you for everything you brought me; may you rest in peace.

25

Grandfather was buried on May 30, 2001 in Secaucus, New Jersey, the town where he and Grandmother had raised my father and Uncle Saul. Several of his friends from Florida had insisted on coming all the way for the funeral.

I was sitting next to my cousins. Alexandra was there, too, one row behind us. I put my hand just behind me and she took it discreetly and gave it a squeeze. I felt strong with her nearby.

I know that later on that day, Woody said to her, "It's a fine love you have for him."

She smiled.

"And you?" she said. "Hillel told me about this girl, Colleen?"

"She's married. It's complicated. I'm not seeing her anymore for now."

"Do you love her?"

"I don't know. I care about her. She makes me feel less alone. But she's not you."

The ceremony was in the image of my grandfather: sober yet full of humor. My father gave a witty speech, where his reference to the boxes of All-Bran caused howls of laughter. Uncle Saul spoke next, more solemnly. This is how he began his eulogy: "This is the first time I've been back to New Jersey. As some of you may know, my relationship with my dad was not always sunny . . . "

This struck me as a strange thing to say. It did not seem to reflect the relationship I had witnessed during the heyday of the Baltimores.

After the ceremony and the meal, Grandmother wanted to go for a drive around Secaucus. I had never been there, so I offered to take her.

Because I wanted to know what Uncle Saul had been referring to, the moment we were alone I put my question to her.

"What was Uncle Saul talking about just now?"

Grandmother pretended not to hear, looking out the window.

"Grandmother?"

"Markie," she said, "this isn't the time for questions."

"Did something happen between them?" I insisted.

"Markie, just keep on driving and be quiet, please. You want to bore me with your questions on a day like this?"

"Sorry, Grandmother."

I said nothing more. She showed me the way to their old house, which was mortgaged when Goldman and Company's financial situation began to falter. Then she asked me to drive her to the old factory. I had never been there so she gave me directions. We drove for a good twenty minutes, leaving New Jersey behind and crossing into New York state, until we reached a deserted industrial zone. Grandmother made me stop outside an abandoned red brick building and waved a finger toward the facade: "That was my office," she said, pointing to a hole in the wall, which must have been a window at one time.

"What did you do there?"

"All the books. I managed the finances. Your grandfather was a peerless salesman, but for every dollar he earned, he spent two. I held the purse strings, both at the factory and at home."

By the time I took Grandmother back to the parking lot at the cemetery, the Baltimores were getting impatient, sitting in the big chauffeur-driven limousine that would take them back to Manhattan. Uncle Saul had booked rooms at the Plaza for Grandmother and all the Baltimores. The Montclairs, on the other hand, would stay in Montclair.

The next day Uncle Saul asked me to come and see him at his hotel, which I did. He convened Woody, Hillel and me in a quiet corner of the bar in the Plaza and informed us that in his last will and testament Grandfather had requested that one of his savings accounts be equally divided among "his three grandchildren". There would be a sum of $20,000 for each of the three of us.

*   *   *

One week after the funeral, I went with Grandmother back to Florida. I took the plane with her and spent a few days in Miami so she wouldn't be alone. Uncle Saul lent me his apartment at the Buenavista.

My being at her old people's home was a great comfort to her. I can still see her as she was the day we got back to Miami, smoking on her patio, staring vacantly out at the ocean. On the table in her tiny living room she had left a shoe box full of old photographs. I picked up a few at random and as I didn't recognize either the people or the places, I started asking her about them. Her replies were halfhearted, and I could tell that I was disturbing her desire for some peace and quiet. But suddenly she started talking about her belongings in the storage warehouse.

"What storage warehouse?"

"Over in Aventura. The address is in the key cabinet."

"And what's there?"

"All the family albums. Since you want to see photographs, you may as well go over there. They're sorted, classified, and annotated. Do what you want with them, just so long as you stop asking all your questions."

To this day I don't know if she mentioned them to me so I would go looking for them, or just so I would go away. My curiosity was aroused, so I went to the storage warehouse and there I found, as she had promised, the lives of the Goldmans in thousands of photographs, sorted and arranged in dusty albums. I opened them at random; I found our younger faces, and everything we used to be. I went back in time, through different eras, and I enjoyed looking for myself. There I was as an infant; there was the house in Montclair with a fresh coat of paint. I saw myself naked in a plastic swimming pool on our lawn. I saw the pictures of my first birthday parties, but soon realized that the most important characters were missing from all these photographs. First I thought it must be just coincidence or a mistake in the way they had been classified. I spent several hours going through the albums but by then I had to face the facts: we were everywhere, they were nowhere. There were Montclairs galore, whereas the Baltimores seemed to be *persona non grata*. Not a single picture of Hillel as a little boy – neither as an infant, nor his birthdays. No photographs of Uncle Saul and Aunt Anita's wedding, whereas my parents were entitled to three whole albums. The first snaps of Hillel dated from when he was at least five. It would seem that for a long time, in my grandparents' archives, the Baltimore Goldmans did not exist.

Grandmother Ruth must have imagined I would stay there in the storage warehouse forever, and she'd be able to sit smoking out on her patio without ever being disturbed. To her dismay, I came back to her tiny apartment with my arms full of family albums.

"Markie, why are you burdening me with all that stuff? If I had known you would do that, I would never have told you about the warehouse!"

"Grandmother, where were they all these years?"

"What are you talking about, sweetheart? The albums?"

"No, the Baltimore Goldmans. Until Hillel turned five, there's not a single picture of any of the Baltimore Goldmans."

Initially she looked annoyed, and she waved her arm as if to banish any hope of a conversation.

"Bah," she said, "leave the past alone, it's better that way."

I thought again of the strange eulogy Uncle Saul had given at Grandfather's funeral.

"But Grandmother," I insisted, "it's as if at some point they disappeared off the face of the earth."

She gave me a sad smile.

"You don't know how right you are, Markie. Did you never wonder why your uncle ended up in Baltimore? For more than ten years, Uncle Saul and your grandfather did not exchange a single word."

26

The academic year was already over when at the end of June 2001, after Grandfather's funeral, Woody went back to Madison. He desperately wanted to see Colleen again.

She wasn't at the gas station. A girl he didn't know had replaced her. He went to wait near her neighborhood. He noticed Luke's pickup outside the house: so Luke was there. Woody sank lower in the seat of his car and waited. There was no sign of Colleen. He spent the night in the street.

The next morning at dawn, Luke left the house. He was carrying a bag. He climbed into his pickup and drove off. Woody followed from a safe distance. They came to the offices of the transport company Luke worked for. One hour later, Luke left again, at the wheel of a huge truck. Woody didn't have to worry for at least twenty-four hours.

He went back to the house. Knocked on the door. No answer. He knocked again, tried to peer through the windows. No-one seemed to be there. Suddenly he heard a voice behind him and he gave a start.

"She's not there."

He turned around. It was one of the neighbors.

"I'm sorry, Mrs —?"

"Are you looking for little Colleen?"

"Yes, Ma'am."

"She's not here."

"Do you know where she is?"

The neighbor had a sad expression.

"She's in the hospital, son."

*

Woody drove at once to the hospital in Madison. He found her in bed, wearing a neck brace, her face swollen. She had been severely beaten. When she saw him, her eyes lit up.

"Woody!"

"Ssh, stay calm."

He wanted to kiss her, touch her, but he was afraid he would hurt her.

"Woody, I thought you'd never come back."

"I'm here now."

"I'm sorry I sent you away. I need you."

"I'm not going anywhere. I'm here now."

Woody knew that if he didn't do something, Luke would end up killing her. But how could he protect her? He asked Hillel's advice, who in turn went to ask Uncle Saul and Patrick Neville for help. Woody had some wild ideas to try and trap Luke: place a gun and some weed in his car, then contact the state police. But everything would point to him. Hillel knew that to corner Luke, he had to be made to leave his father's jurisdiction. He came up with an idea.

* * *

Madison, Connecticut
July 1, 2001

Colleen left her house at the beginning of the afternoon. She put her suitcase in the trunk of her car and drove off. One hour later, Luke came home. He found the note she had left on the kitchen table.

I'm gone. I want a divorce.

If you're prepared to talk calmly, I'll be at the Days Inn motel on Route 38.

Luke flew into a rage. She wanted to talk? Just wait and see. He'd soon make her change her mind. He jumped into his car and drove like a lunatic to the motel. He immediately saw her car, parked outside a room. He rushed over and pounded on the door.

"Colleen! Open up."

She felt a sudden knot in her stomach.

"Luke, I'll only open if you calm down."

"Open this door, now."

"No, Luke."

He pounded on the door as hard as he could. Colleen could not help but cry out.

Hillel and Woody were in the next room. Hillel picked up the phone and called the police. An operator answered.

"There's a guy beating up his wife," Hillel said. "I think he's about to kill her."

Luke was still outside, furiously banging and kicking the door. Hillel, after hanging up, looked at his watch, waited until one minute had gone by, then nodded to Woody, who called Colleen's room. She picked up.

"Are you ready, Colleen?"

"Yes."

"It will be fine."

"I know."

"You're very brave."

"I'm doing it for us."

"I love you."

"I love you, too."

"Now, go ahead."

She hung up, took a deep breath, and opened the door. Luke rushed at her and began to strike her. Her screams could be heard out on the motel parking lot. Woody left his room, took a knife from his pocket, and slashed the rear tire on Luke's pickup, then hightailed it out of there, his stomach twisted in fear.

Luke was still hitting her. And there was no sound of a police siren.

"Stop!" Colleen begged, in tears, curled up on the floor in a fetal position to protect herself from his kicks.

Luke yanked her up by her hair, and figured she had gotten what she deserved. He dragged her out of the room and forced her into the pickup. Alarmed by her screams, guests were emerging from their rooms, but did not dare intervene.

At last they could hear sirens. Two police cars arrived just as Luke was gunning the pickup to tear out of the parking lot. He didn't get any further; his flat tire brought him to a halt. He was arrested in the minutes that followed.

By driving to the motel, he had crossed the border into New York state. That was where he would be incarcerated while waiting to be tried for assault and battery, and false imprisonment.

* * *

The Goldmans took Colleen in for some time in Baltimore. For her, it was a rebirth. During the month of August she came with Woody, Hillel, and me to Florida. Grandmother needed help sorting through Grandfather's affairs.

We did not need to be there all four of us to go through the books and documents Grandfather had left behind. So we sent Woody and Colleen off to spend some time alone. They rented a car and went down to the Keys.

Hillel and I spent a week going through Grandfather's papers.

We agreed that I would deal with the archives and Hillel the legal documents. When I found Grandfather's last will and testament in a drawer I handed it to Hillel without even reading it.

Hillel looked at it slowly. Then he made a strange face.

"Everything alright?" I said. "You look funny all of a sudden."

"I'm fine. Just hot. I'm going out on the balcony to get some air."

I saw him fold the paper in two and leave the room, taking it with him.

27

At the beginning of September 2001, Luke was sentenced to three years' prison in New York State. This was a deliverance for Colleen, who filed for divorce at the same time. She could move back to Madison with complete peace of mind.

This was also the beginning of our fourth and final year at college. And the year Madison's Burger-Shake Stadium became the Saul Goldman Stadium.

I remember the ceremony, when they changed the name; it was on Saturday, September 8. Uncle Saul was beaming. All the university digni‐taries were present. There was a curtain obscuring the massive metal letters, and once the president had given his speech, Uncle Saul pulled on a cord to reveal the letters and the stadium's new identity. For some reason I could not figure out, the only person missing that day was Aunt Anita.

A few days later came the September 11 attacks on New York. Madison, like the rest of the country, was in a state of shock, and only the success of the Titans drove the inhabitants away from their tele‐visions and back to the stadium.

It was the start of an exceptional season for Woody. He was playing his best football. There was nothing, at that point, that gave the slightest hint of what lay in store. This was the year that was going to establish the Titans' reputation. Woody was playing with an extraordinary rage to win. The season had only just started, but the Madison team was already wreaking havoc with the statistics, as they chalked up their victories and crushed their opponents one after the other. Their games attracted a record number of spectators and were always sold out, and Madison was reaping the benefits: restaurants were full, and shops quickly sold out of flags and jerseys with the team's colors. It was like a fever that spread throughout the entire region: everything seemed to indicate that the Titans were on course to win the college championship that year.

Among Woody's admirers was Colleen. Now she could proudly show her face alongside him in Madison. Whenever she could she closed the gas station a little earlier and went to watch him practice. And when he had some free time, he helped out at the gas station. He re-organized the store room, and manned the pumps now and again, and customers would say, "If I had known that a football champ was going to fill my tank today . . . "

Not only did all the students look on Woody as a star, he was also something of a mascot for the town of Madison, and one of the diners even added a special hamburger to the menu, called "The Woody". It consisted of four layers, with so much bread and meat that even a very big eater could hardly finish it. Those who did manage to got their meal for free, along with the honor of having their picture taken with a Polaroid and instantly posted on the wall, to the cheers of the other customers. And the manager would proudly repeat: "This Woody of ours is just like our Madison U Woody: no-one can get the better of it."

At Thanksgiving dinner in Baltimore, Woody asked the family if they would agree to let him change the name on his football jersey to Goldman. There was a flurry of excitement and emotion. For the first time, Woody had transcended us: thanks to him we were no longer Montclairs or Baltimores, we were Goldmans. At last we were all marching to the same tune.

One week later, the *Madison Daily Star*, the local paper, published a feature about the Baltimores, telling the story of Woody, Hillel, Aunt Anita and Uncle Saul. There was a photograph of the four of them, happy and smiling, holding up Woody's jersey with the name GOLDMAN printed on it.

*

While everyone had their eyes on Woody, admiring his path to sporting glory, in Baltimore Uncle Saul and Aunt Anita were slowly slipping into the shadows, and no-one noticed.

For a start, Uncle Saul lost a very important case he had been working on for several years. He had been defending a woman in a lawsuit against an insurance company for non-payment of her diabetic husband's medical care, which had led to his death. Uncle Saul had been suing for several million dollars' compensation. The case was dismissed.

Then sudden, significant signs of tension appeared between Saul and Aunt Anita. She wanted to know how much he had donated to the university to have his name on the stadium. He claimed it was next to nothing, that he had made a deal with the president. She did not believe him. He was behaving oddly. It wasn't like him to put himself forward. She knew he was very generous, and always attentive toward other people; he volunteered at soup kitchens, and never walked past a home-less person without giving them something. But he never spoke of it. Never bragged. He was modest and humble and that was why she loved him. Who was this man who suddenly wanted to have his name on a football stadium?

She did something she had never done in her entire married life: she searched his office, ferreted among his possessions, read his letters and his emails. She had to get to the bottom of this. And when she didn't find anything at home, one day when she knew he would be at the courthouse she went to his office and locked herself in, feeding some pretext to his assistants. She found some binders with his personal accounts and finally uncovered the truth: Uncle Saul had promised Madison University six million dollars. Initially she could not believe her eyes. She had to reread the documents several times over. How could her husband have done such a thing? Why? And above all, where – where had he found the money? What was he hiding from her? She felt as if she were in a nightmare. She waited in his office to demand an explanation, but his reaction to her discovery was calm and unruffled.

"You have no business going through my things. Especially here. I am bound by confidentiality."

"Don't try to evade the issue, Saul. Six million dollars! You promised six million dollars? Where did you find that amount of money?"

"It's none of your business!"

"Saul, you're my husband! How can it not be my business?"

"Because you wouldn't understand."

"Talk to me, Saul, please. Where did you get this money? What are you hiding? Do you have links with organized crime?"

He burst out laughing.

"Whatever gave you such an idea? Leave me alone now, please. It's late already, and I still have work to do."

I didn't know about any of this. When I wasn't at college, I was with Alexandra. I was living a life of total bliss with her. She knew me better than anyone, she understood me better than anyone. She could read my thoughts, and guess what I was about to say before I said it.

She had already finished college the year before and had been trying to break into the music world, but her career was not taking off. I didn't really like the producer she was working with. I thought he was too busy promoting her image rather than her music. He said it was all connected, but I didn't agree. Not with the kind of talent Alexandra had. I tried to tell her, I tried to make her listen to herself above all. She was composing really excellent songs; her producer, instead of helping her blossom further, spent his time reining in her creativity to make her fit a prefabricated mold, one that was supposed to please the greatest number. The structure went: introduction, verse, refrain, second verse, refrain, bridge, pre-refrain, conclusion. The first refrain lasted one minute. The producers committed the same sacrilege with music as with books and films: they standardized them.

Sometimes her discouragement got the better of her. She said she would never make it anywhere. That she'd do better to try something different. I tried to cheer her up: sometimes I would leave college and go to New York just for the night. And as a rule I found her shut in her room, depressed. I made her get changed and take out her guitar, and I took her to a bar with an open mic. Every time it was the same thing: she captivated the audience. The enthusiastic applause that greeted all her performances gave her a boost. She would walk off stage looking radiant. We'd go out for supper. She was happy again. She was once again my lovable chatterbox. She had forgotten her sorrows.

The world was our oyster.

* * *

I went nearly every weekend to Madison to watch Woody play. In the stands of the Saul Goldman Stadium I joined the crowd of his privileged supporters: Uncle Saul, Aunt Anita, Patrick Neville, Hillel, Alexandra, and Colleen.

Given all his victories, rumors began to fly: it was said that scouts from the biggest teams on the N.F.L. were coming to watch him every week. Patrick confirmed that representatives from the Giants would be coming. Uncle Saul assured us that executives from the Ravens were following the Titans very attentively. On game nights, Hillel tried to spot the scouts in the rows of seats in the stadium before he rushed into the locker room to report to Woody.

"Wood," he cried one evening, "I've seen at least one! He was glued to his phone, taking notes. I followed him out to the parking lot. He had Massachusetts license plates. You know what that means?"

"New England Patriots?" Woody asked, not really believing it.

"The New England Patriots, bro!" Hillel said exultantly.

To the cheers of the other players getting changed, they threw their arms around each other.

Twice, after a win, Uncle Saul and Aunt Anita were directly approached by observers from prestigious teams. The evening the Titans crushed the Cleveland Cougars – the only other unbeaten team in the championship that season, and the previous year's victors – Patrick Neville found Woody in the locker room with the scout from the New England Patriots, the same one Hillel had spotted a few weeks earlier. The man handed his card to Woody and said, "Young man, the Patriots would be glad to include you in their number."

"Oh my God! Thank you, sir," Woody said. "I don't know what to say. I have to talk to Hillel."

"Is Hillel your agent?" the scout wanted to know.

"No, Hillel is my buddy. I don't really have an agent, actually."

"I can be your agent," Patrick offered, spontaneously. "I've always dreamed of doing that sort of thing."

"That would be great," Woody said. "You'd do that?"

"Of course I would."

"Then I'll let you deal with my agent," Woody said with a smile to the scout.

The scout gave him a warm handshake.

"Good luck, kid. All you have to do now is win this championship. See you next time in the N.F.L.."

That night, contrary to their usual habit, Hillel and Woody did not celebrate the victory with the rest of the team. They were in their room with the door closed, and with Patrick, who was taking his new role as agent very seriously, discussing Woody's possibilities.

"We have to try and sign an option before the end of the year," Patrick said. "If you win the championship, it shouldn't be too difficult."

"How much will their initial offer be, do you think?" Hillel asked.

"That depends. But last month, the Patriots offered seven million to a college player."

"Seven million dollars?" Woody gasped.

"Seven million," Patrick repeated. "And believe me, kid, you're worth not a penny less. And if it isn't this year, it'll be next year. I'm not worried about your career."

Once Patrick had left, Woody and Hillel stayed up all night. Lying on their beds, eyes wide open, they were stunned by the potential value of the contract.

"What are you going to do with all that money?" Hillel said.

"Split it in two. Half for you and the other half for me."

Hillel smiled.

"Why would you do that?"

"Because you're like my brother, and brothers share everything."

At the beginning of December 2001, when they had just reached the championship semi-finals, the football league had the Titans undergo drug tests.

One week later, Woody did not show up at economics class after his morning practice. Hillel tried in vain to reach him on his cell phone. He decided to go and look for him at the stadium, but as he was crossing the campus he saw Patrick Neville's black Chevrolet Yukon pulling into the parking lot outside the administration building. Hillel realized something had happened. He ran up to Patrick.

"What's going on, Patrick?"

"Woody didn't tell you?"

"What was he supposed to tell me?"

"He failed the drugs test."

"*What*?"

"That idiot has been taking performance-enhancing drugs."

"But Patrick, that's impossible!"

Hillel followed Patrick into the president's office, where he found the president, Woody, slumped on the chair, and across from him an official from the college football league.

When Patrick came into the room, Woody jumped up from his chair, a desperate look on his face.

"I don't get it, Patrick!" he cried. "I swear I didn't take a thing!"

"What's going on?" Patrick said.

The president introduced Patrick to the league representative as

Woody's agent, then asked him to sum up the situation.

"Woody has tested positive for pentazocine. Subsequent tests have all yielded the same result. This is very serious. Pentazocine is an opioid and as such is strictly forbidden by the league."

"I wasn't taking stuff!" Woody shouted. "I swear! Why would I do something like that?"

"Woodrow, calm down, would you?" the official thundered. "Your performances have been too immaculate to be true."

"I caught a cold not long ago and the doctor prescribed vitamins. I only took what he told me to take. Why would I take any of that shit?"

"Because you were injured."

There was a brief silence.

"Who told you that?" Woody said.

"The team physician. You have tendinitis in your arm. And a torn ligament in your shoulder."

"I got in a fight last spring. The police beat me up! But that was at least eight months ago."

"Spare me your tales, Woody," the official interrupted.

"It's the truth, I swear!"

"Really, now? You weren't the victim of overtraining during the summer? I have a report from the team physician which states that subsequent to repeated pain he ordered an ultrasound of your arm that showed a fairly serious tendinitis which was due, according to him, to excessive repetitive motion."

Woody felt hounded. His eyes filled with tears.

"It's true, the doctor wanted me to stop for a while," he said. "But I really thought I could keep my place on the team. I know my body! I was going to get treatment after the championship. Do you really think I would've done something as stupid as doping just before the championship semi-finals?"

"Yes," replied the league official. "Because you're in too much pain to play without a painkiller. I think you took Talacen so you could play.

Everyone knows that it's an effective medication, and that its traces disappear rapidly from the bloodstream. I think you knew that very well and you thought that if you stopped taking it early enough before the championship final, we wouldn't find anything in a drug test. Or am I mistaken?"

There was a long silence.

"Woody, did you take that shit?" Patrick said eventually.

"No! I swear! Maybe the doctor made a mistake when I was sick."

"The doctor didn't prescribe any Talacen, Woodrow," replied the official. "We checked. It was vitamins."

"Then the pharmacy, when they were making up the tablets!"

"That's enough, Woodrow," the president said. "You are a disgrace to the university."

From the wall he took the framed cover of the campus magazine featuring Woody's face and tossed it into the wastebasket.

Patrick Neville turned to the president.

"So now what happens?"

"We have to discuss this. You understand that the situation is of grave concern. League rules call for suspension in these cases, and university regulations stipulate expulsion."

"Do you already have a contract with the New England Patriots?" the official said.

"No."

"It's just as well, because they could have claimed damages for prejudice to their image had that been the case."

There was a heavy silence. Then the official spoke again.

"Mr Neville, we've discussed this at length with the president. Madison's reputation is at stake, as is that of the championship. Everyone has been following Woody's exploits. If the general public gets wind of this doping affair, we will all suffer the consequences, and we want to avoid such a situation at all cost. But that doesn't mean turning a blind eye."

"So what are you suggesting?"

"A compromise that would be acceptable to everyone. Tell them Woody has hurt himself. He has a serious injury and can't play anymore. In exchange, the league will not take the investigation any further, and Madison's reputation will remain intact. Which means that the university's disciplinary council won't have to examine Woodrow and he'll be able to finish his studies here."

"Injured, for how long?"

"Forever."

"But if he stops playing, no N.F.L. club will want him."

"Mr Neville, I think you haven't grasped the gravity of the situation. If you refuse, we will open a disciplinary procedure, and everyone will find out. In the event of a disciplinary procedure, Woody will be expelled from the team and certainly from the university as well. You have the possibility to appeal, but you would lose because the tests are categorical. I am offering you the opportunity to bury the matter right now. *Quid pro quo.* The reputation of the Titans will be intact, and Woody can get his degree."

"But his career as a football player will be over," Patrick said.

"Yes. If you agree to this compromise, I'll give you twenty-four hours to set up a press conference to announce that Woody injured himself during practice and will never be able to play football again."

The official left the room. Woody held his face in his hands, speechless with dismay. Patrick and Hillel went off to confer on their own.

"Patrick," Hillel said, "there must be something we can do! This is crazy!"

"Hillel, he should never have taken the Talacen."

"But he never took any of that shit!"

"Hillel, I really don't think the pharmacy made a mistake when they gave him his vitamins. And his injuries are quite obvious."

"So what, even if he did voluntarily take some Talacen, it's only a painkiller, after all."

"It's a banned substance, according to the league."

"We can appeal."

"You heard the man: he'll lose. I know it and so do you. This is his only chance to save his spot in the university. If he appeals, the doping story will become public. He'll lose everything: the university will kick him out and no-one else will want to take him. He's a resourceful kid, he has to finish his studies. At least with this compromise he'll save his skin."

Just then Woody came out of the office. He planted himself in front of Hillel and Patrick. Wiping his tears with the back of his arm he said, "We won't appeal. I don't want anyone to know. I don't want Saul and Anita to hear about any of this. I'd die of shame if they learned the truth. I've been wearing the Goldman name on the jersey. I don't want to dishonor it."

Patrick scheduled a press conference for the following day.

Ladies and gentlemen, it is my duty to inform you of a development that comes as a severe blow for Madison University and the Titans. Our very promising captain, Woodrow Finn, has been seriously injured during a solo training session in the weights room. He has torn the ligaments in his shoulder and arm, and will probably never be able to play football again. A new captain will be appointed to replace him. We wish Woody a prompt recovery and all the best in choosing a new career.

At Woody's request, we kept the secret. Other than Patrick Neville, the only ones who knew the truth about the end of his career were Hillel, Alexandra, Colleen, and me.

The day of the press conference, Aunt Anita and Uncle Saul hurried to Madison, where they stayed for several days. Unaware of the true reasons behind Woody's retirement, they immediately began to think up ways to treat him. "We'll get you right as rain," Uncle Saul promised. Woody insisted that he was in too much pain to even think of trying to play again someday. Aunt Anita took him in for X-rays, which showed severe lesions: the ligaments of his arm and shoulder were badly damaged, and the ultrasound even showed the beginning of a tear.

"Woody, angel, how could you play in such a state?" Aunt Anita said, horrified.

"That's why I'm not playing anymore."

"I'm not a specialist," she said, "but I'll ask my colleagues at Johns Hopkins for advice. But I don't think it's irreversible. You have to have faith, Woody!"

"I don't have faith. I don't feel like it anymore."

"What's going on, son?" Uncle Saul said, concerned. "You seem really depressed. Even if you have to stop for a few months, there's no reason not to hope that a club will sign you up."

While he admitted to the injury while training during the summer, Woody continued to swear he had never taken any Talacen. And yet, the X-ray results left his ability to play without a painkiller in doubt. For Woody, the only possible explanation that remained was that the team physician had muddled something up when he'd prescribed the vitamins to help him get over his cold.

"His story just doesn't make sense," I said to Alexandra. "He can hardly hold his fork at dinner. I really wonder if he didn't take Talacen on his own initiative."

"Why would he lie to us?"

"Maybe he doesn't want to take responsibility for what he did."

She frowned.

"I doubt that," she said.

"Of course you doubt it! You think butter wouldn't melt in his mouth. You indulge his every whim!"

"Are you jealous, by any chance, Markie?"

I had already bitten my tongue.

"No, not at all," I said, sounding not very sure of myself.

"Markie-moo, I promise you that the day you miss out on seven million dollars and a professional career in football because of some crackpot doctor who got your medication all wrong, you will be entitled to every bit as much attention as Woody is getting right now."

* * *

Woody never did finish his studies.

During the winter vacation that followed his quitting the Titans, Hillel and I tried to cheer him up, but without much success. When classes started up again, he headed for Madison, feeling depressed, but never got further than the edge of campus. He stopped the car just by the first buildings.

"What are you doing?" asked Hillel, who was in the car with him.

"I can't."

"Can't what?"

"All of this . . . " he whispered, waving at the Saul Goldman Stadium there in front of them.

He got out of the car.

"Go on ahead," he told Hillel. "I'm coming. I just need to walk a little."

Hillel did as he asked, not really sure what was going on. Woody never did catch up with him. It was love and tenderness he needed: he walked to the gas station and sought refuge with Colleen. He did not leave her after that. He moved in and spent his days working with her at the gas station. She was now the reason why he was in Madison. Otherwise he would have run away a long time ago; far away.

Hillel went to see him every day. He brought him his class notes and tried to convince him not to give up everything when he was so near the goal.

"Woody, it'll only take you a few months to finish your studies. Don't ruin your chances."

"I just don't have the courage, Hill. I don't believe in myself anymore. I don't believe in anything."

"Woody, did you take the drugs?"

"No, Hillel. I swear I didn't. That's why I don't ever want to go back there, to that school full of liars. I don't want anything to do with them, ever again, they destroyed me."

A few weeks later – it was Thursday, February 14, 2002 – Woody decided to go to the university one last time to pick up his belongings from the room he shared with Hillel.

Colleen lent him her car, and he went to the campus early in the evening. He had tried to reach Hillel, in vain. He was probably in the library, studying.

He knocked on the door to their room. No answer. He still had a key: he took it out of his pocket, turned it in the lock, and opened the door. The room was deserted.

He felt a sudden nostalgia. He sat on his bed for a little while and gazed around the room. He closed his eyes for a moment: he saw himself on campus again, one very sunny day, walking with Hillel and Alexandra, everyone looking at them. After a moment of reverie, he opened the big bag he had brought with him and began filling it with his things: a few books, picture frames, a lamp he liked that he had brought from Oak Park, his running shoes, which had served so well. Then he opened the wardrobe containing his clothes and Hillel's. The top three shelves were his; he emptied them. Then he took a few steps back and looked at the open wardrobe and was overwhelmed by a feeling of sadness: it was the first time he had ever deliberately left Hillel.

He stared at the shelves so long that eventually he noticed something at the back of Hillel's top shelf. He leaned closer and saw a paper bag behind piles of clothes. He didn't know why, but he wanted to see what it was. Something lured him. He pushed the clothes to one side, reached for the paper bag and opened it. He faltered and the color drained from his face.

28

Uncle Saul only ever came twice to my parents' place in Montclair. This I know because for a long time my mother complained that he never set foot in our house. I sometimes heard her grumble about it to my father, particularly when the time came to organize family get-togethers.

"Honestly, Nathan, your brother has never set foot here! You don't think that's shocking? He doesn't even know what our house is like."

"I showed him photos," my father said, trying to placate her.

"Don't play dumb with me, please!"

"Deborah, you know why he doesn't come."

"I know, and that makes me even madder! You really are unbearable with your stupid family squabbles."

For a long time I did not know what my mother was referring to. Sometimes I tried to get involved in their conversation.

"Why doesn't Uncle Saul want to come here?"

"It doesn't matter," my mother always said. "It's complete nonsense."

The first time was in June 2001, when Grandfather died. When Grandmother called to tell us, Saul came all the way to our house, spontaneously.

The second time was Thursday, February 14, 2002, when Aunt Anita left him.

That day, I got to Montclair at the end of the afternoon. It was Valentine's Day, and I was driving all the way from school to spend the evening and the night in New York with Alexandra. As I hadn't seen my parents in a while, I swung through Montclair for a short visit.

Upon my arrival I saw my uncle's car parked in the driveway. I hurried into the house and my mother stopped me at the door.

"What's Saul doing here?" I said, worried.

"Markie honey, don't go in the kitchen."

"What's going on, anyway?"

"It's your Aunt Anita."

"What about Aunt Anita?"

"She's left your uncle. She's gone."

"Gone? What do you mean, gone?"

I wanted to call Hillel, but my mother dissuaded me.

"Don't get Hillel mixed up in this for the time being," she said.

"But what happened?"

"I'll explain everything, Markie, I promise. Your uncle is going to stay here for the weekend, he'll use your room, if you don't mind."

I wanted to go and give him a hug, but I paused by the crack in the kitchen door: I could see he was in tears. The mighty Saul Goldman was weeping.

"Maybe you should go see Alexandra," my mother murmured. "Your uncle needs some peace and quiet, I think."

I didn't leave, I fled. I left Montclair not because my mother had told me I should, but because, that day, I had seen my uncle crying. He was just a Samson-like figure, this man who had been so strong. All it had taken was to cut his hair.

I went to find the one person who could make everything right. Alexandra, love of my life. As I knew she couldn't stand all the Valentine's Day kitsch, I had planned an evening free of any five-course dinners or red roses. I picked her up straight from the studio where she was recording a new demo, and we went to shut ourselves away in a room at the Waldorf Astoria, to watch movies, make love, and survive with the help of room service. In her arms, I was sheltered from the events unfolding elsewhere.

*

That same Valentine's Day evening, Woody sat on his bed and waited for Hillel to come back to his room. It was after ten in the evening when he finally arrived. "Fuck, Woody, you scared me!" Hillel said, startled, when he opened the door. Woody didn't answer. He merely stared at Hillel.

"Woody? Is everything alright?" Hillel asked.

Woody pointed to the paper bag next to him.

"Why?"

"Woody ... I ..."

Woody leapt up and grabbed Hillel by the collar of his jacket. He slammed him hard against the wall.

"Why?" he said again, screaming.

Hillel looked him in the eye, defiantly.

"Hit me, Woody. Go on. That's all you know how to do, anyway."

Woody brandished his fist and held it up for a long time, clenching his teeth, his body trembling. He let out a grunt of anger and rushed out of the room. He ran to the parking lot and climbed into Colleen's car. He pulled away at top speed. He needed to confide in someone he could trust and the only person he could think of was Patrick Neville. He headed toward Manhattan. He tried to reach him, but Patrick's telephone was switched off.

It was eleven when he pulled up outside Patrick's building, parked the car on the opposite side, crossed the street without looking and hurried into the building. The night porter stopped him.

"I have to go up to Patrick Neville's, it's urgent."

"Is Mr Neville expecting you?"

"Call him! Call him, for Christ's sake!"

The porter called Patrick Neville.

"Good evening, sir, forgive me for disturbing you, there is a Mr ..."

"Woody," Woody said.

" ... Mr Woody ... fine."

*

The porter hung up and motioned in the direction of the elevator. When Woody reached the 23rd floor he rushed to the Nevilles' door. Patrick saw him coming through the spyhole and opened the door before he even needed to ring the bell.

"Woody, what's going on?"

"I have to talk to you."

He saw a flicker of hesitation in Patrick's gaze.

"Maybe I'm disturbing you . . ."

"No, not at all," Patrick said.

Woody seemed upset, he couldn't leave him like this. He invited him in and led him to the living room. On his way, Woody noticed a table set for Valentine's Day, with candles, a big bouquet of roses, champagne in a bucket, and two full champagne flutes that hadn't been touched.

"Patrick, I'm sorry, I didn't know you had company. I'll go."

"Not before you tell me what's going on. Sit down."

"But I interrupted—"

"Don't worry," Patrick stopped him. "You were right to come. I'll get you something to drink and you'll tell me everything."

"I'd like a coffee, if you don't mind."

Patrick vanished into the kitchen, leaving Woody alone in the living room. As he was looking around, his gaze landed on a woman's bag and jacket on an armchair. Patrick's girlfriend, thought Woody. She must have gone to hide in a bedroom. He'd had no idea Patrick was seeing someone. But then he thought he recognized the jacket. Uneasy, he got up and walked over. He saw a wallet in the bag, grabbed it, and opened it. He took out a credit card at random: an abrupt wave of nausea came over him. It couldn't be. Not her. He had to find out for sure. He rushed toward the bedrooms just as Patrick was coming out of the kitchen. "Woody, where are you going? Wait!" Patrick put down the tray with the two coffee cups and ran after him. But Woody had already started down the corridor and was throwing open the doors. Finally he found her in Patrick's room: Aunt Anita.

"Woody?" she cried.

He stood there speechless, terrified. Patrick went up to him.

"It's not what you think," he said. "We can explain everything."

Woody shoved him out of the way and stormed out. Aunt Anita ran after him.

"Woody!" she cried. "Woody! Please, stop!"

Rather than wait for the elevator, he took the stairs. She took the elevator. By the time he got to the ground floor she was already waiting for him. She put her arms around him.

"Woody, angel, wait!"

He pulled away from her embrace.

"Leave me alone! Slut!"

He ran out and cried, "I'm going to tell Saul!"

She ran after him.

"Woody, Please!"

He went out the front door, leapt off the curb and crossed the street without even looking, heading straight back to his car. He wanted to get far, far away. Aunt Anita hurried after him and did not see the van coming at full speed; it hit her full on.

Part Three

THE BOOK OF THE GOLDMANS
1960–1989

29

I spent the entire month of April 2012 putting my uncle's house in order. Initially I just sorted a few documents here and there, then I started seriously going through things.

Every morning I left my paradise in Boca Raton to drive through the Miami jungle until I reached the quiet streets of Coconut Grove. Every time I approached the house I got the impression he was there, that he would be waiting for me on the patio the way he had for so long. Reality quickly caught up with me, with the locked door I had to open and the house which, despite the regular visits of the cleaning woman, always smelled stuffy.

I began with what was easiest: his clothes, linens, kitchen utensils; I put everything in boxes and carried them to the Goodwill store.

Then there was the furniture, which was more complicated: whether it was an armchair, a vase, or a dresser, I realized that everything reminded me of some part of him. He hadn't kept any mementos from Oak Park, but I had re-created my own of the five years during which I had spent so much time with him, here in this house.

Then there were the photographs and personal items. In the cupboards I found entire boxes full of family photographs. I immersed myself in them as if in a pool of time, and it was with a certain contentment that I found myself once again with those Baltimore Goldmans who no longer existed. But as I grew steadily closer to them, an ever greater number of questions troubled my mind.

*

From time to time I stopped what I was doing and called Alexandra. She rarely answered. But when she did, we were silent. She picked up and I simply said, "Hi, Alexandra."

"Hi, Markie."

Then nothing more. I think we had so much to say we did not even know where to begin. How many long evenings we used to spend talking! How often, when I took her out to dinner, had we been the last ones there, still talking, while the waiters were sweeping the floor and getting ready to close. After we had missed each other for so long, how could we begin to tell each other our stories? With silence. This powerful, almost magical silence. The silence that had healed our wounds after Scott's death. In Coconut Grove, I sat out on the patio, or under the awning, and I imagined Alexandra in her Beverly Hills living room, looking through the huge picture windows out over Los Angeles.

One day I eventually broke the silence.

"I wish I were there with you," I said.

"Why?"

"Because I like your dog a lot."

She burst out laughing.

"Idiot."

I knew that she was smiling as she said that. The way she often did, for so long, every time I acted stupid around her.

"How is Duke?"

"He's fine."

"I miss him."

"He misses you, too."

"Maybe I could see him again."

"Maybe, Markie."

I figured as long as she went on calling me Markie, there was hope. Then I heard her sniff. She didn't say anything. I realized she was crying. I was sorry to be hurting her, but I could not give her up.

Suddenly I heard a noise in the receiver. And a door opening. Then a man's voice: Kevin. She immediately put the phone down.

The first time we had a real discussion was roughly a week later, after I found at Uncle Saul's the article about Woody from the *Madison Daily Star*, with the photograph of him together with Hillel, Uncle Saul, and Aunt Anita.

I sent her an S.M.S.:

I have an important question for you about the Madison years.

She called me back a few hours later. She was in the car, and I wondered if she had deliberately left her house to have some peace and quiet.

"You wanted to ask me something," she said.

"Yes. I wanted to know why you didn't want me to enroll at Madison, but it was O.K. for Woody and Hillel."

"Is that your important question, Marcus?"

I didn't like it when she said Marcus.

"Yes."

"Honestly, Marcus, how was I supposed to know they came to Madison for my sake? It's true I'd been looking forward to seeing them on campus. Ever since we met up again in the Hamptons, I'd been very fond of them. There was this really strong thing when the three of us were together, and when I wasn't in class I spent most of my time with them. It was only later I found out that they were rivals."

"Rivals?"

"Markie, you know very well. A sort of rivalry sprang up between them. It was inevitable. I remember how tough Woody's training was in Madison. If he wasn't in class, he was on the playing field. And if he wasn't there, then he was out running his ten miles in the forest around the campus. I remember saying to him one day, 'Basically, Woody, why are you doing all this?' And he answered, 'To be the best.' It took me a long time to figure out what he meant: he didn't want to be the best at football, he wanted to be the best in the eyes of your aunt and uncle."

"Best compared to who?"

"To Hillel."

She described episodes of their rivalry I had never heard about. For example, one day Hillel invited Alexandra to meet Woody and him at the concert of a band we liked who were performing in the region. On the appointed evening, when she got to the entrance to the auditorium, she saw only Hillel. He told her that Woody got delayed at practice, and so they spent the evening together just the two of them. The next day when she ran into Woody, she said, "It's a pity you missed the concert yesterday. It was really good."

"What concert?" he said.

"I thought Hillel told you."

"No. What are you talking about?"

A few days later, at the cafeteria, Hillel came with his tray and sat down next to Alexandra, then asked her straight out, "Deep down, Alex, if you had to choose a boyfriend and your only choice was between Woody and me, who would you choose?"

"What a weird question!" she said. "Neither of you. You don't go out with your friends. It spoils everything. I'd rather be an old maid."

"But what about Woody? Do you like Woody?"

"Of course I like him. Why are you asking me?"

"Do you like him or do you love him?"

"Hillel, what are you getting at?"

Then it was Woody's turn to ask, one day when he was in the library with Alexandra: "What do you think of Hillel?"

"He's a good guy, why?"

"Do you have feelings for him?"

"Honestly, why are you asking me that?"

"No reason. It's just you seem very close."

It was as if they were discovering the notion of preference. Those two, who had always been so alike, so inseparable, were now realizing that in their relations with other people, they could not form a single entity, that they were two distinct individuals. Alexandra told me they decided to experiment with the principle of preference by trying to figure out who, between the two of them, Patrick Neville liked better. Who would end up in the limelight? When they went out to dinner together, who would he sit next to? Who would make the greater impression?

According to Alexandra, Patrick preferred Hillel. He was impressed by his intelligence, the brilliance of his remarks. Patrick often asked Hillel his opinion on current affairs, the economy, politics, the crisis in the Middle East, and so on. When Hillel was speaking, Patrick listened. He clearly enjoyed Woody's company a great deal, too, but it wasn't on the same level as with Hillel. Hillel he truly admired.

Patrick invited Woody over one Sunday after a game between the Titans and Columbia. They spent the afternoon together, chatting and drinking whiskey. Woody did not want Hillel to know, and Alexandra realized this too late when she slipped up in the middle of an innocuous conversation.

"Oh really? Woody was at your place on Sunday?" Hillel said.

"You didn't know?"

Hillel was irritated.

"I cannot believe he would do something like that to me!"

Alexandra immediately tried to calm things down.

"Is it really such a big deal?"

He shot her a dark look, as if she were a complete and utter fool.

"Yes. Why didn't you see fit to let me know?"

"Let you know what?" she said irritably. "You make it sound as if I found your girlfriend with another man and didn't tell you."

"I thought we shared things, you and me," he said, frowning.

"Listen, Hillel, just chill out, will you? I'm not responsible for what you and Woody tell each other. It's none of my business. And besides, didn't you take me to that concert without him?"

"That's not the same."

"Oh really? And why not?"

"Because . . ."

"Oh, Hillel, spare me your relationship issues with Woody, please."

But Hillel would not let it go. He decided that if Woody was seeing Patrick behind his back, he had the right to do the same thing. One afternoon when Alexandra was at the cafeteria with Woody, through the picture window they saw Patrick and Hillel leaving the administration building together. The two shook hands warmly then Patrick headed to the parking lot.

"Why was my dad here today?" Alexandra asked Hillel once he joined them in the cafeteria. "You seemed to be having a pretty intense discussion."

"Yeah, we had an appointment."

"Oh, I didn't know."

"You don't know everything."

"An appointment about what?"

"About Friday."

"What's happening on Friday?"

"Nothing. It's confidential."

Alexandra felt very sorry for Woody that day: his expression was both innocent and sad, and it was heartbreaking. She was annoyed with Hillel: she could not stand the hold he had over Woody. Hillel was Patrick's favorite, he'd already won. What more did he want? He wanted her, all to himself, but she hadn't grasped that yet.

Twelve years on, over the telephone, Alexandra added, "Those were just a couple of episodes, and at least while I was with them at Madison they were of no consequence. They had this special, strong bond that always got the upper hand. Something else happened, later, but I don't know what it was. I think it was something to do with your grandfather's death."

"What sort of thing?"

"Hillel found out something about Woody that really upset him. I don't know what it was. I just remember that the summer following your grandfather's death, you went to Florida to help your grandmother, and when he came back he called me. He said he had been betrayed. He never wanted to tell me exactly what he meant."

* * *

When I got back to Boca Raton, after days spent slowly sifting through the memories scattered throughout the house in Coconut Grove, I ran into Leo, who complained he never saw me anymore.

One evening he showed up on my patio with some beer and his chessboard, and he said, "Your story is getting better by the day. You come here supposedly to write a book, but other than connecting with an old girlfriend, stealing a dog, and cleaning up your dead uncle's house, I don't see you're making much progress."

"You're wrong, Leo."

"The day you really start writing, let me know, I would love to see you 'working'."

He noticed photograph albums on the table in front of me. I had brought back my grandmother's old albums, the ones where the Baltimores were missing; I had added the photographs I found at Uncle Saul's.

"What are you up to, Marcus?" Leo said, intrigued.

"It's atonement, Leo. Atonement."

30

Florida
January 2011. Seven years after the tragedy

Grandmother regularly invited Uncle Saul out to dinner. Whenever I was visiting, I would go along.

That evening, she had made a reservation at a fish restaurant north of Miami, and she left a message on Uncle Saul's answering machine to tell him what to wear. "It's a nice restaurant, Saul. Make an effort, please." Before we left, Uncle Saul, who was wearing his blazer – the only one he owned – asked me, "How do I look?"

"You look fine."

That was not Grandmother's opinion. We got there on time, but because she was early she reckoned that we were late.

"In any case, Saul, you are always late. Although this time, since Markie was with you, I figured you were probably stuck in a traffic jam."

"I'm sorry, Mom."

"And just look at you, you could at least have worn a jacket and shirt that go together."

"Markie said it looked fine."

"I did," I said.

She shrugged.

"If Markie thinks it's alright, then it's alright. He's the star. But still, Saul, you could look after yourself a little. You used to be so elegant, before."

"That was before."

"Oh. I had the Montclairs on the telephone just now. Nathan wants us to go and visit this summer. I think it would be a good change of scene for you. He said he'll take care of the plane tickets."

"No, Mom. I don't feel like it. I already told you."

"You're always saying no. You're so stubborn. Nathan is easy-going like I am, but you always wanted to have your own way. Just like your father! That's why you had such a hard time getting along."

"That has nothing to do with it," Uncle Saul said.

"It has everything to do with it. If you had not been so stubborn, the pair of you, things would have turned out differently."

They argued for a short while. Then we ordered and ate in near silence. When the meal was nearly over, Grandmother left the table, on the pretext that she had to go and "powder her nose", but it was to pay the bill, so her son would not be embarrassed. As she kissed Uncle Saul goodbye she slipped a fifty dollar bill in his pocket. She hailed a taxi, the valet brought my Range Rover, and we drove home.

That evening, as he often did, Uncle Saul asked to me to take him for a drive, for the pleasure of it. He gave me no precise directions, but I knew what he wanted. Up Collins Avenue, past the buildings along the seaside. Sometimes I went as far as West Hollywood and Fort Lauderdale. And sometimes I would turn off in the direction of Aventura and Country Club Drive, and we'd drive by the houses from the Baltimores' glory days. Then eventually he would say, "Time to go home, Markie." I never knew whether our drives were moments of nostalgia, or an attempt to run away. I thought he might ask me to turn off and take I-95, the freeway to Baltimore, and drive us back to Oak Park.

As we drove aimlessly toward Miami, I asked Uncle Saul: "What happened between you and Grandfather, that you didn't speak to each other for twelve years?"

31

There was one photograph that always had pride of place on my grand-mother's night table. It was taken in New Jersey, in the mid-1960s. On it are the three men in her life. In the foreground, my father and Uncle Saul as teenagers. Behind them my grandfather, Max Goldman, cutting a proud, fine figure, far removed from the image of a pale, stooped man I had always had of him, confined to his quiet, retired life in Florida. In the background is the pretty white house where they lived at 1603 Graham Avenue, in Secaucus.

In their neighborhood no family was more respected than they were. They were the New Jersey Goldmans. And these were their finest years.

At the head of the family was Max Goldman. He looked like an actor, with his custom-tailored suits. Always a cigarette dangling from his lips. A loyal, honest man, who drove a hard bargain, and whose word was as good as any contract. Loving husband, attentive father, and as a boss, adored by his employees. A man who was respected. Affable, cha-rismatic, he could sell anything to anybody. If a door-to-door salesman or Jehovah's Witness rang at his door, the great Goldman could teach them the art of salesmanship. He would sit them down in the kitchen and give them some theoretical advice, then saunter out with them on their rounds for a practical demonstration.

He had started with nothing. He used to sell vacuum cleaners, then cars, then finally he specialized in medical equipment and set up his own business. A few years later, at the head of Goldman and Company, he was in charge of fifty or more employees and was one of the main providers of medical equipment in the region. This ensured him of a comfortable lifestyle. His wife, Ruth Goldman, was a respected mother, liked by all. She worked behind the scenes, doing all the company's books. She was a gentle, determined woman with a great deal of character. If anyone needed help, her door was always open.

For a number of years Max Goldman had his two sons help out in the company during summer vacation. He did not really need their help, but he wanted to get them involved, in the hopes that they would take over the reins of the business and keep it flourishing. His boys were his pride and joy. They were polite, intelligent, sporty, educated; they were not yet seventeen years of age, but he could tell they were already men. He would take them into his office, set out his ideas and his strategy, then ask them for their advice. My father was very interested in machinery; he thought it was time to expand the use of technology, and develop lighter alloys. He wanted to study engineering. My uncle Saul preferred the planning side: for him this meant coming up with the company's strategic development.

Max Goldman could not have been happier: his two sons complemented each other. They were not rivals – on the contrary, each one had his own business sense. He liked walking with them through the neighborhood on summer evenings. They never turned him down. They would walk and talk and on their way they sat down on a bench. When he was sure no-one could see them, Max Goldman would hold out his pack of cigarettes. He treated his sons like men. "Don't tell your mother." Sometimes they would sit on the bench for over an hour, remaking the world and forgetting the passage of time. Max Goldman spoke about the future, and saw his two sons taking on the whole country. He would put his arms around their shoulders and say, "We'll open a branch on the West Coast, and trucks painted in the Goldman colors will be criss-crossing the country."

What Max Goldman did not know was that his two sons, when they spoke in private, had even bigger dreams: their father wanted to open two factories? What was wrong with ten? They pictured the world on a grand scale. They saw themselves living in the same neighborhood, in two houses near one another, and on warm evenings they would go out for walks together. They would buy a summer house on a lake together, and spend their vacations there with their respective families. In the neighborhood they were known as the Goldman Brothers. They were only one year apart, and had the same liking for excellence. You rarely saw one without the other. They shared everything, and went out together on Saturday evenings. They went into New York City and hung out on 1st Street. You could always find them at Schmulka Bernstein's, the first kosher Chinese restaurant in New York. Standing on their chairs, with Chinese hats on their heads, they wrote the finest pages of their youth; their exploits were magnificent.

* * *

Decades have gone by. Everything has changed.

You can no longer see the buildings that were once the family company. Or at least not as they used to be. Some have been demolished, and the rest left to rot, gone to ruin, ever since the housing project that was supposed to take their place was blocked by an association of local residents. Goldman and Company had been bought in 1985 by a technology firm, Hayendras.

Nor will you find their youthful haunts. Schmulka Bernstein no longer exists, and in its place, on 1st Street, there is a hip eco-restaurant that serves excellent grilled cheese sandwiches. The only trace of the past, on the wall by the entrance, is an old photograph of how the place used to be. There are two teenagers, their features fairly similar, standing on their chairs wearing Chinese hats.

If Grandmother Ruth had not told me otherwise, I would never have imagined my father and Uncle Saul used to be so close. The scenes I witnessed in Baltimore at Thanksgiving or during winter vacation in

Florida seemed light years away from those stories of their childhood. All I had ever noticed about them was how different they were.

I remember when we used to go out, the entire family, in Miami. My father and Uncle Saul would agree ahead of time where to go for dinner, generally choosing from a list of fairly similar restaurants we all liked to go to. At the end of the meal, despite Grandfather's protests, my father and Uncle Saul split the bill equally in the name of an absolutely symmetrical brotherhood. But sometimes, roughly once a year, Uncle Saul would take us to a more upscale place. He would announce in advance, "It's my treat," which was a way of informing the other, somewhat overawed Goldmans, that the restaurant was not the sort of place my parents could afford. As a rule, everyone was delighted: Hillel, Woody and I looked forward to trying out a new place. As for Grandmother and Grandfather, they went into raptures over everything, whether it was the choice on the menu, the exquisite design of the salt shaker, the quality of the dinnerware, the fabric of the napkins, the soap in the restrooms, or the cleanliness of the automatic flush urinals. Only my parents would complain. Before heading to the restaurant, I heard my mother grumble, "I have nothing to wear, I didn't plan on anything fancy. We're on vacation, not at the circus! Honestly, Nathan, you could have said something." After dinner, on leaving the restaurant, my parents would linger behind as the other Goldmans trooped out, and my mother criticized the food, saying it wasn't worth it, and that the service was obsequious.

I could not understand why she had this attitude toward Uncle Saul, instead of being grateful for his generosity. One time I even heard her using particularly virulent terms when referring to him. In those days, there was talk about layoffs at the company where my father worked. I didn't know anything about it, but my parents had almost canceled our vacation in Florida to put money aside just in case, until they decided to go ahead with the trip after all. At times like that I felt resentful toward Uncle Saul, because he made my parents seem diminished. He cast the evil spell of money over them, and it made them shrink until they were nothing but two tiny whining worms, who had to play along with the charade of going out and being treated to food they could not afford. I also noticed how my grandparents' expressions beamed with pride. On the days that followed these evenings out, I would hear Grandfather Goldman telling anyone prepared to listen how his son, the mighty Saul, king of the Baltimore tribe, had done so well in life. "You should have seen that restaurant!" he said. "The most amazing French wine you've ever had, and meat that just melts in your mouth. And all the waiters bending over backwards! You hardly had time to blink before your glass was full again."

At Thanksgiving, Uncle Saul paid for first class tickets for my grandparents to fly to Baltimore. They were ecstatic about how comfortable the seats were, how good the in-flight service was, how the meals were served on real plates, and they loved the fact they could board before everyone else. "Priority boarding!" Grandfather exclaimed triumphantly, relating his travel exploits. "And not because we're old and helpless, but because, thanks to Saul, we're V.I.P.s!"

All my life I had watched my grandparents carrying my uncle shoulder-high, in triumph. Whatever he chose to do was perfection, and his every word was the truth. I saw them come to love Aunt Anita as if she were their own daughter, I saw how they venerated the Baltimores. How then could there have been a period of twelve years during which Grandfather and Uncle Saul did not exchange a single word?

I also remember our trips to Florida, before the Buenavista, back in the days when we all stayed at my grandparents' apartment. Very often our planes landed practically at the same time, and we would arrive together at the apartment. My grandparents would open the door and they always kissed Uncle Saul first. Then they said, "Go put down your suitcases, my dears. Boys, you'll be sleeping in the living room; Nathan and Deborah, in the T.V. lounge. Saul and Anita, you're in the guest room." Every year they would announce the distribution of beds as if it were some sort of grand lotto, but every year it was the same: Uncle Saul and Aunt Anita got the guest room with all the amenities – a double bed and adjacent bathroom – whereas my parents were reduced to the sofa bed in the tiny room where my grandparents watched television. There were two things wrong with this room, in my opinion. First of all, the Goldman Gang had secretly baptized it "the Stinkery", because of the persistent, stale smell (my grandparents never turned on the air conditioning in that room). Every year when we arrived, Hillel and Woody – who believed that luck really did have something to do with the bed lottery – trembled at the thought they might have to sleep in there. So when Grandfather announced who had drawn which room, I would see them holding hands and imploring the heavens as they said, "Please God, not the 'Stinkery'! Please God, not the 'Stinkery'!" But what they never understood was that the 'Stinkery' was my parents' torture chamber: they were doomed to stay there no matter what.

The second thing was not connected to the room itself, but to the fact there were no toilets nearby. Which meant that if my parents had a nocturnal urge, they had to go through the living room where we, the Goldman Gang, were sleeping. My mother cared about her appearance, and she was always elegant; she was always groomed and ready to go out, in my presence. I remember how on Sundays my father and I used to wait ages for her at the breakfast table. I would wonder where she was and my dad always said, invariably, "She's getting herself ready." In Florida, I knew she would be going to the bathroom through our room in the middle of the night, wearing an ugly, wrinkled nightgown, her hair all a mess. For me, it was demeaning. One night, just as she walked past us, her nightgown fluttered up on the breeze and we saw her naked buttocks. All three of us were pretending to sleep, but I know that Hillel and Woody saw her because when she locked the door to the bathroom, once they had made sure I was asleep – which I wasn't – they started giggling and made fun of her. For a long time I hated her for showing herself naked and shaming the Montclairs once again, the ones who slept in the 'Stinkery' and were nighttime exhibitionist sleepwalkers – whereas when Uncle Saul and Aunt Anita emerged from their room with its private bath, they were always impeccably turned out.

In Florida I was also the unwitting witness of the recurrent tension between my parents and Uncle Saul. One day when he thought he was alone with him in the living room, I heard my father say sharply, "You didn't tell me you'd booked first class seats for Mom and Dad. That's the sort of decision we are supposed to take together. How much do I owe you? I'll write you a check."

"It doesn't matter, drop it."

"No, I want to pay my share."

"Honestly, don't worry about it. A few bucks here or there . . . "

A few bucks here or there. It was only years later that I found out that my grandparents could not have survived on the meager retirement benefit Grandfather had been getting since the fall of Goldman and Company, and that their life in Florida was supported solely and exclusively thanks to Uncle Saul's generosity.

Every year after Thanksgiving I would hear my mother enumerate her grievances against Uncle Saul.

"Sure, it's fine for him, buying first class tickets for your parents. But we can't afford it, and he ought to know that!"

"He wouldn't take my check, he paid for everything," my father said, defending his brother.

"And that was the least he could do! Honestly, who does he think he is!"

I hated getting back to Montclair. I didn't like hearing my mother say bad things about the Baltimores. I didn't like hearing her denigrating them, ranting about their incredible house, their lifestyle, their latest model cars; I didn't like knowing that she hated everything that fascinated me. For a long time I believed that my mother was jealous of her own family. This was before I understood the meaning of something she thrust at my father one day, and which would only become clear years later. I'll never forget it: we had just come back from Baltimore, and she said, "For heavens' sake, don't you realize that everything he has is really all down to you?"

32

While tidying my uncle's house, that month of April 2012, I spilled my coffee. To try to limit the damage, I took off my T-shirt and held the stained portion under running water. Then, bare-chested, I took it out onto the patio to dry. It reminded me of Uncle Saul, the way he would dry his laundry on a line behind the house. I can see him removing the clean washing from the machine in a plastic basket, to carry it outside. There was a pleasant smell of fabric softener. Once his clothes were dry he would iron them himself, awkwardly.

When he moved to Coconut Grove, he still had fairly substantial financial means. He hired a cleaning woman, Fernanda, who came three times a week to clean the house and cheer it up with fresh flowers and potpourri. She also fixed him meals and took care of the laundry.

He had to let her go a few years later, when he lost everything. I insisted on keeping her and paying her salary, but Uncle Saul refused. To force his hand, I gave Fernanda six months' salary in advance, but when she showed up Saul sent her away, refusing to open the door.

"I can't afford to employ you anymore," he told her through the door.

"But Mr Marcus sent me. He already paid me. If you don't let me work, it's like I'm stealing from your nephew. You don't want me to steal from your nephew, do you?"

"That's between you two. I can manage fine on my own."

She called me from the patio of the house, in tears. I told her to keep the money, so she'd have time to find a new job.

After Fernanda left, I got into the habit of taking my dirty laundry to the dry cleaners' every week. I begged Saul to let me take his, too, but he was too proud to accept anything. He also did his housekeeping without help. When I stayed with him, he would wait until I'd gone out to take care of it. I would come back from an errand and find him working up a sweat, scrubbing the floor. "It's nice to have a clean house," he said with a smile. One day I said to him, "I feel bad, that you won't let me help you."

He was cleaning the windows with a rag and paused: "Does it bother you not to help me, or to see me doing the housekeeping? You think it's unworthy of me? Who is too good to wash their own toilet?"

He had hit the bull's-eye. And I realized he was right. I admired them in the same way, my uncle Saul the millionaire, and my uncle Saul the bagger at the supermarket: it wasn't a question of wealth, but of dignity. What was strong and beautiful about my uncle was his extraordinary dignity, which made him superior to other people. And his sense of dignity was something no-one could take away from him. On the contrary, it grew stronger with time. Still, to see him scrubbing his floor, I could not help but think back to the Baltimore Goldman days: every day an army of workers would troop through their house in Oak Park to ensure its upkeep. There was Maria, his full-time housekeeper, who had been with the Baltimores since we were children; there was Skunk the gardener; there were people for the swimming pool, for the trees that were too tall for Skunk; there were roofers, and a kindly Filipina lady who came with her sisters to help out with the service during Thanksgiving or big dinner parties.

Among those people in the shadows who made the Baltimore palace shine, Maria was the one I liked best. She was very thoughtful toward me and when it was my birthday she gave me a box of chocolates. I called her the magician. Whenever I went to stay, she would make all the dirty clothes I'd scattered around the guest room disappear, then return them to the foot of my bed that very same evening, washed and ironed. I was full of admiration for her efficiency. In Montclair it was my mother who took care of the laundry and the ironing. She did these chores on Saturdays or Sundays when she wasn't working, which meant it took almost a week for me to get new clean clothes. So, depending on the events I had scheduled that week, I had to choose my outfits carefully, in order not to be caught out if the sweater I wanted to wear on a particular day to impress some girl had failed to show up in my wardrobe.

Even during my years at college, when I went to the Baltimores' for Thanksgiving, Maria found a way to take all my dirty laundry and leave it again on my bed, all clean. After the tragedy, the day before Thanksgiving 2004, Uncle Saul never went back to Oak Park. But Maria continued to go there with unflinching loyalty.

* * *

Florida
Spring 2011

The day after our dinner with Grandmother, I came back from a long run and found Uncle Saul vacuuming.

In the car the night before, he had merely touched on his memories of youth; the fact that we were nearly home had been a pretext to break off his story.

Now I said, "You didn't finish telling me about Grandfather and you, yesterday."

"There's not much more to say. And anyway, the past is the past."

He unplugged the vacuum cleaner, wound the cord and stowed it in a closet, as if none of that mattered. He eventually turned to me and said these stunning words: "You know, Marcus, your grandparents always preferred your father to me."

"What? What on earth are you saying? You always made such an impression on them."

"Impression, maybe. But that doesn't mean they didn't prefer your father."

"How can you think such a thing?"

316

"Because it's the truth. Your father and I were very close until college. Our relationship got complicated when your grandfather wouldn't let me go to medical school."

"You wanted to be a doctor?"

"I did. Grandfather didn't want me to. He said it wouldn't be of any use to the family company. Your father, on the other hand, wanted to be an engineer, which fit in with Grandfather's plans. He sent me to a second-rate school, with low tuition fees, and he invested what he had so that your father could go to a top university. His studies were at the highest level. Your grandfather appointed him director of the company. Even though I was the elder brother, I was just small fry. Everything I did after that was to try and impress your grandparents, so I'd forget they always saw me as inferior to your father."

"But what happened?"

He shrugged, reached for a rag and some detergent, and went off to clean the kitchen windows.

As Uncle Saul did not seem inclined to talk, I decided to bring it up with Grandmother. Her version differed somewhat from my uncle's.

"Your grandfather wanted Saul and your father to run the company together," she explained. "He reckoned your father would know how to deal with technical challenges, while your uncle had the soul of a leader. But that was before the feud between Grandfather and Saul."

"Uncle Saul told me he wanted to go to medical school, but that Grandfather was against it?"

"Grandfather thought that medical school was a waste of time and money."

Grandmother suggested we go out on the balcony so she could smoke. We sat on two plastic chairs and I watched her twiddle a cigarette in her gnarled fingers, place it between her lips, light it, and inhale slowly before she continued.

"You see, Markie, Goldman and Company was your grandfather's baby. He'd fought hard to get that far, and he had very precise ideas on how to go about things. He was a very open-minded man, but he could be inflexible when it came to certain subjects."

At the end of the 1960s, when Uncle Saul wanted to go to med. school, he came up against his father's lack of comprehension. "All those years studying to do what? Your role in the company is to lead it toward new challenges. You have to learn strategy, business, accounting. All that sort of thing. But medicine? Pshaw! What a ridiculous idea!" Uncle Saul had no choice but to obey, and he started studying management at a little school in Maryland. Everything changed when he found out his parents were sending his brother to study at Stanford. He could see that one brother was being preferred over the other, and he was deeply hurt. During family reunions, people were obviously much more impressed by my father, the proud student at the prestigious university, than by my uncle with his second-rate education. Uncle Saul wanted to show what he was capable of. He had established strong ties with one of his teachers, who helped him come up with a development plan for Goldman and Company. One day Saul came home with a thick file: he wanted to go over it in detail with his father.

"I have some ideas for the company's expansion," he said to Grandfather, who looked at him warily.

"Why expand rather than consolidate what we have? You belong to that generation who didn't go through the war, and you take everything for granted."

"Professor Hendricks says that—"

"Who is Professor Hendricks?"

"My professor of business management at college. He says there are only two ways to view running a company: do I want to eat, or be eaten?"

"Well, your professor is wrong. It's when you want to expand at all cost that you go under."

"But if you're too cautious, you don't expand and you end up being crushed by someone stronger."

"Has your professor ever founded a company?" Grandfather said.

"Not that I know of," Uncle Saul said, lowering his eyes.

"Well, I have. And my company is doing just fine. Does your professor know anything about medical equipment?"

"No, but—"

"Typical academic, always spouting theories. Your professor who has never founded a company and knows nothing about medical equipment would like to teach me how to run Goldman and Company."

"No, not at all," Uncle Saul said. "We just have a few ideas."

"Ideas? What sort of ideas?"

"To sell our devices outside the New Jersey region."

"We can already deliver as far away as we need to."

"But do we have clients?"

"Not really. But we've been talking for a long time about the possibility of opening a branch on the West Coast."

"Precisely. That's what you've been saying since we were children, but nothing has come of it."

"Rome wasn't built in a day, Saul!"

"Professor Hendricks thinks the only way to expand is to open branches in other states. You set up a branch with a warehouse for equipment, and you can forge relationships with clients based on trust, and respond quickly to their demands."

Grandfather made a face.

"And where do you find the money to open these branches?"

"You have to open the capital to investors. We could have an office in New York with someone who—"

"Tsk, an office in New York! Now what? Secaucus, New Jersey, isn't fashionable enough for you?"

"It's not that, but—"

"That's enough, Saul! I don't want to hear another word of this nonsense. Am I the boss of my own company, or what?"

Two years went by, and during that time Uncle Saul no longer brought up his ideas about Goldman and Company's expansion with his father. But he did speak about the protest movement. Professor Hendricks was a man of the left, and a militant. Uncle Saul joined in some of his activity. At the same time, he struck up a relationship with the professor's daughter, Anita Hendricks. When he came back to Secaucus, he now spoke of "defending the cause" and "taking action". He began traveling all over the country to accompany Professor Hendricks and Anita on protest marches. This new commitment greatly irritated Grandfather. And it was what led to the argument that stopped them speaking to each other for twelve years.

It happened one night in April 1973, during spring vacation, which Uncle Saul was spending with his parents in Secaucus. It was almost midnight and Grandfather was waiting up for Uncle Saul, pacing back and forth in the living room. There was an issue of *Time* magazine on the coffee table, and he continually picked it up and put it back down again.

Grandmother was upstairs in the bedroom. She had called to Grandfather several times to come to bed, but he wouldn't listen. He wanted an explanation from his son. Grandmother eventually fell asleep – until their shouts woke her up. She heard Grandfather's muffled voice coming through the floor.

"Saul, Saul, for Christ's sake! Do you realize what you are getting into?"

"It's not what you think, Dad."

"I think what I see, and I see you smack in the middle of a load of nonsense."

"Nonsense? And you, Dad, are you aware of what you are doing by refusing to protest?"

The reason why Grandfather was so angry was the photograph on the cover of *Time* magazine: there had been a demonstration in Washington the previous week. Clearly visible in the front row were Uncle Saul, Aunt Anita, and her father, their fists raised. Grandfather was afraid it would all end badly.

"Look, Saul! Look at you!" he shouted, brandishing the magazine in his son's face. "You know what I see in this photograph? Trouble! A mountain of trouble! What is it you want, after all? To have the F.B.I. on your back? And have you thought about the company? Do you know what the F.B.I. will do if they think you are dangerous? They will ruin your life and ours. They will send the I.R.S. to sink the company! Is that what you want?"

"Don't you think you're exaggerating a little, Dad? We're demonstrating for a fairer world, I don't see the harm in that."

"Your demonstrations are pointless, Saul! Open your eyes, for Christ's sake! It's going to end badly, that's all you'll have achieved. You'll end up getting yourself killed!"

"Killed by who? The police? The government? So much for your fine rule of law!"

"Saul, ever since you started spending time in the company of this Professor Hendricks, and above all his daughter, you've become way too obsessed with all causes and protest marches—"

"She has a name, she's called Anita."

"Anita, O.K. Well, I want you to stop seeing her."

"Aw, come on, Dad, why?"

"Because she's a bad influence! Ever since you started going out with her, you have been getting yourself into impossible situations. You've been going up and down the coast to these demonstrations. You'll look real smart if you fail your exams because you spent all your time making leaflets and banners instead of studying. Look out for your future, for heaven's sake! Your future is here, with the company."

"My future is with her."

"Don't be ridiculous. You've been brainwashed by her father. How do you explain the fact that you're suddenly so involved in the protest movement. What happened?"

"Her father has nothing to do with this."

Grandmother could hear them raising their voices, but she did not dare to go downstairs. She thought that perhaps a frank discussion would do them both good. But then the argument degenerated.

"Why won't you trust me, Dad? Why do you always have to control everything?"

"But Saul, you're going off the rails. Don't you see I'm simply worried about you?"

"Worried? Really? What are you worried about? Who's going to take over from you at the factory?"

"I am worried that if you get in any deeper in all these protest movements, you'll end up disappearing one day."

"Disappearing? That is precisely what I will do! I'm fed up with your fucking bullshit. You want to run everything! Control everything!"

"Saul, don't speak to me in that tone of voice."

"Besides, all you're interested in is Nathan. You only care about him."

"At least Nathan doesn't have all these cockamamie ideas that will sink us all!"

"*Cockamamie*? I just want to work for the good of the company, but you never want to listen to me. All you'll ever be is a vacuum cleaner salesman!"

"What did you say?" screamed Grandfather.

"You heard me. I don't want anything more to do with your stupid company. I'll be better off away from you. I'm getting out of here."

"Saul, you're overstepping the mark now. I warn you: if you go out that door, don't bother coming back!"

"Don't worry, I'm leaving and I'll never set foot in this fucking state of New Jersey again."

Grandmother rushed out of her room and went tearing down the stairs, but it was too late: Uncle Saul had slammed the front door and was jumping in his car. She ran outside, barefoot; she begged him not to leave, but he started the car and pulled away. She ran behind him for a few yards, then she knew he wasn't going to stop. He had left for good.

Uncle Saul kept his promise. During Grandfather's lifetime, he never set foot in New Jersey again. He only went there when the old man died in May 2001. Between two puffs of her cigarette, while flocks of seagulls swooped above the ocean, Grandmother told me that the day she called Uncle Saul to tell him Grandfather had died, his reaction was not to go down to Florida, but to rush to New Jersey, where he had grown up; the place he had exiled himself from all those years ago.

33

Because he saw me leaving Boca Raton every morning, Leo was eager to know what I was up to, so he began coming with me to Coconut Grove. He was of no help whatsoever. All he wanted was my company. He would sit out on the patio, in the shade of the mango tree, and say over and over, "Ah, it's really nice here, Marcus." But I did like having him there.

Gradually, the house was emptying out.

Sometimes I went home with a box of things I wanted to keep. Leo would rummage inside it and say, "Come on, Marcus, what are you going to do with all this old stuff? You have a magnificent house and you want to turn it into some sort of flea market?"

"It's just a few memories, Leo."

"Memories are in your head. The rest is just clutter."

I only stopped my methodical tidying of my uncle's things for a few days to go to New York. I had almost finished in Coconut Grove when my agent called me: he'd arranged for me to be on a popular television program. They were due to shoot it that week.

"I don't have time," I told him. "Besides, if they've offered it to me only a few days before the shooting, it means someone else dropped out and I'm just filling in."

"Or that you have a fantastic agent who arranged things so it would happen just like this."

"What do you mean?"

"They're recording two episodes of the program back to back. You're invited on the first one, and Alexandra Neville is the guest on the second. Your dressing rooms will be side by side."

"Oh," I said. "Does she know?"

"I don't think so. So will you do it?"

"Will she be alone?"

"Listen, Marcus, I'm your agent, not her mother. Is that a yes?"

"It's a yes," I said.

I booked a flight to New York for the next day. As I was about to leave for the airport, Leo began to fuss at me.

"I've never seen anyone so lazy. For three months you've supposedly been writing a book, but it's always *mañana, mañana, mañana!*"

"I'll only be gone a few days."

"But when are you actually going to begin that damn book?"

"Soon, Leo. I promise."

"Marcus, am I wrong or are you pulling my leg? I don't suppose you feel anxious, like you're suffering from writer's block, or something?"

"No."

"You would tell me?"

"Of course I would."

"Swear?"

"Swear."

I got to New York the day before the television program. I was very nervous. I wandered aimlessly around my apartment all evening.

The next day, after trying on a dozen changes of clothes, I went relatively early to the television studios on Broadway. They led me to my dressing room, and as I was walking down the corridor, I saw her name on the door next to mine. "Is Alexandra already here?" I said casually to the security guard who was with me. He said no.

I stayed on my own in the dressing room. I couldn't sit still. She would be there soon, but so what? Should I go and knock on her door? And then what? What if she came with Kevin? Then what would I look like?

I felt stupid. I wanted to run away. But it was too late. I lay down on the sofa and listened attentively to the sounds coming from the corridor. Suddenly I heard her voice. My heart began racing. There was the sound of a door opening and closing, then nothing more. I felt my cell phone vibrating. She had just sent me a message.

Are you in the dressing room next door?

I kept my answer simple.

Yes.

I heard a door open and close again, then a dull knocking on my door. I went to open.

"Markie?"

"Surprise!"

"Did you know we were recording the same day?"

"No," I lied.

I stepped back: she came into my dressing room and closed the door. Then she spontaneously threw her arms around my neck and hugged me tight. We held each other for a long time. I felt like kissing her, but I didn't want to risk spoiling everything. I just took her face in my hands and looked at her eyes, which were shining brightly.

"What are you doing this evening?" she said, just like that.

"I don't have anything planned . . . We could . . ."

"Yes," she said.

We smiled.

We had to find a place to meet. Her hotel was swarming with reporters and anywhere public was out of the question. I suggested she come to my place. There was an underground parking lot and from there she could go directly into the building. No-one would see her. She said yes.

I would never have imagined that Alexandra might come to my apartment one day. And yet, I had been thinking of her when I bought it with the money from my first novel. I wanted an apartment in the

West Village, for her sake. And when the real estate agent had shown it to me, I'd fallen in love, because I knew she would love it too. And I was right: she adored it. The moment the elevator doors opened, directly onto the front door, she could not help but give a cry of enthusiasm. "Oh, my God, Markie, this is just the kind of apartment I love!" And I was very proud. Even more so when we sat down on the huge terrace full of flowers.

"Are you the one who does the plants?" she asked.

"Of course. Or have you forgotten I trained to be a gardener?"

She laughed and admired the huge white hydrangea blossoms for a moment, before nestling into a deep outdoor sofa. I opened a bottle of wine. Life was good.

"How is Duke?"

"He's fine. We don't have to talk about my dog, you know, Marcus."

"I know. So how are you?"

"I'm O.K. I like being in New York. I always feel good when I'm here."

"Why did you move to California?"

"It was better for me, Markie. I didn't want to run the risk of bumping into you on every street corner. But for a while now I've been thinking I should buy an apartment here."

"You're always welcome to stay here," I said.

I instantly regretted my words. She gave a somewhat sad smile.

"I'm not sure Kevin would really feel like being your roommate."

"So Kevin is still in the picture?"

"Of course he is, Marcus. We've been together for four years."

"If he was the right one, you'd be married by now . . ."

"Stop it, Markie. Don't make a scene. Maybe I should go."

I regretted saying such stupid things.

"Forgive me, Alex. Could we start the evening over again?"

"Alright."

When I said that, she stood up and left the terrace. I didn't understand what she was doing and I followed her. I saw her head to the door, open it, and go out. For a moment I stood there perplexed, then the doorbell rang. I hurried over to open.

"Hey, Markie," Alexandra said. "I'm sorry, I'm a little late."

"Don't worry, you're fine. I just opened a bottle of wine out on the terrace. I've even poured you a glass."

"Thank you. What an incredible apartment! So this is where you live."

"Yup."

We took a few steps toward the terrace and I put a hand on her bare shoulder. She turned around and we gazed into each other's eyes, in silence. There was that sublime attraction, and we both felt it. I moved my lips toward hers: she did not step away. On the contrary, she took my head between her hands and kissed me.

34

Florida
Spring 2011

All of a sudden, my uncle's behavior toward me changed. He was more distant. From the month of March 2011 on, he began seeing Faith, the manager at Whole Foods, on a regular basis.

Before I found out the truth, I thought they were emotionally involved. She came regularly to pick him up at home and they went off together. They stayed away for a long time, sometimes the whole day. Uncle Saul never told me exactly where they went, and I didn't want to pry. He was often in a bad mood when he came back from his escapades, and I wondered what was going on between the two of them.

I soon got the unpleasant impression that something had changed. For some unknown reason, Coconut Grove was no longer that familiar oasis of tranquility. I noticed that Uncle Saul easily grew impatient at home, and this was not like him.

At the supermarket, too, everything had changed. Sycomorus had not made it onto *Sing!*, and had been depressed ever since he got the letter from the head of production informing him he had not been selected. One day when I was trying to cheer him up, I said, "It's just the beginning. You have to fight for your dreams, Syc."

"It's too hard. Los Angeles is overflowing with actors and singers trying to make it. I get the feeling I never will."

"Look into yourself for the thing that will make the difference."

He shrugged.

"Deep down, what I really want is to be famous."

"You want to be a singer or you want to be famous?" I said.

"I want to be a famous singer."

"But if you could be only one of the two?"

"Then I want to become well-known."

"Why?"

"Because it's nice to be famous. Isn't it?"

"Fame is just a piece of clothing, Sycomorus. And you eventually grow out of it, or it gets worn, or stolen. What matters most is what you're like stark naked."

The atmosphere was morose. When I went to see Uncle Saul on his break, on the bench outside the store, he was taciturn and pensive. Before long I only stopped off at Whole Foods every other day, then one day out of three. In the end Faith was the only one who could get Uncle Saul to smile. He was full of thoughtful little gestures toward her: he gave her flowers, brought her mangoes from his patio, he even invited her over for dinner. To play host, he would put on a tie, something I hadn't seen him do in years. I remembered that in Baltimore he'd had a very impressive collection of ties, which had disappeared since he moved to Coconut Grove.

I was a bit unsettled by Faith's arrival in the twosome I had formed with my uncle. I even ended up wondering whether I was jealous of her, when I should have been happy that my uncle had found someone to distract him from his monotonous life. I began to question the reasons I came to stay in Florida. Was it out of love for my uncle, or to show him that his nephew from Montclair had outclassed him?

One Sunday, when he was in the living room reading, and I was getting ready to go into Miami so he could enjoy his romance in peace, I asked him, "Aren't you seeing Faith today?"

"No."

I didn't say anything more.

"Markie," he said then, "it's not what you think."

"I don't think anything."

*

The first time he put up a barrier between us, I thought it was because of all the questions I was asking him, which annoyed him. It happened one evening after dinner when, as we often did, we were walking peacefully down the quiet streets of Coconut Grove. I said to him, "Grandmother told me about the argument with Grandfather. Was that why you moved to Baltimore?"

"My college was affiliated with the one in Baltimore. I enrolled in law school. I figured it would be a good education. Then I took the bar exam in Maryland and began working in Baltimore. Before long I was making a good living as a lawyer."

"And you didn't see Grandfather after that?"

"Not for twelve years. But Grandmother often came to visit."

Uncle Saul told me how for years, once a month, in secret, Grandmother Ruth came all the way down to Baltimore from New Jersey for the day to have lunch with him.

By 1974 Uncle Saul and Grandfather had not spoken to each other for a whole year.

"How are you, my dear?" Grandmother said.

"I'm fine. Law school is going well."

"So you're going to become a lawyer?"

"Yes, I think so."

"That might be useful to the company . . ."

"Mom, let's not talk about that, please."

"How is Anita?"

"She wanted to join us but she has an exam tomorrow and she has to study."

"I like her very much, you know."

"I know, Mom."

"And your father will like her too."

"Stop it. Let's not talk about him, please."

*

By 1977, Uncle Saul and Grandfather had not spoken to each other in four years. Uncle Saul was completing his specialization, and was getting ready to take the bar exams. He and Aunt Anita had moved into a small apartment in the suburbs of Baltimore.

"Are you happy here?" Grandmother said.

"Yes."

"And you, Anita, is everything alright?"

"Yes, Mrs Goldman, thank you. I've nearly finished my internship."

"She already has a job offer from John Hopkins," Uncle Saul said proudly. "They say they want her at any price."

"Oh, Anita, that's wonderful! I'm so proud of you," Grandmother said.

"How are things in Secaucus?" Anita asked.

"Saul's father misses him terribly."

"My father misses me?" Uncle Saul said, annoyed. "He's the one who threw me out."

"He threw you out, or you left? Talk to him, Saul. Get back in touch, please."

He shrugged and changed the subject.

"How's the company doing?"

"Everything's fine. Your brother is taking on more and more responsibility."

By 1978 Uncle Saul and Grandfather had not spoken to each other in five years. Uncle Saul had just left the law offices where he was working, to open his own practice. He and Anita moved into a tiny villa in a middle-class residential neighborhood.

"Your brother has become the C.E.O. of Goldman and Company," Grandmother said.

"Good for him. That's what Dad always wanted, after all. Nathan was always his favorite."

"Saul, don't go saying stupid things, please. It's not too late to come home. Your father would be so—"

He interrupted: "That's enough, Mom. Change the subject, please."

"Your brother is getting married."

"I know. He told me."

"At least you two are in touch. You'll come to the wedding, won't you?"

"No, Mom."

By 1979 Uncle Saul and Grandfather had not spoken to each other in six years.

"Your brother and his wife are expecting a baby."

Saul smiled and turned to Anita, sitting next to him.

"Mom, Anita is pregnant . . . "

"Oh, Saul, darling!"

By 1980 Uncle Saul and Grandfather had not spoken to each other in seven years.

Hillel and I were born a few months apart.

"Look, this is your nephew Marcus," Grandmother said, taking a photograph from her bag.

"Nathan and Deborah are coming here next week. So at last we'll get to meet the little guy. I'm looking forward to it."

"You're going to meet your cousin Marcus," Anita told Hillel, asleep in his baby carriage. "You have a son now, Saul, maybe it's time to put an end to this feud with your father."

By 1984 Uncle Saul and Grandfather had not spoken to each other in over ten years.

"What are you eating, Hillel?"

"French fries, Grandma."

"You are the cutest boy I know."

"How's Dad?" asked Saul.

"He's not well. The company is doing very poorly. Your father is beside himself, he says they're going to go under."

*

By 1985 Uncle Saul and Grandfather had not spoken to each other in twelve years.

Goldman and Company was on the verge of bankruptcy. My father had drawn up a rescue plan which meant selling the company. He needed help to finalize the plan and he went down to Baltimore to consult his older brother, who was specialized in mergers and acquisitions.

Twenty-five years later, as we drove through Coconut Grove, Uncle Saul told me how one evening in May 1985, the three of them were all standing in the red brick Goldman and Company building in New York State. The factory was deserted, plunged in darkness; the only light was in Grandfather's office, where he was going through his account books. My father opened the door and said quietly, "Dad, I've brought someone who can help us."

When Grandfather saw Uncle Saul in the doorway, he burst into tears, rushed over and flung his arms around him. They spent the days that followed in the Goldman offices working on the purchase plan. During that stay, Uncle Saul did not leave New York State but went back and forth between his hotel and the company, never crossing the New Jersey border, never returning to his childhood home.

Once Uncle Saul had finished his story, we drove back home in silence. Uncle Saul took two water bottles from the fridge and we drank them standing at the kitchen counter.

"Marcus," he said, "I think I'd like to be on my own for a while."

I didn't immediately grasp what he meant.

"You mean now?"

"I'd like for you to go back to New York. I really like having you here, don't get me wrong. But I need to be alone for a while."

"Are you mad at me?"

"No, not at all. I just want to be alone for a while."

"I'll leave tomorrow."

"Thanks."

Early the next morning I put my suitcase in the trunk of my car, hugged my uncle, and went back to New York.

* * *

I was upset by the fact that Uncle Saul had asked me to leave. I made the most of the time I was back in New York to see something of my parents, and one day in June 2011, I took my mother to lunch at her usual restaurant in Montclair and we had a talk about the Baltimores. We were sitting out on the terrace, the weather was magnificent, and my mother suddenly said, "Markie, about Thanksgiving . . ."

"Thanksgiving is five months from now, Mom. Isn't it a little early to be talking about it?"

"I know, but what would make us happy, your father and I, would be if we were all together at Thanksgiving. We haven't spent Thanksgiving together in such a long time."

"I don't celebrate Thanksgiving anymore, Mom . . ."

"Oh, Markie, it makes me so sad to hear you say things like that! You should live in the present, and not so much in the past."

"I miss the Baltimore Goldmans, Mom."

She smiled.

"I hadn't heard that expression for a long time. The Baltimore Goldmans. I miss them too."

"Mom, don't take this badly, but were you ever jealous of them?"

"I had you, sweetie, what more did I need?"

"I've been thinking back about our vacations in Miami, with the Goldman grandparents, how Uncle Saul got the guestroom and you and Dad had to sleep on the sofa bed."

She burst out laughing.

"That didn't bother us, your father and me, sleeping in the T.V. room. You know, it was your uncle who had paid for your grandparents' apartment, so we figured it was perfectly normal for him to sleep in the most comfortable room. Every time, before we went there, your father would call Grandfather to ask him to give us the T.V. room and let Saul and Anita have the guest room. Every time, your grandfather would say that Saul had already called to ask him to stop making his brother sleep in the T.V. room, and to give *him* the less comfortable room. Your father and your uncle ended up tossing for it. I remember one time when the Baltimores got to Florida before we did, Saul and Aunt Anita had already moved into the T.V. room. So, contrary to what you might think, your father and I didn't always sleep there, far from it."

"You know, I often wondered if we too could have become Baltimores . . . "

"We are Montclairs. And that's the way it will always be. Why should we want to change? Everyone is different, Markie, and maybe that's a source of happiness: to be at peace with who you are."

"You're right, Mom."

I thought the matter was closed. We changed the subject, and once the meal was over I drove my mother home. As we pulled up outside, she said, "Park the car for a moment, Markie, please."

I did as she asked.

"Is everything alright, Mom?"

She had an expression on her face I had never seen.

"We could have been Baltimores, Markie."

"What do you mean?"

"Marcus, there is something you don't know. When you were a little boy, Grandfather had to sell his company, because it was failing."

"Yes, I know that."

"But what you don't know, is that at that moment, your father made an error of judgment he would regret for a very long time . . ."

"I'm not sure I follow, Mom."

"Markie, in 1985, when the company was sold, your father didn't take Saul's advice. He missed an opportunity to make a huge amount of money."

For many years I had thought that the barrier between the Montclairs and the Baltimores was the work of the vagaries of time. In fact, it went up virtually overnight.

35

In keeping with the strategy my father and Uncle Saul had come up with, Goldman and Company was sold to Hayendras Inc., a major company based in New York State, in October 1985.

The day before the sale, my father, Uncle Saul, Grandfather and Grandmother all met up in Suffern, where Hayendras had their headquarters. My father and my grandparents had come by car together from New Jersey; Uncle Saul had flown to LaGuardia, then rented a car.

They had reserved three rooms at a Holiday Inn, and they spent all day in the conference room placed at their disposal, attentively re-reading the contracts and making sure that everything corresponded to what had been agreed. By the time they finished it had been dark for quite a while, and Grandfather suggested they go out for dinner at a local restaurant. Over the meal Grandfather looked at his two sons and took them both by the hand.

"Do you remember," he said, "the hours we used to spend on that bench picturing the three of us running the company?"

"You even let us smoke," my father said with a chuckle.

"Well, here we are, boys. I've waited so long for this moment. For the first time, we will preside together over the fate of Goldman and Company."

"For the first and last time," Uncle Saul corrected.

"Well, maybe so, but at least it has finally happened. So let's not be sad tonight: let's drink a toast! To this moment that has finally come!"

They raised their glasses and clinked them together. Then Grandfather asked, "Are you sure it's a good idea, Saul?"

"To sell to Hayendras? Yes, it's the best option. The selling price is not very high, but it's that or bankruptcy. And besides, Hayendras will grow, they have potential, they'll know how to develop the company. They'll take on all the former employees, and that's what you wanted, too, isn't it?"

"Yes, absolutely, Saul. I don't want anyone to be unemployed."

"I've worked it out that after tax there will be two million dollars left over for you," Uncle Saul said.

"I know," said Grandfather. "By the way, your mother, brother and I have discussed it, and we wanted to let you know: this company belongs to the four of us. I founded it in the hopes that one day my two sons would be at the helm, and this evening they are. You have fulfilled my wish and I am eternally grateful to you. The money from the sale will be divided into three equal parts. One third for your mother and me, and one third for each of you."

There was a silence.

"I can't accept," Uncle Saul said finally, suddenly emotional over being brought back into the fold in this way. "I don't want my share, I don't deserve it."

"How can you say such a thing?" Grandfather said.

"Dad, because of what happened, I—"

"Let's just drop all that, okay?"

"Leave the past behind, Saul," my father insisted. "It's thanks to you that today our employees, myself included, will have jobs to go to and that Dad will be able to pay for his retirement."

"That's true. Saul, thanks to your help, your mother and I will be able to move somewhere sunny, maybe Florida. The way we've always dreamt we could."

"I'm going to move to Montclair to be closer to our new offices," said my father. "We found a nice house in a nice neighborhood, just what I always wanted, and I'll be able to finance a loan with my share of the sale."

Grandfather took Grandmother's hand, smiled at his two sons and took some legal documents out of his briefcase.

"I've drawn up the contracts bringing the equal ownership of the business by the three of us into compliance," he said. "The amount from the sale will be divided into three equal parts, in other words $666,666.66 each."

"Over half a million dollars," said my father with a smile.

The next morning at dawn, my father and grandparents were awoken by a call from Uncle Saul, telling them to come as quickly as possible down to the breakfast room. He had to speak to them at once.

"I was talking last night with one of my friends," Uncle Saul said, very excited, between two sips of coffee. "He's a broker on Wall Street. He said Hayendras is not very well known yet but should expand even more than I thought. He said that rumor has it they may go public this year. Do you realize what that means?"

"I'm not sure I fully understand," Grandmother said pragmatically.

"It means that if Hayendras is listed on the stock exchange, the value of the company will skyrocket. It's bound to! A company that goes public increases in value. I thought about it for a long time, and I think we should renegotiate the sale of Goldman and Company to have our parts in shares rather than cash."

"What will that change?" Grandfather said.

"It means that the day Hayendras goes public, the shares will increase in value and our portion will increase. So our $600,000 could be worth more. Look, I've drawn up a proposal for a change to the contract, what do you think?"

He handed out his draft contract, but Grandfather frowned.

"Saul, does what you want mean that in exchange for Goldman and Company I won't get any money, just a piece of paper that says I own a few shares in a company that I don't even know?"

"Exactly. Let me give you an example. Imagine that today Hayendras is worth a thousand dollars. Let's say you have one percent, so your share is worth ten dollars. But if Hayendras goes public and everyone wants to invest money in it, its value will soar. Imagine the value of Hayendras suddenly goes up to ten thousand dollars. Then your share will immediately be worth a hundred dollars. Our money could suddenly amount to a whole lot more!"

"We know how the stock market works," Grandmother said. "I think what your father wants to know is how we're going to pay for shopping and electricity? Theoretical money doesn't pay bills. And besides, if Hayendras doesn't go public or nobody wants it, the shares will tumble and our money will be worthless."

"That's true, it is a risk."

"No, no," Grandmother said decisively. "We need cash, your father and I cannot risk losing everything. We're gambling with our retirement."

"But my friend says it's the investment of the century," Saul insisted.

"The answer is no," Grandfather said.

"And you?" Uncle Saul said, turning to my father.

"I'd rather have cash, too. I don't really believe in the magic of the stock market, it's too risky. And besides, if I want to buy that house in Montclair . . ."

Grandfather could read the disappointment in Uncle Saul's expression.

"Listen, Saul," he said, "if you really believe in dabbling on the stock exchange, there's nothing stopping you asking for your part in shares."

Which was exactly what Uncle Saul did. One year later, Hayendras went public, in spectacular fashion. From what my mother explained to me, in one day the stock price rose fifteen-fold. In a few hours, Uncle Saul's $666,666.66 became $9,999,999.90. Uncle Saul had just made ten million dollars, which he would cash in several months later when he sold his shares. That was the year he bought the house in Oak Park.

One visit to his brother's superb house, and my father was convinced of the benefits of the stock market. At the beginning of 1988 Dominic

Pernell, the C.E.O. of Hayendras, made an in-house announcement vaunting the company's economic well-being and inciting employees to buy shares, and that was all it took to persuade my father. He decided he would use all that was left of his portion from the sale of Goldman and Company, and he persuaded Grandfather to do likewise.

"We should buy shares in Hayendras, too!" my father insisted over the telephone.

"Do you think so?"

"Dad, look how much Saul made: millions! Millions of dollars!"

"We should have listened to your brother at the time we sold the company."

"It's not too late, Dad!"

My father came up with seven hundred thousand dollars: all his savings, and Grandfather's. Their entire war chest. He converted the money into Hayendras shares and, according to his calculations, they should be millionaires in no time. One week later, he got a worried call from Uncle Saul.

"I just spoke to Dad – he told me you invested his money?"

"Oh, take it easy, Saul! I just made an investment, the way you did. For him and for me. What's the problem?"

"Which shares did you buy?"

"Well, Hayendras shares, obviously."

"What? How many?"

"That's none of your business."

"How many? I have to know how many."

"$700,000 worth."

"What? Are you out of your mind? That's almost all your money!"

"So?"

"What do you mean, *so*? That's a huge risk!"

"Well, Saul, at the time we sold the company, you did advise us to get everything in shares. So we're converting it now. I don't see the difference."

"Back then it was different. If anything goes wrong, Dad will lose all his retirement money. And then what will he live on?"

"Don't worry, Saul. Let me decide for once."

The day after their conversation, to my father's astonishment Uncle Saul showed up at his office at Hayendras headquarters.

"Saul, what are you doing here?"

"I have to talk to you."

"Why didn't you just call me?"

"I couldn't tell you over the phone, it's too risky."

"Tell me what?"

"Let's go for a walk."

They went out into the garden next to the building and found a deserted spot to converse.

"The company is not doing well," Uncle Saul said.

"How can you say that? I know all about Hayendras' economic situation: we are doing well, just so you know. The C.E.O. himself, Dominic Pernell, told us as much not long ago, he even told us to buy shares. The share price just went up, as it happens."

"Obviously, the share price went up – all the employees went rushing to buy shares."

"What are you trying to tell me, Saul?"

"Sell your shares."

"What? Not on your life."

"Listen carefully, I know what I'm talking about. Hayendras is tanking, the figures are catastrophic. Pernell should never have told you to buy. Get rid of your shares, now."

"What the hell are you talking about, Saul? I don't believe a word."

"Do you think I would have come all the way from Baltimore if this wasn't really serious?"

"You're just annoyed because you sold your shares and you can't buy anymore, isn't that it? You want me to sell so you can buy them?"

"No, I want you to sell to get rid of them."

"Why don't you just let me breathe a little, Saul? You save Dad's company, you make sure he's got his retirement, you find work for all his employees: he adores you, you're the prodigal son! You've always been his favorite, anyway. And as if that wasn't enough, you won the jackpot along the way."

"But I told you to get shares back then!"

"Don't you have enough, with your career as a lawyer, your big house, your cars? You want more? The C.E.O. in person told us to buy, everyone bought shares! Every single employee! What is your problem? You don't like the fact that I might make some money, too?"

"What? Damn it, why won't you listen to me?"

"You've always felt you had to put me down. Particularly in front of Dad. When we were kids, there on the bench, you were the one he spoke to! Saul this, Saul that!"

"You're talking bullshit."

"You had to be out of the picture before I finally began to matter in his eyes. And even then, when you were not on speaking terms, the number of times he made me feel that the company would have been better run if you were at the helm . . ."

"Nathan, you're raving. If I'm here, it's to tell you that Hayendras is struggling, the figures look bad, and as soon as word gets out the share price will plummet."

"How do you know?"

"I just do. Please, believe me. I've heard it from a reliable source. I can't tell you anything more. Sell everything and above all don't tell anyone. Not a soul, you hear me? I am committing a serious offense by letting you know. If anyone finds out I told you, I will get into trouble, big time, and so will you and Dad. It will be hard enough already to sell such an amount all in one go without raising suspicion. You should do it in several installments. Don't waste a minute!"

My father refused to listen to reason. I think he was blinded by the life his brother led in Baltimore, and he wanted his share. I know Uncle

Saul did all he could, he even went to Florida to see Grandfather and ask him to persuade his son to sell his shares.

Grandfather called my father: "Nathan, your brother came to see me. He said we absolutely have to sell the shares. Maybe we should listen to him."

"No, Dad, for once, please, trust me!"

"He told me he would help us make a better investment elsewhere. An investment that would make money. I have to confess, I am a little worried . . ."

"Why doesn't he mind his own business? Why don't you trust me? I can do things right, too, you know!"

I think my father was gambling his pride. He had made a decision, he wanted it to be respected. He would not budge. Was it out of conviction, or to stand up to his brother? No-one will ever know. Grandfather did not force his hand, no doubt in order not to upset him.

While my mother, sitting there in my car, went on with her story, I recalled a childhood memory. I saw myself at the age of seven, running from the living room into the kitchen and shouting, "Mommy, Mommy! Uncle Saul is on television!" This was his first media event, the beginning of his glory. On the screen next to him was his client, Dominic Pernell. I remember that for several weeks I would proudly tell anyone prepared to listen that Uncle Saul and Daddy's boss were all over the newspapers. What I didn't know was that Dominic Pernell had been arrested by the Securities and Exchange Commission for having cooked the books at Hayendras to make his employees believe the profits were spectacular and in the process sell them millions of dollars' worth of his own shares. He was sentenced to forty-three years in prison by a New York court. In the days that followed his arrest, the Hayendras share price completely collapsed, and its value was divided by fifteen. The company was bought for next to nothing by a major German corporation, which still exists. The $700,000 my grandfather and father had invested was now worth only $46,666.66.

Baltimore became my father's penance. Their house, their cars, the

Hamptons, their vacations in Whistler, the pomp of Thanksgiving, the Buenavista apartment, the private security patrol in Oak Park, looking down on us as if we were intruders: everything was there to remind him that where his brother had succeeded, he had failed.

* * *

That day in June 2011, after talking to my mother, I called Uncle Saul. He seemed happy to hear me.

"I had lunch with my mother," I said. "She told me the story about how Hayendras was sold and Dad lost all his and Grandfather's savings."

"As soon as I heard your father had bought those shares, I did my best to convince him to sell. After the fact, your father reproached me for not having explained the situation to him more clearly. But you have to understand one thing: at the time, Dominic Pernell was already under investigation by the S.E.C., and he'd contacted me to defend him. I knew he had lied to his employees and sold them his own shares. I couldn't tell your father: I'm only too familiar with his sense of justice, and he would have warned his fellow employees. There were thousands of them who, like him, had invested a great deal of money in the shares of their own company. But if it got out, if the S.E.C. had found out that I gave your father that information, all three of us – your grandfather, father and I – would have gone to prison for sure. All I could do was beg him to sell, and he didn't want to listen."

"Was Grandfather very angry with Dad?"

"I don't really know. He always said he wasn't. After all that, there was a wave of layoffs at Hayendras but luckily for him, your dad wasn't among them. Your grandfather, on the other hand, lost all his capital for his retirement. I helped him and Grandmother."

"Did you help Grandfather because of your argument? As a way of asking forgiveness?"

"No, I helped him because he was my father. Because he didn't have a penny to his name. Because I had made my money thanks to him. I don't know what your grandmother told you about the argument, but the truth is that it was all a horrible misunderstanding that I was too stupid and too proud to resolve. That's one thing we have in common with your father: there are times we won't listen to reason, and we go on to regret it our whole life long."

"Grandmother said it was because of your political activism."

"I was never really politically active."

"But what about the photograph on the magazine cover?"

"I went to just one demonstration, for the sake of Anita's father, who was a militant activist. Your aunt and I ended up in the front row with him and, worst luck, there was the photograph. That's all."

"What do you mean? I don't get it. Grandmother said you were always going back and forth to demonstrations."

"She doesn't know the whole story."

"Then what were you doing? And what could have made Grandfather believe you were so militant? After all, you didn't speak for twelve years!"

Uncle Saul was about to tell me, but we were interrupted by the doorbell. He put the receiver down for a moment to go and open: I could hear a woman's voice.

"Markie," he said, getting back on the line, "I have to go, son."

"Is it Faith?"

"Yes."

"Are you two seeing each other?"

"No."

"If you are, you can tell me. You have the right to see someone."

"I'm not having an affair with her, Markie. Not with her, or with anyone. Quite simply because I don't feel like it. I've only ever loved your aunt, and I will always love her."

36

By the time I got back to Boca Raton I was a changed man, after those two days I had spent in New York. It was early May 2012.

"What's going on with you, kid?" Leo said when he saw me. "You look completely different."

"Alexandra kissed me. At my place, in New York."

He said, slightly offhand, "I think that will really help to get your novel going."

"Hide your joy, Leo."

He smiled.

"I'm very happy for you, Marcus. I really like you a lot. You're a good kid. If I'd had a daughter, I'd have done everything in my power to get her to marry you. You deserve to be happy."

A week had gone by since my evening with Alexandra in New York and I had no news. I tried twice to call her, to no avail.

Since I had no news from her, I searched for some on the Internet. On Kevin's official Facebook page, I found out they had gone to Cabo San Lucas. I saw pictures of her by a pool, with a flower in her hair. He had the indecency to display his private life for all to see. His photographs were then copied in the tabloids. I read: *Kevin Legendre has been silencing malicious gossip by publishing photographs of himself and Alexandra Neville on vacation in Mexico.*

I felt incredibly hurt. Why did she kiss me if it was only to go off with him? In the end it was my agent who elucidated the rumor:

"Marcus, have you heard? Apparently things aren't going too smoothly between Kevin and Alexandra."

"I saw pictures of the two of them looking very happy in Cabo San Lucas."

"You saw photographs of the two of them in Cabo San Lucas. Apparently, Kevin wanted to be alone with Alexandra, so he suggested this trip. Things have not been rosy between them for a while, at least that's what people are saying. She was not at all happy that he posted the photographs of the two of them on social media. Apparently she went straight back to Los Angeles."

I had no way of finding out whether what my agent said was true. In the days that followed, I still had no news. I finished emptying my uncle's house. Movers came for the last of the furniture. It was strange to see the place so empty.

"What are you going to do with the house now?" Leo said, inspecting the rooms.

"I think I'm going to sell it."

"Really?"

"Yes. You're the one who said it: memories are in our minds. I think you're right."

Part Four

THE BOOK OF THE TRAGEDY
2002–2004

37

Baltimore
February 18, 2002

Aunt Anita was laid to rest four days after the accident, in the Forrest Lane Cemetery. There was a huge turnout. Many of the faces were unfamiliar to me.

In the front row were Uncle Saul, his face like stone, and Hillel, pale with shock. He stood there like a ghost, his eyes glassy, his tie askew.

I spoke to him, but it was as if he could not hear me. I touched him, but it was as if he could not feel me. As if he were anesthetized.

I watched as the coffin was lowered into the ground, and I could not believe it. None of it felt real. As if it were not my aunt Anita, my beloved aunt, who was in that wooden coffin on which we were tossing clumps of earth. I expected to see her come over and join us. I wanted her to take me in her arms the way she used to when, as a child, I arrived on the station platform in Baltimore and she said, "You're my favorite nephew." How I used to blush with happiness.

She had died instantly. The van that hit her did not stop. No-one saw anything. Or at least not enough to help the police, who seemed to have nothing to go on. After the impact, Woody rushed over: he tried to revive her, but she was already gone. When he understood that she was dead, he began to wail, and held her to him. Patrick was still standing on the sidewalk, wild and distraught.

*

Neither Patrick nor Alexandra were there in the throng of people around the grave. Patrick because of what had happened right outside his house, and Alexandra, to avoid any scandal due to the presence of a Neville at the funeral.

As for Woody, he was hiding behind a tree, watching us from a distance. At first I thought he had not come. I had tried to reach him all morning, in vain: he had switched off his telephone. I only spotted him just as the ceremony was coming to an end. I would have known it was him even from a long way away. All the guests were heading for the parking lot: the plan was to meet back at the house in Oak Park for a light meal. I slipped away discreetly, making for the far end of the cemetery. Woody saw me coming and ran off. I hurried after him. He began to run faster and I found myself tearing after him between the graves, my shoes slipping in the mud. I caught up with him, tried to grab his arm, but I lost my balance and pulled him down with me. We fell to the ground and rolled in the damp, earthy grass.

He fought me off. Even though he was much stronger than me, I eventually managed to sit up and grab the collar of his jacket.

"Fuck, Woody!" I screamed. "Stop acting like an asshole! Where did you go? No sign of life for three days. Why didn't you answer your phone? I thought you were dead!"

"I wish I were dead, Marcus."

"How can you say such a thing?"

"Because I killed her!"

"You didn't kill her. It was an accident."

"Leave me alone, Marcus, please."

"Woody, what happened that night? What were you doing at Patrick's place?"

"I had to talk to someone. And he was the only person I could confide in. When I got to his apartment, I could see he had a date for Valentine's Day. There were flowers on the table, and champagne. But he insisted I stay for a while. I realized his guest had gone to hide in one of the bedrooms to wait for me to leave. At first I thought it was kind of funny. Then I saw her jacket on an armchair in the living room. His guest was Aunt Anita."

I couldn't believe it. So the rumors going around Oak Park were true. Aunt Anita had left Uncle Saul for Patrick.

"But what was it made you show up at Patrick's house at eleven o'clock at night? You're not telling me everything, are you?"

"I had a fight with Hillel. It almost came to blows."

I couldn't imagine Woody and Hillel having a fight, let alone almost hitting each other.

"What did you fight about?" I asked.

"Nothing, Marcus. Leave me alone now."

"No, I won't leave you alone. Why didn't you call me? Why did you say you only had Patrick to talk to? You know I'm always here for you."

"You – here for me? Really? All that changed a long time ago, Marcus. We made a pact, out in the Hamptons. Don't you remember? We weren't supposed to ever get involved with Alexandra. You betrayed our promise, and you betrayed us, Marcus. You chose a girl over the Gang. I suppose you were fucking her that night. Every time you fuck her, every time you touch her, you're betraying us, Marcus."

I tried to act as if I did not hear what he was saying.

"I won't leave you, Woody."

He decided to get rid of me. With a rapid gesture, he pressed his fingers up against my throat, cutting off my breathing. I lost my grip: he was able to get out of my stranglehold and he stood up, leaving me on the ground, coughing.

"Forget about me, Marcus. As far as you're concerned, I don't exist anymore."

He ran away. I started chasing after him again, but I just had time to see him jump into a car with a Connecticut license plate, before it drove quickly out of sight. Colleen was at the wheel.

I went back to the Baltimore house and parked where I could. The entire street was crowded with visitors' cars. I didn't feel like going in, for a start because I was a real mess: I'd been sweating and my suit was covered in mud. But above all, I did not want to see Uncle Saul and Hillel, how desperately alone they would be, surrounded by all these condescending people coming out with their stock phrases, their mouths still full of petits fours: "It will take time . . . " "We're going to miss her . . . " "Such a tragedy," before they turned to swoop down on the dessert buffet for fear there'd be nothing left.

So I sat in the car for a while, looking down the quiet street, my mind full of memories, when a black Ferrari with New York plates appeared: Patrick Neville had had the nerve to show up. He parked on the opposite side of the street and sat for a moment in the car, slumped behind the wheel; he didn't see me. I eventually got out of the car and headed over to him, furious. When he saw me coming, he got out too. He looked terrible.

"Marcus," he said, "I'm glad to see someone who—"

I didn't let him finish his sentence.

"Get the fuck out of here!" I shouted.

"Marcus, wait—"

"Go away!"

"Marcus, you don't know what happened. Let me explain—"

"Go away!" I screamed again. "You have no business here!"

Some guests who heard me shouting came out of the Baltimore house. I saw my mother and Uncle Saul running over. Before long a little crowd of onlookers had hurried outside, holding their wine glasses, and they stared at us, eager not to miss a moment of the confrontation, the nephew castigating his aunt's lover. When I saw my mother's disapproving expression and my uncle's helpless eyes, I felt horribly ashamed. Patrick then tried to explain himself to everyone.

"It's not what you think!" he said again.

But all he got in return was their scornful gazes. He climbed into his car and drove off.

Everyone went back into the house and I followed. From the porch where he had watched the scene, a ghostlike Hillel looked me right in the eye and said, "You should have smashed his face in."

I stayed in the kitchen, sitting at the bar counter. Maria, next to me, was weeping as she filled the trays with *hors d'oeuvres*, while the maids came and went with clean dishes. The house had never seemed so empty.

* * *

My parents stayed in Baltimore for two days after the funeral, then they had to get back to Montclair. I didn't feel at all like going back to school so I stayed in Baltimore a few days longer.

I spoke to Alexandra every evening. I was afraid Hillel might come in during my conversation, so I would make up some errand to run, and I borrowed Uncle Saul's car. I went for a coffee at a Dunkin' Donuts drive-in that was nearby but far enough away so I wouldn't be seen. I stayed out in the parking lot, reclined the seat and called her.

Her voice alone was enough to ease the ache. I felt stronger when I spoke to her.

"Markie, I really wish I was there with you."

"I know."

"How are Hillel and your uncle?"

"Not great. Have you seen your father? Did he tell you about the incident?"

"He really understands, Markie, don't worry. Everyone is on edge at the moment."

"Couldn't he have found someone else to screw besides my aunt?"

"Markie, he says they were just friends."

"Woody told me there was a table all set up for Valentine's Day."

"Anita had something serious to discuss with him. Something to do with your uncle. How long are you staying in Baltimore? I miss you."

"I don't know. All week, in any case. I miss you too."

A strange calm reigned in the house. Aunt Anita's ghost was there among us. The situation was so unreal it was beyond sadness. Maria's busyness seemed pointless. I heard her fussing at herself ("Mrs Goldman told you to clean the curtains," "Mrs Goldman would be disappointed in you"). As for Hillel, he was completely silent. He spent most of the time in his room, staring out the window. I eventually forced him to walk with me as far as the Dairy Shack. We ordered milkshakes and drank them there. Then we headed back to the Baltimore house. When we reached Willowick Road, Hillel said, "You know, all of this is partly my fault."

"All what?" I asked.

"That Mom died."

"Don't say things like that. It was an accident. A fucking accident."

He continued: "It's all the fault of the Goldman Gang."

I didn't know what he meant.

"You know, I think we should try to stick up for each other. Woody is not doing so hot, either."

"Well, good."

"I saw him at the cemetery the other day. He told me you'd had an argument that evening."

Hillel stopped short and looked me in the eye.

"Do you honestly think this is the time to be talking about that?"

I felt like saying yes, but I could not even bear his gaze. We continued walking in complete silence.

That evening Uncle Saul, Hillel and I had a roast chicken Maria had made. We didn't say a word throughout the entire meal. At the end Hillel said, "I'm leaving tomorrow. I'm going back to Madison." Uncle Saul nodded, then shook his head. I could tell that the Baltimore Goldmans were going downhill. Two months earlier, Hillel and Woody had been living it up at Madison University; Aunt Anita and Uncle Saul were a happy couple, brilliantly successful. Now Aunt Anita was dead, Woody was lost, and Hillel was walled up in his silence; as for my uncle Saul, this was the beginning of a new life in Oak Park. He decided to play the role of the perfect widower: courageous, resigned, and strong.

I watched the daily spectacle of neighbors dropping by with food and fine feelings. I saw them troop through the Baltimore house; they would give Uncle Saul their kind embraces, and exchange emotional gazes and long handshakes. Then I overheard the conversations at the supermarket or the dry cleaner's, or at the Dairy Shack: the gossip was flourishing. Saul was the wronged husband, he'd been humiliated. His wife had been killed as she ran out of her lover's apartment building, after her adoptive son caught her there on the evening of Valentine's Day. Everyone seemed to know even the slightest details about Aunt Anita's death. It was all out there. I could hear the scarcely veiled comments:

"But of course, he was asking for it."

"There's no smoke without fire."

"We saw him at the restaurant with that woman."

So I learned there was another woman in the story. A certain Cassandra, from the Oak Park tennis club.

I went to the Oak Park tennis club. It didn't take long to find her: at the reception there was a poster with the pictures and names of the tennis instructors, and one of them was an attractive woman by the name Cassandra Davis. All I had to do was play the charming imbecile with one of the assistants to find out that, lo and behold, she had been giving my uncle private lessons and that, lo and behold, she was off sick that day. I got her address and decided to go and see her.

As I suspected, Cassandra was not sick. When she realized I was Saul Goldman's nephew, she slammed her front door in my face. And as I was pounding on the door for her to open it again, she shouted:

"What do you want with me?"

"I just want to understand what happened to my family."

"If Saul wants to tell you, he'll tell you."

"Are you having an affair?"

"No. We went out for dinner, just once. And nothing happened. But now that his wife has died, everyone thinks I'm the local whore."

I was finding it harder and harder to figure out what was going on. One thing was for sure: Uncle Saul wasn't telling me everything. I didn't know what had happened between Woody and Hillel, or between Uncle Saul and Aunt Anita. I eventually left Baltimore one week after Aunt Anita's funeral, with no answers to my questions. The morning I left, Uncle Saul walked me to my car.

"Are you going to be alright?" I asked him, as I gave him a hug.

"I'll be O.K."

I let go of him, but he immediately grabbed me by the shoulders and said, "Markie, I did something bad. That's why your aunt left."

I drove out of Oak Park, leaving Uncle Saul and Maria behind me as the last residents of the house of my dearest childhood dreams, and I stopped for a long time at the Forrest Lane Cemetery. I don't know if I went there to look for her presence or because I hoped to find Woody there.

Then I took the road to Montclair. It felt good to arrive at my street. The Baltimore castle had crumbled; the Montclair house, small but solid, was standing proudly.

I called Alexandra to tell her I was there. One hour later she was at my parents' place. She rang the doorbell and I opened. I felt so relieved to see her that I let out all the pent-up emotions of the last few days and burst into tears. "Markie . . . " said Alexandra, taking me in her arms. "I'm so sorry, Markie."

38

New York
Summer 2011

The repercussions of Aunt Anita's death had a new resonance nine years after the events, in August 2011, when Uncle Saul called to ask me to be there for the removal of his name from the stadium at Madison University.

I had gone back to New York after he asked me to leave his place in June. He had moved to Coconut Grove five years earlier and this would be the first summer I wasn't going to see him in Florida. It was at that time that I got the idea of buying a house there: if I liked being in Florida, I ought to have my own place. I would find a house where I could write in peace, far from the bustle of New York, and near my uncle's place. Until my last visit I had assumed he enjoyed having me there, but now I realized maybe he, too, needed space to himself to live his life, without having his nephew underfoot. It was understandable.

What was strange was that he rarely got in touch. It wasn't like him. I had always been very close to him; Aunt Anita's death and the tragedy had brought us even closer. For five years I had been traveling down the East Coast on a regular basis to help him out of his solitude. Why had he suddenly severed all ties? Not one day went by without my wondering if I had done something wrong. Was it something to do with Faith, the supermarket manager, whom I had suspected of having an affair with him? Did he feel awkward – as if he were being unfaithful? His wife had died nine years earlier; he had the right to see someone, after all.

He only emerged from his silence two months later when he sent me to the stadium in Madison. We had a long conversation on the telephone the day after his name was destroyed, once I realized that it must be Madison that was at the heart of the mechanism that had been the undoing of the Baltimores. Madison was the poison.

"Uncle Saul," I asked, "what happened during those years in Madison? Why did you finance the maintenance of the stadium for ten years?"

"Because I wanted my name on it."

"But why? That's not like you."

"Why are you asking me all these questions? Are you finally going to write a book about me?"

"Maybe."

He burst out laughing.

"Basically, when Hillel and Woody went away to Madison, it was the beginning of the end. The end of my relationship, to start with. You know that your aunt and I, we loved each other very much."

He gave me a rough description of how he had been a New Jersey Goldman until he met Aunt Anita, and then with her by his side he became a Baltimore Goldman. He told me again how they met, when he went off to study at the University of Maryland in the late 1960s. Aunt Anita's father, Professor Hendricks, taught economics, and Uncle Saul was his student.

They got along particularly well and when Uncle Saul asked for his help with a project, Professor Hendricks readily agreed.

Saul's name often came up in the Hendricks home, until one evening Mrs Hendricks finally asked: "Honestly, who is this Saul who takes up all our conversations? I'm beginning to get jealous."

"My student Saul Goldman, sweetie. A Jewish boy from New Jersey whose father has a medical equipment company. I really like this kid, he'll go far."

Mrs Hendricks told him to invite Saul home for dinner, and it was arranged for the following week. Anita was immediately enchanted by this affable, elegant young man.

The feelings were mutual. Saul, ordinarily impossible to intimidate, was completely tongue-tied in her presence. Eventually he invited her out a first time, and then a second. Then he was invited to dinner at the Hendrickses' yet again. Anita was struck by the impression Saul made on her father. She saw him looking at the young man in a way he usually reserved only for people for whom he had the deepest respect. Saul started coming over on weekends to work on his project; he explained that the aim was to expand his father's company.

Their first kiss was on a day of rain. He was driving her home and, just as he pulled over, the skies opened. He parked a short distance beyond the Hendricks house. A torrential downpour hammered on the roof of the car and Saul suggested they wait for it to calm down. "I don't think this will last," he said knowingly. A few minutes later, it was raining harder than ever. The water streaming down the windshield and windows made them invisible. Saul caressed her hand, she took his, and they kissed.

From that day on, they kissed at least once a day, every day, for thirty-five years.

In addition to her medical studies, Anita worked as a saleswoman at Delfino's, a fairly fashionable store in Washington where they sold ties. Her boss was a bastard. Uncle Saul sometimes dropped in to say hello, just a fleeting visit, not to be a bother, and even then only if there were no other customers. But Anita's boss could not help but make scornful comments, the likes of, "I'm not paying you to flirt, Anita."

As a result, to annoy the man, Uncle Saul began buying ties to make his presence legitimate. He would come in, pretend he didn't know Anita, just say a polite hello, and ask to try on different styles. Sometimes he made his mind up quickly and bought one. More often, he would hesitate for a long time. He tried a tie, then tried it again, doing the knot three times over, then he'd ask Anita to forgive him for being so slow, and she had to press her lips together not to burst out laughing. The entire scenario infuriated her boss, but he did not dare say anything for fear of losing a sale.

Anita begged Saul to stop coming: he didn't have much money, and now he was spending it all on useless ties. But he insisted that, on the contrary, he had never put his money to such good use. He would keep those ties all his life. And years later, in their huge house in Baltimore, when Aunt Anita suggested he get rid of his old ties, Uncle Saul was offended, and assured her that every one of them constituted a particular memory.

When Saul reckoned that his project for giving Goldman and Company a boost was ready, he decided to show it to his father. The night before he was due to go to New Jersey, he rehearsed his presentation with Anita, to make sure everything would be perfect. But the next day, Max Goldman would not hear of expanding his company. Saul realized his father was rejecting his proposal point-blank, and he was devastated. When he got back to Maryland he did not even dare tell Anita's father that he had been sent packing.

Professor Hendricks was very active in the protest movement. Saul was not an activist, but he supported various causes. He occasionally accompanied his professor to a meeting or a demonstration, above all because this was a way of thanking him for all the help he had given him with his project. But before long Saul had become interested for other reasons altogether.

In those days, a wind of protest was blowing over the country: there were demonstrations almost everywhere: against the war, against segregation, against the government. At every university students organized transportation by bus from one state to another to swell the ranks, and Saul, who didn't have a penny to finance the ideas for Goldman and Company's expansion, which his father refused to support, found a way, through these demonstrations, to travel for free and prospect for markets in the name of the family business.

His geographical radius grew ever wider, in keeping with the protest events. There were riots at Kent State, and university strikes against Nixon. Saul planned his trips carefully, and set up meetings with wholesalers, transporters, and hospital authorities in towns where demonstrations were being held. Once he was there, he would disappear into the tumult of the crowd. He would button up his shirt, adjust his suit – carefully removing his antiwar badges – put on a tie and go to his meeting. He introduced himself as the director of development for Goldman and Company, a little medical equipment manufacturer based in New Jersey. He tried to analyze what the various regions needed, what the doctors and hospitals expected or were dissatisfied with, and where Goldman and Company might step into the breach, find a niche. Would it be the speed of delivery? The quality of the equipment? Or of the maintenance service? Should they set up a warehouse in every town? In every state? He looked into rents, salaries, employees' contracts. When he got back to his little room on campus at the University of Maryland, he inserted pages of notes into a big binder and made all sorts of markings on a map of the country he had hanging on the wall. He had but one goal in mind: to prepare, point by point, a development plan for his father's business, a plan his father was sure to be proud of. This would be his moment of glory: he would surpass his brother, the respected engineer. He would be the one to ensure the longevity of the Goldmans.

Sometimes Anita accompanied him on his trips, particularly if her father was taking part in a demonstration. She would stay with her father during the march and keep him busy, making him believe that Saul was either a few rows behind them, or with the organizers up in the front. They would meet again on the bus at the end of the day and Professor Hendricks would say, "Where were you, Saul? I didn't see you all day!"

"It's so crowded, Professor Hendricks, so crowded . . ."

*

1972 was a culminating point for their activism. They were behind every cause: Watergate, women's lib, the Honeywell Project against anti-personnel mines. Which cause it was hardly mattered, as long as Uncle Saul had a good alibi to go on prospecting. One weekend they were at a demonstration in Atlanta, the next one at a meeting on the civil rights committee, and the week after that on a march in Washington. All the while Saul was establishing solid ties with top-level university hospitals.

Saul's parents knew their son was always on the move, but they blindly believed the official version, according to which he was deeply committed to the protest movement. How could they ever have suspected the truth?

In the spring of 1973, Uncle Saul was about to show his father the extraordinary work he had done for the company: there were partnership agreements ready to be signed, potential collaborators they could trust, a list of warehouses they could rent. But then came that one demonstration too many in Atlanta, where Professor Hendricks was a joint organizer. This time, Saul and Anita went on the entire march with her father, in the front row. Nothing would have come of it, had a photograph of them not ended up on the front page of *Time*. Because of that photograph, Max Goldman had a violent argument with his son. And thereafter they did not speak for twelve years. Perhaps it would have been enough simply to explain everything to Grandfather, but Saul was not someone who could swallow his pride.

On the telephone, I interrupted Uncle Saul and said: "So, you never really were an activist?"

"Never, Marcus. All I was trying to do was help Goldman and Company expand so I could impress my father. That was all I wanted: for him to be proud of me. I felt so rejected, so hurt by him. He wanted to run everything his way. Look where it got us."

*

After the argument, Uncle Saul decided to take his life in a new direction. While Anita was studying medicine, he went to law school.

They got married. Max Goldman did not come to the wedding.

Saul took the bar exam in Maryland. As Anita had found a position as an intern at Johns Hopkins, they moved to Baltimore. Saul studied commercial law and before long he was flourishing as a lawyer. At the same time he made some investments that turned out to be very lucrative.

They were so happy together. Every week, they went to the movies, and lazed around on Sundays. When Anita had time off, she would surprise him at his office to take him out for dinner. If, when she got there, she saw through the frosted glass window that he was too busy, with a case or some other matter, she would go to a nearby Italian restaurant, the Stella. She ordered pasta and tiramisu to go and dropped them off with Saul's secretary with a note: *An angel came by*.

As the years passed, the Stella became their favorite restaurant in Baltimore. They befriended the owner, Nicola, and from time to time Uncle Saul gave him legal advice. Woody, Hillel and I got to know the Stella very well too, because Uncle Saul and Aunt Anita often took us there.

During the years that followed their move to Baltimore, the only cloud on the horizon was the fact there were no children. There was no explanation: the doctors they consulted concluded they were both in perfect health. Finally, after seven years of marriage, Anita was pregnant, and that was when Hillel entered our lives. Had the waiting been a whim of nature, or a wink from life, arranging things so that Hillel and I would be born only a few months apart?

On the telephone I asked my uncle: "What does what you've been telling me have to do with Madison?"

"It's the children, Marcus. The children."

* * *

In the months that followed Aunt Anita's death, Hillel and I finished college.

As for Woody, he had abandoned his studies for good. Crushed by guilt, he found refuge with Colleen, in Madison. She showed tremendous patience in looking after him. During the day he helped her at the gas station, and in the evening he washed dishes at a Chinese restaurant to earn some money. Other than going to the supermarket, he kept strictly to those two places. He did not want to run into Hillel. They no longer spoke.

As for me, with my degree under my belt, I decided to set about writing my first novel. For me this was the beginning of a period that was both tragic and wonderful, which would lead to the year 2006: the year my first novel, *G for Goldstein*, was published, the year of consecration that would see the boy from Montclair, the summer visitor in the Hamptons, become the new star of American literature.

If one day you go and see my parents in Montclair, my mother will certainly show you "the room". She has been keeping it intact for years. And yet I have often begged her to make better use of it, but she won't listen. She calls it the "Markie Museum". If you go to their place, she's sure to make you have a look. She'll open the door and say, "See, this is where Marcus did his writing." I wouldn't necessarily have thought of moving back to my parents' place to write had my mother not prepared a surprise for me: she converted the guest room into a study.

"Close your eyes and follow me, Markie," she said, the day I came home from college.

I obeyed and let her lead me to the door of the room. My father was as excited as she was.

"Don't open your eyes yet," she ordered, seeing me flutter my eyelids.

I laughed. Finally she said, "O.K., now you can look!"

I was speechless. The guest room, which I had secretly renamed the garbage room, since over time all the things we didn't know whether to keep or throw away had ended up in there, had been transformed. My parents had cleared it out and redone it: new curtains, new carpet, and a big bookshelf against one of the walls. Opposite the window was the desk that Grandfather used back when he ran the company, and which for a long time had stayed in a storage facility. "Welcome to your study," my mother said, giving me a kiss. "This will be the perfect chair for you to sit in and write." And it was in this room that I wrote the novel about my cousins, *G for Goldstein*, the book of their lost destinies, the book I only started, in fact, after the tragedy. For a long time I let people think that it took me four years to write my first novel. But anyone who looked closely at the chronology would notice a gap of two years, which meant I did not have to explain what I had been doing from the summer of 2002 until the day of the tragedy, November 24, 2004.

39

When Aunt Anita died, it was Alexandra who saved me.

She was my equilibrium, my stability, my mooring in life. By the time I was finishing up my studies, two years had gone by and she'd gotten nowhere with her producer. She asked me what she ought to do, and I said that in my opinion there were only two cities where she could get started in music: New York and Nashville.

"But I don't know anyone in Nashville," she said.

"Neither do I," I said.

"Then let's go there!"

So we went to Nashville.

She came to pick me up one morning at my parents', in Montclair. She rang the bell, and my mother, radiant, opened the door.

"Alexandra!"

"Hello, Mrs Goldman."

"So, it's the big move?"

"Yes, Mrs Goldman. I'm so happy Markie is coming with me."

I think my parents were really glad that I was getting out from under their feet. The Baltimores had always taken up so much room in my life; maybe it was time for me to move on.

My mother thought this was just youthful folly. That it would last two months at the most and we would soon be back, disappointed by our experience. She had no way of knowing what awaited us in Tennessee.

As we drove away from New Jersey, Alexandra said, "You're not too sad to be leaving your new study, Markie?"

"Aw, I'll get around to writing my novel sooner or later. And besides, I don't want to be a Montclair my whole life long."

She smiled.

"And what are you going to be? A Baltimore?"

"I think I just want to be Marcus Goldman."

For me this was the beginning of a magical period: it would last two years and end in glory for Alexandra. It was also the beginning of an extraordinary life together: thanks to a family trust her father had set up, Alexandra received a little monthly allowance. As for me, I had the money I'd inherited from Grandfather. We rented a little apartment, our first home, where she wrote her songs and I started on the first draft of my novel, on the kitchen table.

We didn't question anything: was it too soon for our relationship? Would we be able to weather the vagaries of trying to start our careers as artists? It was a risky wager and it could have all gone wrong. But our closeness transcended everything. It was as if nothing could harm us.

To be sure, we were living in close quarters, but we shared the dream of having a big apartment in the West Village some day, with a big terrace full of flowers. She'd be a famous singer, I'd be a successful author.

I encouraged her to forget about the two years she had spent with her New York producer: she should do as she pleased. The rest hardly mattered.

She wrote a new collection of songs: I thought they were good. She'd found her style again. I urged her to rearrange some of her old compositions. At the same time, she tested audience reaction by performing whenever she could at open mics in Nashville bars. It was rumored that there was one bar in particular, the Nightingale, where producers often came and sat in the audience, on the lookout for new talent. Alexandra sang there every week, hoping she would be noticed.

The days were long. In the evening, after she had been playing in a bar, we were tired, so we went to a diner we liked that was open around the clock, and we'd collapse in one of the booths. We were exhausted and famished, but happy. We'd order huge hamburgers and once we were full, we would go on sitting there for a little while. We felt good. She'd say, "Tell me, Markie, tell me how it will be some day."

I would tell her about our future.

I told her how successful her music would be, how she'd go on tours that would be sold out, filling stadiums, thousands of people coming to hear her. I described her in such a way that I could see her on stage; I could hear the audience cheering.

Then I told her about us. How we'd live in New York, and have a vacation home in Florida. She asked, "Why Florida?" I said, "Because it will be a great place to be."

As a rule, it would be so late that there weren't many diners left in the restaurant. Alexandra picked up her guitar, leaned against me, and began to sing. I closed my eyes. Life was good.

That fall, we found a studio that gave us a good price, and she recorded a demo.

Now we had to get her work out there.

We went to every record company in the city. She would go shyly up to the reception with an envelope in her hand containing a C.D. she had compiled herself, with her best songs. The receptionist would stare at her, not at all accommodating, until Alexandra finally said, "Hi, I'm Alexandra Neville, I'm looking for a record label and—"

"Do you have a demo?" the receptionist said, between two movements of her jaws that offered a glimpse of her chewing gum.

"Uh . . . yes. Here."

She handed her precious envelope to the receptionist, who put it in a plastic basket behind her, already full to the brim with other demos.

"Is that it?" Alexandra said.

"That's it," the receptionist replied, ungraciously.

"Will you call me?"

"If your demo is good, yes, I'm sure we will."

"But how can I be sure that you will listen to it?"

"You know, sweetheart, you can never be sure of anything in life."

Alexandra left the building, crestfallen, and climbed in the car, where I was waiting for her.

"They said that if they like it, they'll call me."

Several months went by, and no-one called.

Other than my parents, no-one really knew what I was doing. Officially, I was in my study in Montclair, busy writing my first novel.

There was no-one who could check on that.

The only other person who knew the truth was Patrick Neville, through Alexandra. I had not been able to mend my fences with him. He was the man who had taken my aunt from me.

That was the only problem in my relationship with Alexandra. I did not want to see him: I was too afraid I would leap at his throat. It was better if I kept my distance. Sometimes Alexandra said: "You know, about my father—"

"Drop it. We just have to let time go by."

She did not insist.

Basically, the only person I wanted to hide the truth from, about Alexandra and me, was Hillel. I was up to my neck in a lie and I could no longer get out of it.

We were only seldom in touch; things were not the way they used to be. It was as if Aunt Anita's death had destroyed our relationship. But it was not only because of his mother's death: there was something else I did not immediately grasp.

Hillel had become serious. He attended his classes at law school and that was enough for him. He had lost his magic. And he had lost his *alter ego*. He had severed all his ties with Woody.

Woody had started a new life in Madison. I called him from time to time: he didn't really have anything to tell me anymore. I finally understood what it was, this bad thing that had overcome them, when he said to me one day, over the telephone: "Same old. The gas station, my job at the restaurant. Daily routine, that's about it." They had stopped dreaming: they had allowed themselves to be swallowed up by a sort of renunciation of life. They had fallen back into line.

They used to defend the oppressed; they had started their gardening business; they dreamt about football and eternal friendship. This was what had kept the Goldman Gang together: we had been first-class dreamers. This was what had made us so special. But now, of the three of us, I was the last one who still had a dream. The original dream. Why did I want to become a famous writer and not just a plain old writer? Because of the Baltimores. They had been my role models, then they became my rivals. My one aspiration was to surpass them.

That year, 2002, I went with my parents to Oak Park to celebrate Thanksgiving. Only Hillel and Uncle Saul were there, halfheartedly toying with the food Maria had prepared.

It was not the way it used to be.

That night I couldn't sleep. At around two o'clock in the morning I went down to the kitchen for a bottle of water. There was a light on in Uncle Saul's study. I went to have a look and I found him sitting in a reading chair, gazing at a photograph of himself with Aunt Anita.

He noticed me there and I gave him a timid wave, embarrassed that I had interrupted him in the middle of his thoughts.

"You're not sleeping, Marcus?"

"No. I can't get to sleep, Uncle Saul."

"Is something bothering you?"

"What happened with Aunt Anita? Why did she leave you?"

"It doesn't matter."

He refused to discuss the matter. For the first time there was an insurmountable barrier between the Baltimores and me: there were secrets.

* * *

August 2011

Who was that uncle I no longer recognized? Why had he banished me from his home?

On the telephone, I could tell his voice was hard.

I had loved Florida because it had restored my Uncle Saul to me. Between Aunt Anita's death in 2002 and the tragedy in 2004, enough had happened to make anyone go into a deep depression. But the move to Coconut Grove in 2006 had transformed Uncle Saul. The Uncle Saul I found in Florida was once again my beloved uncle. And for five years I had known the joy of being with him again.

But now, once again, I felt our relationship was suffering. This uncle was hiding something from me. He had a secret, but what was it? Did it have something to do with the stadium in Madison? Because I kept insisting, over the telephone, he finally said, "Do you want to know why I paid for the maintenance of the stadium in Madison?"

"I do."

"It was because of Patrick Neville."

"Patrick Neville? What has he got to do with any of that?"

Woody and Hillel's departure for college had greater repercussions on Uncle Saul and Aunt Anita's lives than I would ever have suspected. For years the boys had been the existential heart of the Baltimores' lives. Everything had revolved around them: their school tuition, vacations, extracurricular activities. The grownups' daily routine was organized on the basis of the boys'. Football practice, parties and excursions, trouble at school. For years, Uncle Saul and Aunt Anita had lived for them and through them.

But the wheel of life turns: at the age of thirty, Uncle Saul and Aunt Anita had their lives ahead of them. Then Hillel was born, and they bought a huge house. And now twenty years had gone by in a flash. In the blink of an eye Hillel, the child they had wanted for so long, had reached the age to go to college.

One day in Oak Park in 1998, Hillel and Woody climbed into the car that Uncle Saul had just given them and drove off to college. And after twenty years of plenitude, the house was suddenly empty.

No more school, no more homework, no more football practice, no more deadlines. A house so deserted that voices echoed. No more sound, no more soul.

Aunt Anita tried to cook for her husband. In spite of her tight schedule at the hospital, she found the time to come up with complicated, innovative meals. But once they sat down to dinner, they ate in silence. In the old days, conversation had come naturally: Hillel, Woody, school, homework, football. Now there were heavy silences.

They invited friends over, and went to charity events: the presence of other people kept boredom at bay. Conversations flowed more easily. But in the car on the way home, not another word. They might talk about so-and-so, or what's-his-face. But never about themselves. They had been so busy with their children that they did not realize they had nothing left to say to each other.

They walled themselves up in their silence. And as soon as they saw Woody and Hillel again, they came alive. Going to visit them at the university kept them busy. Welcoming them home for a few days filled them with joy. Things started moving again, the house was lively, they had to go shopping for four. Then the boys left, and silence settled back over them.

*

Bit by bit, it was not only the Baltimore house that lost its resonance, with Hillel and Woody deserting it, but also Aunt Anita and Uncle Saul's entire life cycle. Everything was different. They tried to go on doing what they had always done: the Hamptons, the Buenavista, Whistler. But without Hillel and Woody, those happy places became places of boredom.

It did not help that college had gradually absorbed Hillel and Woody. Uncle Saul and Aunt Anita felt as if they were losing them. The boys had their football, the university newspaper, their classes. They no longer had much time for their parents. When at last they met up, all too often the conversation revolved around Patrick Neville.

This was a bad blow for my uncle.

He began to feel less important, less indispensable. He was the head of the family, the counselor, the guide, the wise man, he was all powerful – yet he was losing ground. Patrick Neville cast a shadow. In the desert of Oak Park, Uncle Saul felt he was slowly being pushed to one side in favor of Patrick.

Whenever Hillel and Woody were in Baltimore, they would go on and on about how wonderful Patrick was, and when it was Uncle Saul and Aunt Anita who went to Madison to attend a Titans game, they could see that Patrick and their two children had a special relationship. My cousins had found a new role model, and he was more handsome, more powerful, and richer.

Every time someone mentioned Patrick, Uncle Saul would grumble, "What is so wonderful about that Neville guy?" In Madison, Patrick was on his home turf. If Woody and Hillel needed help, they turned now to Patrick. And when questions about career choice regarding football arose, it was once again Patrick they went to consult. "Why do they always call Patrick?" Uncle Saul said irritably. "Don't we matter anymore? We're not good enough? What has he got that I haven't got, that damned Neville guy from New York?"

*

A year went by, then two. Uncle Saul was getting worse by the day. His life in Baltimore was no longer enough. He wanted to be admired again. He no longer thought about Aunt Anita, but only about himself. They spent several days together at the Buenavista to try to reconnect. But it wasn't the same. Saul missed having his sons there to show their love for him; he missed his nephew Marcus, the way he would stand in awe at the luxury of his uncle's apartment.

Aunt Anita told him she was happy to be just the two of them, that at last they would have some time alone. But so much peace and quiet did not suit Uncle Saul. Eventually she said, "I miss you, Saul, I'm bored without you. Tell me you love me again. Speak to me the way you used to thirty years ago."

"If you're bored, honey, let's get a dog."

He did not notice how anxious she was becoming: she could see in the mirror that she had aged. So many questions were nagging at her: was he neglecting her because of his obsession with Patrick Neville, or because he no longer found her attractive? She could see those twenty-year-old girls in Madison, with their firm bodies, their breasts where they belonged, and she could sense his desire. She even went to consult a cosmetic surgeon, and begged him to help her. To give her a breast lift, erase her wrinkles, firm up her buttocks.

She was unhappy. Her husband felt neglected: consequently he neglected her. She wished she could plead with him not to look away just because they had grown older. She wanted him to tell her all was not lost. She wanted him to love her the way he used to, just one last time. She wanted him to desire her. To take her the way he used to. The way he did in his little room at the University of Maryland, at the Buenavista, at the Hamptons, on their wedding night. The way he had, to give her Hillel, the way he had on a country road on the back seat of his old Oldsmobile, or countless times on a warm night out on their terrace in Baltimore.

But Saul no longer had any time for her. He didn't want to repair their relationship, he didn't want to go back into the past. He wanted a rebirth. Whenever he could, he went off jogging in the neighborhood.

"You've never gone jogging," Aunt Anita said.

"Well, now I do."

At noon he no longer wanted to eat the food she brought from the Stella. He did not want pasta or pizza, he wanted salad without dressing, and fruit. He set up weights in the guest room and a full-length mirror. He began working out at every opportunity. He lost weight, improved his appearance, changed his aftershave, bought new clothes. His clients kept him until late in the evening. Aunt Anita waited.

"I'm sorry, I had a dinner." "Forgive me, but I've got a business trip here and then another one there." "The shipping companies have never been so eager for my services." Suddenly he was in such a good mood.

She wanted to please him, and did everything she could. She put on a nice dress and cooked dinner, she lit candles: the minute he comes through the door, she thought, I'll rush up and kiss him. She waited a long time. Long enough to understand that he wouldn't be coming home. Finally he called and mumbled something about being held up.

She wanted to please him, and did everything she could. She went to the gym, she changed her wardrobe. She bought lacy nightgowns and offered to play-act the way she used to, to strip for him. He replied, "Thanks, but not tonight." And he just left her standing there, stark naked.

Who was she? A woman who had aged.

She wanted to please him, did everything she could. But he no longer looked at her.

He was once again the Saul he had been thirty years earlier: singing, dancing, acting the clown.

He was once again the Saul she had loved so much. But she was no longer the one he loved.

The one he loved was called Cassandra: she gave tennis lessons in Oak Park. She was beautiful, and half their age. But what Uncle Saul liked most about her was that when he spoke to her, her eyes sparkled in response. She looked at him the way Hillel and Woody used to look at him. He could impress Cassandra: he could tell her about his awesome feats on the stock market, or about the Dominic Pernell affair, or his exploits in the courtroom.

Aunt Anita found messages from Cassandra; she spotted her going into Uncle Saul's office with containers of salad and organic vegetables. One evening he left the house to go and "have dinner with clients". When he finally got home, Aunt Anita was waiting for him, and she could smell the other woman on his skin. She said, "I'm leaving you, Saul."

"Leaving me? Why?"

"Because you're cheating on me."

"I'm not cheating on you."

"So what about Cassandra?"

"It's not you I'm cheating on when I'm with her. It's my own sadness."

No-one had any idea, during those years when they were at Madison, how greatly Uncle Saul was suffering from Hillel and Woody's attachment to Patrick Neville.

When Uncle Saul and Aunt Anita went to watch a Titans game in Madison, they felt like strangers. They arrived at the stadium and Hillel was already sitting next to Patrick in a row where there were no more free seats. So they sat just behind. After a victory, they went to join Woody outside the locker room: Uncle Saul was beaming with pride and joy, but his congratulations did not carry as much weight as Patrick Neville's. His opinions were not as precious as Patrick's. When Uncle Saul gave him advice about his game, Woody replied, "Maybe you're right. I'll ask Patrick what he thinks." After the game, Uncle Saul and Aunt Anita would ask Woody and Hillel to go to dinner with them. Most of the time the boys would decline the invitation, saying they wanted to go and eat with the rest of the team. "Sure, have fun!" said Uncle Saul. One day, after the game, Uncle Saul took Aunt Anita to a restaurant in Madison. Just as they walked in, he stopped short and turned back. "What's the matter?" asked Aunt Anita. "Nothing," replied Uncle Saul. "I'm just not hungry anymore." He blocked the way and stopped Aunt Anita from entering. She realized something was going on, and as she looked through the window of the restaurant, she saw Woody and Hillel together at a table with Patrick.

One day, Woody and Hillel showed up in Baltimore in Patrick's black Ferrari. Uncle Saul, disgusted, spluttered: "What the hell? The car I bought you isn't good enough?"

He felt that Patrick Neville had outdone him. All they ever talked about was Patrick's career, Patrick's success, Patrick's amazing apartment in New York and his phenomenal salary. The boys spent their weekends with him in New York. He became their best friend.

And the more they went to Titans games, and the more Woody won, the more abandoned Uncle Saul felt. It was with Patrick that Woody discussed his projects and career opportunities. It was with Patrick that he wanted to have dinner after the game. "But it's thanks to us, after all, that he didn't give up on his football," complained Uncle Saul unhappily, once he was alone in the car with his wife.

Eventually Saul and Anita joined Patrick and the boys for one of their after-game dinners. But when Patrick Neville fixed things on the sly so he could pay the bill, Saul lost his temper. "What the hell does he think? That I don't have the means to take everyone out for a meal? Who does he think he is?"

Uncle Saul had lost.

Uncle Saul flew first class? Patrick Neville flew in a private jet.

Patrick had a car that was worth one year of Saul's salary. His bathrooms were as big as their bedrooms, his bedrooms were as big as their living room, his living room was as big as their house.

*

I listened to Uncle Saul on the telephone. Finally I said, "You're wrong, Uncle Saul. They always loved and admired you, so much. Woody was so grateful for what you did for him. He said that without you he would have ended up on the street. He's the one who asked to have the Goldman name printed on his jersey."

"It's not a question of being wrong or not, Marcus. It's a feeling. You can't control it, or rationalize it. Just a feeling. I was jealous, I didn't feel equal to him. Patrick was a New York Neville; we were just Baltimore Goldmans."

"So you paid six million dollars to have your name on the stadium in Madison," I said.

"Yes. To have my name up there in huge letters, right where you arrived on campus. So that everyone would see me. And to raise that amount of money, I did something very stupid. What if everything that happened was my fault? What if working at the supermarket isn't just punishment for my sins after all?"

40

2003–2004

At the beginning of 2003, Alexandra was performing one evening at the Nightingale and she met someone who would change her life.

When she had finished her gig, she came and joined me. I applauded, and kissed her, and I was about to go and get her a drink when a man came over to us.

"I loved your show," he said to Alexandra. "You are incredibly talented!"

"Thank you."

"Who writes your songs?"

"I do."

He held out his hand.

"My name is Eric Tanner. I'm a producer, and I'm looking for an artist to launch my record label. You're the one I've been waiting for."

Eric spoke in a quiet and sincere manner: he was nothing like those smooth talkers I had met up to then. He had heard Alexandra for only twenty minutes and he was already brimming with ideas. I figured he must be either a crook or a madman.

He handed us his business card, and once we checked his information we had every reason to be suspicious. There might indeed be a company registered under his name, but the address was the same as his house in the Nashville suburbs, and he had not produced the single artist. Alexandra decided not to call him back. He came and found us. He went every night to the Nightingale until he saw us again. He insisted on buying us a drink and we sat down at a quiet table.

He went into a twenty-minute monologue, explaining everything he found so moving about Alexandra, and why he knew she would become a huge star.

He told us he had been a producer with a major record label and had just quit. It had been his lifelong dream to start his own label, but he needed an artist who would be equal to his ambition, and Alexandra was the star he had been waiting for. His conviction, his charisma, and his enthusiasm won her over. When he had finished, she asked to speak to me for a moment and took me to one side. I saw her eyes were shining with joy.

"He's the one, Markie. The right one. I can feel it deep down. He's the one. What do you think?"

"Follow your instinct. If you believe in him, then go for it."

She smiled. She went and sat back down at the table and said to Eric: "It's a yes. I want to make this record with you."

They signed a pledge agreement on a scrap of paper.

It was the beginning of an extraordinary adventure. Eric took us under his wing. He was married, the father of two children, and we spent countless evenings over there for dinner while we were working on Alexandra's first album.

We got a group together, auditioning local musicians in a studio someone had lent to Eric.

Then the long process of recording began, and it lasted several months. Alexandra and Eric chose the twelve songs that would make up the album, and worked on the arrangements. Then there was all the work in the studio.

In October 2003, roughly a year and a half after we had moved to Nashville, Alexandra's first record was ready at last.

Now we had to find a way to get it noticed. There was only one solution for this sort of situation: get in the car and drive all over the country visiting all the radio stations.

And that is what Alexandra and I did.

We drove from one end of the country to the other, from east to west and north to south, from one city to the next, distributing her C.D. to every radio station, and above all persuading the program directors to broadcast her songs.

Every day was a new start. A new city, new people to win over. We slept in cheap motels, where Alexandra managed to charm the staff so she could use the kitchen to bake cookies or a cake for the people in charge at the radio stations. She also wrote long letters by hand to thank them for their attention. She never stopped. She spent all her evenings at it, sometimes well into the night. I would doze on the kitchen counter or a table next to her. During the day I drove and she slept on the passenger seat. Then we'd get to that day's radio station and she would hand out her record, her letter, her cookies. She captivated the radio stations with her youthful, sparkling presence.

On the road we listened attentively to the radio. With every pause before a new track, our hearts would be pounding with the hope that it might be one of her songs. But it never was.

Until finally one day in April we got into the car, I switched on the radio, and there she was. One of the stations was playing her song. I turned the volume up as loud as it would go, and I saw her burst into tears. Tears of joy streamed down her face; she reached for me and kissed me for a long time. She told me that it was thanks to me, all of it.

We had been together almost six years, and all that time we'd been happy. I thought that nothing could ever part us. Except the Goldman Gang.

* * *

It was Alexandra who brought the Goldman Gang back together again.

She was still in touch with Woody and Hillel. One day in the spring of 2004 she said, "You have to talk to Hillel, he has to know about us. He's your friend, and mine, too. Friends don't lie to each other like this."

She was right, so I did as she said.

At the beginning of May I went to Baltimore. I told him everything. When I had finished talking, he smiled and gave me a hug.

"I'm really happy for you, Markie."

His reaction surprised me.

"Honestly?" I said. "You're not mad at me?"

"Not a bit."

"But we made that pact, in the Hamptons . . . "

"I've always admired you," he said.

"What are you talking about?"

"It's true. I always thought you were better looking and more intelligent, and more gifted than me. The way girls look at you, the way my mother used to talk about you after you had come to stay. She would say, 'Let Markie be an example to you.' I've always admired you, Markie. And then your parents are great. Look at that, your mother made you a study so you could become a writer. In my case, my father has always been pestering me to become a lawyer, like him. So that's what I'm doing. To make my father happy. The way I always have. You're a special guy, Marcus. And the proof is that you don't even realize it."

I smiled. I felt very moved.

"I want us to get together with Woody again," I said. "I want us to start the Gang again."

"I do, too."

The Gang's reunion, which took place at the Dairy Shack in Oak Park, make me realize how strong the bond between my cousins and me was. One year had been enough to ease the suffering and criticism, and give way to that powerful, immutable feeling of fraternal friendship that united the three of us. Nothing could destroy it.

We met around the same table, sipping our milkshakes the way we used to as kids. Hillel, Woody and Colleen, Alexandra and me.

*

I realized that deep down Woody was happy in Madison with Colleen. She had calmed him down, healed his wounds, made him whole again. He had managed to move on from Aunt Anita's death.

As if to ward off an evil spell, after the Dairy Shack we all went to the Forrest Lane Cemetery. Alexandra and Colleen stayed behind, at a distance. Woody, Hillel and I sat down next to her tombstone.

We had become men.

The photograph of the three of us wasn't the one I had imagined ten years earlier.

We had not become those larger-than-life people I had dreamt of. The great footballer, the famous lawyer. We hadn't become as extraordinary as I had hoped. But they were my cousins, and I loved them more than anything.

In Oak Park, in the big house on Willowick Road, Uncle Saul was no longer the man I had known. He was lonelier, sadder. But at least I was in touch with him again, too.

I began to wonder if I was the one who, as a child, had done all their dreaming for them. Whether I had not seen them differently from who they really were, in the end. Had they indeed been those amazing people I admired so much? Had it not all been my imagination? And had I not, myself, always been my own Baltimore?

We spent the evening and night together in the Baltimore house, which had plenty of room for us all. Uncle Saul was delighted to have us there.

It must have been midnight and we were out on the patio by the swimming pool. It was very warm. We were gazing at the stars. Uncle Saul came out and sat down with us. "Boys," he said, "I thought maybe we could all meet up here for Thanksgiving."

What a joy to hear him talking like that! It gave me a shiver to hear him say "boys". I closed my eyes and saw us the way we had been twelve years earlier.

His suggestion met with general approval. We were excited at the mere thought of seeing the table set for Thanksgiving. The months would have to go by quickly.

But there would be no Thanksgiving that year.

Two months later, at the beginning of July 2004, Luke, Colleen's husband, got out of jail.

He had served his sentence.

41

Madison, Connecticut
July 2004

The word began to spread the moment he set foot in town. Luke was back.

He arrived one morning, acting triumphant, making sure everyone saw him at the tables outside the bars in Madison. "I'm a reformed man now," he said with a chuckle, to anyone who would listen. "I don't hit people anymore." And he laughed hysterically.

He moved into his brother's place, and his brother was the contact for his probation officer. Thanks to his network in town, he immediately got a job as a warehouse clerk in a hardware store. The rest of the time he wandered around town all day long. He said he had really missed Madison.

Colleen was terrified at the thought that Luke was free. She could no longer walk around town without the risk of running into him. Woody was afraid, too, but he didn't want to tell her, and he tried to reassure her. "Listen, Colleen, we knew he'd get out sooner or later. He's not allowed to go anywhere near you anyway, otherwise they'll send him back to jail. Don't let yourself be intimidated by him, that's just what he wants."

They tried to act as if everything were normal. But before long Luke's omnipresence meant they had to avoid public places. They went shopping in the next town.

Their hell had only just begun.

For a start, Luke took the house back.

His divorce from Colleen had been finalized during his imprisonment and he was challenging the division of property. He had bought the house with his own savings so he decided to contest the decision of the divorce court, which had determined that the house would belong to his ex-wife.

He got a lawyer who managed to halt the procedure. The decision to give Colleen the house would be suspended until a further judgment, and for the time being the house was restored to its initial owner: Luke.

Woody and Colleen had to move out. Uncle Saul referred them to a lawyer in New Canaan who could advise them. He said it was just a matter of time, that by the end of summer they would get the house back.

In the meantime they rented an ugly little place on the edge of town. "It's only temporary," Woody promised Colleen. "We'll get rid of him soon."

But Colleen had no peace of mind.

Luke retrieved his pickup truck, which he had left with his brother. Every time she saw him drive by she felt a knot in her stomach.

"What are we going to do?" she asked Woody.

"Nothing. We're not going to let fear drive us away."

Everywhere he went he thought he saw the pickup. Outside their house. On the parking lot of the supermarket in the next town. One morning Colleen saw it parked in front of the gas station. She called the police. But by the time Luke's brother showed up in his squad car the pickup had vanished.

Colleen was constantly on edge. Woody was working every evening washing dishes and she stayed at home alone, worried. She was forever looking out the window, down the street, and she would not move from one room to another without taking a kitchen knife with her.

One evening she wanted to go out and buy some ice cream. Initially she did not dare even think of going out. Then she decided she was being foolish. She could not go on letting herself be terrorized like this.

She could have found ice cream just about anywhere, but in order not to run into Luke she went to the supermarket in the next town. On the way back, she got a flat tire. Just her luck. She was on a deserted road: she'd have to change the tire all by herself.

She put the jack under the car and hoisted it up. But when it came time to remove the tire with the wrench, she found she couldn't. The lug nuts were screwed on too tightly.

She would have to wait for a passing car. Before long she saw headlights in the darkness. She gave a wave and the car stopped. Colleen walked closer and she recognized Luke's car. She recoiled.

"What's the matter?" he said through the open window. "Don't you want my help?"

"No, thanks."

"Fine. I won't force you. But I'll wait for a while, just in case no-one goes by."

He stayed parked on the shoulder. Ten minutes went by. No-one.

"Fine," Colleen said, eventually. "Please help me."

Luke got out of the car with a smile.

"I'm glad to help. I paid my debt, you know. I served my time. I'm another man now."

"I don't believe you, Luke."

He changed Colleen's tire.

"Thanks, Luke."

"You're welcome."

"Luke, I still have a few things at the house that I'd like to have. I'd like to come and get them if you don't mind."

He grimaced and acted as if he were thinking.

"You know, Colleen, I think I'll hang on to those things of yours. I like to sniff your clothes from time to time. It reminds me of the good old days. You remember when I used to throw you out in the middle of nowhere and you had to go home on foot?"

"I'm not afraid of you, Luke."

"You should be, Colleen. You should be."

He stood before her, menacing. She ran to her car and drove off. She went to Woody's restaurant.

"You're not supposed to leave the house at night," he said.

"I know. I just wanted to buy something."

The next day, Woody went to a gun store and bought a revolver.

* * *

We were a long way from Madison, and Luke's threats.

In Baltimore, Hillel and Uncle Saul went on living their peaceful life.

Little by little, Alexandra's songs began to get air time all over the country. People talked about her, and she had been asked to be the opening act for a number of important groups on tour. She was getting one concert date after another, playing acoustic versions of her songs.

I went with her to several of the concerts. Then it was time for me to go to Montclair. My study was waiting, and now that Alexandra's career was taking off, it was time for me to start writing my first novel, and I hadn't come up with a subject yet.

* * *

In the days that followed, Colleen thought she saw Luke's pickup following her again.

She got strange telephone calls at the gas station. She felt as if someone was watching her.

One day, she did not even open the gas station, and stayed hidden in the storeroom. She could not go on living like this. Woody had to come and get her. He had his gun tucked into his belt. They had to get away from Luke, far away, before things got out of hand.

"We'll leave tomorrow," he told Colleen. "We'll go to Baltimore. Hillel and Saul will help us."

"Not tomorrow. I want to get my things. They're at the house."

"We'll do it tomorrow evening. Then we'll leave right away. And go away forever."

Woody knew that Luke went every evening to hang out in a bar on the main street.

The next day, as he had told Colleen they would, they parked on Luke's street far enough away not to be noticed; they would wait until he left.

At around nine o'clock they saw Luke come out of the house, climb into his pickup and drive off. Once he had turned the corner, Woody got out of the car. "Hurry!" he ordered. Colleen tried to open the front door with her key but she couldn't: Luke had changed the lock.

Woody took her hand and led her around the back. He found an open window, climbed in, and opened the door for Colleen.

"Where are your things?"

"In the basement."

"Make it quick," said Woody. "Do you have stuff anywhere else?"

"Check the closet in the bedroom."

Woody hurried in and grabbed a few dresses.

Luke's brother drove along the street and slowed down outside the house. Through the bedroom window that looked onto the street he saw Woody. He stepped on the gas and headed for the bar.

Woody put the dresses in a bag and called to Colleen. "Are you done?" She didn't answer. He went down to the basement. She had taken out all her things.

"You can't take everything," Woody said. "Just the minimum."

Colleen nodded. She began folding her clothes. "Just stuff it all in the bag!" Woody said. "We can't hang around."

*

Luke's brother found him at the bar counter. He murmured in his ear, "That little asshole Woodrow Finn is in your house right now. I think he's getting Colleen's stuff. I figured you would want to take care of him yourself." Luke's expression lit with fury. He put one hand on his brother's shoulder to thank him and walked quickly out of the bar.

"Come on, let's get going, now!" Woody shouted, as Colleen finished filling a second bag of clothes. She stood up and grabbed the bags. One of them tore and spilled out onto the floor.

"Never mind!" Woody shouted.

They ran up the stairs from the basement. At that very moment Luke pulled up right outside the house and rushed in. He met Woody and Colleen head on as they were about to leave by the back door.

"Run!" Woody shouted to Colleen before throwing himself on Luke. Luke punched him, then jabbed him in the face with his elbow, and Woody fell to the floor. Luke began kicking him ferociously in the stomach. Colleen turned around. She was on the threshold: she couldn't leave Woody behind. She snatched up a knife from the kitchen counter and held it above Luke, threatening.

"Stop, Luke!"

"What are you going to do?" Luke jeered. "Kill me?"

He took a step closer, she didn't move. Then he grabbed her arm and twisted it. Colleen cried out in pain and dropped the knife. Luke took her by the hair and banged her head against the wall.

Woody tried to stand. Luke reached for a lamp, yanked out the power cord and threw the lamp at him. Then he picked up a little side table and battered him with it.

He turned back to Colleen, dragged her by the shirt and began punching her.

"This is for trying to act smart around me!" he cried.

He did not stop hitting her, but he had his eye on Woody. Woody summoned all his remaining strength and managed to leap up and rush at Luke, landing a surprise punch. Luke grappled Woody and wanted to throw him against the coffee table, but Woody hung on to him and they both fell to the floor. They struggled wildly, then Luke managed to put his hands around Woody's throat and he squeezed as hard as he could.

Woody could not breathe. He saw Colleen crumpled behind him on the floor, bleeding. He had no choice. He managed to raise his back from the floor and reached for the revolver in the elastic waist of his pants. He pressed the barrel into Luke's belly and pressed the trigger.

A shot rang out.

42

July 2004

The night Luke died, Madison got no sleep.

Locals clustered behind the police tape to try to glimpse what they could of the spectacle. Beams from the police cars swept up and down the street. Agents from the Connecticut State Police crime squad were dispatched from New Canaan to take charge of the investigation.

Woody was arrested and transferred to State Police headquarters in New Canaan. He was allowed one telephone call, so he made it to Uncle Saul.

Uncle Saul called a lawyer colleague in New Canaan and set out at once with Hillel. They got there at one o'clock in the morning and were able to see Woody. He had superficial injuries and the ambulance paramedics had treated him at police headquarters. Colleen had been taken to the hospital. She was in a bad way.

Woody, groggy, told them in detail what had happened in Luke's house.

"There was nothing else I could do," he said. "He was going to kill both of us."

"Don't worry," Uncle Saul reassured him. "This was legitimate self-defense. We'll get you out of here in no time."

Uncle Saul and Hillel went to stay at a hotel in New Canaan for the night. Woody was due to be brought before the judge the next morning. In light of the circumstances, he was let out on one hundred thousand dollars' bail, which Saul paid, and the trial was scheduled for October 15.

*

Hillel told me what had happened and I immediately left for Connecticut. Woody was not allowed to leave the state. Nor could he stay in Madison, after what had happened.

Hillel and I found him a little rental in a quiet place, in a town nearby, where Colleen could go and be with him once she got out of the hospital.

* * *

The two and a half months until the day of Woody's trial went swiftly by.

Hillel and I took turns keeping him company. He couldn't be left alone. Fortunately Colleen was there, and was kindness itself. She knew what he needed. She kept watch over him. She was his life saver.

But the only person who could actually get through to him was Alexandra. I saw as much when she too came to the house in Connecticut.

Around us, Woody was silent most of the time. If he answered our questions, it was only out of politeness, in an effort to put on a brave face. When he wanted to be alone, he went running. But when Alexandra was with him, he talked. He was a different man.

I could see that he loved her. The way I had, ever since we all first met her in 1994 – he loved her. Passionately. She had the same effect on him as on me. They had the same endless discussions. More than once they stayed out on the little wooden deck in front of the house, talking for hours.

I walked around the house and sat in the grass in a spot where they could not see me. I listened to them. He was confiding in her. He opened up to her in a way he had never opened up to us.

"It's not like it was when Aunt Anita died," he was saying. "I don't feel anything for Luke. I'm not sad, I have no remorse."

"It was legitimate self-defense, Woody," Alexandra said.

He did not seem to be convinced.

"You know, I've always been violent. Ever since I was little. The only thing I know how to do is hit people. That's how I met the Baltimores, because I had gotten in a fight. And that's how I'm going to leave them."

"Leave them? Why do you say that?"

"Because I can tell I'm going to be convicted. I can tell this is the end."

"Don't say things like that, Woody."

She took hold of his face, looked him straight in the eyes and said, "Woodrow Finn, I will not allow you to say things like that."

I was jealous of those moments of closeness I had spied on. She spoke to him the way she spoke to me. With the same tenderness. She called me by my first and last name, too, when she wanted to scold me. She would say, "Marcus Goldman, stop being stupid." It was her way of pretending to be angry.

But sometimes she really did get angry. And her anger was something to behold. Rare, but magnificent. She flew into a rage when she found out I had been spying on her moments with Woody, and that on top of it I was jealous.

When she caught me, since she didn't want to make a scene there in the house, she said to Woody and Colleen, "Marcus and I are going to the supermarket." We got into the rental car, she drove until we were well out of sight, then she pulled over and began shouting: "Marcus, have you completely lost your mind? You're jealous of Woody?"

And I was foolish enough to try and protest. I told her she paid too much attention to Woody, and that she was calling him by his first and last name. "Marcus, Woody killed a man. Do you realize what that means? He's going to be tried for murder. I think he needs his friends. And what sort of friend are you, bloated with this ridiculous resentment toward your cousins!"

She was right.

Woody was the only one who thought he would go to prison. Uncle Saul went several times to Connecticut to prepare his defense, and he was convinced of the contrary.

It was only once he got access to the indictment that he realized the situation was more serious than he had thought.

The prosecutor's office did not buy the presumption of legitimate self-defense. On the contrary, they maintained that Woody had entered Luke's house illegally and that, moreover, he was armed when he did so. It was possible to consider that Luke was the one who had acted in legitimate self-defense by trying to overcome Woody. The prosecutor's office charged Woody with murder. As for Colleen, she was in danger of being prosecuted as an accessory to the murder. A criminal investigation would also be conducted.

A sudden wind of panic blew through the house in Connecticut, where until then they had felt sheltered from the storm. Colleen said she could not tolerate the idea of going to prison. "Don't worry," said Woody again. "You have nothing to fear. I'll protect you, the way you protected me after Aunt Anita's death."

We did not understand what he meant until the trial had actually begun. Woody, without telling Uncle Saul or his own lawyer, accused himself of having forced Colleen to go with him to Luke's house. He claimed she had tried to dissuade him, but as he went on into the house anyway, she had followed him to try and get him to leave. Then Luke arrived and jumped on them.

During the recess, Woody's lawyer tried to reason with him: "You're crazy, Woody! What's come over you, accusing yourself in this way! What's the use of me trying to defend you if you go ruining your chances?"

"I don't want Colleen to go to prison."

"Let me do my job and no-one will go to prison."

On the basis of testimonies from Madison residents, Woody's lawyer was able to confirm that Luke had put Colleen through an excruciating ordeal. But this merely incited the prosecutor to launch another attack: it wasn't Colleen who had killed Luke, and the violent nature of her relationship with Luke was not material in order to determine whether

Woody had acted in self-defense. The prosecution maintained that Woody had not fired the gun to stop an attack, and thus had not acted in self-defense. He was already armed when he entered Luke's house. It had been his intention right from the start to finish him off.

The trial was developing into a nightmare. After two days of deliberations, there was no longer any doubt that Woody was going to be convicted. To avoid too heavy a sentence, Uncle Saul suggested they enter into a plea bargain with the prosecution: Woody would plead guilty to murder in exchange for a reduced sentence. When they met in closed session to hammer out an agreement, the prosecutor was uncompromising.

"I won't go below five years of prison," he said. "Woodrow waited at Luke's house and shot him down."

"You know that isn't true," Woody's lawyer raged at him.

"Five years," the prosecutor repeated. "You know I'm doing you a favor. He could easily get ten or fifteen years."

Uncle Saul, Woody, and his lawyer had a lengthy meeting after that. There was a gleam of panic in Woody's eyes: he did not want to go to prison.

"Saul," he said to my uncle, "do you realize that if I say yes, they're going to put handcuffs on me right then and there and lock me away for five years?"

"But if you refuse, you might spend a good chunk of your life inside. In five years you won't even be thirty years old. You'll have time to start a new life."

Woody was devastated: he had known from the beginning what was at stake, but now it had become reality.

"Saul, ask them not to arrest me right away," he begged. "Ask them to give me a few days of freedom. I want to go to prison as a free man. I don't want to be chained up like a dog fifteen minutes from now and dragged off to a paddy wagon."

The lawyer presented Woody's request to the prosecutor, and he accepted it. Woody was sentenced to five years of prison without immediate incarceration, and would start serving his sentence at the State penitentiary in Cheshire, Connecticut, on October 25, one week from that day.

43

Baltimore, Maryland
October 24, 2004

Woody is going to prison tomorrow. He'll be there for the next five years.

As I drive from Baltimore airport to Oak Park, the neighborhood where he grew up and where I'm about to join him for his last day of freedom, I can already imagine him standing outside the gate of the imposing penitentiary in Cheshire, Connecticut. I can picture him going through the doors, being stripped and searched. I can picture him putting on his prison uniform and being led to his cell. I can hear the doors slamming behind him. He walks on, surrounded by two guards, holding sheets and a blanket in his arms. He walks past other prisoners, who stare at him.

Woody is going to prison tomorrow.

Alexandra has come with me. She is in the passenger seat, looking at me intensely. She can see I'm lost in thought. She puts her hand behind my neck and, very tenderly, strokes my hair.

When we reach Oak Park, I slow down. I drive through the neighborhood where we were so happy, Woody, Hillel, and I. We drive past an Oak Park patrol car and I make the secret sign. Then I turn into Willowick Road and pull over by the Baltimore house. Woody and Hillel, my two cousins, my two brothers, are sitting on the steps outside the house. Hillel is holding a photograph and they are gazing at it.

It's a photograph of the four of us that was taken the day Alexandra moved away, nine years ago. Hillel sees us coming and protects the photograph by slipping it into the pages of the book next to him. They stand up and come over to greet us. All four of us hug each other for a long time.

There is only one month left until the tragedy, but we don't know it yet.

Woody had no right to be in Baltimore. The law said that while waiting to start his term he had to stay in Connecticut. But Woody figured that if he couldn't spend his last days of freedom wherever he liked, it was as if he were already in prison.

To avoid having his I.D. checked, he had not taken the plane. Hillel had gone to get him in Connecticut with the car, and they would leave again during the night. They would spend one last sleepless night in each other's company, they would watch the sun rise, eat a huge breakfast of pancakes and maple syrup, scrambled eggs and hash browns, and then in the morning Hillel would drive him to the penitentiary.

That day had only just begun. The weather was magnificent. Oak Park wore the red and yellow colors of fall.

We spent the morning on the steps of the house enjoying the balmy day. Uncle Saul brought us coffee and donuts. At noon he went to get some hamburgers at one of Hillel's favorite restaurants. The five of us ate outside.

Woody seemed serene. We talked about everything, except prison. Alexandra told us that her tour of the radio stations was continuing to bear fruit: her songs were getting an ever wider distribution, and her album was beginning to sell. She had already sold more than ten thousand copies. Every week it crept a bit higher on the hit parade.

"When I think of you, here, ten years ago!" Hillel smiled at her. "You gave us concerts in your bedroom. And now here you are on the threshold of success." He reached for his book and took out the picture of the four of us. We laughed, recalling the years of our youth.

After lunch Hillel, Woody, and I went for a walk in Oak Park. Alexandra said she wanted to help Uncle Saul clean up after lunch so that the three of us could have some time alone.

We wandered through the quiet streets. A team of gardeners were raking fallen leaves from the sidewalks, and it reminded us of the Skunk era.

"That was a great time, the Goldman Gang," Woody said.

"It still is," I said. "Nothing is over. The Gang is eternal."

"Prison changes everything."

"Don't say that. We'll come and see you all the time. Uncle Saul said you're sure to get a reduced sentence. You'll be out of there in no time, and we'll be here."

Hillel nodded.

We walked around the neighborhood and soon we were back outside the Baltimore house. We sat down on the steps again. Woody suddenly revealed to me that he had left Colleen. He did not want to put her through five years of visiting rooms. Deep down I thought that if he had left her it was because he did not really love her. He had felt less alone with her, but he had never loved her the way he loved Alexandra. So I felt obliged to mention her.

"I'm sorry I betrayed you guys by going out with Alexandra," I said to my cousins.

"You didn't betray anything," Hillel reassured me.

"The Goldman Gang is eternal," Woody said.

"When you get out, Wood, we'll take a trip, the three of us. A long trip, together. We could even rent a house in the Hamptons and spend all summer there. We could rent a house together every summer."

Woody gave a sad smile.

"Marcus, there's something I need to talk to you about."

Uncle Saul interrupted us, opening the door.

"Oh, there you are," he said. "I thought I'd barbecue a few steaks tonight, how does that sound? I'll go shopping now."

We offered to go with Uncle Saul, and Woody murmured in my ear that he'd talk to me later.

We all went to the Oak Park supermarket. It was a happy moment; it reminded us of the days we used to go shopping with Aunt Anita and she let us fill up the cart with all our favorite things.

Later, out on the patio, I helped Uncle Saul prepare the barbecue, to let Woody and Alexandra have some time on their own. I knew it was important to him. They went for a walk. I think Woody wanted to go and see the Oak Park basketball court. Hillel went with them. It occurred to me that they were actually the Madison gang. And the Goldman Gang, that was the three of us.

It was one o'clock in the morning when we parted.

The evening we had spent together was almost too normal. As if what was about to happen in a few hours' time could not be real.

It was Hillel who said it was time to leave. They had four hours on the road ahead of them. We put our arms around each other. I squeezed Woody very tight. I think that was the moment we realized what was happening. We all left Uncle Saul at the same time; he stood there on the porch outside his house, on the steps where we had spent the day. He was weeping.

Alexandra and I got into our rental car and followed Hillel's car to the edge of Oak Park. Then they turned to the right to head for I-95, and we went left toward the center of town, where we had booked a hotel room. Uncle Saul, obviously, had offered to put us up, but I didn't want to stay in Oak Park. Not that night. It wasn't meant to be a night like any other. It was the night I would be losing Woody for five long years.

In the car, I tried to picture us – Alexandra, Hillel, and me – five years down the road. I wondered what would have become of us by October 25, 2009.

* * *

The next day, Alexandra and I flew to Nashville very early in the morning. We had an important meeting that day with Eric Tanner, her manager.

I wanted to talk to Woody one last time before he went into the Cheshire penitentiary. But I couldn't reach him. His phone was switched off, and so was Hillel's. I spent all day trying. To no avail. I was beginning to have a bad feeling. I called the Baltimore house, but there was no answer. Eventually I called Uncle Saul on his cell phone: he was with clients and could not talk to me. I asked him to call me back as soon as he could, but he did not call until the following afternoon.

"Marcus? Uncle Saul here."

"Oh, hey, Uncle Saul. How—"

He interrupted me.

"Marcus, listen carefully: I need for you to come to Baltimore right away. Don't ask any questions. Something very serious has happened."

He hung up. At first I thought that we'd been cut off so I called him straight back: he did not pick up. I kept trying, and he eventually answered, only to say: "Come to Baltimore."

And then he hung up again.

44

October 26, 2004

Woody had not shown up at the penitentiary.

Uncle Saul filled me in when I got to his place that evening, after taking the first available flight to Baltimore.

He was nervous, in a panic. I had never seen him like that.

"What do you mean, he didn't show up?"

"He's run away, Marcus. Woody is a fugitive."

"And Hillel?"

"He was with him. He has vanished, too. He left at the same time as you the day before yesterday, and he never came back."

Uncle Saul told me that already, the day before, he had wondered if something was wrong when he was not able – as I had not been – to get through to Hillel or Woody. A U.S. marshal had come to the house in Oak Park that morning. He questioned Uncle Saul at length.

"Do you know where Woodrow might have gone?" the officer said.

"No. Why would I know?"

"Because he was here the night before he was due to go to prison. The neighbors saw him. They are categorical. Woodrow did not have the right to cross the Connecticut state line. You're a lawyer, you should know."

Uncle Saul saw that the Marshal was one jump ahead of him.

"Listen, I'll be frank with you. Yes, Woody was here the night before he was due to go to prison. He grew up in this house, he wanted to spend one last day here before going to rot in prison for five years. Nothing very serious. But where he is now, I don't know."

"Who was with him?" the officer wanted to know.

"Friends. I don't remember exactly. I didn't want to get too involved."

"There was your son, Hillel. Neighbors identified him, too. Where is your son, Mr Goldman?"

"At the university, I suppose."

"Doesn't he live here?"

"Officially, yes. But in fact he's never here. He's always off somewhere with a girlfriend. Besides, I work long hours, I leave in the morning and come back late at night. As a matter of fact, I was about to leave for my office."

"Mr Goldman, you would tell me if you knew something?"

"Obviously."

"Because we will find Woodrow. People don't usually get away from us. And if I find out that you helped him in one way or another, that would make you an accessory. Here's my card. Ask Hillel to give me a call when you see him."

Uncle Saul had had no news from Hillel all day.

"Do you think he's with Woody?" I said.

"Everything would appear to indicate that he is. I couldn't tell you that over the phone. The line might be tapped. Don't tell anyone about this, Marcus. And above all, don't communicate with me by phone. I think Hillel went to help Woody hide somewhere and that he'll be back. We have to play for time with the investigators. If Hillel comes back tonight, all he has to say is that he was at the university all day. The police might question you. Tell them the truth, don't get yourself in trouble. But try to avoid mentioning Hillel, if you can."

"What can I do, Uncle Saul?"

"Nothing. Above all, stay out of all this. Go home. Don't talk to anyone."

"And what if he contacts me?"

"He won't contact you. He won't take the risk of getting you involved."

*

A thousand miles from Baltimore, Woody and Hillel drove past Des Moines, Iowa.

Already on our last evening they knew they would not be going to the prison in Cheshire. Woody could not bear the idea of prison.

They had slept in motels along the freeway. They paid everything in cash.

Their plan was to drive across country to Canada, by way of Wyoming and Montana. Then they would go through Alberta and all of British Columbia as far as the Yukon. They would settle there, find a little house and start a new life. No-one would come looking for them there. In a bag that, as a rule, Woody looked after, they had $200,000 in cash.

Back in Nashville the next day, I told Alexandra what had happened. I handed on the instructions Uncle Saul had given me. Not to talk about it to anyone, particularly over the telephone.

I wondered if I should go looking for them. She dissuaded me. "Woody isn't lost, Markie. He ran away. It's what he wants, for no-one to find him."

*   *   *

October 29, 2004

Hillel had not reappeared.

The Marshal came back to question Uncle Saul.

"Where is your son, Mr Goldman?"

"I don't know."

"He hasn't been seen on campus for several days."

"He's of age, he can do what he wants."

"He emptied his savings account one week ago. Where did he get so much money, anyway?"

"His mother died two years ago. He had a share of the inheritance."

"So your son has disappeared with a great deal of money at the same time as his friend who is wanted for murder. I think you can see what I'm driving at."

"Not at all, officer. My son does what he wants with his time and his money. This is a free country, after all."

Hillel and Woody were twenty miles from Cody, Wyoming. They found a motel where they paid cash and the manager didn't ask any questions. They did not know how they would make it across the border without getting caught. At least in the motel they were safe.

There was a little kitchenette in the room. They could cook without having to go out. They had stocked up on pasta and rice, things that were easy to keep and didn't go off.

They kept thinking about the Yukon. That was what kept them going. They imagined a log cabin by a lake. The wilderness of nature all around. They would earn a living going to Whitehorse from time to time to do odd jobs for people, the way they used to during the Goldman Gardeners days.

I thought of them constantly. I wondered where they were. I looked at the sky and thought they must be looking at that same sky. But from where? And why didn't they tell me about their plans?

* * *

November 16, 2004

They had been on the run for three weeks.

Hillel was accused of aiding and abetting a fugitive, and was also wanted by the U.S. Marshals Service. They had one thing going for them: the search was not very intensive. The Feds had far more important criminals to hunt down, and they had limited means for trying to find Woody and Hillel. In this type of case, the fugitive nearly always got caught during an I.D. check, or was made to slip up for lack of money. This was not going to be the case for Hillel and Woody. They did not leave their room, and they had plenty of money.

"As long as we don't show our faces, we'll be fine," Hillel told Woody.

But they could not stay locked in the room indefinitely. It was like being in prison. They had to try and cross the border, or at least change motels, to get a bit of fresh air.

Two days later, they headed for Montana.

The landscape was breathtaking. A foretaste of the Yukon.

In Bozeman they met a man in a bikers' bar who told them he could fix them with fake I.D.s for $20,000. It was a huge amount, but they went along with it. Quality fake documents would be a guarantee of invisibility, and therefore of survival.

The man said he would accompany them to a nearby warehouse to take their I.D. photos. The man led the way on his bike, they followed in the car. But the meeting was an ambush: when they got out of the car they were surrounded by a group of armed bikers. They were searched, guns pointed at them, and the bikers made off with their bag of cash.

* * *

November 19, 2004

They had only a thousand dollars left which Hillel had hidden in an inner pocket of his jacket. They spent the first night in the car in a freeway rest area.

The next day they drove north. Their plans were completely screwed. They wouldn't get far without money. Gas ate into the little they had left. Woody said he was prepared to stage a hold-up. Hillel dissuaded him. They badly needed to find work. Anywhere. But the main thing was not to attract attention.

*

They spent the night of November 20 in a parking lot in Montana. At around three o'clock in the morning they were woken by a pounding on the window and a blinding light. It was a policeman.

Hillel ordered Woody to keep quiet. He rolled down the window.

"You're not allowed to overnight on the parking lot."

"Really sorry, officer," Hillel said. "We'll get going right away."

"Stay right where you are. I need to see your driver's license and an I.D. for the person there with you."

Hillel could read the panic in Woody's eyes. He whispered to him: "Do it." He handed the documents to the policeman, who went back to his squad car to proceed with the identity check.

"What are we going to do?" Woody said.

"I turn the ignition and we get out of here."

"In five minutes, we'll have every policeman in the state after us, there's no way we can escape."

"So what do you suggest?"

Woody didn't answer. He opened the door and got out.

Hillel heard the policeman shout, "Get back in the car! Get back in the car right now!"

Woody suddenly pulled out a revolver and fired. A first time, then a second: the bullets hit the windshield. The policeman dove behind his car for protection, and to take out his gun, but Woody had already caught up with him, and fired again. A first bullet hit him in the throat.

Woody fired four more times. Then he ran back to the car. Hillel was aghast. He had his hands over his ears. "Go!" Woody shouted. "Go!" Hillel obeyed and the car pulled away, tires squealing.

They drove for a while without meeting any cars. Then they turned off onto a forest track and only stopped when they were sure they were invisible among the trees.

Hillel got out of the car.

"You are completely crazy!" he screamed. "What have you done, for Christ's sake, what have you done?"

"It was us or him, Hill. Us or him."

"We killed a man, Woody. We killed a man!"

"It's only the second one for me," Woody said, his tone almost cynical. "What did you think, Hillel? That we were going to run away and live the life of Riley? I'm a fucking fugitive."

"I didn't even know you had a gun. Where the fuck did you get it?"

"I stole it, O.K.?"

"Give it to me, now."

"Not on your life. Just imagine if you get caught with it."

"Give it to me. I'm going to get rid of it. Give it to me, Woody, or else we go our separate ways."

After a long hesitation, Woody handed him the gun. Hillel disappeared among the trees. There was a river below them and Woody heard the gun splash into the water. He came back to the car. He was pale.

"What's the matter?" Woody said.

"Our I.D.s.... we left them with the cop."

Woody held his face in his hands. In the heat of the moment he had completely forgotten to take them.

"We have to leave the car here," Hillel said. "The cop had the papers for the car, too. We have to continue on foot."

*　*　*

This time the Marshal went to see Uncle Saul at his office.

It was the first news we'd had.

"Woodrow Finn killed a policeman last night in Montana, during a routine identity check on a parking lot. The dashboard webcam recorded the whole thing. They were in a car that is registered in your name."

He showed him a print taken from the video recording.

"That's the car Hillel uses," Uncle Saul said.

The Marshal corrected him: "It's your car."

"How can you possibly suppose I was in Montana last night?"

"I'm not implying you were with Woody, Mr Goldman. The driver of the car was your son, Hillel. They found his driver's license there. He is now an accessory to the murder of an officer of the law."

Uncle Saul went pale and hid his face in his hands.

"What do you want from me, officer?" he asked.

"Your complete cooperation. If they get in touch in any way, you have to inform me. Otherwise, I will be obliged to arrest you for aiding and abetting fugitives and murderers. And as you can see, we have the proof."

* * *

November 22, 2004

After they abandoned the car they walked until they found a motel. They paid cash, and a little extra so that the manager wouldn't ask for their I.D. They took a shower and got some rest. Then, for fifty dollars, a man gave them a lift as far as the Bozeman bus station. They bought Greyhound tickets to Casper, Wyoming.

"Then what are we going to do?" Woody said.

"We'll go to Denver, and get a bus to Baltimore."

"What are we going to do in Baltimore?"

"Ask my father to help us. We can hide for a few days in Oak Park."

"The neighbors will see us."

"We won't leave the house. No-one will suspect we're there. Then my dad can drive us somewhere. Canada, or Mexico. He'll find a way. He'll give me money. He's the only one who can help us."

"I'm afraid I'll get caught, Hillel. I'm afraid of what will happen to me. Will they execute me?"

"Stay calm. Nothing is going to happen."

After two days on the road, they reached the Baltimore bus station in the late morning on November 24. It was the day before Thanksgiving.

*　*　*

November 24, 2004
Day of the tragedy

They took public transport to Oak Park.

They had bought two baseball caps which they kept pulled down tight on their heads. But at that time of day the streets were deserted. Children were in school, and adults at work.

They hurried down Willowick Road. Before long they could see the house. Their hearts beat faster. They were almost there. Once they were inside, they would be safe.

They reached the house at last. Hillel had the key. He opened the door and they disappeared inside. Uncle Saul wasn't there. He was at his office, like every day.

Out in the street, sitting low in his car, the Marshal had just seen Woody and Hillel go into the house. He reached for his radio and called for backup.

They were famished. They headed straight for the kitchen.

They made sandwiches with toast bread, cold turkey, cheese, and mayonnaise. They wolfed them down. They felt better now that they were home. Their two days on the bus had been exhausting. They wanted to have a shower and get some rest.

Once they'd finished lunch, they went upstairs. They stopped outside Hillel's room. They looked at the old pictures on the walls. On his childhood desk was a photograph of the two of them at the Clinton campaign stand during the 1992 elections.

They smiled. Woody left the room, walked down the corridor and went into Uncle Saul and Aunt Anita's room. Hillel glanced out the window. His heart stopped beating: policemen wearing balaclavas and flak jackets were lining up in the garden. They'd found them. They were cornered.

Woody was still in the doorway of his parents' room. He had his back to Hillel and hadn't noticed anything. Hillel walked quietly up to him.

"Don't turn around, Woody."

Woody obeyed and didn't move.

"They're here, is that it?"

"Yes. There are policemen everywhere."

"I don't want them to get me, Hill. I want to stay here forever."

"I know, Wood. I want to stay here forever, too."

"You remember Oak Tree School?"

"Of course I do, Wood."

"What would have become of me without you, Hillel? Thank you; you gave meaning to my life."

Hillel was crying.

"Thank *you*, Woody. Forgive me for everything I did to you."

"I forgave you long ago, Hillel. I'll always love you."

"I'll always love you, Woody."

Hillel took Woody's revolver from his pocket. He hadn't gotten rid of it. He had thrown a big stone into the river.

He held the barrel behind Woody's head.

He closed his eyes.

They could hear a terrible commotion down on the ground floor. The S.W.A.T. team had just broken down the front door.

Hillel fired a first time. Woody collapsed to the floor.

There were shouts downstairs. The police thought they were being targeted and retreated.

Hillel lay down on his parents' bed. He buried his face in the pillows, burrowed into the sheets, found the smells from his childhood. He pictured his parents in the bed, on a Sunday morning. He and Woody bursting triumphantly into the room, surprising them with trays laden with breakfast. Sitting down on the bed with them, sharing their painstakingly prepared pancakes. There was laughter. From the open window the sun bathed them in a warm light. The world was their oyster.

Hillel put the gun to his temple.

Everything ends as it begins.

He pulled the trigger.

And everything ended.

Part Five

THE BOOK OF ATONEMENT
2004–2012

45

June 2012 was hot and muggy in Florida.

My main occupation consisted in finding a buyer for Uncle Saul's house. I knew I had to let it go. But I didn't want to sell it to just anybody.

I'd had no news from Alexandra and this troubled me. We had kissed at my place in New York, but then she went to Cabo San Lucas to try again with Kevin. According to the rumors that came my way, her stay in Mexico had quickly turned sour, but I wanted to hear it from the horse's mouth.

Finally she called to tell me she was going to spend the summer in London. She had been planning the trip for a long time. She was working on her new album, and part of it would be recorded in a prestigious studio in London.

I had hoped she would suggest we meet before she left, but she didn't have time.

"Why are you calling me if it's just to tell me you're leaving?"

"I didn't call to say I'm leaving. I called to tell you where I'm going."

Inanely, I said, "And why is that?"

"Because that's what friends do. They keep each other informed of what they're up to."

"Well, if you want to know what I'm up to, I'm selling my uncle's house."

There was a sweetness in her voice that I found annoying as she said:

"I think that's a good idea."

In the days that followed, a real estate agent brought some would-be buyers I liked. A charming young couple who promised to look after the place and fill it with children and life. We signed the contract there at the house; it was important to me. I handed over the keys and wished them fair winds. I was free of everything. Now there was nothing left of the Baltimore Goldmans.

I got back in my car and returned to Boca Raton. When I got home, I found Leo's notebook outside my door, the famous *Notebook No. 1*. I leafed through it. It was blank. I took it with me and went to sit down in my study.

I reached for a pen and let it glide over the paper of the notebook open before me. That was how I started *The Baltimore Boys*.

46

Baltimore, Maryland
December 2004

Two weeks after the tragedy, Woody and Hillel's bodies were returned to us and we were able to bury them.

They were laid to rest on the same day, side by side, at the Forrest Lane Cemetery. The winter sun was brilliant, as if nature had come out to greet them. Only the closest friends attended the ceremony: I made my speech in the presence of Artie Crawford, my parents, Alexandra, and Uncle Saul, who was holding one white rose in each hand. From under the smoked lenses of his glasses, tears were streaming down his face.

After the funeral we had lunch at the restaurant in the Marriott where we were all staying. It was strange not to be in Oak Park, but Uncle Saul was not ready to go home yet. His room in the hotel was next to mine and after the meal he told me he was going up to have a nap. He stood up from the table and I saw him searching in his pocket to make sure he had his magnetic key card. I followed him with my gaze, and could not help but see his torn sleeve, his tired gait, and the stubble on his cheeks, soon to become a beard.

He had said, "I'm going up to my room to get some rest," but when the elevator doors closed on him I wanted to cry out that his room wasn't there, that his room was ten miles to the north in the neighborhood of Oak Park, on Willowick Road, in the splendid, luxurious, and comfortable Baltimore home. A house that was full of the joyful singing of three children bound by the Goldman Gang's solemn promise, three boys who loved each other like brothers. He had said, "I'm going up to my room to get some rest," but his room was three hundred miles further north, in a wonderful house in the Hamptons that had witnessed our hours of happiness. He had said, "I'm going up to my room to get some rest," but his room was a thousand miles further south, on the 26th floor of the Buenavista, where the lunch table was set for five – the four of them, and me.

He had no right to say that this room with its dusty carpet and sagging bed on the seventh floor of the Baltimore Marriott was his room. I couldn't stand it, I couldn't accept the fact that a Baltimore Goldman was sleeping in the same hotel as the Montclair Goldmans. I got up from the table, apologizing, and I asked if I could take the rental car to run an errand nearby. Alexandra came with me.

I drove as far as Oak Park. I passed a patrol car and made the secret sign of our tribe. Then I stopped outside the Baltimore house. I got out of the car and stood for a moment gazing at it. Alexandra put her arms around me. I said to her, "You're all I have left, now." She held me close.

We wandered around Oak Park for a while. I went by the Oak Tree School, I saw the basketball court, which hadn't changed. Then we went back to the Marriott.

Alexandra was not in good spirits. She was overwhelmed with sadness, but I could sense it wasn't just that. I asked her what was going on, and all she said was that it was because of losing Hillel and Woody. She wasn't telling me everything, I could sense that.

My parents stayed two more days, then they had to go back to Montclair. They couldn't miss work any longer. They invited Uncle Saul to come and visit with them for a while in Montclair, but he declined their offer. Just as I had done after Aunt Anita's death, I decided to stay on in Baltimore. At the airport, as I was dropping off my parents, my mother kissed me and said, "That's good you're staying with your uncle. I'm proud of you."

Alexandra went back to Nashville one week after the funeral. She had said she wanted to be with me, but I thought it would be more useful, more important if she went on promoting her album. She had been invited to appear on a number of television programs, on important local channels, and she still had a few opening acts to prepare.

I stayed in Baltimore until Christmas vacation. I watched as my Uncle Saul gradually started going to pieces, and it was very difficult to bear. He remained shut away in his room, lying flat on the bed, with the television for background noise, to fill the silence.

As for me, I spent my days between Oak Park and Forrest Lane. I was catching memories in the butterfly net of reminiscence.

One afternoon when I was in the center of town I decided to stop off at the law office. I figured I might pick up Uncle Saul's mail; maybe it would occupy him and get his mind on something else. I knew the receptionist well: she gave me a funny look when she saw me come in. I asked her if I could go into my uncle's office. She asked me to wait and she left her desk to go and get one of the partners. I found her behavior odd enough not to obey her: I went straight to Uncle Saul's office and opened the door, expecting to find the room empty: much to my surprise I found a strange man in possession of the place.

"Who are you?" I said.

"Richard Philipps, esquire," the man answered curtly. "Allow me to inquire who you are."

"You're in the office of my uncle, Saul Goldman. I'm his nephew."

"Saul Goldman? He hasn't worked here in months."

"What are you talking about—"

"He was dismissed."

"What? That's impossible! He founded this law office."

"The majority of the partners called for his departure. That's life, old elephants die and the lions eat their corpses."

I waved a threatening finger at the man. "You're in my uncle's office. Leave at once!"

Just then the receptionist hurried in with Edwin Silverstein, the oldest partner in the office and one of Uncle Saul's best friends.

"Edwin," I said, "what's going on?"

"Come with me, Marcus, we have to talk."

Philipps chuckled. I shouted, full of rage, "Did this shitbag take my uncle's position?"

Philipps was no longer chuckling.

"Stay polite, alright? I didn't take anyone's place. As I told you, old elephants die and—"

He didn't have time to finish his sentence because I rushed at him and grabbed him by the collar, and I said, "When lions get too near old elephants, young elephants come and stomp them into the ground!"

Edwin urged me to let Philipps go and I did so.

"That guy is nuts!" Philipps shouted. "I'm going to press charges! I'm going to press charges! There are witnesses!"

Everyone on the floor had come running to see what was going on. I wiped his desk with my arm, sweeping everything onto the floor, including his laptop, then I stormed out of the room like a man looking to kill someone. Everyone stepped aside as I headed for the elevator. "Marcus!" Edwin called, making his way through the throng of onlookers with difficulty to catch up with me. "Wait for me!"

He followed me into the elevator.

"Marcus, I'm sorry. I thought Saul told you what happened."

"He didn't."

Edwin took me to the cafeteria, where he bought me a coffee. We stood leaning against a high table with no chairs and he said, as if telling me a secret:

"Your uncle committed a grave misdeed. He fiddled with some of the law office's accounts and made fake invoices, in order to misappropriate funds."

"Why on earth would he do such a thing?"

"I have no idea."

"When did this happen?"

"We discovered the fraud roughly a year ago. It was cleverly done. He had been siphoning money off for years. It took us until a month ago to figure out that it was your uncle. He agreed to reimburse part of the amount so we have decided not to press charges. But the other partners demanded your uncle's head, and they got it."

"But he's the one who created the office!"

"I know, Marcus. I did all I could. I tried everything. Everyone was against him."

I lost my temper: "No, Edwin, you didn't do everything. You should have gone out and slammed the door with him, and started a new venture. You shouldn't have let this happen."

"I'm sorry, Marcus."

"Yeah, it's real easy to be sorry when you're sitting comfortably in your leather armchair, while that bastard shithead Philipps has taken my uncle's place."

I walked out, seething with rage. I went back to the Marriott, and pounded on the door to Uncle Saul's room. He opened it.

"Did they throw you out of your office?" I cried.

He lowered his head and went to sit on the bed.

"How did you find out?"

"I went by the office to see if there was any mail for you and I found that piece of shit at your desk. Edwin had to tell me everything. When were you going to tell me?"

"I was ashamed. I'm still ashamed."

"But what happened? Why did you take that money?"

"I can't talk about it. I got myself into a bad situation."

I was on the verge of tears. He saw this, and took me in his arms.

"Oh, Markie . . ."

I could not stop crying, I just wanted to get out of there.

* * *

To get my mind on other things, over the holiday season Alexandra used the earnings from her album to invite me for ten days' vacation in a dream hotel in the Bahamas.

A bit of rest far away from everything would be good for her, too. The events had left their mark on her. We spent the first day on the beach. It was the first time in ages that we had been together in a quiet place, but I could sense a strange tension between us. What was going on? I went on thinking she was hiding something from me.

That evening, before we went to dinner, we had a cocktail at the hotel bar and I started hounding her. I wanted to know. Finally she said: "I can't talk about it."

I got annoyed.

"I'm fed up with all these little secrets. Can't somebody be honest with me for once?"

"Markie, I—"

"Alexandra, I want to know what you are hiding."

Suddenly she burst into tears right there in the bar. I felt stupid. I wanted to put things right so I said, more gently, "Alexandra, angel, what is going on?"

Floods of tears were pouring down her cheeks.

"I can't hide the truth from you anymore, Marcus! I can't keep it to myself."

I was beginning to have a sense of foreboding.

"What's going on, Alex?"

She tried to get hold of herself, then looked me straight in the eye.

"I knew what your cousins were planning to do. I knew they were going to run away. Woody never had any intention of going to prison."

"What? You knew? But when did they tell you?"

"That evening. You were busy with the barbecue with your uncle, and I went for a walk with them. They told me everything but they made me promise I wouldn't tell."

I said again, wildly, "You knew from the start and you didn't tell me?"

"Markie, I—"

I stood up.

"You didn't warn me about what they were going to do? You let them go and you didn't tell me? Who are you, Alexandra?"

All the other people in the bar were staring at us.

"Calm down, Markie," she pleaded.

"Calm down? Why should I calm down? When I think of the act you put on the whole time they were on the run!"

"But I was really worried! What did you think?"

I was trembling, overwhelmed with fury.

"I think we're through, Alexandra."

"What? Markie, no!"

"You betrayed me. I don't think I can ever forgive you."

"Marcus, don't do this to me!"

I turned my back on her and walked out of the bar. Everyone was staring at us. She followed me and tried to grab my arm; I pulled away and shouted, "Leave me! I said, leave me!"

I charged through the hotel lobby and went out.

"Marcus," she cried, weeping with despair, "don't do this."

There was a taxi outside the hotel. I climbed in and locked the door. She ran over, tried to open the door, banged on the window. Leaving everything behind me, I told the driver to head for the airport.

She was still pounding on the window, screaming and crying. "Don't do this, Marcus," she begged. "Don't do this to me!"

The taxi accelerated away and she had to give up. I threw my cell phone out the window and gave a cry, screaming my rage and anger, disgust at life's unfairness, how it had taken all those who mattered the most from me.

At the airport in Nassau I bought a ticket for the first flight back to New York. I wanted to disappear forever. And yet I missed her already. And to think I wouldn't see her again for eight long years.

* * *

I often recall that scene. How I left Alexandra. Now in this warm month of June 2012, alone at my desk in Boca Raton, retracing the meanders of our youth, I was thinking of her in London. I had only one desire: to go and be with her. But it was enough to see her as she was, in tears, running after my taxi, to not want to do anything. What right did I have, after eight years had gone by, to show up in her life and turn everything upside down?

Someone knocked on the door to the room. I gave a start. It was Leo.

"Excuse me, Marcus. I took the liberty of coming in. I never see you these days, and I was beginning to worry. Is everything alright?"

I picked up the notebook I was writing in and I looked at him with a friendly smile.

"Everything's fine, Leo. Thank you for the notebook."

"It's yours by right. You're the writer, Marcus. Writing a book is a lot more work than I realized. I owe you an apology."

"Don't worry about it."

"You look a little sad, Marcus."

"I miss Alexandra."

47

January 2005

In the weeks that followed the breakup with Alexandra, I spent most of my time in Baltimore. It was not so much to visit Uncle Saul as to hide from her. I had put her behind me, I had changed my cell number. I didn't want her to come to Montclair.

Over and over I replayed in my head the scene of the departure from Oak Park, when Hillel and Woody's car turned off to head for the freeway. They were about to go underground. If I had known they planned to run away, I could have made them change their minds. I would have reasoned with Woody. What was five years? Both a long time, and nothing at all. He wouldn't even be thirty years old when he got out. He had his whole life ahead of him. And besides, he might have gotten a time off his sentence for good behavior. He could have used those years to finish his studies by correspondence. I would have convinced him: we had our life ahead of us.

Since their death, everything seemed to have gone to pieces. Starting with Uncle Saul's life. The bad patch he was in had only just begun.

Word got around about his dismissal from the law offices. It was rumored that the real reason he left was a significant embezzlement of funds. The disciplinary commission of the Maryland State bar had already begun proceedings; they held Uncle Saul's behavior, if proven to be true, to be a disgrace to the profession.

For his defense, Uncle Saul sought Edwin Silverstein's support. I ran into him regularly at the Marriott. One evening he took me out to dinner at a Vietnamese restaurant in the neighborhood.

I asked him, "What can I do to help my uncle?"

He replied, "Honestly, not a great deal. You know, Marcus, you have guts. Not everyone is that fortunate. You're a really good kid. Your uncle is lucky to have you."

"I'd like to do more."

"You've done enough already. Saul told me you want to become a writer?"

"Yes."

"I don't think you can really concentrate that well, here. You should also think about yourself and not spend too much time in Baltimore. You should go and write your book."

Edwin was right. It was time for me to start on the project that meant so much to me. So during that month of January, when I came back from a stay in Baltimore, I began writing my first novel. I had understood that if I wanted to bring my cousins back, I would have to tell their story.

The idea came to me at a rest area on I-95, somewhere in Pennsylvania. I was drinking a coffee and rereading my notes when I saw them come in. It couldn't be. But it was them. They were joking happily, and when they saw me, they rushed over.

"Marcus," Hillel said, giving me a hug. "I thought that was your car!"

Woody joined in the hug, wrapping his huge arms around both of us.

"You're not real," I said. "You're dead. You're two dead bastards who left me all alone in this shithole of a world!"

"Oh, stop moaning, Markie-moo!" Hillel said, mocking, ruffling my hair.

"Come on," Woody said, with a consoling smile. "Come with us."

"Where are you going?"

"To the Paradise of the Just."

"I can't go with you."

"Why not?"

"I have to go to Montclair."

"O.K., then we'll see you there."

I wasn't sure I understood. They gave me a hug and turned to go. Before they went through the door, I called out:

"Hillel, Wood! Was it my fault?"

"No, of course it wasn't," they answered, as one.

They kept their word. I found those adored cousins of mine back in Montclair, in the study my mother had set up for me. No sooner did I sit down at my desk than there they were, dancing around me. They were just the way I had always known them to be: noisy, magnificent, overflowing with tenderness.

"I love your study," Hillel said, sprawled in my armchair.

"I love your parents' house," Woody said. "Why didn't we ever come here?"

"I don't know. And it's true . . . You should have."

I showed them around the neighborhood; we went all around Montclair. They thought everything was great. The three of us, together again: it filled me with immeasurable happiness. Then we went back to my study, and I picked up the thread of my story.

Everything came to a halt when my father opened the door to the room.

"Marcus, it's two o'clock in the morning. You're still working?" he said.

The two of them vanished through the cracks in the floor like frightened mice.

"Yes, I'll go to bed soon."

"I didn't want to disturb you. I saw the light and . . . is everything alright?"

"Everything's fine."

"I thought I heard voices . . . "

"No, maybe it was the music."

"Maybe."

He came and gave me a hug.

"'Night, son. I'm proud of you."

"Thanks, Dad. Goodnight to you, too."

He went off and closed the door behind him. But they were gone. They had vanished. They were my vanished cousins.

* * *

Between January and November 2005, I wrote continuously in my study in Montclair. Every weekend I went down to Baltimore to see Uncle Saul.

I was the only Goldman who regularly went to see him. Grandmother said it was too much for her. My parents made a quick visit from time to time, but I think they had trouble accepting the situation. And besides, you had to be able to put up with Uncle Saul—the ghost of himself, refusing to set foot outside the perimeter of the Hotel Marriott in Baltimore where he was living.

It did not help matters that in February, upon the decision of the disciplinary commission of the state of Maryland, Uncle Saul was disbarred. The mighty Saul Goldman would never be a lawyer again.

I started going to see him, not expecting anything. I didn't even warn him I was coming. I left Montclair and drove to the Marriott. The more often I went, the more I felt at home at the hotel: the staff called me by name, I could go straight into the kitchen and order what I wanted. When I arrived, I would go up to the seventh floor and knock on the door to his room, and he opened, looking haggard, his shirt wrinkled, the television on for background noise. He said hello to me as if I had just come from the next street over. I didn't mind. Eventually he gave me a hug.

"Markie," he murmured. "My little Markie! I'm glad to see you."

"Are you O.K., Uncle Saul?"

Often when I asked him this, it was because I hoped he would suddenly be invincible again, that he would laugh off his troubles the way he used to in the time of our lost youth, and that he would say everything was fine, but he merely shook his head and said, "It's a nightmare, Marcus. A nightmare."

He sat down on the bed and picked up the phone to call reception.

"How long are you staying?" he said.

"As long as you like."

I heard someone pick up at the other end, and Uncle Saul said, "My nephew is here, I need another room, please." Then he turned to me and said, "Just the weekend. You have to get ahead with your book, that's important."

I could not understand why he didn't go home.

Then, early that summer, I went for a drive one day to Oak Park, looking for inspiration for my book, and to my horror I saw a moving van outside the Baltimore house. A new family was moving in. I found the husband busy giving orders to two big guys who were moving a panel.

"Are you renting?" I asked him.

"I bought the place," he said.

I went straight back to the Marriott.

"Did you sell the house in Oak Park?"

He gave me a sad look.

"I didn't *sell* anything, Markie."

"But there's a family moving in, and they say they bought the house."

He repeated, "I didn't *sell* anything. The bank *took* it."

I was flabbergasted.

"And your furniture?"

"I got rid of it all, Markie."

He also told me that he was about to sell the house in the Hamptons so he would have some cash, and he would let go of the Buenavista and use the capital to set himself up with a new house and a new life somewhere else.

"You're going to leave Baltimore?" I was incredulous.

"I have nothing more to do here."

Soon there would be nothing left of the grandeur of the Baltimore Goldmans. My only response to life was my book.

Thanks to books,
  Everything is erased.
  Everything is forgotten.
  Everything is forgiven.
  Everything is atoned for.

In my study in Montclair, I could relive the happiness of the Baltimores forever. So much so that I did not want to leave the room, and if I really did have to go out, I was all the more eager to meet up with them again upon my return.

And when I went to the Marriott in Baltimore I distracted Uncle Saul from his television by telling him about the book I was writing. He was always wanting to know how I was getting on, and how soon he could read an excerpt.

"It's the story of three cousins," I told him.

"The three Goldman cousins?"

"The three Goldstein cousins," I corrected him.

In books, people who are no longer with us can meet again, and embrace.

I spent ten months stitching up my cousins' wounds by rewriting our story. I finished the novel about the Goldstein cousins the day before Thanksgiving, 2005, exactly one year after my cousins died.

In the final scene of the novel about the Goldsteins, Hillel and Woody drive down to Baltimore from Montreal. They stop in New Jersey to pick me up and we continue on our way together. In Baltimore, in a magnificent house full of light, the unsinkable couple, Uncle Saul and Aunt Anita, are waiting for our return.

48

All through the summer of 2012, thanks to the magic of the novel, I found them again just as I had done seven years earlier.

One night at around two o'clock in the morning I couldn't sleep, so I went out on the patio. The heat was tropical, but it felt good to be outdoors. The night was lulled by the chirr of the crickets. I opened my notebook and started writing her name. That was all it took for her to appear before me.

"Aunt Anita," I murmured.

She smiled and tenderly put her hands on my face.

"You are still so handsome, Markie."

I stood up and put my arms around her.

"It's been such a long time," I said. "I've missed you so much."

"And I've missed you, angel."

"I'm writing a book about you. A book about the Baltimores."

"I know, Markie. I came to tell you that you have to stop tormenting yourself with the past. First you wrote the book about your cousins, now it's the book about the Baltimores. It's time for you to write the book about *your* life. You're not responsible, and there's nothing you could have done. As for the culprit, if we need a culprit for the chaos of our lives, then we are the culprits, Marcus. We alone. We are each of us responsible for our own life. Responsible for what we have become. Marcus, my nephew, my darling, none of it, do you hear me, none of what happened was your fault. And none of it was Alexandra's fault. You have to let the ghosts go."

She stood up.

"Where are you going?" I said.

"I can't stay."

"Why not?"

"Your uncle is waiting for me."

"How is he?"

She smiled.

"He's fine. He said he always knew you would write a book about him."

She smiled, gave me a little wave, and vanished into the night.

49

When my book was published in 2006, its success restored my cousins to me. They were everywhere: in bookstores, in readers' hands, on buses, subways, airplanes. They followed me loyally all across the country during the book tour that followed publication.

I was no longer in touch with Alexandra. But I saw her countless times without her knowing it. Her career had taken off, spectacularly. All through 2005 her first album had continued to climb the charts and by December she had sold a million and a half copies, and the title track had ended up number one on the American hit parade. Her fame had skyrocketed. The year my book was published coincided with Alexandra's second album. It was an absolute triumph. Both her audience and the music critics were enthralled.

I had never stopped loving her. I had never stopped admiring her. I went regularly to see her in concert. Hidden in the darkness of the auditorium, anonymous among thousands of other spectators, I moved my lips in time with hers as she recited the words of the songs I knew by heart: most of them had been written in our little apartment in Nashville. I wondered if she still lived there. Almost certainly not. She would surely have moved to the fashionable Nashville suburbs where, back in the day, we used to go together and admire the houses, wondering which one we would live in someday.

Did I have regrets? Obviously. They were killing me. Seeing her there on stage, I closed my eyes so I would only hear her voice, and my thoughts went back through the years. We were on the campus in Madison, and she was pulling me by the hand. I asked her, "Are you sure no-one will see us?"

"Of course not! Come on," I said.

"What about Woody and Hillel?"

"They're in New York, at my dad's place. Don't worry."

She opened the door to her room and shoved me inside. The poster was there on the wall. Like in New York. Blessed Tupac, our eternal matchmaker. I threw her onto the bed, she burst out laughing. We cuddled up against each other and she murmured, as she took my face in her hands, "I love you, Markie-moo Goldman."

"I love you, Alexandra Neville."

In 2006, Uncle Saul had just moved into the house in Coconut Grove, which he had bought thanks to the sale of the Buenavista, and I started going regularly to Miami.

Uncle Saul could have lived comfortably on the money from the sale of the house in the Hamptons, which he had converted into very profitable shares. To keep busy, he joined various reading groups, went to all the talks at a nearby bookstore, and tended his mango and avocado trees.

But it didn't last. As for many other people, my uncle's financial security came to an abrupt end in October 2008, when the global economy was rocked by the subprime mortgage crisis. Markets collapsed. Investment banks and hedge funds went under, one after the other, losing all their clients' money. From one day to the next, people who had been rich had nothing left. This was the case for my uncle Saul. On October 1, 2008, his share portfolio was worth six million dollars. By the end of that month, it was worth sixty thousand.

I found this out when I went to visit him at the beginning of November, in the run-up to Thanksgiving – which neither of us celebrated now. I found him in desperate straits. He had nothing. He had sold his car and now he was driving an old Honda Civic that was on its last legs. He counted every penny. He wanted to sell the house in Coconut Grove, but it wasn't worth anything anymore.

"I paid $700,000 for it," he told the broker who came to value it.

"A month ago, you would have sold it and made a profit," the broker said. "But that's all over. The bottom has fallen out of the housing market."

I offered to help Uncle Saul. I knew that Grandmother and my parents had also offered. But he had no intention of moping or letting life get him down. That was why I admired him: not for his financial or social standing, but because he was a real fighter. He needed to earn his living, so he began looking for any job he could get.

He found a job as a waiter in an upscale restaurant in South Beach. It was tedious work and physically hard on him, but he was ready to overcome everything. Except for the humiliation he suffered at the hands of his boss, who was forever shouting, "You're too slow, Saul!" "Hurry up, the customers are waiting!" Sometimes in his haste he broke a plate, and they deducted it from his salary. One evening he reached breaking-point, and he resigned then and there, throwing his apron to the floor and striding out of the restaurant. He wandered through the pedestrian streets of the Lincoln Road Mall and ended up on a bench, sobbing. No-one paid any attention, except for a tall black man who was walking around singing and who seemed touched by his distress. "My name is Sycomorus," the man said. "You don't seem to be doing too hot . . ." Sycomorus was already working at the Whole Foods in Coral Gables, and he mentioned Uncle Saul to Faith: she found him a job bagging at the supermarket checkout.

50

In the quiet of Boca Raton, as the weeks passed, I made headway with my new book.

That summer of 2012, had I invited the Baltimores into my mind to relive the past, or to evoke Alexandra?

Leo continued to follow the evolution of my work. I let him read my pages as I progressed. At the beginning of August he asked, "Why this book, Marcus? Didn't you already write about your cousins in your first novel?"

"This one is different," I explained. "It's a book about the Baltimores."

"It may be different, but basically, nothing has changed where you're concerned."

"What do you mean?"

"Alexandra."

"Oh, for pity's sake! Don't go bringing that up again."

"Do you want my opinion?"

"No."

"I'm going to give it to you anyway. If the Baltimores were still alive, Marcus, they would tell you it's time for you to be happy. It's not too late. Go find her and ask her to forgive you. Start your life together again. You're not going to spend your whole life waiting! You're not going to spend your whole life going to her concerts and wondering what it might have been like if you had stayed together! Call her. Speak to her. Deep down, you know that's what she's waiting for."

"It's too late," I said.

"It's not too late, Marcus!" Leo shouted. "It's never too late."

"I still think that if Alexandra had told me what my cousins were going to do, they would be here today. I would have stopped them. They would be alive. I don't know if I can ever forgive her."

"If they weren't dead," said Leo solemnly, "you would never have become a writer. They had to go away so that you could fulfill your dream."

He went out of the room, leaving me to my thoughts. I closed the notebook. In front of me was the photograph of the four of us: it never left me.

I picked up the telephone and called her.

It was the end of the day in London. I could tell from the way she answered that she was happy to hear my voice.

"So, it took you all this time to call me," she said.

I could hear a noise behind her.

"Am I disturbing you? I can call back later if you want."

"No, not at all. I'm in Hyde Park. I come here every day after the studio. There's a little café by a lake, and it's a very soothing sort of place."

"How's the album coming along?"

"We're making progress. I'm pleased with the results. And your book?"

"Fine. It's a book about us. About my cousins. About what happened."

"And how does the story end?"

"I don't know. I haven't finished it yet."

There was a silence, and then she said, "Things didn't happen the way you imagine, Marcus. I didn't betray you. I wanted to protect you."

And so she told me what had happened on the evening of October 24, 2004, the last night of Woody's freedom.

She had gone with Hillel and Woody for a walk around Oak Park, while Uncle Saul and I were preparing the barbecue.

"Alex," Woody said, "there's something you ought to know. I'm not going to prison tomorrow. I'm going to run away."

"What? Woody, you're crazy!"

"Hell, no. It's all planned. I've got a new life waiting for me in the Yukon."

443

"The Yukon? In Canada?"

"Yes. This is probably the last time we'll meet, Alex."

She burst into tears.

"Don't do this, please!"

"I have no choice," Woody said.

"Of course you do. You can serve your sentence. Five years would go by in no time."

"I'm not cut out for prison. Maybe I'm not as tough as everyone always thought."

She turned to Hillel and pleaded with him.

"You have to make him give up this idea, Hillel."

Hillel looked down.

"I'm going too, Alexandra. I'm going with Woody."

She was appalled.

"What is the matter with the two of you?"

"I committed a crime that is much more serious than Woody's," Hillel said. "I destroyed my family."

"Destroyed your family?" Alexandra echoed, now completely at a loss.

"If Woody has reached this point, if my mother died, it's all because of me. It's time for me to pay. I'll take Woody to Canada. It's my way of asking him to forgive me."

"Forgive you for what? What are you talking about?"

"All we're trying to say, Alex, is goodbye. And to tell you we love you. We love you in a way you could never love us. Maybe that's another reason why we're leaving."

She was in tears.

"Please don't do this, I beg you."

"Our minds are made up," Hillel said. "We've sealed our fate."

She wiped her eyes.

"Promise me you'll think it over during the night. You won't spend even five years in prison, Woody! Don't ruin everything."

"We've thought it all through," Woody said.

They both seemed very determined.

"Does Marcus know?" Alexandra said eventually.

"No," Woody said. "I wanted to tell him earlier, but Saul interrupted us. I'll talk to him in a while."

"No, don't, please. Don't tell him anything. Both of you, I beg you, don't tell him!"

"But he's Marcus, we can't hide it from him."

"I'm just asking you one last favor. In the name of our friendship. Don't tell your cousin."

Alexandra's story left me devastated. I had always believed that Woody and Hillel had only confided in her, that they had deliberately hidden their plans from me. I had always thought that in sharing their last secret with her, they had excluded me from the Goldman Gang. But they had wanted to tell me and Alexandra had stopped them.

"Why?" I asked her now. "Why did you convince them not to tell me? I would have stopped them. I would have saved them."

"You couldn't have stopped them, Markie. Nothing, nobody, could have persuaded them to give up their plan. I could see it in their eyes, and that's why I pleaded with them not to tell you. You would have gone with them, Marcus. I know you would have. You wouldn't have abandoned the Goldman Gang. You would have followed them, and you would have been on the run, too, you would have ended up getting yourself killed. The way they did. I begged them not to say anything to you, because in fact I was begging them to spare you. I knew you would leave with them, Markie. I didn't want to lose you. I couldn't bear it. I wanted to save you. But I lost you all the same."

After a moment of silence, I murmured, "What did Hillel do that was so terrible that he had to go with Woody? What was it he had to atone for, in such a way?"

"I have no idea. But it's the sort of thing you should ask my father."

"Your father?"

"He's not the man you think he is. And I get the impression he knows a lot, even if he never wanted to tell me about it."

"Your father meddled with my family. He humiliated my uncle by trying to impress Woody and Hillel at all costs."

"Whatever you might think, my father never felt he had to impress Woody and Hillel in order to exist."

"And what about the Ferrari? And all his trips? And the weekends in New York?" I said angrily.

"I'm the one who asked him to do all that," Alexandra said. "My father really did like Woody and Hillel, that much is true. Who didn't? But if he did all that for them, it was to protect you and me. To give us the freedom to enjoy our relationship in peace. He knew that if he lent them his car, they would go off and have fun and not pay any attention to either you or me. It was the same thing when he took them to the Giants games, or invited them to his place. It meant so much to you, for your cousins not to find out about you and me. Marcus, my father did everything he could to keep your secret. There was never any rivalry with Saul. The rivalry your uncle experienced was with himself. Everything my father did was to keep your cousins away from us. And that's what you wanted."

I was dumbfounded.

And then she said: "I left Kevin two weeks ago, Marcus. Because of you. He came here without telling me he was coming. He wanted to make it a surprise. When he knocked on the door to my hotel room, initially I thought it was you. I don't know why. When I saw through the spy hole that it was him I was so disappointed. I realized I had to be open with him, and break it off with him. He deserves to find someone who really loves him. As for you, Marcus, I can't go on waiting for you. You're a wonderful person, and I spent the best years of my life with you, and it's thanks to you that I have become who I am. But you spend so much time rehashing the past that you don't realize what's been clear to me all along."

"And what's that?"

"The Montclair Goldmans: they were the best."

The day after my conversation with Alexandra, I took the first flight to New York. I had to speak to Patrick Neville at once.

I arrived at his building during the morning. He had already left for work. The doorman agreed to let me wait for him, and I sat on the sofa in the hall most of the day, except to go briefly for a bite to eat or to the restroom. It was six in the evening when he came in. I stood up. He stared at me for a moment, then gave a friendly smile and said, "Long time no see."

He took me upstairs and made me a coffee. We sat down in his kitchen. It was strange to be there: it was the first time I'd been back since Aunt Anita died.

"I'd like to ask your forgiveness, Patrick."

"What for?"

"Because of the way I behaved after my aunt's funeral."

"Bah, I forgot about it a long time ago. More than anything, Marcus, I want you to know that I never had an affair with your aunt."

"So what happened, then, the night she was here? Why was she here?"

"She had just left your uncle."

"Yes, I know that."

"But you don't know why. If she came to me that night, it was to ask for my help. She wanted me to help Woody and Saul."

"Woody and Saul?"

"A few months earlier, Woody got kicked off the Madison football team."

"I remember."

"The official version was that he had torn his ligaments, and he would no longer be able to play. Your aunt and uncle immediately came to Madison. Woody wouldn't tell them anything, but I told them the truth. I told them that Woody had tested positive for Talacen. If your aunt came to see me here in New York on February 14, 2002, it was because she had just found out two things that really upset her."

And so, ten years after the events, Patrick told me at last what had happened that Valentine's Day.

Aunt Anita had taken a day off from the hospital to prepare a romantic evening for herself and her husband. Early that afternoon, she had gone to the Oak Park supermarket to do some shopping. She also stopped off at the pharmacy.

The head pharmacist, whom she knew well, brought her what she wanted and then asked her for the prescription he had been waiting for – it had been months.

"What prescription?" she asked.

"The prescription for the Talacen," the pharmacist said. "Your son asked for several boxes last fall. He said you'd bring in the prescription."

"My son? Hillel?"

"Yes, Hillel. And as I know you well, I agreed. To do him a favor. In principle, it's something I never do. I do need that prescription, Dr Goldman."

She suddenly felt weak in the knees. She promised she would be back with a prescription by the end of the day and she went home. She felt like throwing up, it was a nightmare. Had Hillel bought the Talacen at Woody's request? Or had he forced it on him, unknowingly?

The telephone rang. She answered. It was the bank. Regarding the mortgage payment on the house in Oak Park. Anita said there must be a mistake: the mortgage had been paid off long ago. But the caller from the bank insisted: "Mrs Goldman, you took out a new mortgage in August. Your husband brought me the documents, they have your signature. The house has been mortgaged for six million dollars."

Uncle Saul had financed the stadium by borrowing six million dollars. The house in Oak Park had been sacrificed to mend his wounded ego.

She felt a rush of panic. She hunted through her husband's desk and all his personal things. In the sports bag he used when he went to play tennis she found some accounting statements she had never seen.

She immediately called Uncle Saul. They had a violent argument over the telephone. She told him she couldn't stand it anymore and that she was leaving him. She got in the car and took the accounting statements with her; at first she drove around aimlessly, then finally she called Patrick Neville to ask him for help. She was absolutely distraught and he suggested she come to New York.

Patrick had planned to have an intimate dinner that evening with a young woman he worked with whom he fancied. He canceled the dinner. When Aunt Anita saw the champagne on the table, she felt bad about disturbing Patrick on the evening of Valentine's Day. He insisted she stay. "You're not going anywhere," he told her. "I've never seen you so upset. You're going to tell me what is going on."

She told him everything: about the Talacen and the mortgage. If it was Hillel who had been doping Woody without him knowing, she wanted Patrick to intervene with the university to have Woody rehabilitated. She hoped she could still save his career. She also wanted Patrick to find a way to terminate the contract between Saul and the university, so they could get back as much of their money as possible and save their house.

Then she showed him the documents she had brought with her. Patrick studied them carefully: they looked like nothing so much as fraudulent accounts.

"It looks like Saul is siphoning money from the law office into one of his private accounts. He's concealed it by changing the amounts on his clients' invoices."

"But why would he do such a thing?"

"To absorb a sizeable loan he might be having trouble reimbursing."

Patrick invited Anita to stay for dinner. He told her she could stay at his place as long as she liked. Suddenly the telephone rang: it was the doorman. Woody was downstairs and wanted to come up. Patrick asked Anita to hide in one of the bedrooms. Woody arrived at the apartment.

What happened next was already history.

When Patrick stopped talking, I was speechless for a long while, stunned. And there were more surprises in store. Patrick went on to tell me he had confronted Hillel about the Talacen. He went to see him in Madison and wormed it out of him.

Hillel's story was that on the evening of February 14 he'd had a terrible argument with Woody. Woody had found what was left of the Talacen, hidden at the back of a closet. For some reason Hillel had hung on to it.

"You were doping Woody without him knowing?" Patrick said, in despair.

"I wanted to get him kicked off the football team. I found out which were the banned products, and Talacen was the easiest to get hold of. All I had to do was mix the tablets with the protein and food supplements he was taking."

"But why would you do such a thing?"

"I was crazy with jealousy."

"You were jealous of Woody?"

"He was my parents' favorite. It was so obvious. He got all their attention. I realized it when they separated us and I had to go to the special school. My parents sent me away from Baltimore. But they kept Woody with them. Dad taught him how to drive, he encouraged him to play football, he took him to the Redskins games. And where was I, all that time? One hour away, stuck in that shithole of a school! He took my parents, then he took my name. At college he decided to call himself Goldman. He got my parents' blessing to have our name printed on his jersey. Now he was the mighty Goldman, the football champion. He owed us everything, we picked him up off the street. For as long as I can remember, when someone asked him who he was, he'd say, 'I'm Hillel Goldman's friend.' I was his reference. But now at college when people heard my name they said: 'Goldman? You mean like Woody, the football player?' I didn't want to see him play anymore, I didn't want to hear his fake-Goldman name. At the end of the summer, after my grandfather died, I decided to do something about it. In the middle of tidying up Grandfather's things, I found his will. My father had told us that according to Grandfather's last wishes, Woody, Marcus, and I would share sixty thousand dollars. That was a lie. In my grandfather's will there was no mention of Woody. But my father – to make sure Woody, his little treasure, wouldn't feel bad – decided on his own authority to include him.

"Woody was taking up too much room: I had to do something."

The shock was devastating.

So it was Hillel who had destroyed Woody's career. It was because of him that on the evening of February 14, after their argument, Woody went to Patrick Neville's and found himself face to face with Aunt Anita, and she died.

As for my Uncle Saul, the reason he stayed so long at the Baltimore Marriott after the tragedy was not because he didn't want to go back to the house in Oak Park, but because it no longer belonged to him. He had been jobless all the while, for months, short on cash, and he couldn't keep up with the mortgage payments. So the bank foreclosed on the house.

Then I asked Patrick, "Why didn't you tell me anything?"

"Your uncle had enough troubles as it was. Woody and Hillel knew the truth about the Talacen. What use would it have been to involve your uncle in that? Or for Hillel to find out that his father had embezzled money and mortgaged the house to pay for the stadium in Madison? All your uncle had left was his dignity. I wanted to protect him. I've always loved your family, Marcus. I have always wished you well."

51

Coconut Grove, Florida
September 2011

Roughly three weeks after I went to attend the removal of his name from the stadium, Uncle Saul called me up. His voice was weak. All he said was, "Marcus, I don't feel well. You'd better come." I could tell it was urgent so I booked a seat on the next flight to Miami.

I got to Coconut Grove early that evening. The Florida heat was baking. I found Faith sitting outside my uncle's house on the steps to the porch. I think she had been waiting for me. The way she took me in her arms to greet me I understood that the situation was not good. I went into the house. I found Uncle Saul in his room, in bed. When he saw me, his face lit up. But he seemed very weak and had lost a lot of weight.

"Marcus," he said, "I'm really glad to see you."

"Uncle Saul, what's going on?"

The grouchy uncle of recent months, the uncle who had sent me away, was an uncle who was unwell. Early that spring he been diagnosed with pancreatic cancer, and it was already clear at that time that he would not recover.

"I tried to treat it, Markie. Faith helped me a lot. When she used to come to get me at home and we went off like that, it was because we were going to my chemo sessions."

"Why didn't you say anything?"

He regained his spark for a moment and burst out laughing.

"Because I know what you're like, Markie. You would have driven me crazy taking me around to every doctor imaginable, you would have sacrificed everything to look after me and I didn't want that. You mustn't spoil your life for my sake. You have to live."

I sat down on the edge of his bed. He took my hand.

"This is the end of the road, Markie. I won't recover. These are my last months. And I want to spend them with you here."

I took him in my arms and held him close. We both had tears on our face.

I will never forget those months we had together, from September to November 2011.

Once a week I went with him to see his oncologist at Mount Sinai Hospital in Miami. We never talked about his illness. He didn't want to discuss it. I just asked him on a regular basis, "How do you feel?"

And he would answer, cloaking himself in his legendary aplomb: "Couldn't be better."

Sometimes I managed to question his physician: "Doctor, how much time does he have left?"

"It's hard to say. His morale is good. Your being with him is doing him a lot of good. The treatment can't cure him, but it can keep him going for a while."

"When you say a while, do you mean days, weeks, months, years?"

"I understand this is distressing for you, Mr Goldman, but I can't venture an opinion. Maybe a few months."

I watched him getting weaker by the day.

At the end of October, there were a few warning signs: one day he began vomiting blood, and I took him at once to Mount Sinai, where he stayed for a few days. He came out feeling very weak. Walking wore him out. I rented a wheelchair and took him for walks through Coconut Grove. It reminded me of Scott Neville in his wheelbarrow. I told him so, and he had a good laugh. I liked it when he laughed.

By early November he had difficulty getting out of bed. He hardly left it. His face was ashen, his features marked. The nurse came to the house three times a day. I stopped sleeping in the guest room. He never found out, but I spent my nights in the corridor near his open door, so I could keep an eye on him.

His physical weakness did not stop him talking. I remember the conversation we had the day before he died – the day before Thanksgiving.

"When was the last time you celebrated Thanksgiving?" he said.

"Before the tragedy."

"What do you mean by tragedy?"

His question surprised me.

"I mean when Woody and Hillel died," I said.

"Stop this tragedy business, Marcus. There is not one tragedy, there are tragedies. There's your aunt's tragedy, and your cousins'. The tragedy of life. There have been tragedies, and there will be more, and you'll have to go on living in spite of everything. Tragedy is inevitable. On the grand scale of things, it's not that important. What is important is how you manage to overcome it. You won't overcome your tragedy by refusing to celebrate Thanksgiving. On the contrary, you'll just sink further into it. You have to stop doing that, Marcus. You have a family, you have friends. I want you to start celebrating Thanksgiving again. Promise me."

"I promise, Uncle Saul."

He coughed, and took a sip of water. Then he went on: "I know you've been obsessed by these Baltimore Goldman and Montclair Goldman stories. But in the end there's only one Goldman, and that's you. You are one of the Just, Marcus. Many of us try to give meaning to our lives, but our lives only have meaning if we can fulfill these three destinies: to love, to be loved, and to know how to forgive. The rest is just a waste of time. Above all, go on writing. Because you are right: you can atone for everything. My nephew, promise me you will atone for us. You will atone for the Baltimore Goldmans."

"How?"

"Bring us back together. You alone can do that."

"How?"

"You'll find a way."

I wasn't really sure what he meant, but I promised. "I'll do it, Uncle Saul. Count on me."

He smiled. I leaned closer and he put his hand on my hair. His voice was high and thin, but he gave me his blessing.

The next day, on Thanksgiving morning, when I went to him in his bedroom, he didn't wake up. I sat next to him and put my head on his chest, my face streaming with tears.

The last Baltimore was gone.

52

In mid-August 2012, two days after my conversation with Patrick Neville, Alexandra called me. She said she was in Hyde Park, sitting on the terrace at the Serpentine Bar, by the lake. She was drinking a coffee and Duke was dozing at her feet.

"I'm glad you finally spoke to my father," she said.

I told her everything I had learned. Then I said, "In the end, in spite of what happened between them, all that mattered to Hillel and Woody was the happiness of being together. They couldn't stand being angry or apart. Their friendship made up for everything. Their friendship was a hundred times greater than the tragedy. That's what I have to remember."

I could tell she was moved.

"Are you back in Florida, Markie?"

"No."

"You're still in New York?"

"No."

I whistled.

Duke raised his ears and leapt up. He saw me and bounded toward me, frightening a flock of seagulls and ducks. He jumped up on me and knocked me over.

Alexandra stood up from her chair.

"Markie?" she cried. "Markie, you came!"

She rushed over. I got up and took her in my arms. Before laying her head against my chest she murmured, "I missed you so much, Markie."

I held her very tight.

I thought I could see, dancing in the clouds, my two cousins, laughing.

Epilogue

Thursday, November 22, 2012
Thanksgiving Day

And that is how this book comes to an end, the last page turned, on Thanksgiving Day, 2012, outside my parents' house in Montclair. I parked the car in the drive. Alexandra and I got out and walked up to the house. It was the first time I would be celebrating Thanksgiving since my cousins died.

I paused outside the front door. I took from my pocket the photograph of Hillel, Woody, Alexandra, and me, taken in Oak Park in 1995, and gazed at it.

Alexandra rang the doorbell. My mother came to the door. When she saw me, her face lit up.

"Oh, Markie! I wondered if you were actually going to come!"

She covered her mouth with her hands as if she couldn't believe it.

"Hello, Mrs Goldman," Alexandra said. "Happy Thanksgiving."

"Happy Thanksgiving, children! It's so good to be together again."

My mother took both of us in her arms and hugged us for a long time. I could feel her tears on my cheek.

We went into the house.

Patrick Neville was already there. I greeted him warmly then set down on the living room table the bound ream of paper I had brought with me.

"What's this?" my mother said.

"*The Baltimore Boys.*"

One year after his death, I had kept my uncle's promise. By telling their story, I had brought the Baltimores together again.

I had written the last words the night before.

*

Why do I write? Because books are stronger than life. They are the finest revenge we can take on life. They are the witnesses from the impregnable wall of our mind, the unassailable fortress of our memory. And when I'm not writing, once a year I drive back to Baltimore and spend a while in Oak Park, and then I drive to the cemetery in Forrest Lane, to see them. I pile little stones on top of their graves, to go on building their memory. And I sit there quietly thinking. I remember who I am, where I am going, and where I have been. I kneel next to them, put my hands on their carved names, and kiss them. Then I close my eyes and they are alive, inside me.

My Uncle Saul, may his memory be blessed. *Everything is erased.*

My aunt Anita, may her memory be blessed. *Everything is forgotten.*

My cousin Hillel, may his memory be blessed. *Everything is forgiven.*

My cousin Woody, may his memory be blessed. *Everything is atoned for.*

They are gone, but I know they are here. I now know that they reside forever in this place that is called Baltimore, the Paradise of the Just, or perhaps simply in my memory. It doesn't matter. I know they are waiting for me somewhere.

There you are, Uncle Saul, my beloved uncle. The book I promised you, here before you.

In atonement.

JOËL DICKER was born in Geneva in 1985, where he studied Law. *The Truth about the Harry Quebert Affair* was nominated for the Prix Goncourt and won the Grand Prix du Roman de l'Académie Française and the Prix Goncourt des Lycéens. It has sold more than 3.6 million copies in 42 countries. *The Baltimore Boys*, at once a prequel and a sequel, has sold more than 750,000 copies in France.

ALISON ANDERSON is an author and translator. Her books include *The Summer Guest*, *Darwin's Wink* and *Hidden Latitudes*. Her translations include works by Muriel Barbery, J. M. G. Le Clézio and Amélie Nothomb.